something remains

D0294305

something remains

hassan ghedi santur

DUNDURN PRESS
TORONTO

Copyright © Hassan Ghedi Santur, 2010

All rights reserved. No part of this publication may be reproduced, stored in a retrieval system, or transmitted in any form or by any means, electronic, mechanical, photocopying, recording, or otherwise (except for brief passages for purposes of review) without the prior permission of Dundurn Press. Permission to photocopy should be requested from Access Copyright.

Editor: Michael Carroll
Designer: Jennifer Scott
Printer: Transcontinental

Library and Archives Canada Cataloguing in Publication

Santur, Hassan Ghedi
    Something remains / Hassan Ghedi Santur.

ISBN 978-1-55488-465-0

I. Title.

PS8637.A67S65 2009   C813'.6   C2009-903004-7

1   2   3   4   5   14   13   12   11   10

  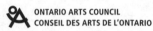

Conseil des Arts du Canada   **Canada Council for the Arts**   Canadä   **ONTARIO ARTS COUNCIL CONSEIL DES ARTS DE L'ONTARIO**

We acknowledge the support of the **Canada Council for the Arts** and the **Ontario Arts Council** for our publishing program. We also acknowledge the financial support of the **Government of Canada** through the **Book Publishing Industry Development Program** and **The Association for the Export of Canadian Books**, and the **Government of Ontario** through the **Ontario Book Publishers Tax Credit program**, and the **Ontario Media Development Corporation**.

Care has been taken to trace the ownership of copyright material used in this book. The author and the publisher welcome any information enabling them to rectify any references or credits in subsequent editions.

J. Kirk Howard, President

Printed and bound in Canada.
www.dundurn.com

Dundurn Press
3 Church Street, Suite 500
Toronto, Ontario, Canada
M5E 1M2

Gazelle Book Services Limited
White Cross Mills
High Town, Lancaster, England
LA1 4XS

Dundurn Press
2250 Military Road
Tonawanda, NY
U.S.A. 14150

Mixed Sources
Product group from well-managed forests, controlled sources and recycled wood or fibre
www.fsc.org Cert no. SW-COC-000952
© 1996 Forest Stewardship Council
FSC

To my mother,
for sacrifices too many to mention

LANCASHIRE COUNTY LIBRARY	
3011811946462 0	
HJ	12-Apr-2010
AF	£12.99

acknowledgements

To paraphrase that African proverb, it takes a village to raise a child; it also takes a village to publish a novel. I would like to thank everyone at Dundurn Press, and in particular, my deep gratitude to my editor, Michael Carroll, for his faith and guidance.

I would also like to thank the Toronto Public Library for its wonderful writer-in-residence program. It was through that program that I met Dennis Bock, Eliza Clark, and Helen Humphreys. Special thanks to Helen Humphreys for her kindness and generosity. To get the encouragement and critique of these talented writers meant so much to me. Thanks also to the wonderfully supportive members of my former writing group: David Whitton, Nitin Deckha, and Shari Lapena. I have so many fond memories of our monthly meetings. To Debbie Wolgelerenter, Bernice Landry, and Mary O'Connell, thank you for your friendship, support, advice, and ideas.

During my years at York University, I was blessed with many amazing professors, but I would like to give particular thanks to Marie Rickard and Janet Lewis for seeing a potential in me I didn't know I had.

But most of all, my deepest gratitude and love to my mom, my brothers, and my sisters — they are that special something that always remains.

Though nothing can bring back the hour
Of splendour in the grass, of glory in the flower;
We will grieve not, rather find
Strength in what remains behind ...

—William Wordsworth,
"Ode on Intimations of Immortality from
Recollections of Early Childhood"

Grief moves us like love. Grief is love ...
Love as a backwards glance.

— Helen Humphreys, *The Lost Garden*

I

hellos and handshakes

I wish I had my camera, Andrew Christiansen thinks to himself as he leans against the wall-to-wall glass window that offers a perfect view of the Metropolitan United Church and the little park in front. The trees in the park blow in the strong winds of the autumn storm that has been battering Toronto for three days.

Andrew is thirty-six, long-limbed, angular, and wears his thick dark hair combed back close against his skull. He berates himself for thinking about taking a photograph at a time like this. An hour has passed since Dr. Farshad has updated him, his sister Natalie, and father Gregory about his mother's grave condition and disappeared into the ICU, saying he will do his best in response to Natalie's plea not to let their mother die.

One painful hour and still neither the doctor nor the nurses have shown their faces in the waiting room on the fourth floor of the hospital where they, the Christiansen family, are the only people at ten-thirty in the morning. Having paced the long, narrow room for what felt like an eternity and registering his sister's livid glare, silently imploring him to sit, Andrew finally stopped moving and slouched against the glass wall, directly facing his sister and father who are sitting on the poorly upholstered sofa, their tense bodies shifting every once in a while, choosing a posture and holding still as if constructing a tableau vivant.

It is their current posture that makes Andrew wish he brought his camera, which is locked in the glove compartment of his car. Andrew's father sits hunched, elbows pressed against thighs, head lowered as if pouring all his attention into a small hole on the floor between his feet. Natalie sags against their father's large frame, resting her head on the left side of his back, her round, olive-skinned face severe and expressionless.

It is a perfect representation of grief, poignant in its apparent powerlessness but also revealing a slight, palpable undertone of hope that their beloved Ella will rally one more time as she has done on several occasions already in the past year. Andrew is almost moved to tears by the simple arrangement of their limbs: father bowing his head as if silently praying to a God he has lost faith in but turns to now out of desperation; sister, exhausted, empty of tears, propped against her father, if not for strength, then consolation.

Andrew tries to ignore the small part of him that is jealous of Natalie's ability to unselfconsciously seek and find warmth and comfort — however small — from physical contact with their father. He wishes it were as easy for him to do the same. Why is it that such a simple intimacy between men as leaning against each other in times of great need looks awkward and unsightly? Andrew has always felt the existence of a shaky bridge between himself and his father, and its crossing is, he realizes, at best clumsy and forced, at worst, downright needy and undignified.

He remembers when his father called him in Helsinki and told him that his mother had been diagnosed with stage four ovarian cancer. Six days later his father picked him up at Pearson International Airport. Dragging a large black suitcase, a heavy knapsack perched on his shoulders, Andrew came out of the terminal to find his father waiting by the grey Volvo. He quickened his pace, and his father did the same. When they finally stood face to face after a three-year absence, all they could do to show how much each missed the other was a strong handshake and a hug that consisted of the merest contact of their chests before recoiling and busying themselves with the luggage.

As Andrew stares at his sister and father now, he longs to know what that kind of contact feels like. Of all the people he knows, there are few, if any, he admires more than his father. Gregory was the one person whose respect and approval Andrew sought the most, from the time he was a boy and lived for those Sundays when the two of them rode bicycles through the nearby park or played baseball together, all the way to the day he left home for university and desperately yearned to tell his father how much he would miss him, only to have words fail him.

His mother's love, on the other hand, Andrew never had to seek. He would have had it whether he won the Nobel Prize or sat in a prison cell. Andrew went to sleep at night and woke up every day with the certainty that his mother loved him. Even if Gregory didn't mean it intentionally, Andrew always believed he had to work hard to get the same attention from his father. And now that he is in his mid-thirties, now that he can no longer lobby for his father's affection as shamelessly as he did when he was a boy, he feels hopeless that they will ever go back to the way they were. For the Christiansen men these are the days of hellos and handshakes.

Andrew's thoughts on the state of affairs between himself and his father are cut short when he sees Dr. Farshad walking in the centre of the shiny hallway toward them. Springing away from the wall he has been slumping against, Andrew prompts his father and sister to jump out of their seats, violently destroying their beautiful tableau. All of them now stand in the middle of the waiting room, eyes watching the small-framed man in the white coat heading their way. They look to his eyes for some sign, but find nothing, only the neutral, exhausted gaze of a medical professional.

With the air of a man who has become too used to striding into waiting rooms full of bereaved families praying for miracles, Dr. Farshad stands before them and in a tone of distant tenderness says, "I'm very sorry. I'm afraid we've lost her. We've tried everything, but her heart just gave out." A long silence fills the room. "For what it's worth, the end was peaceful, she didn't ..." The doctor's words trail off, as if he can't bring himself to actually say that she didn't suffer. Instead, he simply raises his hand, lightly pats Gregory's shoulder, and repeats, "I'm so very sorry." Then he turns and makes his way back along the corridor, the squeaky sounds of his Nikes against the well-scrubbed ivory linoleum floor dying off with each step.

Andrew tries his best to stand still and not crumple under the weight of the doctor's words of finality: "Her heart just gave out." He feels powerless, like an astronomer glimpsing Venus tip off its axis, defy the gravitational laws of the galaxies, and head straight toward Earth, with nothing he and all the science in the world can do to prevent it from crashing.

Natalie, whose face has already convulsed into despair, runs after the doctor, as though by following him she can reverse time. Andrew tries to reach for her hand to stop her, but she is too fast and all he can do is watch her rush by. His father — too weak or too shocked to sprint — ambles in the opposite direction toward the exit. Andrew doesn't know where his father is headed, but he knows that shuffling away and being alone for a while is how Gregory handles extreme emotions. So he makes no attempt to hinder his father.

Alone in the waiting room, Andrew collapses onto the nearby sofa, finally digesting the news that his mother, the woman around whom everyone and everything he knew and loved orbited, the woman to whom they all looked to for comfort, guidance, and validation has, after fighting for two years, surrendered and quietly slipped out of their lives forever.

2

action

Before Sarah knows it, his tongue is in her mouth and they are kissing with the intimacy and intensity of long-lost lovers. They are lying on a bed, he on top of her, his crotch grinding against hers. Both are naked except for the flesh-coloured patch of nylon material attached to their crotches with double-sided tape. Her raised legs are wrapped tightly around him.

"Cut!" yells the director, his booming voice resonating throughout the small set.

Christopher Hastings, a stocky man of fifty with a shiny, shaved head and a greying goatee, strides away from the small monitor from which he has been observing the scene. He comes over to the bed where Sarah and her fellow actor lie and leans over them, resting his palms on his knees.

Everyone else on the set is motionless, waiting to see what wisdom the director will impart to these actors about the secret art of pretend-fucking for film. Since this is a closed set, there aren't many people around, only the minimum, consisting of the director, the cinematographer, the boom mike operator, the focus puller and script supervisor, and one or two other necessary individuals.

Very few, indeed, considering the number of crew and the team of producers who would otherwise swarm the set had they not been shooting the most explicit sex scene of a film filled with frank depictions of sex.

Staring into his eyes, Sarah senses that her loud but otherwise amiable director, who came to filmmaking via art direction, is a bit uncertain, which isn't surprising since he has never directed a movie let alone two nude actors. It seems pretty clear to her that he doesn't really know what he is doing, but she appreciates his attempt to appear confident.

"Brilliant guys, just brilliant," he tells them as if he has read every book on directing he could get his hands on. No doubt, she thinks, the one thing every book advised was to compliment actors after each take, even after a rubbish one. Actors are a sensitive, fragile bunch, these books must have instructed, and they are prone to unprovoked hysterical outbursts, so be wary of them.

"That was brilliant," he tells them again in case they didn't hear him before. "But I'm not seeing the passion. I'm not feeling it. Remember, Constance and Mellors have been dying to make love ever since they laid eyes on each other."

Sarah, playing the part of Constance Chatterley, nods as if she is hearing this for the first time, as if he is giving her a piece of information without which she could never gain insight into the complex interior life of her character.

"Let's give it another go, shall we?" Christopher requests in his fake Cockney accent, no doubt to hide his ridiculously posh background. "This time, gimme more. Give me more. Give me everything." He wobbles over to a little monitor and stands behind it, excited, eager to see the result of his great direction. "More sweat," he demands, and suddenly an obliging production assistant in his early twenties with long, oily black hair that appears not to have seen shampoo in months materializes out of nowhere, runs over to Sarah and Ian, and sprays them with water from a Windex-like container. He squirts liquid rather liberally on Ian's back, making it seem as if the actor is dripping with perspiration, the kind that comes from a hot, passionate romp.

Shit! Sarah curses silently as she and Ian exchange a glance, as if to ask: "What the fuck does 'give me more, give me everything mean'?" This sort of vacuous direction infuriates her. She wants to scream: "Give me an action. For fuck's sake, give me an action to play." But her fear of being labelled "difficult" doesn't permit her to make such a demand, even if it would help her do the job better.

Sarah can understand action because she has spent the better part of her life trying to interpret human behaviour, why people do the crazy things they do. But today, it seems, she will have to settle for "give me more."

"Set!" the camera operator yells.

A bell goes off, more like an annoying beep than a ring, which means a red light is flashing on the stage door, instructing people not to enter or exit until the shot is completed.

"Rolling!" the first assistant director cries.

Christopher places the headset on his tiny red ears and takes a quick look around to see if everything is to his liking. All is quiet. Nervous expectation hovers. *"Action!"* he shouts.

Sarah and her scene partner go at it again. Since the dialogue track has been stripped out, Christopher feels free to comment without worrying about his voice being recorded. "Go slower," he whispers to Ian. "You're rushing it. Slow is good here."

Ian does as he is told, slowly kissing Sarah on the mouth, then making his way down to her neck and breasts.

How strange, Sarah thinks as she feels Ian's lips enclose her nipples. What a miracle that she can trick her body into responding to the stimulation of a stranger. Her brain and all its complicated neurons and sensors, it appears, can't tell the difference between real lovemaking and make-believe.

Ian's task is to kiss, lick, and nibble his way down Sarah's belly slowly, but he has rushed this on every take. Maybe his nerves are getting to him. Maybe he is uncomfortable about kissing the naked breasts of a woman he barely knows. Whatever his reason, he is going too fast for the director's liking.

"Stay there a little longer, Ian," Sarah hears Christopher say in his unbearably loud voice. "Don't head down too fast. Now circle your tongue around her nipples. Yes, that's brilliant. And, Sarah, dig your nails into his back. I want to see marks on his back. Yes. Very good, indeed." There is a creepy trace of fatherly pride in his voice.

Magically, Sarah Turlington, the celebrated stage actor making her feature film debut, and scene partner, Ian Harmer, the hunky movie star, pull off the tricky scene. Despite their director's blow-by-blow commentary and booming voice, they accomplish what good actors always strive for but rarely achieve — a synchronicity of action and emotion, of give and take, so much so that for a moment they convince the onlookers on the set, and themselves, that they are indeed lovers lost in bliss. With increasing speed and passion they gyrate in unison, their moans rising to a crescendo like the high notes of an aria. She kisses his mouth and forehead, tasting the mixture of sprayed-on water and sweat. She bites the side of his neck. Suddenly, she feels him get hard. His erection, thankfully still covered by the modesty patch, presses against her. Since this is a master shot that shows their entire naked bodies, it is imperative that they keep in constant contact to give the impression of intercourse.

Sarah is gripped by a strange combination of discomfort and excitement. She desperately wants to remain in the moment and not ruin the sense of intimacy they have been trying to achieve for the past eight takes, but she also can't help the excitement, the sense of actual sex invading, contaminating, what should be a completely platonic relationship between professional actors. Sarah does her best not to register his hardness, not to mention the increasing friction of his hips against hers.

During the fleeting moments between *action* and *cut*, Sarah and Ian are Lady Chatterley and her lover. Not wanting to take herself and her partner out of the loop, Sarah continues in this dangerous fashion, waiting and hoping to hear the director's voice cry, "Cut!" But the command never comes. She imagines Christopher sitting in his chair, staring at the little monitor, lost in the flickering vision of untamed passion before his eyes, mesmerized by its theatricality, its staged realness. Sarah knows a good director wouldn't cut a scene this good, this authentic, but she hopes Christopher will, anyway.

Red with embarrassment, Ian continues his vigorous humping. Sarah, now lost in this strange terrain of real/fake orgasm, clings to her partner, desperately trying not to betray what is happening — that she is really feeling something she should only be experiencing in theory. A part of her also cherishes this delicious secret like a kid stealing candy and getting away with it. Of course, in the past she has sensed the overlapping of her real sentiments and those of her characters' as she portrayed anger and sadness and all other human emotions onstage night after night, but never has she encountered this extraordinary meeting of her own sexual awakening and that of a character — the infamous Lady Chatterley no less.

The director finally yells, "Cut," when the scene reaches its natural conclusion and he gets what he needs: a genuine sense of two people drawn to each other so viscerally that they have no choice but to surrender. As uncomfortable a situation as it is, Sarah understands why she and Ian have to be pushed to such extremes of passion. More important, she knows they must be willing to force themselves to do whatever is needed if the audience is expected to buy the scene.

"Print!" Christopher shouts to no one in particular. "That's a wrap! Thanks, everyone." He runs to the two actors, who scuttle to cover their nakedness. "That was bloody beautiful. Brilliant work, guys." This time Sarah almost thinks his compliments are genuine, but he has said those very words so many times before that they now sound hollow.

Having already changed into her comfort clothes — a pair of blue jeans and a cream cashmere sweater — Sarah stands in front of the mirror in her trailer. She studies her face, delight flashing in her eyes for handling what could have been a difficult day rather well. Sarah is also happy about how she looks. Although people have been telling her how lovely she is all her life, she has never allowed herself to believe it, or more accurately, never permitted herself to take joy in it because she has always thought one should be proud of one's accomplishments, not a blessing as random as physical beauty. She is quite Puritan that way. But of late, especially after her thirty-third birthday a month ago, she has become much more interested in herself, not only in her intellect and emotions to which she has always paid utmost attention but in her body, as well — its appearance, the way she feels in it, and the many pleasures it has to offer.

Hers is a beauty composed of parts that are individually ordinary, even flawed. The neck is a centimetre or so too long, the nose too thin and pointed. The ears have an elfish, upward drift that makes them stick out more than she cares for, the lips appear too plump, almost collagenated, and the skin is fairer than is fashionable.

Add these oddities, however, and the effect is stunning yet approachable, with a kind of Audrey Hepburn vulnerability that makes everyone around her either want to fuck her or protect her from those who want to fuck her. As she stares in the mirror, apparently fascinated with herself, Sarah ties her brown hair in a high, loosey-goosey ponytail, puts on her coat, and leaves.

When she steps out of the trailer, which is parked outside a closed-off street, she finds Ian at the foot of the vehicle. For a moment he looks like a star-struck teenager waiting for an autograph from his favourite actress. Ian offers his hand and helps her down the trailer's steep steps.

"I thought you'd gone home," Sarah says.

"Before I left, I just wanted to thank you for a really amazing day."

At first Sarah doesn't read much into this compliment. She knows how obnoxiously self-congratulatory actors can be and that they say this sort of thing to one another all the time, especially on the first days of a shoot. But something in Ian's eyes, the way he gazes at Sarah but quickly turns away as if the gratitude he feels is too overwhelming, convinces her of his sincerity. She stands close to him, peers into his eyes, and kisses him on the lips softly, barely touching them. "You're so sweet, you know that? You've waited just to tell me that?"

"That and ..."

"And what?" she prompts.

"I ... well, the thing is. Back then, when we were making love, I mean, pretending to ... I just want to say I'm sorry."

"Sorry? What for?"

He hesitates as though trying to find a discreet way to speak his mind.

"What on earth are you sorry for?" she asks again.

"For getting, you know ..."

"Oh, that …" she says with a smile of sudden recognition — a perverse grin, actually.

"I just wanted to assure you that it was no disrespect on my part. I'm sorry if I made you uncomfortable. I couldn't help myself."

Sarah finds his clumsy apology endearing, touching even. "You're so very sweet."

This behaviour isn't what she anticipated from a man who has become a box office sensation by playing bigger-than-life heroes who save East Coast cities from psychopathic Arab terrorists or who single-handedly terminate giant bloodthirsty bugs invading from South America, wavy brown hair blowing beautifully in the wind. Sarah expected him to strut around the set, sweet-talking female crew members out of their pants, charming them into making a pilgrimage to his sizable trailer. Sarah even figured he would attempt a quick on-set fling with her. She didn't imagine herself standing in front of a man so shy, so quiet, that she can barely hear him.

Suddenly, Sarah is overcome by guilt for almost refusing to take the role in the film when she discovered that Ian Harmer would be her co-star, that her first foray into cinema would be alongside a man whose movies she can only bring herself to watch when she takes her godchildren and even then finds it difficult to sit through them. But having actually done some scenes with him now, she sees that underneath the matinee idol is a good actor who could someday be great if only he challenged himself more often. She feels a strong physical attraction toward him. Her desire made sense when he was naked and she was touching his beautiful body, feeding off his reaction to her, but fully clothed outside her trailer on a cold, rainy September night, she can't make sense of it.

"Would you like to have dinner with me?" Sarah asks him, almost before the thought fully forms in her head. "The food at

the hotel is … well, let's just say I'm not looking forward to it."
She realizes she might have stepped over an invisible line whose
crossing could have very serious consequences, especially only
two weeks into principal photography. *What if something does actually happen between us?* she wonders.

Sarah doesn't entertain that idea any further, for there is
Michael, her husband, to consider. It is Michael who really makes
her think twice about what lies on the other side of desire. If she
had an affair with Ian, it would break Michael. She knows he
would find out, too, not due to his own cleverness but because
she could never keep something as big as that to herself. No matter how hard she tried to wipe away the residue of another man
such a secret would manifest itself in some unforeseen way.

A part of Sarah admires people who possess the peculiar talent of taking from others what they can't get from their husbands
or wives while at the same time holding on to those things they
cherish most in their spouses, those things that made them say "I
do" in the first place.

Could I be one of those people? Sarah asks herself as she and Ian
walk side by side on the wet, shimmering pavement on their way
to dinner, shoulders occasionally touching. There is one thing she
knows, though — her capacity to surprise herself.

3

maybe tomorrow

For a brief moment Zakhariye thinks he is having a nightmare as the sound of George W. Bush's voice talking about spreading freedom and democracy throughout the Middle East ricochets in his head. He jolts up, popping his head from under the pillow. It dawns on him that it isn't a nightmare. He fell asleep with the television on last night while watching CNN and has awoken to the sound of Bush's self-righteous voice as the president gives another speech on the campaign trail.

When he opens his eyes, Zakhariye is blinded by the harsh morning light flooding the room. *We really should get heavier drapes,* he thinks. But how will he sell the idea to Thandie? His wife adores these sheer cream curtains that she chose — at a hefty price per metre — more for the sophisticated elegance they bestow on their lives than the shelter they provide. If he does ask his wife about putting up heavier drapes, then that would make their sleeping arrangement official. So far, for the past month, his sleeping downstairs on the sofa has had an accidental appearance. When she recently asked him why he was sleeping on the couch, he told her that since he was watching the news so late at night he didn't want to disturb her, thus portraying himself as a self-sacrificing husband rather than a man more comfortable sleeping by himself in the living room than on his side of their bed next to his wife of nine years.

Zakhariye sits up on the sofa and cranks the volume to hear what the experts are saying about the previous evening's presidential debate. He watched it and was thrilled at how well John Kerry did, but he wants to know if everyone else saw what he did or if his hatred for George Bush clouded his objectivity. The longer he listens the clearer the victor of the debate becomes to him.

Even though Kerry has won two debates in a row, Zakhariye hears the wholesome, all-American TV announcer reading the latest polls, indicating that if the election were held today, Bush would win. The prospect of George W. Bush returning for four more years as the leader of the free world saddens Zakhariye in a way that scares him. Such anguish over an American presidential election makes him worry about his mental state.

The time on the bottom right side of the TV screen above the CNN logo reads 8:04 a.m., and Zakhariye knows his wife will be coming downstairs any moment dressed in faded blue jeans and a sweater, with a knapsack on her back to carry her scrubs. Exactly as estimated, Thandie sprints down, full of energy and enthusiasm for the day ahead. Zakhariye represses a surge of resentment at his wife's tampon commercial perkiness. He wonders if he, too, would be so giddy if he took his multivitamins as religiously as she does. They exchange quick smiles as she makes her way toward the kitchen and he folds the blanket he covered himself with the previous night and puts it in the linen closet next to the kitchen.

Zakhariye's eyes fix on her willowy neck that would make her look so regal if it were a bit shorter but in actuality makes her seem fragile, almost childlike. He turns his attention to the small amount of cereal she helps herself to in the green ceramic bowl they bought together at Pottery Barn. Zakhariye wants to tell her to eat more, that she is getting too thin, but he doesn't. They have had many conversations, arguments even, about her not eating enough, and he recalls how much she disliked the fatherly tone of his voice. He doesn't want to go back to the way things were following the accident, so he glances away instead.

"Busy day?" he hears himself ask, surprised that he wants to know.

She turns to him but remains silent, as if caught off guard by the resumption of the usual morning chitchat that once filled their home. "Yeah," she says, and starts eating.

In the old days, as they ate breakfast, she leisurely munching on her cereal while he and Alcott enjoyed large, syrup-drenched pancakes Zakhariye woke up early to make, they would compare and contrast what lay ahead, telling each other how busy things were going to be at work as if competing for the title of whose day would be the most demanding.

Thandie would tell their son in great detail about the three or four people booked for surgery that day, all the people that she, as the anesthetist, would gently usher to sleep. And he would inform Alcott about the editorial meetings he would have to endure or the many squabbles between the writers and art department that he as the managing editor would have to intervene in. Alcott, the whole time, would turn his gaze from one parent to the other, always paying special attention to his mother's stories because to a seven-year-old boy operations sounded far more "awesome" than squabbles over heads, decks, and cover lines.

Zakhariye remembers how Alcott loved asking his mother about the operations and how she relished describing the pains-taking work of removing a bad kidney or repairing a defective heart, all the while making her modest part in the whole danger-ous endeavour more heroic.

But today as Zakhariye drinks coffee, as he leans on the ivory marble kitchen counter while his wife eats at the nearby table, nothing is shared, no comparisons are made about the coming day. He gestures to refill her coffee. She smiles, silently indicating that she would like that. He does so, and she thanks him with another gesture — a simple nod — so elegant in its precision that it would make a tango dancer proud. Lately, most of their communication has taken the form of these gestures. A stranger observing them would find beauty in the way they distilled complex language into mere gestures.

This graceful series of movements is separated by uncomfortable silences punctuated every so often by an overly polite *please* or *thank you* as if anything resembling a real conversation might open another abyss. They lived in that dark, horrifying place for months after they buried Alcott, so they avoid anything that might throw them back there — talking especially. Words have a way of leading them astray into unwanted memories of when things were good and happy and the particles of their lives were securely in place.

Watching their boy's small body draped in a simple white cotton sheet — in keeping with Islamic burial — being lowered into the ground did things to them individually. It shattered something that could never be repaired. But it also did something to them as a couple. It stopped them from being on the same team. These days they are as estranged from each other as he feels from their previous life. From the moment they found out that Alcott didn't make it out of the emergency surgery to stop internal hemorrhaging, whatever love and affection Zakhariye and Thandie had for each other had leaped into their past and become inseparable from memories of their son. Regaining even an ounce of what they once felt for each other now means remembering their lost son.

As Zakhariye sips his hot coffee, he glances at the morning newspaper.

His wife gets up, puts her bowl and coffee mug in the dishwasher, grabs her knapsack, and heads for the door. Just before she leaves the kitchen, she stops and says, "Bye."

"Have a nice day, sweetie," he replies, barely shifting his attention from the paper.

Zakhariye glances at his watch — time for him to go to work, too. But there is something else he really wants to do now that he has the whole house to himself and doesn't have to fear his wife giving him another one of her subtle but reproachful looks for wasting so much time in front of the TV. He desires nothing more than to take another cup of coffee, sit before their plasma screen TV in the middle of their beautifully decorated living room, and lose himself in world events where the good guys and bad guys are clearly labelled. Bush and Blair good, Osama and Saddam bad. There is great comfort in such irrefutable clarity.

Deep down inside he knows world affairs are never as simple as the talking heads on CNN, MSNBC, BBC, and the other twenty-four-hour-news channels he watches would have him believe. But since he can't find an expert, a priest, or an imam who can explain why he had to bury his son instead of the other way around, he gladly consumes the news because it, like a well-made Hollywood flick, makes sense. If he puts aside all that he knows about the world and the corrupt men who run it, he really can find some order.

As much as he wants to vegetate in front of the TV, he knows he can't risk being late for work again. He has a meeting with the publisher of his magazine at ten to discuss sagging sales and stagnant circulations, and he can make it on time if he grabs a quick shower and jumps into a cab. So he, too, throws his mug into the dishwasher and heads for the bedroom. He tries to sprint up the stairs like his wife, but his back is sore. Weeks of sleeping on the sofa have compromised his much-admired posture.

His posture was the thing Thandie noticed about him when she first met him. She told him that over dinner one night during the initial months of their courtship. "I loved the way you held yourself," she said, giggling as she confessed to him. "Just fell for those broad, pushed-back shoulders." He almost chuckles now recalling that evening as he takes cautious steps up the stairs.

In the bedroom he pulls the T-shirt over his head and throws it into the laundry basket that sits behind the door of the walk-in closet. With a single smooth motion he strips off his pajama bottoms and chucks them into the basket, as well. Striding back into the room on his way to the bathroom of the master bedroom, its luxurious ivory carpet under his feet, he catches his naked body in the dresser mirror. He turns to face it and inspects his nakedness. *Gotta hit the gym, man,* he instructs himself.

All is not lost, though. There is still time to salvage his once beautifully toned physique. Sure, his six-pack, the centrepiece of his own marvellous creation, is barely visible. There is the hint of love handles, and his former rock-hard chest has softened, reinforcing his current state as a man who has at last come to terms with his distinctly average looks. For years he managed to look way above average by sheer hard work and the belief that it was his moral duty to co-operate with Mother Nature and do his bit to make life more beautiful.

As Zakhariye studies his naked self, he lets his eyes wander to his crotch, stopping to focus on his limp penis. Once the centre of his universe, it now appears neglected, unimportant, no longer the facilitator of unimaginable pleasures. *It is true,* he thinks. *The less you do it the less your body desires it.* Placing a hand on his genitals, he tries to muster a reaction. A moment later he gives up, disappointed but resigned to the fact that he is a different man these days. He is no longer that guy who lived in the smithy of his body, perpetually delighting in all its pleasures great and small.

Standing over the bathroom sink, still naked, Zakhariye shaves, a task he loathes but has to do today because of his meeting with the publisher. He works up a good lather and takes the triple-blade razor to his face. Starting from the top of his sideburns, he glides the sharp metal along his skin until he strips the last strand of three-day growth. When he begins to rinse the razor, he notices a large drop of blood in the white sink moving toward the drain. He wonders whose blood it is. Startled, he inspects his face and discovers he has nicked, very badly, a shaving bump under his chin. A thin stream of blood trickles down his collarbone. He dabs a finger and holds the blood-covered finger to the light, surprised by its vivid redness. It sparkles. *Wow, I didn't even feel a thing.*

A peculiar rush at seeing his own blood grips Zakhariye. It is the kind of thrill foreign to a peaceful, middle-aged, middle-class man who has never witnessed the shedding of his own blood. His delight is heightened by the delayed sting of the cut that his brain now registers. This is the strongest bodily sensation he has had in so long that the elation he experiences overwhelms him. It feels as if his nervous system has finally jumped up from its long hibernation and screamed, "Wake up!" But he is dismayed by the ephemeral nature of his newfound aliveness. As soon as the blood stops flowing and the sting of the aftershave subsides, the joy ceases.

Zakhariye longs for more. He would give anything to have that rush again. Independent of his intelligent, rational mind, he watches his hand, the one clutching the razor, move toward his face. He runs the middle finger of his other hand along his chin in search of another bump. When he finds one just under his jawbone, he rests the blade on it, relishing the moment before the skin ruptures. With a quick gesture he drags the blade over it and feels the bump open. A guttural scream escapes him. This time what he feels is sheer pain minus the exhilaration that accompanied the first cut. Disappointment, as with everything else in his life, sullies the whole enterprise.

He wants to find another bump to see if he can re-experience, recapture, the bliss of the first nick, but his nerves fail him. *Maybe tomorrow,* he thinks, regarding himself in the mirror, *maybe tomorrow.*

4

bowling in peace

Gregory Christiansen has never been in a bowling alley. Less than an hour ago he stood in a hospital waiting room where a kind, soft-spoken doctor told him that his wife of thirty-nine years was dead. Now he finds himself in a rundown bowling alley whose geographical location in the city is a mystery to him and how exactly he got there an even bigger riddle.

He remembers leaving the hospital waiting room, desperate to get out of the building as if by escaping the scene he could somehow erase the fact that the centre of his life around which he and the rest of his family congregated has vanished. Gregory also recalls getting lost in the hospital and ending up in the surgery wing where a willowy Ethiopian-looking nurse in scrubs stopped him, telling him he shouldn't be there and pointing him in the direction of the elevator. Then there was the sensation of finally rushing out of the building and the cold, damp air hitting his face. But that is where his memories end.

Gregory doesn't remember getting into his car, if he did, or what made him come into this place, since he has never had a desire to enter a bowling alley. He also doesn't recollect paying at the counter or sitting on one of the blue-and-white chairs to put on the silly shoes he is wearing now, which make the ground beneath his feet shaky and untrustworthy.

Much to Gregory's annoyance some loud people two lanes down are relentlessly teasing one another. The unruly bowlers are likely office co-workers on a team-building excursion to get acquainted outside their usual roles and duties. Just as Gregory gets ready to roll the ball on the long, narrow strip in front of him, the place explodes into sudden, shrill cheers coming from the noisy bowlers, making Gregory miss the pins by a mile. Never stopping to consider that his failure to topple any of the pins might have more to do with the fact that he has never bowled before, he shoots an angry, self-righteous glare in their direction much like the ones he and his wife used to aim at chatty couples who always sat next to them whenever they went to a stage play, which was often.

He glowers at one of the rowdy bowlers — a fifty-something woman with blond hair so puffed up it resembles an actual bee-hive. She shoots him a screw-you look. Gregory returns to his solitary game, convinced that if he had a quiet moment to concentrate, he would be able to knock over the pins before him. They seem to mock him, as if they, too, are involved in a vast conspiracy against him.

Gregory wants to ask them why of all the bowling alleys in the world this flock of office nobodies had to invade this one in his hour of need. He desperately needs to flatten some pins as though that mere accomplishment has the power to put the rest of his life back together in a recognizable form, one that resembles the way the world was when his wife was still in it.

Taking a deep breath, his sausage-like thumb barely fitting in the hole of the navy blue ball, Gregory positions himself, making a great effort not to slip and slide in the unfamiliar shoes. As he is about to release the ball, a member of the raucous group executes a perfect shot, sending all the pins crashing. The successful bowler celebrates his triumph with a long chicken dance, complete with squawks in his opponent's face. The man's office comrades cheer him on loudly.

That's it! Gregory thinks. *A man can only be pushed so far, then it's war.*

Gregory drops the ball on the hardwood floor. It thuds so loudly that everyone turns to stare at him. He scurries over to the man doing the chicken dance. When he reaches the guy, he pushes him back with the open palms of both hands on the man's thick chest, feeling the warm, cushy fat of the thick chest under the golf shirt. "Have you people no respect?" Gregory cries.

The other bowlers surround him, ready to protect their man. The chicken-dancing fellow stumbles backward under the force of Gregory's fury, then yells, "What the fuck's your problem, buddy?"

"Don't call me *buddy*. I'm not your *buddy*. A little peace — that's all I'm asking." Gregory's fists are now closed, ready for a fight. "I just want to bowl. Is that too goddamn much to ask?" He grabs the man by his shirt collar and shakes him. "I just want to be left alone. Why won't you do that?"

Gregory is surprised and frightened by the secret source of strength that enables him to manhandle this beefy bowler like a rag doll. One of the men in the offending fellow's group, fortyish with big arms and even bigger belly, seizes Gregory from behind and pulls him away, while one of the women, a black lady with large cornrows, shouts in a heavy Jamaican accent, "Oh, sweet Jesus, he gonna kill him! Patty, run, girl, and get security. Oh, sweet lord, he gonna kill him."

The big-bellied guy yanks Gregory so hard that he loses his balance and falls to the floor. As Gregory struggles to get up, the chicken-dance man and his plump comrade push him back onto the floor, then sit on him. When Gregory hears boots pounding on the floor, he twists his head, presses a sweaty cheek against the cold, dusty floor, and spots two twenty-something security guards in black uniforms approaching.

"All I wanted to do was play," Gregory tells the security guards as they extricate him from the tangle of limbs. "They wouldn't let me play," he says, practically sobbing. "Why won't they let me play?" The guards ignore his questions as they hustle him out of the building.

As the security men drag him away, Gregory remembers how hopeful he felt early that morning when he drove to the hospital to continue reading Edith Wharton's *The Age of Innocence* from where he had left off the previous day. He is astonished that he can recall the precise spot where he stopped reading to his wife — at the end of the scene after Newland Archer and Countess Olenska's accidental meeting in Boston where Newland tells the countess, "You gave me my first glimpse of a real life, and at the same moment, you asked me to go on with a sham one. It's beyond human enduring."

Ella wanted him to continue reading, but when she shut her eyes, strength clearly waning, he closed the book and said, "Tomorrow, my dearest. We'll continue tomorrow." Then he chuckled. When his wife asked what was so funny, he lifted the book and told her, "Now you got me talking like one of *them*."

His wife laughed, something that had become harder and harder to elicit from her in those last days. So, on the rare occasions when he made her smile or chuckle, he relished it. She said the chemotherapy made her tired and humourless, but he knew there was more to it. The end was nearing. They both realized that, but neither dared to acknowledge it.

When he parked his car in the hospital lot earlier today, he was eager to sit on the edge of her bed and resume their daily reading, perhaps even find out what happened to Newland and the countess. Gregory had learned to lower his expectations of what counted as a good day. That morning he walked into her room with a hopeful smile only to discover that Ella had gone into cardiac arrest and had been moved to the ICU where she perished alone.

"We perish each alone," Gregory says aloud as he is hauled out of the bowling alley. *Who said that? Where did he read that?* He can't remember. His desire to bowl, which was so strong, so all-consuming a few minutes ago, now seems small and ridiculous to him, causing him to howl with laughter.

5

small triumphs

Andrew's heart sinks as he listens to the man on the other side of the telephone saying, "This is Constable Abraham of 51 Division. May I speak with Andrew Christiansen, please?"

He can't imagine losing two parents in one day but knows it is possible. It is not statistically impossible, nor is he so special as to be karmically immune to great misfortunes. Andrew also knows that given the bereaved state his father was in, he could have easily run the Volvo into a light pole or driven off a bridge. Such horrifying scenarios are within the realm of possibility. Therefore, when Constable Abraham asks him to come to the police station to post bail for his father who is sitting in a cell charged with assault, it is the last thing he expects.

A little later, as Andrew parallel-parks outside the police station, he is overwhelmed by a deluge of emotions. His heart breaks for his father who will have to learn how to live without a wife and constant companion. Andrew also feels the numbing shock of his mother's death, not to mention the fatigue of being on his feet since the morning. Underneath all that is the guilt of forgetting to call his wife to tell her about his mother's passing.

However, his most immediate reaction as he opens the heavy glass door of the police station is sheer gratitude that his father is safe, held in a cell where the man can't be a danger to himself or anyone else.

After posting the $3,000 bail, Andrew waits in the reception area. "Huh?" was all he could say when the policeman told him about the bowling alley brawl. But his surprise that his father was in a bowling alley of all places took a back seat to the charge of assault. His father, the pacifist, the believer in non-violent solutions to world problems, the man who drove all the way to Washington, D.C., to demonstrate against the Vietnam War, who voted for any politician advocating the banning of guns, now sits in jail for smashing another person's face. *Unbelievable!* Andrew thinks as he waits for his father to emerge. And the more he ponders the situation, the less he feels he knows his father.

When the glass door finally slides open and Andrew's father steps out, he seems too frail to have beaten anyone. Andrew smiles, trying his best not to appear disapproving. However, Gregory's dirt-covered khakis, the torn pocket of his blue shirt, and the cut over his left eyebrow make it impossible not to judge. They stare at each other for a moment, then without a word walk side by side out of the building.

As Andrew drives north on Parliament Street toward his father's house near Bathurst Street and Eglinton Avenue, he wants to ask Gregory what possessed him to attack another man in a bowling alley. But he doesn't. Andrew can see that whatever the cause, just or unjust, his father seems sorry about the outcome. Besides, they have more pressing matters to worry about. They have a funeral to plan, relatives to notify, an obituary to write, not to mention getting a good lawyer to sort out the bowling alley mess.

"Natalie has called Aunt Doris, who said she'd call everyone else, and Uncle Dave is flying in tomorrow," Andrew says without taking his eyes off the road. "I'm going to take care of the funeral home and the obituary, and Natalie will handle the rest."

"What about me?" Gregory asks.

"You're in no condition."

"Bullshit."

"Dad, you need to rest."

"Don't treat me like an invalid."

"I'm not. I'm just worried about —"

"I'll find the funeral home. You'll take care of the rest, and that's final."

Andrew knows better than to argue with his father, a man whose stubbornness has always been formidable under the best of circumstances. He pulls the cab into his father's driveway and turns off the engine. Reaching for the door lock to get out, he notices that his father isn't moving, so he remains seated, gazing at the red garage door in front of them. They sit in this fashion for quite a while. It feels so long that Andrew begins to worry. He wouldn't put it past his father to stay in the car all night, so he makes the first move. Touching Gregory's wrist to be certain his father is still awake, he suggests, "Dad, why don't you go in? You must be starving."

"I should paint that door," Gregory says.

"What?"

"The garage door." He moves his chin up a little to point to the door in question. "Your mother nagged me to repaint it for months."

"Don't worry. I'll paint it."

"Before the funeral. We have to do it before the funeral. She would hate people visiting us with a door like that."

Andrew tries to hide a surge of impatience. "I'll paint the door, Dad."

They stare at the garage door as if waiting for it to tell them what to do next.

"We really should go in," Andrew says at last, putting authority in his tone. "Natalie's worried to death in there."

Gregory finally gets out of the car. Andrew follows him, registering a tinge of pride for his display of strength against his father's childish obstinacy.

When they stroll in the front door, they are confronted by a dishevelled Natalie. Her hair is mussed and her blouse is covered with large red stains. She hugs her father with relief.

"What the hell happened to you?" Gregory demands.

"I was cooking. I wanted to have something ready to eat when you came home. We'll have to order pizza, though."

"I'm not hungry," Gregory mutters as he climbs the stairs, leaving his children in the mustard-yellow foyer.

They watch him trudge up. Once alone, Andrew turns to Natalie and chuckles. "You tried to cook?"

"Oh, shut up!" Natalie snaps as they head toward the kitchen to inspect the damage.

Andrew feels a jolt of happiness that he can still get satisfaction from teasing his sister even on a day such as this one.

Standing in a corner of the elevator, Andrew stares at the changing red digital numbers above the door. It occurs to him that he hasn't shed a single tear yet for his mother, who he imagines lying in the hospital morgue, body growing colder with each passing minute. He is dismayed by his lack of emotion. It is as if his heart hasn't caught up with the dizzying speed with which the events of the day have occurred. And the day still isn't over. Turning the key in the door to his apartment, he tries to construct the words to tell his wife that his mother is dead. His mother liked Rosemary — a lot. She told him so when he informed her that Rosemary was two months' pregnant with his child.

"Marry her, you fool," his mother said to him as she struggled to sit up in bed, exhausted from another chemotherapy dose earlier that morning. "She's a sad girl, no surprise considering her parents, but she's kind and hard-working. If that doesn't make a good wife, then I give up."

Rosemary once lived two houses down from the Christiansen family, with a bipolar mother who spent most days watching Portuguese soap operas while knitting miles and miles of colourful bedspreads no one ever bought. Her father used his job driving a Greyhound bus as an excuse to be away from home most of the year. So it was natural for Andrew's mother to develop a soft spot for the shy, scrawny girl whose flat chest made her unpopular with boys at school, and more dismayingly, with girls, as well. Because Andrew was the only guy among his peers who was nice to her, and because they were neighbours, Rosemary found a second home with the Christiansens where after school she would watch *Wheel of Fortune* — a game she beat everyone at — or help Ella prepare supper.

Given all that, Andrew wasn't surprised to hear his mother say, "Marry her, you fool" — especially since Rosemary was carrying his child, the result of many evenings driving her home when she visited his mother at the hospital. It had started with one awkward kiss on Rosemary's porch and had progressed to what could only be described as several months of comfort sex, the type two sad, lonely people share as a temporary refuge.

As Andrew now enters his apartment and quietly closes the door, he knows he will probably find his wife in one of the two bedrooms of their tiny apartment at the corner of Finch Avenue and Yonge Street where they are a visible minority among the upwardly mobile yuppies occupying much of the building. Just as he suspected, Rosemary is on their queen-size bed. They wanted a king, but the room that pretends to be the master suite doesn't accommodate anything larger than a queen. His wife is propped against the bed's headboard, her reading glasses perched on the tip of her nose as she reads another romance novel.

Andrew once made the mistake of suggesting that since Rosemary spent so much time reading, why not make the effort worthwhile by reading something good. She didn't speak to him for three days. Instead of perceiving his suggestion as innocent, albeit pompous, Rosemary interpreted it as a comment not so much on her intelligence, for she was confident in her intellect, but a cowardly reminder that she lacked the kind of sophistication her husband found sexy in a woman. Andrew has come to realize that his wife's homeliness is a particular sore point with her. Also problematic are his world travels as a photojournalist and all the adventures and exotic love affairs such a career rightly or wrongly implies. A background like that makes the differences between them all the more striking.

After his comment about his wife's choice of reading material, Andrew learned to keep his mouth shut. He truly believes that one of the reasons his wife is so unhappy, and as a result angry, is that she reads romance novels in which all the men are wealthy and dashing and all the women are long-legged and gorgeous. If she stopped reading those novels, Andrew feels, she would be content with the mediocrity of her life. Or, failing that, she would learn to value its many quiet virtues.

Andrew knows Rosemary wasn't reading before he arrived. More likely she was pacing the kitchen floor, anxiously awaiting his return. However, his wife would rather eat a rotting octopus than let on she was fretting. But despite her attempt to seem nonchalant, he always finds her waiting to tell him how horrible he is for not doing the hundred and one things she asks him to do on any given day.

Normally, Andrew takes exception to her complaints about his shortcomings, but tonight he, too, would concur with her. This morning when his father called and told him to rush to the hospital, Andrew turned off his cellphone and hasn't checked the countless messages his wife has likely left by now. To make matters worse, he was so overwhelmed by the events of the day that he forgot to let Rosemary know that Ella, the woman who had been more of a mother to her than a mother-in-law, was dead.

Andrew sits on the edge of the bed gingerly looking at his wife, doing his best to seem guilty. He takes his shirt off as Rosemary carefully puts the novel on the night table and folds her arms. Andrew can sense the coming recriminations.

"Before you say anything, I just want to ask you a simple question," Rosemary says slowly as if talking to one of her more difficult fourth-grade students. "Do I or do I not have the right to be angry? You're always accusing me of being angry, that I make too much out of —"

"Honey, I'm really sorry. I have —"

"Andrew, *no!* First, I want you to acknowledge the validity of my feelings and make a genuine effort to understand why I feel the way I do before you try to pacify me."

He hates the inane therapy jargon she uses on her emotionally troubled students, but this isn't the time to bring that up. Instead he plays it safe. "Sweetie, I do understand how you feel —"

"Fuck you, Andrew. You have no fucking idea how I feel."

He is always shocked when his wife swears, even though he has spent more than a year listening to her curse as if she were auditioning for a Quentin Tarantino flick.

"I left you seven goddamn messages and not once did you bother to call me. Didn't it occur to you there might be a legitimate reason for my calls? I could've been raped, for fuck's sake. I could've been strangled and left to die, for all you knew. Hanna could've fallen out of her crib and —"

Andrew's heart leaps with fear. "Is Hanna all right?"

"No, your daughter's fine," Rosemary says quickly as though realizing that bringing Hanna into the fight is a low blow. "But that's not the point, Andrew."

"Then what the fuck is the point?" He recently noticed that he only swears when fighting with his wife — her casual use of expletives gives him the permission to do likewise.

"*The fucking point* is you wouldn't know if she wasn't okay. I could've been scraping her brains off the goddamn floor and you wouldn't know because you didn't bother to pick up the phone. *That's the fucking point.*"

Andrew, who has now taken his pants off, leaving on his blue boxers, gets off the bed and goes over to the closet where he throws in his jeans and sweater and takes out a wrinkled grey T-shirt. He sniffs it to check if it is clean. It could use a spin in the washing machine, but he is too tired to be picky tonight, so he puts it on. Then he returns to the exact position on the bed where he was sitting.

"Well?" Rosemary says.

"Well what?"

"An explanation would be nice."

"I turned my cellphone off. Is that enough explanation?"

"What's the point of paying for the thing if you're just going to shut it off?"

Andrew doesn't respond. He is too exhausted for tit-for-tat tonight. The death of a loved one has a way of making winning an argument inconsequential. On the edge of the bed he bows his head, lets his shoulders slump, and dangles his arms as if they were deflated balloons. "My mother's dead," he whispers, finally giving into the fatigue of this wretched day.

Rosemary doesn't reply. Either shock or just plain not having a clever comeback has rendered his otherwise cantankerous wife speechless. After a moment, Andrew glances up to see if she heard what he said. Her slap-on-the-face expression indicates she did.

"What the fuck, Andrew!" she screams. "When were you going to tell me? I mean, you could've told me the minute you came through the door."

"You didn't give me a chance. Besides, you could've asked me."

"What should I have said exactly — hi, hon, is your mother dead yet?"

Andrew glares at her menacingly.

"I'm sorry, I'm sorry. That was horrible. All I'm saying is that you could've told me rather than let me bitch about the stupid messages. Do you really think I'm so heartless that it wouldn't have made a difference to me?"

"No, I don't think that. I'm sorry. I don't know what I'm doing." Actually, Andrew isn't really sure if that is true or not.

"Of course, you don't. How can you?" Rosemary crawls on the bed over to Andrew. She wraps her arms around him from behind, encircling her bony, pasty legs around his waist as she kisses him on the back of the neck and whispers how sorry she is. Andrew turns his head, his face meeting hers. They kiss. It is a sweet, consoling, sexless kiss, the kind he has longed for all day. Rosemary starts to cry.

Andrew wipes her tears with the open palm of his hand. "Don't cry," he whispers. "Don't cry."

"I loved her. She wasn't an in-law to me. She was a like a mother." Her voice cracks.

Andrew knows Rosemary's words are heartfelt, that her sentiments aren't the hollow kind people are compelled to offer to the relatives of the dead no matter what their true feelings are. He has always despised false tributes — like the time he was watching the funeral of Richard Nixon in a hotel room in Kinshasa and he threw the can of yogurt he was eating at the television because he couldn't stand the sight of Jimmy Carter and Bill Clinton and so many other dignitaries pretending to be sad for the loss of one of the most loathsome presidents in American history. So when Rosemary says that his mother was like another mother to her, he knows she is sincere and is moved.

"When did it happen?" Rosemary asks after her tears subside.

"This morning Dad called me on my cell, just as I started working. I meant to call you, but I had to drive to my parents' place to pick up Natalie, who flew in late last night. We rushed to the hospital, and by the time we got there, Mom was already in the ICU. We didn't get to see her alive." Andrew glances at his wife, who now seems sadder than he has ever seen her, even more than she was on their high school prom day when her date stood her up and his mother asked, actually demanded, that he take her instead. And he complied begrudgingly but was glad he did, not because it made him feel compassionate or heroic but because they ended up having such a nice time as friends without all the weird expectation of customary prom-night sex.

They sit silently for a minute, holding each other, then change positions. Now she sits at the foot of the bed, side by side, takes his head in her hands, and rests it on her lap.

Her cool cotton nightgown feels so good on the side of Andrew's face. He looks up at her face. "After we found out that she passed away, we lost Dad."

"Lost Dad?"

"He ran away, and we looked for him all over the hospital."

"Did he go home?"

"That's what we thought, so we went home, but he wasn't there. Natalie wanted to call the police and report a missing person, but I told her to wait a little longer."

"When did he come home?"

"He didn't. I had to pick him up at the police station."

"What? Why?"

"He beat up some guy in a bowling alley."

"A bowling alley? What on earth was he doing there?"

"Bowling, I gather."

"I don't understand."

"Neither do I, honey."

"Wow!"

"I know."

"Now do you see why I forgot to call you?"

"I do. I'm sorry. I did go nuts on you, didn't I?"

Andrew nods.

She bends and kisses him on the lips. "What a day you've had."

Andrew sighs. "I just want it to end. Make it go away."

Rosemary pulls his head off her lap. "Lie down and get some sleep."

"I can't sleep. I have to write an obituary for the newspaper tomorrow."

"Don't they have people who do that?" she asks, clearly unfamiliar with the rituals of death.

"Dad wants it to be personal. He doesn't want a complete stranger writing it."

"That's understandable. I wouldn't like someone who's never met me to write about me when I'm dead."

"I don't even know what to say. Where do I start?"

It is one-thirty in the morning. Andrew nurses a glass of whiskey he poured himself ten minutes ago with the hope of lubricating his mind so he can write his mother's obituary. All he has done, though, is stand by his eighth-floor living-room window and stare down at Finch Avenue, giving him a perfect view of the long, narrow bus bay of the subway station.

Andrew watches several people waiting for a bus in the cold, wet September night. As he takes another slow sip of whiskey, he wonders who these people are and where they are going at this late hour. He often finds himself doing that — gazing at people in the midst of their lives. Whether from behind the lens of his camera or through the windshield of his cab, he is always captivated by the sight of other human beings rushing to work, walking their dogs, kissing in the a park under a tree, or lingering at a city intersection, pausing for a light to change.

Witnessing the private stories of others playing out in public isn't just a hobby but a compulsion. Something about the simple act of observing others moves him. He is touched not so much by their activities, for they are almost always banal, but the very fact that they exist, that out there, at any given moment in Toronto, in any city in the world, are millions of private little narratives unfolding, some beginning, others ending, all adding up to an unfathomable master narrative whose ultimate conclusion is anybody's guess.

One of the people waiting for a bus is a tall African man who could pass for the doppelganger of Andrew's friend Zakhariye, which reminds him that he should tell Zakhariye about his mother. Watching people is what made Andrew a good photojournalist. He has never had what could be called a technique or artistic vision, but he does possess the gift of observation. As he takes another sip of his drink, Andrew thinks about the millions of stories that need to be written, painted, photographed, captured in some way for others to see and maybe find consolation in.

A bus finally arrives and parks next to the line of people. They board the vehicle, but it idles for a while. Suddenly, a heavy-set woman with a long blond mullet emerges from the station. She is holding two plastic bags in each hand and starts running. Andrew knows that catching the bus will make the difference between getting home to a warm bed or standing in the cold for thirty or forty minutes, maybe longer. The woman tries to move faster, but her weight holds her back. Andrew thinks about the blank page that still waits for him. He shakes his head.

He spent the past hour at the dinner table attempting to compose a short obituary to inform Torontonians about the life and death of a woman most of them never met and couldn't care less about. Andrew doesn't understand the point of the exercise. Its apparent futility makes him even sadder. But his father was adamant that it be done, that they inform whoever is out there about the special woman this town has lost.

Andrew wonders what his father thinks writing an obituary will accomplish. Does he imagine someone out there, perhaps an old friend she lost touch with or one of the young men she dated before she married him, will read the newspaper and discover his wife's death, share his loss, and grieve with him from afar?

Already Andrew has tried three drafts and found the task of distilling his mother's life into a few sentences next to impossible. How does one sum up a full, rich, well-lived life? Frustrated and feeling unequal to the task, Andrew now finds himself watching an obese woman frantically trying to catch a bus. He notices he has been holding his breath as he follows her progress. The bus has been idling for sometime now and could drive away at any minute. But she is so close. *What a shame it will be*, he thinks, *what a shame if she doesn't make it after such a valiant effort. Does God see our efforts?*

Andrew isn't even sure if he believes in God anymore. His former life as a photojournalist took him to the gaping mouths of dug-up mass graves in Bosnia and villages in Bangladesh drowned by nature's indifference, making it difficult to accept a supreme, benevolent being watching over everyone.

Gazing out the window, he wants to believe there is a God who sees how hard people try — like the fat woman racing for the bus — how much everyone strives only to fall a little short. Tonight, though, one woman does succeed. She reaches the bus's rear door and boards the vehicle. The bus comes to life and slowly turns westward on Finch. He tilts his neck as far as he can to track the bus until it disappears, then smiles.

Andrew is so happy for her. Whoever she is, wherever she is going, his heart is glad for her small triumph. He takes the last sip of whiskey, relishing its sweet aftertaste in the contours of his mouth. Then he returns to the blank page on the table, hopeful that he, too, will have his own small victory and find the right language to pay tribute to the life of Ella K. Christiansen.

As if by sheer inspiration, the words, good, solid, truthful ones about his mother, tumble onto the page. Andrew's previous attempts produced what sounded to him like overly sentimental rubbish, and now here it is — a brief, honest, unembroidered account of his mother's life. As he puts the finishing touches on the piece, the shrill, start-stop-start crying of his daughter drifts out of her room. Although he yearns to finish the obituary, he is happy for the urgent intrusion of the living upon the final affairs of the dead.

Andrew goes to his daughter's room and opens the door. He stands over the dimly lit crib where Hanna, a chubby-faced, seven-month-old girl, sits cross-legged in the middle like a Buddhist monk. She has recently learned to sit on her own and takes every opportunity to use her newly discovered independence. As soon as she sees Andrew, she raises her arms, a gesture she performs with perfection. Hanna is supremely confident of the outcome of her action — that her father will pick her up.

And she is right; it never fails. Andrew sweeps her up in one smooth motion and holds her warm, soft body close to him. He kisses her head, its soft curls pressing on his lips. The scent of baby oil hits him, making him dizzy with joy.

"She must be hungry," Rosemary says.

He turns to find his wife standing behind him. "I've got her. Go back to sleep. I'll warm up her bottle."

Rosemary wobbles back to their bedroom as Andrew carries his daughter to the kitchen. Hanna's bottle of formula milk has already been prepared for a late-night feeding like this. He puts the bottle in the sink, runs hot water over it for a minute, then tests the milk by pouring a little on his hand. Happy with its temperature, he takes a seat at the kitchen breakfast nook. Holding Hanna on his lap, he places the bottle in her waiting mouth. She wraps her tiny pink fingers on the bottle as if to say to her father: "I can hold it myself, thank you."

As she sucks on the bottle, her brown eyes — the exact shade of her father's — focus on him. Hanna tilts her head up slightly as if trying to remember who the man with the bottle is. Then her little red lips curl into a big grin in recognition.

6

great many things
and many great things

Sarah has heard many film actors complain about the endless hours spent preparing for a scene rather than actually doing one. She is beginning to understand the source of that frustration. Working in film, she has discovered, is a lot like getting ready for a battle — the preparation long and boring and the actual battle brief and overwhelming.

Today, for instance, the driver picked her up from the hotel at six in the morning, and now at nine-fifteen, they have yet to film a single frame. She has already been to the wardrobe trailer, already had her morning meeting with the director as she was getting fitted for her costume for the big climactic confrontation scene for which he gave her several suggestions that are the complete opposite of her vision for how the scene should be played.

The scene in question is the emotional centrepiece of the film in which Clifford confronts Constance about her lover. It is a long, complicated sequence riddled with many shifts in tone and points of view requiring a great deal of coverage, and they only have two days to shoot it.

In this adaptation of the novel, Clifford's confrontation with his wife takes an interesting, unexpected, but wholly believable turn at the end. What drew Sarah to the script, what made her decide to play the part, is this very scene she is getting made up for now. It is a scene of heartbreaking realization on Clifford's part. After the anger and betrayal subside, without words, without a tedious monologue, he lets Connie, as he likes to call her, know that as much as it hurts him, he would rather see the woman he loves happy, even if it is with another man.

This bittersweet gift to his wife, her lover, and their future child — and the silent gratitude with which Constance accepts Clifford's bestowal of understanding — is what made Sarah take the role. She read the script in the London subway on her way to a matinee performance of the play she was doing in the West End, and when she got to the final page, she burst into tears, prompting the woman next to her to get up and sit a couple of seats away from her.

Another thing Sarah loves about this version of *Lady Chatterley's Lover* is that unlike the previous screen adaptations, which have been period pieces with a capital *P*, this one is positively modern. The corsets, for instance, are far less frilly, the hair less ornate, and to Sarah's delight, there isn't a goddamn bonnet in sight.

Everything about the production, from the art direction to the costume design to the cinematography, is lean, almost austere. Sarah has always hated those earnest period films in which the actors are mere models for the elaborate costumes and the women all sport precious little bonnets to match their frocks.

Sitting in the makeup trailer in front of a large vanity mirror and sipping green tea, Sarah reads the day's newspaper. Sandy, a heavy-set woman in her late twenties with long, silky hair and soft, baby-like skin, is busy doing Sarah's face, while Vita, a muscularly compact woman with a shaved head and drawn-on eyebrows, blow-dries Sarah's hair, which she then lengthens by attaching extensions.

Sarah likes to read the newspaper while the hair and makeup department work their magic, which can take anywhere from forty-five minutes to an hour and a half, depending on the scene. During this process, some actors read the script as a last-minute preparation. Sarah, on the other hand, knows her lines beat by beat at this stage of the game, and instead likes to read the morning paper, which has the unique effect of taking her out of herself and immersing her in the lives of others.

When she is in a play, her prep routine is different. As she does her own makeup in the dressing room, she likes to listen to the chatter of the audience as the theatre fills up. Sarah uses the sounds of each night's audience as a soundtrack, an audio portal into the emotional journey she is about to take. The one thing she asks the stage manager to do is to feed the noises in the theatre directly into her dressing room, which can usually be achieved by putting a discreet microphone in the auditorium and connecting it to a speaker in her dressing room. While preparing for the night's approaching performance, she drinks in the voices of the crowd, absorbing the energy as if by osmosis and making a connection with the audience even before she utters her first line.

Working on a film set, however, presents a different set of challenges that requires another kind of ingenuity. In the absence of a live audience with whom to give and take from, she exploits the technological demands of the medium. Sarah loves to confine her energy and release it slowly like an IV drip, according to the size of a shot. For a close-up she releases emotional energy in microscopic bursts, intensifying the audience's thrilling, beat-by-beat discovery of her character. In a master shot, though, she can afford to be more liberal, allowing herself freedom of movement, of gesture, of play, by using her entire body to tell the story, something she has tried to learn from her idol, Meryl Streep. Sarah is astounded by Streep's ability to summon every limb to play a character while never compromising that character's inner life. Many times she has watched the actress on film and whispered to herself: "How does she do it?"

By the time Vita finishes putting in the hair extensions, Sarah has reached the last pages of the newspaper, having taken her time with the articles and op-ed pieces in the politics section while merely skimming entertainment. She has little patience for the way entertainment is covered in most newspapers. The sort of who-is-screwing-who chatter that passes for entertainment journalism revolts her. As for the sports section, she couldn't tell rugby from hockey to save her life, so she skips it altogether.

Sarah finally reaches the obituaries and takes her time there. She got in the habit of reading the obituaries several years ago when her father passed away suddenly from a severe brain aneurysm. Sarah took it upon herself to write his obituary. The following day she bought the newspaper, read her father's obituary, and then scanned all the other ones published that day. Since then she has been inexplicably drawn to them. No matter which city she is in, what is happening in her life, whether she is happy or sad, she checks every obituary in the paper. She always feels better — no, not better, somehow less alone, more connected to others. It is as if through the act of reading about the departed she can silently pay tribute to them, be a witness to the fact they were once here.

Finally, Sarah comes to Ella Christiansen, the last obituary of the day. She continues to read, not recognizing the name. Only after she finishes does it hit her. She studies the obituary again as if to confirm what her eyes are telling her:

CHRISTIANSEN, Ella Kotsopoulos, of Toronto, Ontario, passed away on Monday, September 6,

2004, at St. Michael's Hospital. Ella was the daughter of Frank and Edna Kotsopoulos. She was also
the beloved wife of Gregory Christiansen and the
loving mother of Andrew and Natalie Christiansen.
A former stage actress and theatre teacher, Ella
taught drama at Thistledown Collegiate Institute
and later at York University. She also founded
her own drama school, The Playroom. Ella loved
the theatre and devoted most of her professional
life to understanding and teaching acting to the
hundreds of students who studied with her over
the years. She will be greatly missed by the many
people whose lives she touched with her love,
humour, and devotion to excellence. The family will receive visitors on Thursday, September 9,
from 6:00 to 8:00 p.m. at Botti Funeral Home,
570 Danforth Avenue, east of Pape Avenue. A private ceremony will be held on Saturday at 12.00
p.m. at the Christiansen residence.

After Sarah finishes the last sentence, her heart misses a beat
when she realizes this woman was her former drama teacher.
Her magnificent teacher, supporter, and encourager passed away.
Sarah meant to call her, tell her she was in town, take her out to
dinner or maybe invite her to the set. She has been in town for
three weeks, and every day calling Ella was in the back of her
mind. Now it is too late.

Ella was the woman who taught Sarah to respect her craft,
who pushed her to dig deeper, who told her the one thing all
serious, aspiring actors long to hear: that she was good enough
to be great. However, the one compliment from her teacher that
Sarah clung to throughout the lean years was: "Young lady, you

have in your future great many things and many great things."
And now that woman is lying dead somewhere in the city, waiting to be buried, and it shatters Sarah in a way even the death
of her own father didn't. Tears come with surprising speed, and
it isn't long before she completely breaks down, ruining Sandy's
hour-long makeup job, which will mean reapplying foundation
and eyeliner all over again, maybe start everything from scratch.

"Sweetie, what is it?" Sandy asks, putting a long emphasis on the
weeee, stretching it to an almost comical length. "Now look what
you've done to your pretty face," she says lugubriously, as though
Sarah has taken a sharp blade to her face and scarred it for good.

Sarah tries to give a genuine apology without getting into the
reason for the tears. "I'm sorry, Sandy. I'm so sorry I ruined all your
work." Sarah should know better, though. She knows that the one
thing hair and makeup people love more than hair and makeup is
a juicy story and that these girls aren't happy with a simple apology without a good story to go with it. Sandy wraps her arms
around Sarah, pushing her gigantic breasts into Sarah's back as if to
say, "There, there, sweetie." If she could, however, she would really
rather say, "Now hush up, bitch, and let me do my work!"

Looking at Vita and Sandy, Sarah senses bemused contempt
beneath their words of sympathy. She can only imagine what these
two women who have likely had a rough ride in life truly think
of her. Surely, they must see her as another overpaid, fucked-up,
drugged-up actress in desperate need of emotional pampering.

7

what if ...

"The five greatest love novels of all time," says Charles Cartwright, large black eyes widening as if experiencing a mystical revelation. "That's what I'm thinking for the January issue."

Charlie is famous for his unabashed enthusiasm among this small group of young, hip staff writers whose wardrobes are as limited to black and grey as their temperaments are to unjustified melancholy and cynicism. Charlie, the son of a farmer from Manitoba, is the odd man out among these prematurely disenchanted urbanites. He was the last of the three staff writers to join the magazine two years ago, and his excitement at these story meetings hasn't diminished with time.

"We can get, oh, I don't know, five contemporary writers to create lists of their top five love novels of all time and then each writer votes out the other's pick till we're left with ... the greatest love novel of all time." Charlie turns to his boss, Zakhariye, his moist, round eyes hungry for approval.

Zakhariye, who has been nodding the whole time, more out of benevolent encouragement than interest, is amazed at Charlie's ability to find pleasure in coming up with these story ideas. The man grows enthusiasm for his job the way others grow hair, always springing up from some never-ending source. For a fleeting moment Zakhariye hates Charlie for having a love for the job that he has lost and doesn't know how to regain.

"Why not just ask them to choose their favourite love novel of all time and be done with it?" Daniel Barnum asks with his usual derisive smile that always makes his fellow staff writers fidgety. He has a singular talent for belittling them and their ideas with just a grin, not even bothering to show his nicotine-stained teeth.

"But then it wouldn't be a list," Charlie says, avoiding eye contact with Daniel as if merely looking at him might bring tears to his eyes.

"Precisely," Daniel cuts in. "Haven't we already done enough lists? The ten greatest Canadian novels of all time. Top five Maritime novels. Top three this, top five that. It's as if the entire culture has become incapable of judging the value of anything without ranking it, without putting it on a list and pitting it against something else."

Zakhariye sits up in his chair and clears his throat a little in an attempt to assert his authority before things disintegrate into a shouting match. He shares Daniel's loathing of lists. Having lists in his magazine reminds him of those "Ten Quick Moves to Flatter Abs" he always sees on the cover of every men's exercise magazine. Or even worse, the "Eight Ways to Drive Your Man Wild" lists always splashed across the cover of his wife's *Cosmopolitan*.

Despite his hatred of lists, at least one ranking of some kind inevitably finds its way into every issue of his magazine. The publisher loves them. For some reason readers respond to lists. But aside from his dislike of lists, Zakhariye doesn't care. In fact, he hasn't actually read the magazine out of interest for a long time, in contrast to the old days when he read every page, not only because they had to do a post-mortem after each issue but also because he genuinely enjoyed reading it. He loved what the magazine was about, still about — the art of good storytelling and the people who devote their lives to it.

In a feeble attempt to reduce the combative atmosphere, Zakhariye speaks at last. "What do you have in mind for the January cover?" He glances at Anna Winterbottom, a slender blonde with sharp, birdlike features who has a tendency to sit so low in her chair at these meetings that Zakhariye often wonders if she is even in the room.

"Well …" Anna begins, then clears her throat twice as if to dislodge a giant walnut. "Well, since we have Colm Tóibín as our cover story, I've been playing around with images of Henry James and Tóibín, a sort of collage, a superimposed collage, if you will, of …"

As Ms. Winterbottom delves into the details of what is no doubt the fantastical and poetic image she has in mind for the January cover, her slight, quavering voice is lost altogether on Zakhariye. He nods knowingly in all the appropriate places, occasionally saying "Hmm" or "Ah." Zakhariye can see her lips moving, but all he hears is the screeching, metal-against-metal grinding of a streetcar on Queen Street and the rhythmic *thump-a-thump* of his heart.

He has been experiencing these odd sensations a lot lately in which he loses his hearing as if walking on an ocean floor like a deep-sea diver and all he can perceive are his breathing and the beating of his heart inside the pressure suit. *I should see Dr. Owen,* he thinks. *Could be a brain tumour.* Zakhariye doesn't know what the particular symptoms of brain tumours are, but he imagines they include this sort of general, indefinable feeling of being submerged. Besides, he recently watched an episode of *Medical Miracles* about a woman who waited thirty years to have a tiny tumour in her abdomen removed until the thing ballooned to eighty kilograms.

The same thing happens later that day when Zakhariye talks with Virginia Kisor, the senior art director, an over-tanned, over-wrinkled, fifty-something woman famous for her colourful French scarves, which she ties around her neck as if they alone possess the power to give her the easy Parisian elegance she so desperately craves. That unmistakable feeling of submergence washes over him again as Virginia launches into a long justification for why she thinks they should go with a smaller, simpler font for the cover lines against the beautifully stark black-and-white photograph of Ian McEwan — their cover boy for the next issue — rather than the usual large, red, attention-grapping fonts. The longer he ignores the sensation the deeper he feels himself slipping away until he finally says to her, "Excuse me for a minute," and starts for the door. But he makes sure he pats her back as if to say, "Nothing personal, but I don't give a shit."

Slowly, Zakhariye makes his way across the office, passing a line of cubicles full of hard-working interns who get paid nothing and who are frequently reminded how grateful they should be for the chance to be associated with the glamorous world of magazine publishing. As he heads toward the men's room, his feet make more noise than he likes on the creaky hardwood floor of the sun-drenched, loft-like office with exposed red-brick walls that accentuate the self-conscious aren't-we-so-hip decor.

Once inside the men's room, Zakhariye shakes his head vigorously to snap out of the spell or whatever it is that has come over him. He yawns repeatedly in an exaggerated fashion until he catches a glimpse of himself in the mirror, which prompts him to stop immediately. To give his brain one last good shake, he tilts his head to the side and whacks the top of his skull a couple of times with an open fist the way he did after swimming on the beaches of Mogadishu as a boy to empty his ears of sea water. But the trick that worked for him as child doesn't do him any good now.

Desperate for a remedy, Zakhariye paces the narrow, grey-tiled space that separates the sinks and stalls. Mysteriously, his head responds well to the pacing, at least better than the violent yawning or the head banging. Zakhariye has noticed that as long as he keeps moving the spells aren't so bad. When his body is in motion, the numbness isn't so all-consuming.

Zakhariye got a wonderful jolt of life, however transient, from nicking the two bumps under his chin during shaving, but he has no more bumps to slice and even the last cut didn't give him the exhilarating rush he felt after the first accidental one. When he became aware of what he was doing, it seems, the delicious thrill was lost. That's the trouble with being as self-aware as he is — he can never find his own self-destructive remedy among the countless "cures" people indulge in to cope. He is always too aware of their futility while in the middle of doing them. Like the time he was dumped by his first love for another man. To numb the agony that came with the realization of his utter replace-ability, he went to a prostitute. However, he stopped midway because he couldn't expunge from his head the knowledge of why he was there long enough to find any pleasure in being there. The trick, he now realizes, is not to see himself in the act.

The same thing happened this morning as he stood over the sink, finger pressed on the slash, trying to staunch the bleeding. He imagined himself as a guest on a daytime talk show, perhaps an episode entitled "Men Who Cut Themselves with Shaving Razors." And that was when the pathetic futility of what he was doing hit him. He was too old to be a guest on a Jerry Springer–style show, so he stopped what he was doing at once.

As Zakhariye now paces in circles, he realizes how strange it would seem if a colleague — God forbid, Daniel sporting his permanently smug grin — were to enter and see him going around and around in the men's room. Zakhariye remembers a quiet, tree-lined street off Queen that would be perfect for the sort of anonymous, vigorous pacing he has in mind. He knows he needs to get back to his meeting with Virginia, imagines her sitting in her cramped office, waiting for him to return, endlessly rearranging that damn scarf of hers. But he fears what he might do if he goes back to that airless office. No telling what might result from an hour-long dissertation on font size and background colour.

The worst-case scenario is that during one of three meetings he has scheduled later in the day he will let loose with a sudden, deafening scream that will cause everyone in the office to hide their scissors and letter openers. He can't take that risk. So he leaves the washroom, quietly passes Kisha, the receptionist, and escapes out the big glass door toward the elevator, trying hard to avoid Virginia altogether.

Zakhariye's desire for movement, his need not to be pinned to a chair, has started to affect the customary dinner with his wife. It is a custom they started in the early days of their marriage as an antidote to their hectic, overscheduled lives. Although implicit, they agreed that no matter how chaotic things got, they would always make time for a proper family meal at the table, complete with good china and conversation. To their credit, Thandie and Zakhariye have maintained this tradition even after everything unravelled following Alcott's death. Out of defiance, stoicism, or plain desperation to hold on to something familiar, they have continued to come home in time for dinner, sit face to face, eat, and talk. Or at least try.

Tonight, as they sit across from each other eating pasta and thinly sliced, well-cooked steak, the only sound in the room is the clatter of silverware against the fine china they received as a wedding gift. Unlike some couples who reserve the good china for company, Zakhariye and Thandie believe they are worthy of eating from their expensive plates.

He watches his wife absent-mindedly play with the long bangs of hair that rest on her forehead, and for a moment he sees the horizontal scar that runs across her forehead just under the hairline. Thandie grew the bangs to cover the scar the day before she returned to work four months after the accident. Recently, Zakhariye caught her poring over a website about plastic surgery on her computer, presumably doing research into having the scar fixed. He wanted to tell her she looked beautiful just as she was, but he couldn't bring himself to say the words.

Fidgeting has become a serious problem for Zakhariye. Whenever he has to sit at a table for a meeting or a meal, the constant rearranging of his limbs and how to conceal it from others takes up so much of his thinking that he often has trouble following a simple conversation. As he sits across from his wife, his thoughts are consumed by what to do with his elbows. He puts them up on the table, but that feels terribly wrong. It goes against all the etiquette his mother instilled in him and that he tried to encourage in Alcott.

Zakhariye can almost hear Alcott's voice saying, "Your elbows are on the table, Daddy." So he lets his arms dangle as he chews the steak. This, too, feels wrong. All the blood in his upper body seems to drain into his hands, and the weight is unbearable. *Fuck etiquette,* he thinks, placing his elbows back on the table. A little sigh of relief escapes from his lips after he does that.

Thandie turns to him. "Are you okay?"

"Sure." Zakhariye attempts to hide the irritation in his voice. "Why?"

"I don't know. It seems like you have something on your mind."

Zakhariye shakes his head, his chewing more animated now from the effort of trying to look nonchalant. A moment later he puts his fork down. "I had an interesting thought today."

"Oh?"

Zakhariye doesn't know how to interpret his wife's non-committal "Oh." She could be saying, "Oh, who gives a shit." Or perhaps she means: "Oh, that's wonderful. Tell me more, hon." Unable to decide, he continues to eat silently.

A moment later she glances at him. "Well, would you like to share your interesting thought with me?"

Damn! He is wrong again. Lately, he has been misreading her little gestures and code words such as "Oh," "Uh-huh," and "Hmm."

"I took a long walk in the middle of the day," he finally says. "I was supposed to be in a meeting. But I took a walk instead."

"Hmm. Must've been a good walk."

"And as I was walking, the thought occurred to me. What if I quit the magazine?"

Thandie puts down her fork. "But you love your job."

"*Do* I love my job? Or is it that I never really knew any other work, never really investigated other avenues?"

"Are there other avenues you want to *investigate*?"

"No, you're right. I love my job. I don't know. It was one of those moments, you know, those weird what-if moments." He tries to smile.

"I had a what-if moment myself."

"Oh?"

"We were prepping a triple bypass. A thirty-nine-year-old architect, can you believe that? So I put the anaesthetic in, and he's counting down, eight, seven, six, and I thought to myself … what if we did something with the room?"

"The room?" Zakhariye knows exactly what room she is referring to.

"Well, we don't really have a guest room."

"We never have guests."

"We could invite guests."

"You want to turn Alcott's room into a guest room so we can invite guests?"

"It doesn't have to be a guest room. How about a home office? You could work from home when the weather's really bad."

"I don't want a home office."

"Well, anything then. We can turn it into anything you fancy."

"I don't fancy anything. I want it to stay as it is — Alcott's room." Zakhariye longs for the old days when there weren't so many minefields to navigate, when they could talk, even debate, about anything that popped into their heads and the only outcome would be more talk. He gets up from the table with his plate, walks to the nearby kitchen, scrapes the uneaten food into the garbage bin, and puts the plate in the dishwasher. On his way to the living room he passes Thandie, who is still sitting at the dinner table, staring at her food.

Zakhariye flops onto the couch, puts his feet on the coffee table next to an expensive blue-and-yellow ceramic bowl, and turns on the television. It is already tuned to CNN, and since it is eight o'clock, he is in time for the headlines. There is a snippet of a speech by George Bush attacking John Kerry, and then a sequence of Kerry indignantly lashing back, or at least trying. *How does Kerry hope to be president when he can't even muster a good old-fashioned political finger-wagging?* Zakhariye thinks.

Next there is a rather artless segue into a piece about insurgent attacks in Iraq. Thirty-four dead. Seventy wounded. Mostly Iraqis. The reporter is a bulletproof-vested, all-American young man. Dust covers his blond hair and face as though he just had a good roll in the desert sand before the camera started rolling. *Where is Christiane Amanpour when you need her?*

Zakhariye switches to BBC World News where a story on Israel's security barrier is in progress. A reporter makes a point about Ariel Sharon's insistence on building the wall despite European Union objections. He chuckles. *Like they give a shit about the EU.* When he turns to MSNBC, *Hardball* with Chris Matthews is on. A conservative and a liberal are going at it about family values. The conservative, a chubby, balding man in a striped suit several sizes too small, rants about how abortion is destroying the soul of the nation.

Shaking his head in disgust, Zakhariye flips to Newsworld and a segment about the parliamentary debate on North American missile defence. Canadian politics doesn't inspire revulsion in him, but it doesn't arouse much else, either. It isn't that he finds Canadian affairs boring — well, maybe a little — it is just that they are so inconsequential ... on a global level. Who gets elected south of the border has severe repercussions around the world in a way that it doesn't in Canada.

He continues flicking from one news channel to another, fingers expertly gliding over the digits on the remote to locate the right buttons without looking. The fidgeting returns. Lately, even the news has lost its ability to pacify him. He needs a little bit of the rush he experienced earlier today when he escaped the office to walk. *I'll go for a jog,* he thinks as he switches back to *Hardball* where Jerry Falwell is now pontificating on the so-called East/West clash, saying that Western values and identity are in danger from Islamofascism. *Where do they come up with these phrases?* Pithy political phrases like "enduring freedom" confound him. When did freedom become a hardship to be endured? He tries to listen to Falwell, and the longer he does the more appealing an evening jog seems. Zakhariye can't understand how intelligent human beings can seek spiritual guidance from a man who believes that Teletubbies have a secret agenda to turn the toddler boys of America into raving queens.

Sighing, he turns off the television. Thandie has retired to their bedroom, so he climbs the stairs to tell her he is going for a jog. She will probably think he has lost his mind, what is left of it, but he won't be discouraged. When he opens the bedroom door, he finds it dark, his wife deep in REM sleep. There was a time when they watched the news together after dinner, shared their thoughts on the major world events of the day, then tuned to a movie channel.

In those days they rarely made it to the final credits. Their hand-holding during the movie inevitably turned into a full-blown make-out session on the living-room couch, ending with quiet but passionate lovemaking, fearful of letting go, afraid to wake Alcott, but also savouring the rush of silent orgasms magnified by the effort to suppress them.

Zakhariye's thighs are wobbly, and the ache in his knees that started out dull and general has now become a sharp pain localized to specific points in his knees. It has been months since he has done anything more vigorous than a walk, and his body reminds him of this fact every way it can.

His lungs burn. Each inhale is a flame across his chest, and his heart beats so hard that it sounds like a foreign object with an engine of its own. Despite all these complaints, Zakhariye presses on. He jogs at the steady pace of a cunning marathon runner trying to outpace his opponents. Who the opponents are, he hasn't quite figured out yet. Zakhariye has been running for ten minutes now, can already feel beads of sweat dripping between his shoulder blades and down the small of his back under his matching navy blue Nike sweatpants and zip-up top. He has travelled from his townhouse near Jarvis and Wellesley and made an eastward turn on Bloor Street. A road sign to the left reads MOUNT PLEASANT. He knows that road is bound to be quiet at this time of night, so he makes a sharp left turn down the bridge.

Zakhariye's persistence against his body's protests seems to pay off, since he no longer struggles for breath the way he did a while ago. It is as if his heart has accepted the sudden demands of the night and has decided to co-operate with its unkind owner. As he passes the intersection of Moore and Mount Pleasant, he wonders why he hasn't done this before. All the cells in his body have risen to the challenge and conspire with their host's desire to escape.

As Zakhariye races past the rows of houses lining either side of the street, he glimpses their inhabitants in their living rooms bathed in the flickering blue light of televisions. He wonders who these people are, what sort of jobs they have. Are they making love on their couches with the laugh tracks of sitcoms in the background? Or are they like him and Thandie — enduring lonely celibate marriages?

Forging on, Zakhariye is astounded by the beautiful mechanics of his body: how his brain commands his legs to move in perfect synchronicity, the dignified way his abdomen and the muscles of his back and torso collaborate to hold him strong and steady, how his once-muscular thighs aid in his attempt to flee. *What an amazing instrument the human body is,* he thinks as he passes the dark, leafy cemetery.

Zakhariye has always loved Mount Pleasant Cemetery in autumn — the way it injects a brilliant splash of colour into the city like an amber-and-crimson paintbrush streaked across a bleak grey canvas. Whenever he takes the subway on the Yonge line northward, he sits by the window on the right to get a view of the cemetery as the train whips past the immaculately kept grounds and the tall trees that shelter the dead.

something remains

As he jogs up Mount Pleasant toward Davisville away from his home and slumbering wife, Zakhariye thinks about how much farther he has gone than he planned when he began. He knows he should return and get some sleep. He also knows that his untrained body will ache badly for days to come. But his desire to keep running away and out of his life trumps all other realities.

8

interpreter for the dead

"What were her favourite flowers?" the woman sitting in front of Gregory asks.

Gregory stares at her, unable to decipher the significance of the question.

"We try our best to make the ceremony a true reflection of the deceased," the man next to the woman adds, their kind gazes trained on Gregory. They talk soothingly as though how gently they speak to the widower in front of them is a direct measure of their sympathy.

Do they teach these people how to talk like this in mortuary school? Gregory wonders. A narrow coffee table with a nicely arranged vase of hydrangea separates Gregory and the couple. Gregory sips from the glass of water they offered him when he arrived.

"Are you married?" he asks the couple, who glance at each other, then back at him as if they have never heard such a question.

"Yes," the man says.

"Well, technically, no," the woman corrects. "But we've been together for five years and we're engaged." She wiggles a finger to show off the diamond engagement ring.

"We've been so busy taking over the business for my parents when they retired that we never got around to setting a date," the man says.

The couple is about the same height and weight, which strikes Gregory as odd. He can't figure out why this should seem so strange. Perhaps because he was much taller and weighed a lot more than Ella, he expects the same of all couples.

"When did your parents retire?" Gregory asks the man, not really giving a damn about the answer.

"Last year," the man replies. "Did you know my parents?"

"My wife came here when her father died four years ago. She was very happy with the service she got."

"We can assure you, Mr. Christiansen, we'll do our best to match the level of service your wife received." The man glances at his partner, expecting her to concur. She does so with a smile.

"If you can't remember your wife's favourite flowers, which is of course completely understandable given your situation, we can make the floral arrangements," the woman says.

Gregory remains quiet for a moment.

"You must still be in shock," the man adds.

Gregory's wife was seriously ill for two years. Part of him was prepared for the possibility of sitting across from people like this talking about his wife's favourite flowers to make the funeral service "a true reflection of the deceased," as they put it. So it wouldn't be completely true to tell them he is still in shock. What he really feels, however, is rage — pure and undiluted.

Ever since running out of the hospital after the doctor told him his wife was dead, Gregory has experienced an array of emotions, more than he even knew existed, most of which cancelled one another out. Except rage. It remains without being transmuted into something else. It has been ubiquitous and unrelenting. What or who he is angry at hasn't become clear with time.

He is even enraged at this nice, colour-coordinated couple sitting before him, even though they appear to desire nothing more than to help him give a funeral service befitting his wife. So why is he so infuriated at them? All he can do is stare at them and silently curse the way they smile and finish each other's sentences, how they nod appreciatively at each other's suggestions. They have gotten under his skin, and he wants to smack them silly. To Gregory everything they do comes off as shameless gloating.

"Did your wife leave a will?" the man asks.

"Excuse me?"

"We only ask because sometimes people leave specific instructions for the sort of funeral they want. You know, the music they want played and such …"

Gregory almost asked his wife to tell him what he should do if the end came. It was on a hot August Friday afternoon after a particularly bad week when even the doctors had little hope. But since Ella never brought up the subject, he didn't have the heart to ask her. It seemed to him as if his wife believed that any discussion of a will or funeral arrangements was a resignation, an acceptance of defeat. So he, Andrew, and Natalie rallied around her in a display of willful denial.

"No, she left me no specific instructions," Gregory says.

"In that case, you'll have to help us decide." As she speaks, the woman turns to her partner for another supportive nod. "Since you knew her best, you'll have to act as … an interpreter of sorts."

Gregory thinks about what is being asked of him. He doesn't know whether to laugh or cry or both at the thought of being an interpreter for the dead. Suddenly, his anger shifts from the funeral home couple to his wife for putting him in this position. "Okay," he says, accepting the task, face flushed with shame for being mad at his wife. She isn't even buried yet and he has failed her already.

"For starters, have you thought about what kind of casket your wife would have wanted?" the woman asks.

"She wouldn't have wanted one. If she had a choice, I'm sure she'd rather not be in one. Don't you think?" Gregory watches the woman cringe with embarrassment. He feels the momentary thrill of victory, of making her feel guilty for her stupid question.

"I'm very sorry. I didn't mean to —"

"No, I'm sorry," Gregory interrupts, his triumph shifting into sorrow for taking his anger out on this poor woman trying to do her job. If he believed in psychotherapy or ordered self-help books on Amazon.com, he would have the tools, the emotional lingo, to understand the source of his rage and know where to direct it at. Instead he is incensed at himself, at God, at the universe, at whomever is ultimately responsible for who dies and who lives. Somebody has to pay, and since he can't see God, it might as well be this nice woman in the brown turtle-neck sweater.

"We have an excellent collection of caskets to choose from," the man says, attempting to rescue his partner.

The woman rises, picks up a huge binder from a table in the corner of the room, and hands it to Gregory. "You can leaf through it and select the one you like," she tells him.

Does anyone actually like *picking out a casket?* Gregory wants to ask her, but he knows he has already been rude enough for one day. As a grieving widower, he is probably allotted a certain amount of impoliteness before people think he is an asshole. So he quietly flips through the binder's pages, which display caskets and their prices.

The man clears his throat. "The prices range from $1,400 to over $18,000."

Gregory glances up from the picture of the casket he is studying and frowns.

"We want you to pick the one you're most comfortable with," the man says.

Bullshit, Gregory thinks. *You want me to choose the one that's going to add the most to your bank account.* He continues to browse the binder until he comes across a beautiful black casket. The price is $8,911. *How absurd to spend so much money on a box only to bury or burn it.*

Gregory once read that Muslims inter their dead wrapped in a simple white cotton sheet. At the time he thought it was disrespectful to the dead; now it makes perfect sense. "This one," he says as he hands the binder to the woman and indicates the black casket.

"An excellent choice," she says.

"Indeed," the man concurs. "One of our most popular."

Gregory has to get out of the stuffy room. One more minute with this couple and their friendly toothpaste commercial smiles and soft, consoling voices and he will scream. He might even grab the pretty vase of hydrangea on the coffee table and hurl it at them. *That ought to wipe the sympathy smiles off their faces,* Gregory thinks. However, two assault charges in one week would be pushing luck even for a bereaved widower.

"You said your wife wanted to be cremated, correct?" the man asks.

Is this ever going to end? Gregory wants to scream. "Well, I don't know about always," he says instead in a pleasant tone, surprising even himself. "But she did express an interest in cremation once." For the first time in ages, he remembers when his wife actually talked about her death and what kind of burial she would like. Strange that it was two days into their honeymoon rather than when she got sick and was on the cusp of the hereafter. She didn't tell him what she wanted when it really counted, when death was no longer a hypothetical, way-in-the-future abyss.

———

Gregory and Ella were really keen on going somewhere fancier — Rome, Cairo, or even reliable old London — but in the end the Grand Canyon won. As small as the wedding was, it was still expensive, and the down payment they put on their first home, a fixer-upper off Bathurst Street near Eglinton Avenue, had pretty much depleted their collective savings. Europe could wait, they agreed, so they rented a car and set out on a road trip. Three days on the highway, three days camping at Grand Canyon, and three more days driving back. It was exhausting, sometimes boring, and often plain rough. But one morning at the edge of the canyon when they managed to awaken as the sun came up over the cliffs made all the trouble worth it.

As Ella and Gregory stood side by side near the metal railing that separated them from the great chasm, they stared straight ahead, the sun casting its first rays on the mind-boggling void and rendering them speechless. That wasn't much of an accomplishment for Gregory, since silence was the state in which he spent much of his days, but it was a shocking new experience for Ella. For close to ten minutes she gazed ahead as if stunned by the vista.

Almost frightened by her reaction, Gregory put his arm around her shoulder. "You okay there?" he asked with a slight but benevolent smile.

Tears welled in Ella's large black eyes, which were almost as dark as her hair. There were no tears in her eyes on the first night they had made love in his small, sparsely furnished apartment three weeks after they met. Nor were there any tears when he proposed to her a year later, and most surprisingly, even on their wedding day. Gregory used to think all women cried at weddings, especially their own, but Ella proved that theory wrong. It took a geological freak of nature to bring tears to his wife's eyes.

"This is it," Ella said finally. "This is where I want to be buried."

"Honey, I don't think that's legal."

"I don't mean literally," she said, giving him a slight, scolding push with her shoulder against his rib cage. "God, sometimes you can be so damn literal. I meant my ashes, my remains."

Remains? Gregory repeated to himself. He hated that word. It sounded like something a serial killer left behind. Gregory turned away from the scenic wonder and peered into Ella's watery eyes, so open and already familiar to him as though he had known them all his life. "That's a pretty morbid request on your honeymoon, isn't it?"

"It feels like home," she said as undramatically as if she were talking about her favourite sweater. "Puts it all into perspective, doesn't it?"

"How so?" he asked, instantly regretting the question. He often felt like a complete ignoramus around her. She was always thinking five steps ahead of him.

"Oh, I don't know — life, death, divorce, bankruptcy, a bad case of syphilis, a flooded basement, all of it. This —"she pointed with her chin "— dwarfs everything else. What's a single life's ups and downs in the face of billion-year-old rocks?"

After that they sank back into their respective reveries as the sun slowly revealed more and more of the red cliffs and pits of the canyon.

"It's amazing isn't it, God's patience?" she said without looking at him.

Ever the scientist, Gregory wanted to say, "What's God got to do with it?" But he remained silent as they held hands and stared ahead.

———

"She wanted to be cremated and scattered over Grand Canyon," Gregory says to the undertaker couple. Then he grins devilishly. "Me, I want to be buried, mud, dirt, and all. Why deny the crawly suckers their feast? That's my philosophy."

A quick peal of laughter escapes the woman and stops immediately as though she remembered that merriment in the presence of a grieving widower goes against everything they taught her at mortuary school.

Finally, after saying goodbye to the couple, Gregory steps out of the funeral home and into the blinding September sun, feeling relieved. It is mid-afternoon, and Danforth Avenue is alive with people going about their business. A young mother with a pierced eyebrow pushes a double stroller. A willowy black teenager, possibly Haitian, almost bumps into Gregory. He notices the teen is reading a tattered copy of Virginia Woolf's *Mrs. Dalloway*. An old Greek woman in a black skirt, a black sweater, and a black head scarf sits on a bench, hands folded, gazing intently at something unseen as though trying to figure out how she got there.

Gregory takes a couple of deep breaths as he walks toward his car, which he parked in a lot a block away. He is so happy to be out at last and into the sunlight. *What sweet lark it is,* he thinks, *to find one's self plunged deep in the midst of life.* A sudden pang of guilt hits him. *How heartless,* he thinks, *to revel in life, to breathe it so shamelessly, so joyously.*

9

how to be where we are

Andrew would rather be at home making Hanna laugh by doing funny faces. It astonishes him how much pleasure can be had by this simple activity. And pleasure is something he is in dire need of right now, considering that his mother is lying in a funeral home being embalmed, powdered, and lip-glossed in a feeble attempt to make her not look as dead as she is. At the moment he is in his taxi parked on Elizabeth Street outside Toronto General Hospital where he often waits to pick up customers. Thanks to his father's bowling alley freak-out, he had to charge $3,000 on his Visa and now has to work extra hours to pay it off.

He is listening to Joni Mitchell oldies. Joni's and Nina Simone's music are all he plays while working. Something about their voices adds a little zip to his days. As he shifts in the fake leather seat of his cab, he thinks about Helli for the first time in weeks. Maybe the orange dusk sky over the city's office towers reminds him of her. Sunset was her favourite time. Or perhaps the recent events in his life have made him think of her. He can't help wondering what his life would be like if he hadn't left Helsinki because of his mother's illness.

His old life with Helli seems like paradise now. But what he really longs for isn't so much Helli but her cozy, warm apartment in which they spent most of their free time cooking, reading, and making love. And then there were their weekend getaways to her parents' lake cottage two hours southeast of Helsinki. Everything he left behind beckons him now. Andrew forces himself to stop his futile pondering and redirects his thoughts back to Hanna. Only she has the power to make him feel he is where he needs to be. Because of her he is still intact. Because of her he is well on his way to mastering the one thing most of people have trouble learning — how to be where they are.

He glances at the car clock. It reads 6:46 p.m. He wonders what his daughter is doing. Knowing her schedule as well as he does, he figures she has just awakened from her nap and is being fed dinner, spitting everything out and driving her mother crazy in the process. He smiles to himself as he pictures the sweet chaos play before him like a silent movie.

Andrew takes his cellphone from the side pocket of his denim cargo pants and speed-dials home but hangs up before making a connection. Since Hanna isn't going to pick up, it means he would have to speak to his wife and ask her to put the phone near Hanna's mouth. Normally, he has no objection to talking to his wife, but he can imagine the mood she is in now as she struggles to feed their baby after a long day of teaching kids who are referred to as "special needs." This is the time of day when he tries his best to stay out of Rosemary's way. He does the same early in the morning when she gets ready for work. The weekends are usually okay unless something unexpected happens or she returns from one of her biweekly visits to her mother, who lives in London, Ontario.

Just as Andrew puts the phone back into his pocket, a Middle Eastern woman with a mass of unruly curly hair covering much of her face approaches his window. "Can you take me to Islington and Dundas West, please?" she asks, pulling as many curls away from her face as she can.

"Hop in," Andrew says, starting the engine.

As the woman climbs into the back of the taxi, he sets the meter. The rush-hour traffic is beginning to ease in the downtown core but is still heavy enough to require him to take some creative alternative routes. Most cabbies gladly sit in traffic even though if they tried they could easily think of less-congested avenues to save their customers time and money. But Andrew would hate the nagging guilt that would eat away at him if he knew of a quicker way and didn't use it. So he takes several smaller streets in the core until he hits Bloor Street West.

Manoeuvring expertly through traffic, he occasionally peers at the rearview mirror, which gives him a perfect view of the young woman's face. He is struck by how large her eyes are and the long arc of her eyebrows. Surely, they are the longest eyebrows hc has ever seen.

"Is it someone close to you?" Andrew asks.

"What?"

"In the hospital, I mean. Is it someone close to you?"

"My brother," she says with a deep, velvety voice that reminds him of Lauren Bacall, albeit with a Middle Eastern accent.

"I'm very sorry," Andrew says, surprised he can feel such sympathy for someone he has never met. "Will he be okay?"

"He should be. That's what the doctor says ... unless there are complications."

"I see they gave you the famous *unless*. What's wrong with him?"

She turns to look out the side window. "He had an operation."

Andrew takes this as a hint that he is getting too nosy, so he concentrates on the road ahead. Joni Mitchell's "River" comes on, and he quietly sings along with it, trying not to let the woman in the back hear him.

"It's a little too early for Christmas music, no?" she says, making eye contact with him through the rearview mirror.

"It's included on this greatest hits CD I'm listening to."

"It's good. I like it. Sad song, but I like it."

They listen to it quietly until the song ends and "Chinese Café" replaces it. Andrew watches as she bobs her head to the beat. "I hope it all turns out well for your brother."

"Me, too," she says, laughing. It is nervous, hesitant laughter that increases in volume.

"What's so funny?"

"It's not funny. I shouldn't laugh. Really, it's not funny." But she continues to laugh, anyway. Finally, she forces herself to stop. "It's the surgery. I'm laughing about my brother's surgery."

Andrew is confused.

"He had his … his … you know … removed."

Andrew is still puzzled.

"You know …" she repeats as if that is all that needs to be said. "His thing, his dick … he had it removed." She breaks into another fit of laughter, then covers her mouth with her hand, but the hilarity refuses to be contained.

As Andrew turns north on Christie Street, he wonders what would make a man do such a thing. Like most guys, the thought of a knife near that general area makes him cringe. "Why would he do that?" he asks, immediately realizing how dumb he must sound to her. He has lived in big cities all his life; he should be able to make such a simple deduction.

"He's having, uh, what do they call it …?" She searches for the right words. "Gender-reassignment surgery."

"Wow!" Andrew says.

"He's already had the counselling and the hormone injections. Today was the last step."

"Wow!" Andrew repeats.

"It's common nowadays, no?"

"I'm sorry. I don't mean to sound so —"

"It's okay. My father had the same reaction. Must be a male thing."

"And your mother, what was her reaction?"

"She disowned him."

"Wow!"

"You like saying *wow* a lot, no?"

"Yes ... I mean, no."

"You would think a mother would be more understanding, more loving, yes?"

Andrew nods emphatically. He finds the way she ends her sentences with a question confusing but charming. *Very French!* he thinks.

"So he's been living with me in my tiny apartment for two years, saving for the big day. A brother moved in with me and now I have a sister. Very strange, yes?" She laughs again.

Andrew laughs with her.

"Don't get me wrong. I love my brother, but sometimes I don't know how to deal with the whole thing. Sometimes you just don't want to deal with your family and all their crazy shit. Know what I mean?"

"Sure do!" Andrew turns west on Dupont Street.

"I left Montreal to live in a city I hate just to get away from it all. But their shit follows me no matter where I go."

"You hate Toronto?"

"I miss Montreal."

"That's where you're from?"

"Originally, we're from Lebanon. We fled after the civil war broke out and lived in Marrakesh for eleven years, then moved to Montreal. Now I'm here. But all my real friends are in Marrakech. Nabil, Ismail, Nazra, Moen, the whole gang. She's a hooker, you know?"

87

"Who, Moen?"

"No, Nazra. Moen is a man, silly."

"Oh."

"But she got tricked into it."

"How do you get tricked into something like that?"

"Hassan, her bastard loser boyfriend, got her into it. He's addicted to opium. He got her addicted, too, and since he didn't work, she had to support both of them. That's how. She says she loves him. It's amazing, no?"

"What is?"

"The things we find ourselves agreeing to in the name of love."

Andrew nods and reflects on the truth of that statement as he turns onto Dundas Street West.

But she doesn't give Andrew any time to ponder. "Look at my situation. Yonis, my brother — oh, excuse me, Jasmine, that's his name now. Sounds like a cheap stripper name, no? He doesn't pay a dime. I pay for the apartment, eleven hundred a month to be exact. He doesn't even buy his own bras. He has to take mine. And that's not even the worst part."

"It gets worse?"

"For two years I had to put up with all his boyfriends. He brings over these hairy, super-macho men in leather who look like they're auditioning for the reunion of Village People. That's what he's into. Me, I can't stand hairy men."

Andrew can't help laughing. He examines his arms to see if he is someone she can't stand.

She catches him in the act. "Oh, don't worry. You're not too hairy."

"Good to know I don't repulse you."

"You're so funny." She releases another giggly laugh. "Where was I? Oh, yes, and I put up with all his shit, why?"

"Why?" Andrew prompts.

"Because I love him. Because he's my brother."

"Sister now," Andrew corrects her.

"Right. Because he's my sister and I love him, her. So there."

"So there indeed." Andrew parks at Dundas and Islington with the meter at $31.75. "Well, here you are."

"Thank you." She hands him $35. "Keep the change."

Andrew watches as she gathers her two leather purses, a small one and a larger one. He wants to ask why she has two purses but is afraid that will set her off again about her brother. "Listen," he asks instead, throwing caution to the wind, "can I take your picture?"

She gawks at him as if he asked for one of her kidneys.

"I'm doing this project, a photography project ... portraits. A sort of visual chronicle of my customers, of the citizens of the city, if you will." He wants to smack himself for sounding so grandiose about his simple but potentially interesting project.

She tilts her head as if baffled by the request but is giving it due consideration. "Okay," she finally says.

As always such compliance amazes him — the fact that most of his fares are so willing to let a complete stranger photograph them. Although a few people decline, the majority he asks gladly pose for him. As he tells them to sit naturally, to be themselves, that he is really interested in revealing them as they are, they settle back and offer themselves and their stories, happy to be asked, almost grateful for the opportunity to demonstrate to the world that they exist. Tonight it is this woman's chance to show the world her face, her olive skin, her hair pulled back to reveal subtle features.

"I'm Nuura, by the way." She giggles as she tilts her face playfully, displaying her pretty profile as if she were a contented queen.

"Thank you, Nuura," he says flirtingly, the sound of the camera shutter and the light of the flash filling the taxi.

"Make me look beautiful now, promise?"

"Oh, that won't be too hard to do." He clicks away fast, desperate to capture "it," the thing that comes through in a photograph every once in while, the quality that makes a viewer stand straighter and pay attention.

Later, after Nuura has departed, Andrew finds himself waiting at the intersection of Bloor and Islington for the light to turn green. Then, out of the corner of his eye, he thinks he spots someone he knows. He turns to get a better look. For a moment he can't tell if his mind is playing tricks on him or if he really does glimpse his mother crossing the street. She walks in slow motion, radiant in a red trench coat, long black hair blowing in the wind. When she turns toward him, they lock eyes and she smiles.

The blaring horns of the cars behind him jolt Andrew back to reality. The light is green, and the cars in the lane next to him are moving. He peers at the rearview mirror, realizes he is holding up traffic, and steps on the gas. As he drives toward downtown, he knows he is in no shape to be on the road tonight. It is a miracle he hasn't run a red light or hit someone already. So he decides to call it a night. He is far short of what he needs to earn for the day to be profitable, but to continue working would endanger lives. Andrew doesn't want to go home yet, though. He likes to work until eleven at night and arrive home when Rosemary is already in bed and at the threshold of sleep. At that time of day their relationship is at its most pleasant. They are both too exhausted to talk, fight, make love, or do any of the things couples do after a long day. Instead they slump into bed, assume the spoon position, and drift off to their private dreamlands.

Andrew also doesn't want to go to his dad's house where his father, Natalie, Aunt Doris, and her daughter are probably busy phoning relatives to tell them about the funeral, calling caterers, or doing the numerous other things that have to be done before

Saturday's service. It is selfish of him not to help, but he can't deal with any of that tonight. So he decides to contact Zakhariye to see if they can get together for drinks. He extracts his cellphone from his pocket, searches for Zakhariye's number, and speed-dials it. Several rings later his friend's voice comes on the line.

"Hey, Zakhariye, it's Andrew. How are you? I'm all right. How's Thandie? Good. Glad to hear that. Listen, I was wondering if you can come out for a drink. I'm in your neighbourhood. Great. I'll pick you up in fifteen."

Andrew hangs up, makes a U-turn, travels east on Bloor until he reaches Jarvis, then makes a right turn, followed by a left turn on Earl Place, a tiny street he would surely miss had he not come here several times already. He passes a row of townhouses of different styles, some old and ivy-covered, others brand-new. When he gets to the end of the lane, he spots Zakhariye locking his front door. He is wearing navy jeans, a red sweater, and a black leather jacket. Andrew waves at him, and Zakhariye returns the gesture with a smile. He is so happy to see his friend smiling at last.

Several months after the death of Zakhariye's son, Andrew and Zakhariye met for drinks a couple of times. Then a mere smile seemed to require a summoning up of all of Zakhariye's strength. Andrew recalls going home to Rosemary and telling her that he had been out with the saddest man in the world. So seeing Zakhariye now smiling so freely lifts him in a way he doesn't completely comprehend.

Their friendship started quite by accident and progressed very fast, or at least more rapidly than most male bondings, which can require years of playing baseball or basketball or some other kind of game before getting to the things that really matter. Maybe it was their age or where they were in their lives, but staying on the surface of things didn't hold much appeal for either of them.

By their second get-together at a pool hall during an intense game of billiards, which they both like and are equally skilled at, they talked about everything — their pasts, their unrequited dreams, their marriages and careers. It didn't take long to get to the raw, well-hidden layer that takes most men years, decades even, to reach. The strangest part of their friendship isn't even the speed with which it developed but rather the way it began. It was as accidental as two lovers meeting on a train.

It was back in February 2003. Having just gotten his cab driver's permit, Andrew was going by the intersection of Richmond Street and Spadina Avenue when Zakhariye, who was ill-dressed for a storm that had dumped twenty centimetres of snow on the city, hailed his cab. If Andrew was driving a little faster, or if Zakhariye had come to the intersection ten seconds later, they would never have met. Zakhariye was shivering when he climbed into the back of the cab and asked Andrew to turn up the heat.

"Nasty day for a jacket like that," Andrew said.

"Yeah, should've listened to my wife. She told me to wear my winter coat."

"Think of all the trouble we'd save ourselves if we just listened to them."

They both chuckled knowingly.

"Where to?" Andrew asked.

"Seven Earl Place, near Jarvis and Wellesley, please."

Andrew headed up Spadina and made a right turn onto College Street. After a few minutes of driving, it became clear he had made a mistake taking College. Traffic was normally bad enough on this street on a good day, but during a winter storm there was no telling how long an otherwise ten-minute ride could take.

"Sorry, man," Andrew said as he made eye contact with Zakhariye via the rearview mirror. "I'll try to find an alternate route as soon as I can."

"Don't worry about it. It's bad everywhere."

Happy to hear that, Andrew put on one of his favourite Nina Simone CDs to ease the long ride ahead. Zakhariye asked if Andrew could tune to the six o'clock news. When Andrew switched to CBC Radio, the theme music for the news was just starting. The lead was a story about the United Nations Security Council's failure to pass a resolution permitting the use of force to topple Saddam Hussein. A short audio clip played in which George Bush said that he and the coalition of the willing would go to war regardless of the U.N. resolution. Zakhariye chuckled sarcastically as he muttered, "Coalition of the willing." Next was a sound bite of Prime Minister Tony Blair in the British Parliament, yelling over the din of opposition MPs as he warned about the grave threat of nuclear weapons in Iraq. The clapping and cheering of his supporters drowned out Blair's voice.

Zakhariye snorted. "God, these people have no shame, do they?"

"It's their job, actually, when you think about it," Andrew said nonchalantly.

"What is?"

"To sound morally indignant and resolute. They're just doing their job."

"Are you defending these crooks?"

"It's not about defending them. I'm talking about not letting them get to you."

"Even when they're feeding us bullshit? And we're not talking about some benign bullshit here. This isn't Bill Clinton saying, 'It depends on what the meaning of the word *is* is.' People are going to die, thousands, possibly hundreds of thousands, based on some

93

ridiculous claims of imminent threat to our civilization. Doesn't that get to you?"

Andrew shrugged. "I'm talking about politicians feeding us black-and-white certainties. We don't vote for politicians because of their ability to analyze the complexities of the world and then get back to us with a grey portrait. That's not comforting."

"Comforting?"

"Yes, comforting. Isn't that why we elect these guys? People come home from a long day at work, they're tired and anxious about losing their jobs, about their kids experimenting with drugs or failing algebra, and when they sit down to watch the news, they don't want to see Bush or Blair looking conflicted about the thousands of innocent deaths their decisions will cause. No, we want them to say with confidence — 'You're safe because we're protecting you. We'll get Saddam, Bin Laden, Al-Zawahiri, and any other evil guy of the month. That's what we vote them into office for. So that we can go to bed every night with the illusion that somebody's out there policing the big bad world."

Zakhariye frowned. "More like a delusion if you ask me. They're not policing the real threat. Saddam didn't attack the U.S. He had nothing to do with 9/11."

"And you don't think they know that?"

"And Saddam doesn't have nuclear weapons. The very experts they hired to find out told them just that."

"They also know that," Andrew said.

"I suppose you're going to say they also know they'd have much better luck eliminating the threat of WMDs falling into the wrong hands by focusing their attention on a breakaway nation of the former Soviet Union rather than bombing Baghdad."

"Bingo! They know all that. Look, these people aren't idiots. They have the smartest intelligence gatherers out there, but focusing on an obscure breakaway nation or fighting a shadowy, fluid enemy like Al-Qaeda won't do the trick. You can only get so much press mileage out of that. They have a much better chance defeating Al-Qaeda by overthrowing the Saudi royal family than getting rid of Saddam. But that's too long-term, too complex. Voters want action and assurances, and they want them now."

Zakhariye shivered. "You make people sound so bloodthirsty."

"No, the people aren't bloodthirsty. They've been made to feel afraid, so naturally they want their leaders to protect them, to make it all go away so they can get back to their kids' soccer games and Thanksgiving dinners, the things that really matter to them."

"So what are you saying? We should just watch the world going to hell in a handbasket and not do anything?"

"The world has always been going to hell in a handbasket. The only difference now is that we have CNN and Al Jazeera to tell us about it with pictures and bulletins 24/7. When in human history were things ever good and safe? If it wasn't the plague or the potato famine killing millions, it was the transatlantic shipping of tens of millions of people as slaves, or two world wars, or atomic bombs being dropped on innocent civilians. We've always been on the brink of some great calamity. Maybe the problem isn't with the world."

Zakhariye raised an eyebrow. "Oh? What do you suggest? Let me guess — going inward and meditating?"

"If that does it for you, why not? I mean, what do you suggest?"

"Fight back."

"Anarchy?"

"Demonstrate. Yell! Chant! I don't know. Whatever it takes."

"Millions of people have done just that from Sydney to London to New York and right here in Toronto. But in a few weeks the war will happen regardless and thousands of innocent people will die."

"So how do you sleep at night?"

"Actually, I haven't really been sleeping all that well, but not because there's going to be a war. There have always been wars, there will always be wars. That's just what we do — we fight."

"So why aren't you sleeping then?"

Andrew didn't answer.

"Sorry. I don't mean to pry."

"No, it's all right. My mom's pretty sick. She has cancer."

"Oh, man, I'm very sorry to hear that."

Andrew shook his head. "Yeah, what can you do? It's always something, right? If it's not cancer, it's El Nino or killer bees or some other shit." The traffic got worse as they approached the intersection of College and Yonge.

"You know the part that infuriates me the most?" Zakhariye asked. "It's not that the Americans and Brits suddenly developed a conscience about Saddam. Where was their conscience when he was slaughtering a million Iranians with the very weapons they gave him? And it's not even the whole spreading democracy in the Middle East crap when their closest allies, Egypt's Mubarak and Jordan's King Abdullah, are the biggest autocrats in the region. The part that really gets under my skin and drives me insane is the idea that their lives are so much more valuable that they have absolutely no moral qualms about condemning thousands of innocent Iraqis to certain death and destruction in order to protect American and British lives from a hypothetical threat."

"But isn't that human nature?" Andrew asked. "You make it sound like the Americans and Brits invented the concept that their lives are more valuable or more worthy of safety and security. If people truly believed their lives had the same value, there would never be wars and we'd never have genocide, slavery, oppression, occupations, suicide bombings, and all the other horrible things we do to one another. Instead we'd see that other people were more like us and not obstacles to our economic and geopolitical objectives. If we could all imagine ourselves into the lives of others, I mean, really feel what it's like to be someone other than ourselves, we wouldn't be having this discussion now. After all, isn't that the very essence of morality?"

"So it's the survival of the fittest then?" Zakhariye said with resignation. "You sound like a man who's made peace with it all, about human nature, I mean."

"Buddy, it's either that or drive yourself insane, and I don't know about you, but I want to hold on to what little sanity I've got for as long as I can." Andrew made a left turn on Jarvis. "What's your name, by the way?"

"Zakhariye. I guess the Canadian version would be Zachary."

"And what version is yours?"

"Somali."

"I thought so. You have that Somali look."

"The Somali look? Do we have signs on our foreheads?"

"No, I meant, it's different. Unique. I was there once."

"No kidding. Really? What were you doing there?"

"Work. I was sent there after Barre was overthrown and the civil war just broke. I'm … I was a photojournalist."

"Really? You used to be a photojournalist and now —"

"And now I'm a cab driver — go figure."

"No, I think it's fascinating." Zakhariye pointed at Earl Place and asked Andrew to make a right turn into the unpaved lane.

Andrew could barely keep the tires of the car straight. Finally, he came to a slow stop in front of Zakhariye's townhouse.

Once he paid the fare, Zakhariye shook hands with Andrew. "It was a pleasure talking to you, even if I don't buy your eat-or-be-eaten theory. I never got your name, though."

"Andrew. I enjoyed talking to you, too. And remember, the world has always been going to hell in a handbasket."

"I'll try to remember that." Zakhariye gathered his briefcase and got ready to get out of the cab.

Andrew turned to him. "Listen, man, I'm doing this thing, a photography project. I'm taking pictures of people I pick up. I'd really appreciate it if I could take a couple of shots of you in the back seat. Just a simple portrait, really."

"I'd love to, but my wife and son are waiting to have dinner with me. I'm late as it is." Zakhariye fished for something in his wallet and handed a business card to Andrew. "Give me a call when you're around."

"Cool. Thanks. Have a nice dinner with your family. How old is your son?"

"He just turned seven. Quite the troublemaker. Well, good night."

Now Andrew watches Zakhariye lock his front door and get into the front seat of the cab. They head to their usual pool hall at the Elephant & Castle at King West and Simcoe Street.

"So how have you been?" Zakhariye asks.

"Okay."

"I'm glad you called. I was wondering how you were doing. How's your mother?"

Andrew doesn't answer. He should tell Zakhariye what happened. He certainly intends to. But at the moment he just wants to get away from anything to do with his mother's funeral. So he grins at his friend. "Ready to get your ass whipped?"

Zakhariye aims the cue ball at the centre of the triangle of balls. A perfect break. The balls fly every which way on the table. "Stripes," he says, and chooses a striped ball near a corner pocket. It is too easy, so he picks another striped one. This ball requires a little more ingenuity. He walks around the table, mulling over the perfect angle. "So how's the project coming along? When's the big unveiling?"

"Oh, it'll be a while before you see it. I've been having a shitty time finding subjects."

"Are the citizens of our city not beautiful enough for you?"

Andrew takes a gulp of icy beer. "It's not about finding beautiful people, Zakhi. If that were the case, I wouldn't have taken *your* picture."

They laugh.

"I keep picking up the same type of people — bored, depressed, uninteresting sorts. Or worse, happy ones. Copies of the same person over and over again. Till today."

Zakhariye misses a shot. "Oh, and who changed it all?"

"I picked up this girl from Lebanon whose brother is in a hospital for a sex-change operation."

Zakhariye grimaces. "Yikes!"

"Yeah, I had the same reaction. But there was something about her. She was … I don't know … very unusual. A bit neurotic, but also very generous — the way she talked about her brother. Just when I thought I had her figured out, she'd say something completely unexpected. There was this dichotomy between the person she appeared to be and the lives she's led. She struck me as a connoisseur."

"Of what?"

"Of lifestyles."

Zakhariye nods like a man who understands what it means to try different lives on for size with the hope that one day he will discover the authentic one.

Andrew misses his shot. He is as good a player as Zakhariye and has no business flubbing such an easy shot, but his heart isn't really in the game. He just wanted to hang out with his friend and talk. Playing pool was merely the excuse. It seemed like a good idea at the time. Now he isn't so sure.

Zakhariye grins. "What the hell was that? Are you letting me win? Come on now. Don't insult me."

"Sorry. I got distracted." Time to change the subject. "So what about you? How have you been?"

"Same old." Zakhariye walks around the table, surveying the best angle.

"Does it get easier … with time, I mean?" Andrew asks, wanting to know about the stages of grief and whether there is an expiration date for the constant hollowness that nothing seems to fill and which follows him around wherever he goes. That is how Zakhariye described it one night when they got together two months after Alcott died.

"The grief does," Zakhariye says. "Well, not easier, just duller. It loses its sharpness, becomes, I don't know, less piercing. Like you know when you dive into the deep end of the pool and your head starts to ache from the pressure of the water and it feels like it's going to explode any minute, but it doesn't? The mourning ends, but the grief … it never really goes way."

Andrew nods as if he understands, but he doesn't really. Only a few days have passed since his mother's death, and he hasn't gotten to that place where he can differentiate the nuances between grief and mourning. Andrew regrets starting a discussion that makes him even more depressed, the very thing he was hoping to alleviate when he called Zakhariye and invited him for drinks. "How's work?" he asks as he takes his turn to shoot.

"I had an interesting thought the other day," Zakhariye says.

"Oh, yeah?"

"For the first time in seven years I wanted to quit the magazine."

"Do it," Andrew says, making a perfect shot.

"You sound so certain."

"I'm certain because I did it — walked away from it all. Best decision I ever made."

"But it's all I know how to do. I was a failed academic. The magazine's the only job I've ever had."

"I know." Andrew takes another successful shot and is now two away from winning the game. "That's the problem. People hold on to their jobs like identity cards."

"Aren't we what we do?"

"To some degree. But we're so much more than our work. We are what we think, feel, eat, and dream, and we're definitely what we fear."

"So you don't miss it? You don't open a newspaper or a magazine and see a great photograph you wish you'd taken?"

Andrew's streak comes to an end. Zakhariye takes over. He, too, has only two balls left on the table.

"I don't read newspapers." Andrew realizes his answer might seem facetious, but it is true. He no longer views the world through the lens of mass media.

"So just like that you quit a whole way of life cold turkey?"

Andrew nods, then gulps some beer. But what he doesn't tell his friend is that it wasn't that easy. His decision to quit war photography percolated in him for several years. It started in Rwanda when he and Nigel Northam, a British photographer who worked for Associated Press, were walking along a river they had been told was a nightly dumping ground for bodies. The tip had sounded a bit dubious, but Nigel and Andrew had decided to look into it.

Then, at the crack of dawn, bodies began to float by, and Nigel and Andrew started clicking away. Some of the mutilated corpses were missing arms, legs, or heads. Andrew stopped taking pictures and pressed his camera against his mouth. He can still taste the repugnant sense of utter impotence. The evil and sorrow in the world were so vast, and his camera and all his good intentions were no match for them. His vision was clouded by the tears in his eyes as he heard the fast shutter of Nigel's camera. Slowly, he walked backward from the edge of the river, leaving Nigel behind. He scurried to his tiny motel room, locked himself in the bathroom, and wept.

Andrew continued to take assignments in war zones, but by the time he was sent to cover the Second Intifada, something had changed in him forever. He was running around the streets of Qalqilyah in the West Bank, dodging bullets and covering his eyes against the tear gas while trying to take a picture of a bleeding boy when he thought one word: *Enough!* Andrew no longer wished to add to the library of human suffering that had been accumulating in his head for more than a decade. That was the last war assignment he accepted.

Zakhariye is staring at Andrew, seemingly worried about his long silence. "So how do you keep up?" he finally asks.

"Keep up with what?"

"The world."

"Why do you need to keep up with the world?"

Zakhariye sighs with frustration. "Because you live in it. Because you're a citizen of it."

"Yeah, but just because I live in it doesn't mean I have to be *of* it."

"What the hell does that even mean?"

"It means I can live in the world and move about it without becoming subsumed by its fucked-up, destructive, and cruel nature. I lived in that far too long. I've seen first-hand what it does to people. In Bosnia, Rwanda, Somalia, I've seen it." Andrew is no longer concentrating on the game. He blows his chance to pocket the black ball and win the game. Zakhariye, though, still has two balls left.

"So you're just going to hide from it all?" Zakhariye presses. "I've done that, too. I've buried my head in books and theories of the world till I had theories coming out of my ass. I spent seven years of my life in libraries, reading everything from Heidegger to Whitman and Dante to Donne, and look at me. What good has that done me? I was as mystified by it all when I came out as I was going in." He puts away his two remaining striped balls. The game is now tied with just the black ball left.

"I'm not talking about hiding away in books, Zakhi."

"Or in your head. It's the same thing. At some point you have to get out of yourself and join others. More and more I'm becoming convinced that going out there and contributing in some tangible way to something larger than our little lives, or our kids and wives, is the way to go." He misses the black ball.

"Charity starts at home, Zakhi." Andrew aims for the black ball but also fails to pocket it. The last ball is always the hardest.

"I'm not talking about charity. I'm talking about being engaged, being part of something bigger than your thoughts and feelings, your inner life." Zakhariye chalks the tip of his stick. "Take you, for instance."

"Okay, let's take me."

"Don't mock me, asshole."

Andrew smiles. "I'm not. Go on."

"Okay, you had a job, you were out there in the middle —"

"More like no man's land."

"Just hear me out. You had a profession that gave you the privilege of showing idiots like me what's happening out there, the horrors and atrocities being committed every day. With a single picture you made us aware so that we wouldn't be able to say we didn't know it was happening. Give me one example of a war you've covered."

Andrew thinks for a second. "Rwanda."

"A perfect case in point. That's exactly what I'm talking about. Didn't you feel like you were doing valuable work? Weren't you showing the West, the U.N., and everyone else the very thing they vowed never to allow after the Holocaust?"

"Yeah, and to what end? People saw what was happening. Clinton saw the pictures every day of nearly a million people being butchered, and even then they still didn't call the thing what it was — genocide. We've all seen famous war photographs like the execution of Nguyễn Văn Lém the minute before the bullet hit his head. We've seen Phan Thị Kim Phúc running naked from the bomb fires, her skin peeling from her body. We've all seen the horrors of Auschwitz in countless photographs, but then we also saw the same thing in Cambodia, Srebrenica, and Rwanda. So tell me, Zakhariye, what good have all those photographs done?"

Zakhariye doesn't answer. He positions himself for the last play and gently taps the white ball with his stick. It brushes against the black ball sitting at the edge of the far corner pocket. Andrew watches helplessly as the black ball disappears into the hole. He takes a final sip of his now-warm beer to ease his defeat.

Back in his cab, with Zakhariye in the passenger seat, Andrew is overwhelmed by thoughts of his mother and the approaching funeral. He feels irresponsible for not being with his father, sister, and aunt, helping them with whatever needs to be done. His guilt for not being there is soon replaced by remorse for not telling Zakhariye about his mother's passing. It is as if he has deceived his friend, that their evening of pool and abstract discussion was a big lie. As Andrew gets closer to Zakhariye's house, he knows he can't let him leave without telling him about his mother. "Look, Zakhi, there's something I've been meaning to tell you."

Zakhariye gasps. "You've been cheating on me."

They both laugh.

"My mother passed away."

Any trace of gaiety instantly vanishes. "Fuck, Andrew."

"I know. I should've told you."

"I'm so sorry, man. When did it happen?"

"Three days ago. The viewing service is Thursday night."

"Why didn't you tell me earlier? You let me babble on and on about my stupid theories and the whole time you had this —"

"I know. I'm a jerk. I just wanted to get away from it all."

Zakhariye nods. They drive silently for the rest of the trip. When they arrive at Zakhariye's townhouse, Andrew gets out of the taxi as Zakhariye walks around the vehicle and faces him. They shake hands.

"Thanks, man," Andrew says.

Unexpectedly, Zakhariye hugs him. They hold each other for a long time. At last they let go of each other. Andrew watches as Zakhariye opens his front door. Before his friend goes in, Andrew raises his hand a little and waves. Zakhariye returns the gesture, then closes the door. Andrew gets back into the taxi, executes a U-turn, and drives away, feeling strangely buoyant.

I O

holy war

Zakhariye can't understand how he could have gotten through almost forty years without painting a wall, a patio chair, or anything else requiring a new coat. He feels as though he has failed his transcendentalist credo on the value of manual labour and all the simple joys it can afford. He missed a good opportunity seven years ago when he and Thandie moved into their house, which needed to be painted. She was seven months' pregnant with Alcott, and so rather than going through the trouble of painting the house themselves, he hired several Serbian professionals that a co-worker recommended.

Now, as he applies the roller to the garage door, he remembers his call to Andrew this morning. He asked Andrew if he could do anything for him. After all, Andrew really helped him get though the first months after Alcott died. Andrew phoned him often, took him out for drinks several times, and listened to him when he needed to talk or sat next to him when he didn't want to speak. So this morning when Andrew asked him if he could help repaint his dad's garage door, Zakhariye was happy to get a chance to do something, however small.

Having already stripped the dry, chipped paint from the door and having just applied the first coat, Zakhariye understands why Andrew's old man wanted to do this job. The deep red paint has a strikingly rejuvenating effect not only on the door but the whole facade of the house.

Zakhariye is amazed by the relative quiet all around him. Even though the house is near the busy intersection of Bathurst and Eglinton, he feels as if he is tucked deep in the country because of the large, sheltering trees in the neighbourhood. All he hears are the sounds of birds chirping and the wind rustling the leaves. After their initial burst of talkative energy, Zakhariye and Andrew have fallen into an oddly comforting silence.

Disturbing their peace, Natalie comes out of the house, carrying two cups of coffee on a silver tray. "Take a break, fellows."

Zakhariye puts down the roller and takes one of the cups. "Thank you."

"My pleasure."

He and Andrew sip their coffee as they lean against the taxi in the driveway and face Natalie, who is busy appraising the garage door.

"Coming along nicely," she says. "I see a whole new career for you guys."

Andrew and Zakhariye glance at each other and chuckle.

"What's so funny?"

"My friend here is considering a career change," Andrew says.

"Oh, what did you have in mind?" Natalie asks, holding the tray against her chest like a schoolgirl clutching textbooks.

"Well, it's more a change from my current line of work rather than a change to something else," Zakhariye says, trying not to sound as directionless as he feels. He has always hated the whole midlife crisis cliché, but secretly he is petrified it might just be happening to him.

"What do you do now?"

"I'm the managing editor of a book magazine."

Natalie raises her eyebrows.

Zakhariye can't tell if she is genuinely impressed or if she is merely being polite. "Ever read a magazine called *Scio*?"

"Can't say I have."

"You'll have to forgive my sister, Zakhi," Andrew says. "She has no use for fiction."

"I do, too. Don't listen to him."

"Oh, yeah, quick, what was the last novel you read cover to cover?"

Zakhariye glances back and forth between them, entertained by their banter but also touched by it. It reminds him of his sister who lives in Jowhar, Somalia, taking care of his widowed mother. A sharp pang of guilt hits him. *I should be there with them,* he thinks.

"The only books she has any use for are ones on viruses," Andrew says.

"Viruses?" Zakhariye asks.

"I'm doing my doctorate on them."

"Wow!" Zakhariye says. "Where?"

"At Brown Medical School."

"Not bad."

"Yeah, it's this neat interdisciplinary program. You can combine biochemistry, immunology, and microbiology — a wide array of disciplines. It's a really progressive program."

"What's your specialty?"

"Bacteriology."

"My sister's had a lifelong love affair with bacteria," Andrew interjects. "Tell him about it, big sis."

"Well, I'm looking into the role bacterial genetics plays in epidemic patterns, why a certain disease breaks out at a particular time and place, kills a bunch of people, and then goes away on its own and hides for decades, centuries even. What is it in its genetic code that makes it do that? Is it a survival mechanism or something more complicated? I'm studying their life cycles so that we can better understand them and hopefully better prepare against them."

"That's incredible work," Zakhariye says. "Worthwhile."

"Well, mostly it's pretty dry lab stuff and case studies, but every step of the process is crucial. You can't skip the boring parts."

Turning to Andrew, Zakhariye asks, "How come you're not as smart as her?"

"She got the brains. I got the looks."

"I better let you guys get back to work before it gets too dark," Natalie says, gazing at the already indigo sky. She collects their empty mugs on the tray.

"Thanks for the coffee," Zakhariye says.

"Any time."

"How's Dad doing?" Andrew asks, prompting Natalie to turn back.

"He's sleeping. Aunt Doris gave him one of her sleeping pills. He needed it. I checked in on him a little while ago."

"Thanks," Andrew says. Then he and Zakhariye start putting a second coat of paint on the garage door.

"How has he been taking it?" Zakhariye asks.

"Wish I knew. He doesn't talk. Doesn't open up to me or Natalie. He's just so angry all the time."

Zakhariye nods.

"Were you angry?" Andrew asks, then flinches as if he has stepped over an invisible line that shouldn't have been crossed.

"I was too drowned in apathy to be angry," Zakhariye says.

Andrew stops painting and turns to him.

"I turned cold. Something froze. All the things that used to move me, that meant anything to me, ceased to. Cold! Just like that." Zakhariye starts painting, prompting Andrew to continue, as well.

"I tried to watch all my favourite films to see if I could feel anything again. Have you ever seen a movie called *Make Way for Tomorrow?*"

Andrew shakes his head.

"Great film! You should see it. There's a scene at the end where this old couple realizes they have nowhere to live and no one to take care of them and that they have to live in separate seniors' homes. As he gets on a train, the man tells his wife he'll go to California, get a job, and save some money so they can live together. They both know that will never happen, but they decide to hold on to the lie. No matter how many times I saw that movie, that scene used to always make me cry. To test myself I put in my VHS copy of it and watched the entire movie. And nothing. I thought maybe I just saw it way too many times.

"So I reread all my favourite Walt Whitman poems, especially the parts that used to move me. There's this passage from 'Crossing Brooklyn Ferry.'" Zakhariye recites from memory: "'These and all were to me the same as they are to you, I loved well those cities, loved well the stately and rapid river, the men and women I saw were all near to me, others the same — others who look back on me because I look'd forward to them. The time will come, though I stop here today and tonight.' And just when I got to 'What is it then between us? What is the count of the scores or a hundred of years between us? Whatever it is avails not — distance avails not, and place avails not,' I'd get a lump in my throat and tears would fill my eyes. I don't know what it was about that poem or that passage that always got to me. I think it was the idea — however wishful thinking — that we're all connected in a way that transcends time and place that moved me to tears. But now I can read it and I might as well be reading Aramaic. It's dead to me."

They paint in silence for a long while, the breeze in the trees the only sound that accompanies the soft swooshes of their wet rollers against the door.

"What do you think happened?" Andrew asks, turning away from the door and looking at his friend. "Why have they stopped affecting you?"

Zakhariye shrugs, his eyes wide and sad like a schoolboy who has forgotten the answer to two plus two. "Do you understand it now? Why I can't do my job anymore? Do you see why I can't look at another goddamn profile of some twenty-year-old ingenue and her debut novel about her drug-induced hallucinations? I just don't believe in that stuff anymore."

"Then don't," Andrew says. "If you told me six years ago that I would quit being a photojournalist, I would've said you were out of your fucking mind. I couldn't conceive of my life without my work. Now look at me. I couldn't be further away from my old job, and I feel more myself than I ever did before."

"So you don't miss it? Any part of it?"

"Yeah, I miss some things about it, but it doesn't mean it was right for me. There are many more things about it I'll never miss than I'll miss."

"Like what?"

Andrew is silent for a moment as though ranking all the things he will never miss about his old job. "There's one thing I never did get the hang of. I'd be on the scene of some horrible thing, a mass grave or family home being demolished as its owners looked on helplessly and people wept in front of me. Then I'd run out of film and I'd have to reload my camera or check the light meter, some other mundane but necessary business, while a human tragedy unfolded in front of me. And in order to do my job well I had to build a bubble around me. I hated that ... that wall. So is there something you always wanted to do but just never gave yourself the chance to do?"

Zakhariye stops painting. "I've always wanted to write. Fiction, I mean. I had this amazing experience on a train to Dublin once.

I met this old man, the saddest guy I ever saw in my life. Up until then, anyway. I wanted write about him."

"Great! So why don't you write about it?"

"I did. I tried. I wrote one short story. Then I realized that loving stories isn't enough. Being a writer requires something I don't have or don't have the discipline to develop. It calls for a kind of patient dedication to a never-ending, never-perfected task with no other inducement than the hope of getting it right someday. I'm afraid I need a little more inducement for that amount of work. It was a great learning experience, though."

"Fair enough," Andrew says. "You gave it a shot. That's all that matters. Now you can delete that from the list of possibilities. What's next on the list?"

"Not a clue, man. Not a fucking clue." For the first time in his life Zakhariye doesn't have a five-year-plan for the future.

"Go wild, man. Surprise yourself. You might just stumble on the dream you never knew you had. Or not! Change is doable, though. Reinvention is possible."

Zakhariye frowns. "Reinvention?"

"I know, I know, it sounds vulgar. It sounds like something an aging pop star does. But I see it more as, oh, I don't know, rebirth."

They look at each other for a moment and burst into riotous laughter.

"Okay, that didn't come out right," Andrew admits. "Rebirth? Man, talk about sounding fucking pompous."

"Hey, you're talking to a man who named his first-born after Amos Bronson Alcott."

"Amos Bronson Alcott? Who's that?"

"He was a great teacher, a Transcendentalist, and the father of Louisa May Alcott, the author of *Little Women*. Because of his ideas about education and the way he interacted with children, I wanted him to be the father I never had. My father passed away when I was a year old, so I never got to have a dad, a man I could look up to, who could teach me about the world and what it meant to be a man. I had to figure it all out for myself. So when I learned about Amos Alcott, he was like the mentor I'd been searching for. So that's why I named my son after him."

"As good a reason as any I've ever heard," Andrew says.

They resume their painting. When they finish, they stand a metre or so away from the garage door and take in their work.

"Our work here is done, my friend," Andrew says.

"Well done us."

"Well done us!" Andrew repeats. He starts putting away the rollers and places the lid back on the can of paint. "You said your hero Amos was a Transcendentalist. What's that all about?"

"Ralph Waldo Emerson, Henry David Thoreau, those guys. I bought into them hook, line, and sinker."

"Bought into what?"

"All of it. Not so much the obvious stuff, you know, the whole metaphysical aspect of it, transcending the physical and empirical realities of our daily existence and that crap. I completely and passionately believed in the idea or at least the possibility that we can experience life through the mind, that we can see the truth, you know, the big picture — God, life, death, love, loss, all of it through this bit of grey matter we carry around in our skulls."

"Surely you're not dismissing the inner life."

"But the inner life doesn't exist without the outer. One is created by the other."

"Oh, I don't know about that, Zakhi."

"We can build all the inner life we want for ourselves, but there's this parallel reality, the world outside that exits right along with it, and the latter can blow the former to smithereens in a way the former can't do to the latter. Simple physics, I think."

"So it all comes back to action versus thought?"

"More like fantasy versus reality. Dream versus the fucking truth. Sorry. I don't mean to sound so angry."

"Why not if that's what you feel," Andrew says.

"It's not so much anger that I feel. More like idiocy, really, like I've been had. I don't know. It's hard to explain. I think more than anything else that I'm angry at myself for separating the world as *me* and *not me*. Inside and outside. Somehow I made independence my religion. I accepted without question Emerson's declaration that he wanted no followers, that he would be disappointed if his ideas turned men, like me, into a hanger-on. But I never asked independence from what? The world? Others? You know, the 'Inner Spark,' the 'Oversoul,' the 'Float,' and all the rest are nothing if they're not connected to the outside world, to who's hungry, who has too much, who has too little, who's robbing whom, who's trying to control who has sex with whom, and who can marry whom. All the 'Inner Spark' can't save you from those fuckers out there who want to steal from you, imprison you, take your land, invade your country …" Zakhariye notices Andrew staring at him. "Sorry. I'll shut up now."

"No, man, go on. I like seeing you all riled up like that."

Zakhariye takes a deep breath as if to recharge for a second round. "I guess I'm just pissed at my naïveté for thinking they cracked it —"

"Who's they?"

"Them, they, all of them — Emerson, Thoreau, Kant, all those fuckers. I thought they cracked it wide open. The whole question of human happiness."

"Oh, man, happiness, that tricky one. I guess you could say I'm a let-happiness-come-to-me sort of guy. Every time I consciously went after it, every time I did something with the sole purpose of making me happy, I ended up getting screwed."

"Someone should've warned us."

"No kidding. But you know what gives me that warm and fuzzy little feeling but doesn't screw me in the end?" Andrew asks with a mischievous grin.

"I'm afraid to ask."

Andrew goes into his taxi and comes out with an Altoids box.

"Peppermint makes you happy?" Zakhariye asks.

Andrew opens the box ceremoniously as if expecting a white dove to fly out. Inside are eight expertly rolled joints.

"Well, now," Zakhariye says with glee.

They each take a joint, light up, and sit on the hood of Andrew's cab. As they lean on the windshield and gaze up at the overcast, starless sky, they take long, luxurious drags.

"Did I ever tell you what happened to me the first time I ever got high?" Zakhariye asks as he releases a long silver trail of smoke.

"No, what happened?"

"I had to be rushed to the hospital."

"What?"

"I had a major freak-out. My heart started beating so fast it felt like it was going to explode. My limbs were jumping and jerking on their own, and the worst part was —"

"It got worse?"

"My jaws completely shut. Whenever the paramedics asked me anything, I answered in sign language."

"You know sign language?"

Zakhariye snorts. "Fuck, no!"

Later that night, while Zakhariye prepares a bowl of cornflakes in the kitchen before going to bed, he sees a bit of red paint on his arm, goes to wash it off in the sink, and starts thinking of his conversation earlier with Andrew about his chance meeting with Mr. O'Brien on a train to Dublin. He hasn't thought about O'Brien in years.

Zakhariye wonders what became of the old man as he eats the first spoonful of cornflakes. He tries to remember where he put the story he wrote about the old man, his sole attempt at creative writing. Zakhariye always dreamed of writing, but having interviewed so many great writers for the magazine over the years, he came to understand there was a world of difference between being a good writer and admiring good writing. It took him a while to realize that he fitted into the latter category.

That realization might have been painful had it occurred in his twenties, but it came well into his thirties — a good age to accept one's limitations. Suddenly, he recalls where he put the story. He springs away from the kitchen table and heads for the storage closet upstairs where he keeps all his notebooks and papers in clearly labelled boxes. One of the boxes contains his half-finished Ph.D. dissertation on the evolution of the *Bildungsroman*, which he abandoned when he took a one-year sabbatical. He never went back. Zakhariye sits on the floor, opens the box, and skims some of the pages of his thesis. Then his eyes fall on a large quote in the middle of the page. It reads:

> More than any other literary form, more perhaps than any other type of writing, the novel serves as the model by which society conceives of itself, the discourse in and through which it articulates the world.... Words must be composed in such a way that through the activity of reading there will emerge a model of the social world, models of the individual personality, of the relations between the individual and the society.... Our identity depends on the novel, what others think of us, what we

think of ourselves, the way in which our life is imperceptibly moulded into a whole. How do others see us if not as a character from a novel? The novel is the primary semiotic agent of intelligibility.

Zakhariye glances at the footnote to see where this quote comes from, for he has no recollection of it. Apparently, it is from an essay entitled "Poetics of the Novel" in a book called *Structuralist Poetics* by Jonathan Culler. He tries to remember ever having read this book or who Culler is. Nothing comes to him. In fact, his whole Ph.D. pursuit seems to have vanished into a little black hole in his being, and the only evidence of it is this box in front of him full of many ideas and declarations on life that are alien to him now.

Back in at the kitchen, he resumes eating the cereal that is now tasteless and mushy. He starts to read "Holy War," the story he retrieved from one of the boxes. It is the only short story he ever wrote, the one he thought would be the first of many, maybe even the title of a small but well-crafted collection that would garner him rave reviews and put him in the company of those he most admired.

As I walked on the station platform toward the train, it occurred to me that it would only be a matter of twenty-one hours before I was home in the arms of my wife and before my son was in my arms. The more I thought about them the more I quickened my pace toward the train that would get me closer to home.

The train was old and revealed its age by the stuffy, musty scent that permeated every particle of its interior. The seats had the feel of having been sat on, rubbed in, and moved about by a thousand travellers. I felt as if each seat had a story to tell about who had sat on it, how they had come to be there, and where they were destined. Once in my seat, next to the large window, I closed my eyes and starting rubbing my hands up and down on the arms of my seat.

It was right about the time that the train conductor's voice disturbed the stillness to announce we would be in Dublin in a little over three hours. It was also at that time that I opened my eyes to find a pale-faced man in his mid-sixties sitting next to me. He had a stern, studious look about him, and his perfectly tailored grey-striped suit and the stiff-collared shirt underneath the suit did little to soften his image. His ashy skin was sprinkled with generous amounts of freckles, and when he took off his hat, I noticed that the skull showing through his rapidly thinning hair was speckled with large liver spots. I couldn't help but think that he looked utterly anachronistic in his well-crafted suit and his 1930s hat. Here we were in the late 1990s and this man was wearing a hat to match his suit the way they did in those old Hollywood film noirs. I thought: *So this is what Humphrey Bogart would've looked like had he continued to play, well into his sixties, the strong, silent detective who solves the crime and gets the girl in the end.*

The old man might have resembled Bogart — past his prime — but his presence was the opposite of what I had silently prayed for: several uninterrupted hours to work. It seemed that every time I travelled, which was more often than I cared to, I had the bad luck of sitting next to some old and occasionally young person who condemned me to a never-ending, one-sided conversation. And against my better judgment, I always indulged them for the sake of good manners. Sitting at the window seat of the train comforted me a little in that at least I had the option of gazing at the distant horizon as if lost in profound contemplation, thus giving the old man a hint.

I started to think about how two weeks had already passed since I had come to Ireland in search of the man behind the poet whose beautifully confounding, generously illuminating words I read, reread, analyzed, and reflected on. It wasn't too long before it became apparent to me just how much I had come to love and enjoy my short stay in this country. Perhaps *enjoy* was the wrong word, for it belittled the solemnity of my experience here. *Treasure? Value? Cherish?* Perhaps they were much closer to what I felt, but even those words didn't precisely get at how I felt about this country. But then again, language always has a way of failing us, doesn't it? Of falling just short of what we yearn for it to do: paint the multitudinous colours and shapes of our emotions.

Ireland, as I had come to discover, was a place of many para-doxes and ambiguities. Yes, it was a country of immense beauty. Not the beauty of other regions I had visited such as those sleepy towns in Provence whose tiny squares and cobblestone roads I loved so much, or the immaculate sandy beaches of Hawaii where people far wealthier and prettier than I went for their hon-eymoons. Ireland had the kind of haunting, majestic beauty that made one glad to be a human being, able to behold such beauty and possibly be changed by it. For instance, I was awestruck by the way the various shades of green melted into one another: dark green tree leaves dissolving into paler green grass; barren, rocky hillsides gradually giving way to smooth green hills; white sand dunes transforming into lush yellow-green fields of oilseed. And all that happened without one ever becoming conscious of the exact moment and place the change occurred, much like the inexplicable way the phases that make up our lives bleed into one another: the past into the present and the present into the past.

The ugly paradoxes of this place also became painfully obvi-ous to my foreign, untutored eyes. In the populated areas I was disoriented by endless identical houses made of red or dirty brown bricks that monotonously lined up for as far as the eye could see. The result of this was that a labyrinth of human shabbiness and lack of ingenuity became too difficult for nature's beauty to conceal. The dreary ambience of these towns was sometimes so acute that it called into question my faith in the very existence of human creativity and imagination.

My thoughts on the conflicting qualities of Ireland were cut off rather abruptly by the raspy voice of the old man who sat next to me.

"What time is it?" he asked in a thick, droopy Dublin accent that was different from the other accents I had heard in the countryside. His accent had a liquid quality in which the words melted into one another.

"Five-thirty," I replied, trying to conceal the inconvenience of having to check my watch.

The old man looked out the window. "Heavy rainfall, that's what they predict."

Unable to find a suitable reply, I said, "I happen to be very fond of rain."

He glanced at me with a perplexed expression that made me ashamed to lie to a man old enough to be my father. "You aren't from around here, are you? Your accent and the fact that you love rain tell me that."

"You're right. I'm definitely not from this part of the world." I had expected him to ask me where I was from, because that was the sort of question that naturally followed such an answer. But the old man remained quiet for some time and stared blankly ahead as if he had forgotten what he was thinking about. He seemed to me to be a man whose only care in the world was to be near a loved one who needed his comforting, or perhaps a loved one whose comforting he was in need of. It was at that precise moment that I realized this was a man I might possibly have something in common with.

"Ayuub," I said. "My name is Ayuub Ahmed."

The man extended his hand, and we shook. "Stephen O'Brien," he said, still clasping my hand.

"I'm from Toronto," I ventured in an effort to seem polite.

"Where on earth's that?"

That was a question I didn't expect to hear from him, for I was used to taking a healthy amount of pride in Toronto as a city of certain international renown. As we continued our awkward but unhurried talk, it became clear to me that there were many people in the world who had never heard of Toronto, and that as far as they were concerned, my hometown could very well be in South America or even the Far East. As Mr. O'Brien and I conversed, I understood that he was a man whose life hadn't afforded him the easy pleasures of knowing about faraway places. One could only enjoy such privileges when one's life lacked the drama or rather the tragedy of one grave misfortune followed by another, as I discovered was the case with this freckled old man.

I also ascertained that O'Brien and I shared a destination. We were both headed for Dublin. He had spent the past two weeks taking part in a national mourning of sorts. This "collective mourning," as some of the local newspapers had dubbed it, was brought about by a car bomb detonated in a busy market in Omagh on August 15, 1998. Omagh, a town of equal Nationalist and Unionist factions, was about a hundred and twenty kilometres west of Belfast. All the national newspapers, including the copy of the *Belfast Telegraph* I carried in my knapsack, showed the bloody pictures and told the stories of twenty-nine souls lost in an instant so brief in duration but everlasting in the shadows it cast on the lives of thousands of people. During the past two weeks of my stay, this country had been living and breathing a tragedy whose magnitude only its citizens could comprehend, and even they were often unable to make sense of the random and indiscriminate nature of who was killed, who was maimed, and who was spared the deadly carnage dreamt and actualized with such lethal exactitude.

About an hour into our conversation I discovered that Mr. O'Brien's mourning had been much greater than that of his fellow countrymen. He told me that his son, James O'Brien, was one of the individuals killed in the bombing.

Hearing the words *individuals, wounded, killed,* their cold impartiality combined with the distant and tranquil tone with which he uttered them continue to haunt me even as I write this story in the warm safety of my townhouse. Here amid so many sweet and familiar things I sit in my brown leather armchair, under the glow of the fireplace, and I'm consoled by the company of my two-year-old son who sleeps peacefully in his playpen, his chest effortlessly rising and falling with each breath. I'm sorry that the world he'll inherit is one of car bombs, suicide bombs, smart bombs that obliterate at the touch of button. I'm sorry he'll have to grow up with anaesthetized phrases like "ethnic cleansing," "collateral damage," and "holy war" and not understand the horrors they conceal.

One day he'll come home from school and ask me what holy war means, and I hope to God I have a good answer for him, because I certainly don't understand all the holy wars being waged all around us — holy war in the name of holy lands and holy war in the name of God and holy war in the name of enduring freedom and democracy, holy wars that seem to do nothing but make an unholy mess of so many lives. I'm sure that in due time he'll become well acquainted with human atrocities, but for now I'm happy for his ignorance. For now I'm happy he sleeps utterly oblivious to human cruelty and all the other maladies that plague his race.

As I continue to write about my short journey with Mr. O'Brien, memories of him flood my consciousness. He seemed to be a man who had struggled greatly but finally made peace with the mocking arbitrariness of his misfortunes. Without any sense of drama the old man had chosen to make me privy to the private ebb and flow of the tumultuous relationship with his now-deceased son, James, whom he affectionately called "Little Jamie." It wasn't until the end of our journey that I discovered that Little Jamie wasn't so little either in appearance or in character.

"Little Jamie left home barely seventeen," Mr. O'Brien told me. "It wasn't till his twenty-seventh birthday that he called home."

I was overcome with an odd sense of being unworthy of the privilege, the honour, of being the chosen stranger entrusted with the intimate truths of this frail old man's family, a man who seemed to me to be in need of not the pity but the company, however temporary, of another human.

"Why have you come to Ireland, if you don't mind me asking?"

"I work for a literary magazine," I replied, grabbing my knapsack and fishing for a copy. I produced an old issue of the magazine that had been the object of my life's undivided attention for the past four years. Below the name of the magazine, written in the large red letters, was a photograph of Toni Morrison. "This is the magazine I work for," I said rather proudly. Then it hit me, the absurdity of trying to impress an old man I would probably never see again. "I came to interview an Irish novelist and poet," I added.

"Is she the one?" he asked, pointing at the regal lady with the luminous white braids and mischievous smile on the cover of the glossy magazine.

With an exaggerated emphasis I replied, "Oh, no!" I must admit I was surprised that he didn't recognize the author on the cover, a surprise I somehow managed to hide. Later on, however, I was filled with a dull but incessant shame for having been so egocentric as to assume that this man would know about this most pre-eminent author, who I not only admired greatly but worked hard to conduct an interview that befitted her. This was further proof of something I had often been accused of, mostly by my wife.

My wife often pointed out this particular shortcoming of mine, especially when she wanted to get back at me for an unkind, inconsequential remark of my own. She sometimes, with certain wifely disapproval and disappointment, told me about my presumptuous attitude that whatever or whoever I valued should likewise be valued by others. I usually shrugged off this accusation and paid no further thought to it. But that day, sitting next to Mr. O'Brien, I accepted that this was indeed chief among my character defects and made a mental note to rectify it. Someday.

After ridiculing myself for my colossal egotism, I continued my conversation with Mr. O'Brien, saying, "I spent the last two weeks near the Derryveagh Mountains interviewing the writer I told you about."

"What a coincidence," the old man said with renewed interest in our conversation. "My bride was born and buried in Gweedore, right beneath the Derryveagh Mountains."

When I attempted to extend my sympathies for the death of his wife, O'Brien told me, with a weary sigh, that she died while giving birth to Little Jamie.

Suddenly, a man in a uniform came by and asked to see our tickets, interrupting our talk. I was a bit annoyed with the man because I was becoming interested in the story of my friend in travel. When the official moved on to the passengers behind us, I eagerly resumed our conversation and asked Mr. O'Brien to tell me more about his son.

He volunteered a great deal of information as though it were a taxing burden he needed to part with. The more he told me the more I wondered how he could be so unguarded with a person he had known a mere hour. Then I thought that perhaps, unlike me, he didn't have the luxury of going to a therapist to remedy all his psychological aches and pains. Perhaps this was his only means of release. And if that were the case, I was more than happy to oblige.

Mr. O'Brien said his son was one of the people responsible for the explosion in the Omagh market. Just as I was beginning to recover from the shock that "Little Jamie" was one of the men that everyone referred to as "the terrorists," the old man astonished me further by relating the gruesome business of how James was accidentally killed in the blast, that his body was burned beyond recognition, and that the police could only identify his remains by analyzing his dental records.

Once the identity was confirmed, the police were ecstatic because they could finally stop hunting James H. O'Brien, who according to their files was one of Ireland's most wanted men. How fascinating, I thought, that this man, of all people, would have such a great tale to tell. Soon after that notion crossed my mind I was overwhelmed by shame again for seeing this old man's great misfortune as another story, another tale to entertain a reader or two. Occupational hazard was my only defence.

"The fool didn't get far away from the car quickly enough, so he got a taste of his own venom," Mr. O'Brien continued.

I couldn't figure out why he said this with such deep but calm anger in his voice. Was it because his son didn't do the job right and therefore disappointed him once more? Or was his anger sparked by the knowledge that his own flesh and blood, the son he had sacrificed his days and nights to teach him hot from cold, right from wrong, good from evil, would end up destroying the lives of so many innocent people? As O'Brien continued his story with decreasing guardedness, it dawned on me: the reason for the bitter disappointment in his tone was much less complex. He was simply a man whose bones and limbs ached for the loss of his one and only son. O'Brien did have another child, a girl named Maureen who succumbed to leukemia when she was barely nine. The hope of one folk remedy was replaced by the futility of another until finally O'Brien lost faith and shipped his small family to Dublin to be closer to city doctors. After he personally buried Maureen's frail, cancer-ridden body, he decided to stay in the city where he made a living from a small cigar shop on a corner of Bond Street and raised James by himself.

Although he knew he could never do as good a job as Molly Hackett, the woman he still called his bride, O'Brien cared for his son the best way he knew how. And for a short while, until those infamous teen years, his best seemed good enough. With tough love and the grace of God, O'Brien managed to do it well all by himself. Or so he thought.

Our talk was interrupted by hunger for food, so we decided to search for something edible in the train restaurant, which didn't offer much, but our choices were limited, considering we were trapped in a moving steel tube that hurled us southward across the island.

While I ate brown bread and fried fish and washed it down with bitter tea, O'Brien told me about his reaction when his son woke him from a restless sleep one night to tell him he had joined a small group he called freedom fighters who answered to the IRA and that he was ready to be buried for their cause. Shattered that his only son was now a part of a movement the rest of the world viewed as callous and evil, O'Brien disowned his only son. And it wasn't until three years later that he received from James a curt, matter-of-fact letter containing nothing more than the necessary information that he was alive and well and asked his father not to worry about him. As if that were an option.

The bittersweet taste of the cheap tea still lingered in my mouth when O'Brien pointed out the irony of everything. He had spent a great deal of his life indoctrinating James with the righteousness of the very cause that ultimately tore them apart. When James was barely old enough to comprehend the complexities of his nation's troubles, his father often took him to the local library where they spent hours upon hours reading about and reflecting on the contributions and disgrace of Charles Parnell, the heroism and so-called betrayal of Michael Collins's Anglo-Irish Treaty, and the many other facts and fiction that were indignantly argued and fought about by fathers and sons, friends and lovers, from coast to coast. O'Brien himself was an avid supporter of the uprisings in the 1970s. However, as the 1980s approached, he became less political and more philosophical, thus the vigour in his arguments and his passion for the cause vanished bit by small bit.

During heated debates among the patrons of his cigar shop, made up mostly of old friends and neighbours, he often stopped them in the middle of their fierce arguments to ask if it was all worth it. Over their indignant protests, O'Brien would raise his voice to explain that in the final analysis, nationalities and religious denominations were about as consequential to the value of a man's soul as what he ate for dinner. Needless to say, his theory was met with nothing more substantial than a sarcastic chuckle or a laugh.

During dessert, as we savoured cheap custard pudding, O'Brien said, "My biggest regret is that I now know I could have been a better father. I had it in me to be the kind of father a troubled boy like James needed."

I was struck by an immense respect and admiration for a man so willing to acknowledge and mourn his shortcomings without excuses and without timidity. O'Brien's attitude plunged me into a deep sense of failure for not being with my own son who was growing and learning so much about the world despite my absence. The fact that the whole Atlantic separated me from my son almost moved me to tears. I distracted myself by changing the subject and telling O'Brien about the author I had come to Ireland to interview. I went on and on about this poet, this recluse, this ultimate man's man who lived on an enormous farm with a bunch of sheep, a brood of collies, and a typewriter without the company and distraction of people.

The manner in which O'Brien's face lost its life, the way his eyes began to wander around the train, told me he wasn't keen about wasting our brief time together talking about a man who made up stories for a living. I stood, took my wallet out of the right pocket of my khaki trousers, and produced a small photograph of my little boy.

It was a picture I had taken the day he uttered his first word. The word was indecipherable, but I was convinced he was trying to say "Daddy." My wife, on the other hand, was equally convinced he was saying "Mommy." For the remainder of that day we bickered over the precise meaning of *saani*. Even now that he has learned many different words, *saani* still remains my favourite sound ever to drool out of his small, round lips.

That day, before I put my son down for his afternoon nap, I took the photograph I now held in my hand. I didn't tell my wife that I had an overwhelming desire to photograph our son that particular day, nor did I know why I felt that need. However, months later I stumbled upon the real reason I took the photo that afternoon. It was simple and painful. I didn't trust myself to remember the day my son uttered his first word. In retrospect I understood that it was a pathetic attempt to solidify, somehow immortalize, the event. It pained me to know I would probably forget about that day if I didn't always carry with me this small, permanent memento.

When I finished telling O'Brien the history of that beloved photograph, I saw that he was overcome by the intangible force of my little tale, a power that could only be felt by another father who yearned for his son. His eyes welled with tears, and he immediately hid his face from the rude scrutiny of my gaze. A few seconds later he abruptly got up to use the toilet.

As I saw the old man slowly make his way down the narrow aisle of the train upon his return from the washroom, it occurred to me that I had inadvertently committed the sin of causing a grown man to cry. When he approached our seat, I saw that his large green eyes weren't only red but that in them lingered remnants of tears. Just as O'Brien relaxed into his seat, the deep, comforting voice of the conductor resonated throughout the car, informing us we were at the threshold of Dublin.

We remained quiet for the next few minutes until we started to see the old structures of the city loom high in the slate sky. The fog and heavy rainfall of that warm early September day made Dublin appear even gloomier and more haunting.

I couldn't help being depressed by the sudden silence that permeated that brief moment in our shared existence. I thought about the reason for the painful hush that had draped itself over us like a silk shawl. The best answer I could come up with was that O'Brien and I separately, simultaneously, dreaded the approaching moment when we would have to part. He would go back to his flat in the heart of Dublin, and I would catch a flight from Dublin to Toronto the following morning. How would we say goodbye? Would we be manly and therefore casual? Would a mere farewell be adequate to say all that we wanted to? Or would we be more human and acknowledge that we had achieved something people often try to but rarely succeed at — connecting with another human being — and that our lives had, in some peculiar, indefinable, but long-lasting way, converged? Should we exchange addresses and vow to keep in touch?

As the old train rolled along the wet tracks of Dublin, it passed ancient churches and little houses with windows covered by white lace curtains. Through the rain-spattered windowpane I stared at a sprawling green cemetery and wondered about the countless souls dwelling there.

I envisioned the dead. Some seemed to gasp for air, suffocating without anyone to witness their eternal suffering. Others sat silently, peacefully, as if waiting for a call to rise and take their rightful place in the hereafter, a summoning to restoration and the transmigration of their souls according to their karma. It occurred to me that waiting was precisely what all the passengers on this train were doing. Waiting, it appeared, was how we spent much of our short time here, waiting for something to happen, for some event to take place so that we could at last comprehend that we weren't alone, that there were people like us in the most faraway places, in the least likely places, people who felt as we did, as was the case with O'Brien and me. Even at that moment we were waiting for a voice to tell us we had at last arrived in Dublin.

When the train crawled into Connolly Station, O'Brien and I wore similar sad expressions on our faces. We both realized we had come to the end. So much had transpired, yet oddly enough nothing had changed. I would go on with my busy and insignificant life of deadlines, schedules, and story meetings. O'Brien would continue with his lonely and insignificant shopkeeper's life. Before the train halted completely, the old man wiped the dignified wrinkles on his face with a neatly folded handkerchief, gazed through the rain-spattered window, and bid me farewell.

Since I had a lot of luggage, I took more time to assemble it. By then the old man had already left. Before I got off the train I checked our seat once more to see if I had forgotten anything. There was a small photograph remarkably similar to the one of my son that I showed O'Brien. I picked up the snapshot. It depicted a red-headed young man of about fifteen standing next to a youthful O'Brien. The young man's green eyes stared directly into mine as if he knew that someday, I, a stranger on a train, would come to know all about the extraordinary drama of his short-lived life.

Armed with the instinctive knowledge of how valuable the picture I held in my hand was to O'Brien, I hurried off the train and ran after the old man. On Amiens Street, just outside the station, I got a glimpse of him walking away. I dashed after him, wanting desperately to return the priceless photograph I held in my hand.

A few metres away from him I had it on the tip of my tongue to call out his name. However, some mysterious force prevented me from returning the photo. This thing, whatever it was, made me question how a single snapshot had found its way out of the rest of O'Brien's belongings to be left behind. Realizing the improbability of such an accident, I accepted the picture for what it was — a heartbroken father's last-minute attempt to ensure that his son's life didn't end with an untimely demise, that his Little Jamie, however misguided and destructive, wasn't the devil incarnate, as people called him. I also interpreted the photograph as a gift from an old-fashioned man who didn't know how to give so much to a stranger he met on a train to Dublin.

At that moment I ceased running and stood there, frozen amid the heaving crowd of that busy street. By then it was dusk, that transitory moment when the light of day was no more, the dark of night was yet to come, and everything between the earth and the heavens took on an indigo hue. I watched O'Brien trudge off, shoulders slightly hunched by a lifetime of disappointment, failure, and regret.

I I

something closer to love

It is eight-thirty in the morning, and Sarah's hotel room, with
its impressive view of Lake Ontario, is aglow with sunlight. The
first fully conscious thought she has this morning is of Ella
Christiansen, her beloved teacher. She remembers that according
to the obituary she stumbled upon the viewing is this evening.

Sarah rises and walks over to the door of her room where she
picks up a manila envelope that is slipped under her door every
morning. She opens the envelope and extracts a pink letter, a call
sheet, and her schedule for the day, complete with scene numbers
to be shot and time and place.

The call sheet advises her that filming of the scene they started
yesterday, the big confrontation sequence with Clifford, will be
picked up tonight. That means she will have to be in makeup by
5:30 p.m., thus forcing her to miss her one opportunity to say goodbye to the woman to whom she owes much of her career. Asking
Simon, the first assistant director, to rearrange the schedule is out
of the question, but one way or another she has to bid Ella farewell.

———

Consulting the neatly folded obituary page she cut out from the newspaper, Sarah strolls eastward on Danforth Avenue, going against the easterly wind, which at mid-morning has a sting to it despite the warm early-autumn weather. She wears a simple long black dress and a black wool cardigan over it, making her appear more elegant than she had in mind when she left her hotel room. Glancing at the dark sky, she sees the sun flashing through thick clouds. *It's one of those days,* she thinks, *when it rains one minute and shines the next. Anything can happen on a day like today.* She relishes this feeling of not knowing.

Sarah checks the address on the page again and peers at the doors of the buildings that line the street. She wonders if she ever came to this part of town when she lived in Toronto, then it dawns on her that she never did. Sarah is surprised by her limited knowledge of her hometown. She never bothered to discover all the great little nooks of the city while she lived here — so many different neighbourhoods and enclaves that she never explored. Instead she spent her days in drama classes deciphering Shakespearean soliloquies, and her nights fantasizing about the Broadway stage. Regret courses through her for all the years she wasted thinking about far-off places, for all the time she squandered dreaming rather than living.

At last Sarah finds the Botti Funeral Home. She is surprised by the unassuming Victorian building sandwiched between a low-rise condo and a drugstore. Sarah expected a huge, well-decorated home with calming wall-to-wall beige carpets. In her imagination she saw a fancy corporate funeral home, not a small family-owned business. Once inside, the hardwood floors, the red Persian rugs, and the richly detailed olive-green floral wallpaper exaggerate the discrepancy between what she pictured and what actually is.

Sarah strides down a narrow hallway that leads directly to what seems like the reception hall where she finds a man, tall and heavy with a slight hunch to his shoulders. She watches him, his back turned to her. He is arranging a huge bouquet of different types of irises. She clears her throat. He turns around. He has a long nose and sad, sunken eyes. A fitting look for a place like this, it seems to Sarah.

The man inspects her for a moment. "Viewing doesn't start until six, ma'am."

"I know. Um, I understand. But the thing is …" Sarah approaches him, right hand already extended. They exchange a firm, confident handshake. "My name is Sarah Turlington. I'm pleased to meet you."

"Yeah, nice meeting you, too," he mutters shyly, but also seeming to enjoy hearing a pretty woman say she is pleased to meet him.

How remarkable, Sarah muses, *the way a friendly handshake, a little human touch, disarms people, making them more inclined to grant favours.* "Like I was saying, the thing is, I can't be here during the official viewing hours. But Mrs. Christiansen meant a great deal to me. I'd really be grateful if I could just have a moment to, you know …"

It doesn't look as if he knows, so she presses on. "The thing is, I must be on a flight at five tonight, and it would mean the world to me if you'd be kind and give a few minutes to …" *To what?* Sarah wonders. She hasn't really thought about what she plans to do here. "Please?" she implores.

He considers her plea for a few seconds. Then a slight smile creases his face. "Five minutes. Only five minutes. I need to finish these flowers, get this place ready."

Sarah nods and smiles gratefully. He walks out of the reception room, leaving her alone with the closed casket at the front. She takes several cautious steps toward it. Now standing over the casket, she places both palms flat on the smooth curve of its lid.

It feels cool on her clammy hands, and she leaves imprints of her palms on its sleek surface.

She has a strong urge to lift the casket's lid so she can see what has become of her favourite teacher, the woman who pushed her to try harder, to not settle for being just an actor when she had it in her to be an artist. Sarah wants to see what that woman looks like now. She tries to lift the lid, but it is much heavier than she expected. When she manages to raise it slightly, she changes her mind.

Her curiosity to see what the dead look like is replaced by her desire to keep the image of her teacher as she once was — alive and passionate, long, unruly charcoal hair always trailing behind. Sarah doesn't want that image of Ella to be replaced by one of a cold, steely corpse. So she slowly lowers the lid back to its original position. She longs to touch Ella, to kiss her on the forehead, so she places the side of her face on the casket, her cheek resting on its cool surface. Memories of Ella flood her mind — the sound of the woman's strong, raspy voice full of authority and dignity.

"Acting is about behaviour," Ella often repeated as she paced before the class, gesturing with both hands for emphasis. Ella encouraged her students to study the various acting theories, but everyone knew it was Sanford Meisner who reigned supreme in her class. "It is *not* about the words!" she often shouted. "It's *not* about how you say the words! You can sing the words, scream the words, fucking mime them for all I care. Find the action and commit to it, and I promise you, whatever you have to say, whatever you're carrying around inside of you, will be out in the open for all to see and it will be more truthful and powerful than anything you could ever say with mere words." That simple but profound precept has saved Sarah many nights onstage.

The voice of a man coming from the back of the room disturbs Sarah's reminiscences of her teacher. The voice sounds familiar. She turns and sees a man staring at her.

"You shouldn't be here," he says. "The service doesn't start till tonight."

Sarah quickly wipes tears from her face. Like his voice, she also finds his face familiar. She can't place it, but she knows she has seen him somewhere, or at least a version of him.

"Did you know her?" he asks, moving a little closer.

"She was my ... Andrew?"

"Yes?"

"Oh, my God, it's me!" She laughs a little, mostly out of sheer surprise and happiness to see him.

"Sarah Turlington, is that you? Is that really you? It is you."

They stand a metre apart, motionless, their feet seemingly glued to the floor. Andrew takes a couple of steps toward her, then stops as though not sure what etiquette dictates in a situation like this. Sarah answers for him by extending a hand, and they shake slowly, taking their time. This feels wholly unsatisfying to her, so she moves closer and kisses him on his stubbly cheek.

Andrew finally breaks the silence. "What are you doing here?"

"I heard about your mother's ..." She suddenly forgets the word. Those awful euphemisms people employ flood her mind at breakneck speed. "I heard about your mother's death. I'm so very sorry."

"Thank you. I meant, what are you doing in Toronto? Didn't you move to —"

"New York. Yes, I still live there. I'm here for work. What about you? Didn't you move away, too? Your mother told me you were in — oh, where did she say you were?"

"I moved back recently," Andrew says as he glances at his watch.

Sarah takes that as a subtle hint. "Please don't let me hold you up. I was just paying my respects. I can't be here tonight, so I thought ... I hope it's okay."

"Oh, yeah, that's fine. I just need to find the owner of this place. I came to deliver a cheque for the services. I'm just going to give this to him quickly. Don't go anywhere. I'll be right back." He moves backward, still keeping his eyes on hers, looking bewildered, apparently stunned that Sarah Turlington has walked back into his life.

When they leave the funeral home, Sarah sees that the sky has become completely overcast with clouds so dark and low they seem to hover above them. She fastens the buttons of her wool cardigan against the chilly wind.

"Stay here," Andrew says. "I'll get the car."

She nods and watches him walk away. He looks somehow diminished to her, leaner and more elongated than she remembers. The last time she saw him he was more muscular. He had the body of a young man who lived in the gym. Now, in his present physical condition, it is clear he has been altered as if by disease or trauma. As she thinks about what could have changed him so radically, she hears the jarring sound of a car horn blaring close to her. She turns and spots a navy blue taxi. Andrew waves to her from the driver's seat. Surprised, Sarah hops into the passenger seat.

When Andrew offered to give her a ride back to her hotel, she didn't think he meant in his taxi. The last time Sarah spoke to his mother she told him he was a photojournalist living in Europe. What changed? Was it a case of a mother trying to make her only son sound more successful? She finds herself disappointed that Ella, of all people, needed to puff her son up. Sarah thought Ella knew her better, that she wasn't the kind of person who judged a man by his career ... or lack of one.

Andrew heads west on Danforth Avenue, driving slowly as though wanting to stretch this ride for as long as he can. Sarah studies his profile while he focuses on the road. She notices the greying of his hair around the temples. The effect is sexy with substance. Sarah is surprised that the physical attraction she once felt for Andrew is still strong, perhaps even greater now. Without warning Andrew turns away from the road and catches her gazing at him. Quickly, she averts her eyes.

"What hotel did you say you're staying at?" he asks.

"The Westin Harbour Castle." Sarah notices a large black camera in the space between the passenger and driver's seat. She picks it up, surprised by its heaviness. Looking through the lens, she points the camera at Andrew. Something in his face, the look of solemnity in his eyes, moves her. "A serious camera for a serious fellow."

"Sorry. The past couple of days, well, actually, the past couple of months, have been … pretty serious."

Sarah feels her face flush with embarrassment. "I'm sorry. That was stupid of me. I don't know why I said that."

"It's okay."

"You seem to be handling it quite well, though. I don't know what I would do if my mother —"

"Where is she, your mother?" Andrew asks as though desperate to change the subject.

"She lives in Orlando. After my father passed away she —"

"When?"

Andrew's habit of asking cold, abrupt questions irritates Sarah. "Four years ago," she answers, doing her best not to show annoyance. "A brain aneurysm. So she moved to Florida to be closer to her sister. She's pretty happy there, the warm weather and all."

A lull settles over their conversation as they cross the Don Valley Bridge. Andrew breaks the silence. "What's it about?"

"What's what about?"

"Your movie? You said you're working on one here."

"Oh, it's about a woman who falls in love with her husband's employee."

Sarah looks at him, trying to read the expression on his face. She isn't sure if it represents interest or disdain for the type of story she is involved in telling.

"Haven't we seen enough of those?" Andrew asks, turning his gaze away from her and back onto the road.

Let me out! she wants to say. *Let me get off here. I'll take the bus.* Instead she sits quietly, still holding his camera on her lap. She puts it back where she picked it up from.

"What's your movie called?"

"It's not my movie," she snaps, no longer caring to be polite.

"What's it called?"

"Lady Chatterley's Lover."

Andrew is quiet again. Sarah finds these spells of silence unbearable. She wants to know what he is thinking. She would like to ask him but fears he will think she cares.

Then he comes to life again. "I like D.H. Lawrence. I liked that novel."

"You'll probably hate the movie then."

"Oh, and why's that?"

"They've taken liberties with it."

"Liberties? Like what?"

"The setting for starters. It's no longer in England."

"You've taken Lawrence out of England?"

"It's in Pennsylvania now. The mining region of Pennsylvania."

"A Yankee Lawrence? Hah, now there's a movie I'd pay to see."

Sarah is confused again. She finds it impossible to read him. Is he being facetious now? Or does he really like the idea but just doesn't know the proper way to express his feelings? She wouldn't be surprised if that was the case. With the exception of her husband, who is terrifyingly eloquent about feelings, most of the men she has known have been horrendously bad at articulating them.

"They've taken Shakespeare around the world, why not Lawrence?" she says, trying not to sound too defensive.

"You play the lady herself then?"

Sarah nods vigorously, making sure to show him she is proud to be involved with the project in question despite his seeming disapproval.

Andrew whistles. "Pretty racy stuff, no?"

"What's wrong with racy?"

"Nothing. I like racy." He grins boyishly.

Sarah laughs. To her delight and relief this is the first thing he has said since she got into his taxi that hasn't either perplexed or irritated her, sometimes simultaneously. She leans back into her seat at last, no longer eager to leap out of the car. "So what's with the camera?"

"I'm a photojournalist. Well, I was. Now I just take pictures."

"And the cab driving?"

"An experiment."

"An experiment?"

"Something new to do. A new experience and it pays the bills."

At last they arrive at the hotel. Andrew makes a left turn and parks at the entrance. They sit still for a couple of minutes.

"Can you drive me somewhere?" Sarah asks. "It's not very far."

"I thought you wanted to go to your hotel."

"I did. But now I don't. I just don't want to sit in my room watching Oprah till they pick me up. There's a walking path along the lake I discovered a couple of days ago. You don't have to drive me back. I'll walk."

"That's a long walk."

"I did it the other day."

Andrew nods and gets back onto Queen's Quay, then turns into Lake Shore Boulevard. Out of nowhere, without any warning or warming up to it, Sarah twists her upper body so that she can face him and asks, "Why didn't you call me?" She winces and turns away, her voice shriller and more accusatory than she intended.

"What?"

"Never mind. I don't know why I asked. No, I know exactly why. I gave you my number. I asked you to call me. You never did. Why is that?"

Caught off guard, Andrew doesn't answer. Sarah takes that as a hint not to probe further.

Andrew changes the subject. "So did you and my mother keep in touch?"

"We tried. I wrote to her whenever I got a part I really wanted or had an interesting experience or met an actor we both admired."

"Yeah, like who?"

She thinks for a moment. "I once met Liv Ullmann. She came to my dressing room after the opening night of a play I was doing in London. I had so many things I wanted to ask her. I wanted to know all about Ingmar Bergman and what it was like to work with Ingrid Bergman and about the making of one of my favourite Bergman films, *Autumn Sonata*. But instead I giggled like a schoolgirl the whole time. I wrote to your mother and told her what an ass I made of myself in front of the great Liv Ullmann."

"You must be very happy. Out of all the students my mother taught, I don't know of any who went on to have a successful career."

"Most actors never really do."

"You must be pretty talented then."

"There are other things."

"Ambition?"

"Luck."

"Looks."

"Hard work."

"I'm sure being beautiful doesn't hurt."

"I wouldn't know."

"Bullshit!"

Sarah is startled by his response, its bluntness, its crudeness. She is intimidated by him and is annoyed at herself for allowing it. Sarah has worked with some of the most intense, brutally frank, opinionated people and never allowed them to bully her or make her feel off-kilter. But sitting in the passenger seat of this pine-scented taxi with a man she hasn't seen in years but has thought about frequently, even fantasized about, renders her speechless. With his single word *bullshit*, said so aggressively, so unapologetically, he compels her to explain herself, modify her statement. "I'm sure looks help," Sarah says, "but I try really hard not to base my work —"

"You don't have to convince me. I believe you."

"Then why the hell did you say *bullshit* like that?"

"I wanted you to know," he says with a devilish grin.

"Know what?"

"That you're beautiful, that I didn't buy you saying you didn't know."

Bewildered, Sarah shakes her head. She doesn't know if she should simply thank him for the compliment or tell him to go fuck himself. Her inability to read him accurately and respond accordingly infuriates her. "I guess I'll take that as a compliment."

"Good. I meant it as one."

Andrew makes a sharp left U-turn on Lake Shore Boulevard and enters a small parking lot. It is mostly empty, with a few cars scattered about. There is an equally tiny park next to the lot. It, too, is deserted except for several elderly couples taking afternoon strolls. Sarah climbs out of the car and walks around to the driver's door. Andrew gets out, and they exchange awkward, silent glances. She doesn't know how to bring this odd and mostly uncomfortable chance meeting to a dignified conclusion to which she can look back at years from now and say that it was a scene well handled.

"I'd ask you to join me for a walk, but I'm sure you have a million things to do before the services tonight," Sarah says.

"Actually, I don't. The funeral home is taking care of everything. I just have to put on my clip-on tie and be there on time."

"A clip on tie?"

"That was a joke. C'mon, work with me here. I'm trying."

"Sorry. I'm just having a little trouble figuring you —"

"Then let me join you on your walk and then you can figure me out."

Sarah wonders if he knows how nervous and oddly vulnerable he seems. Does he think she might say no? "If you wish," she finally tells him, taking her turn to be aloof.

Andrew locks the taxi, and they hike toward a jogging trail that runs surprisingly close to the lake. They head eastward. The downtown skyline is visible in the midday haze. They walk close together, hands almost touching with each leisurely step they take.

They are quiet, but it isn't one of the painful silences they were falling in and out of in the cab. Those were silences born of tension and misunderstanding. This lack of words has a more serene quality. After a few minutes, Sarah decides to be brave and risk ruining their newfound peace. "The last time I spoke to your mother she told me you were living in Europe."

"I was living all over, really. A few years in Johannesburg, two years in Turkey, and later I settled in Helsinki."

"Helsinki? Sounds great."

"I hated it. Cold and windy."

"Then why did you stay there?"

"There was … someone."

"Ah, fell in love with a Finnish woman, did we?"

"Worked with any movie stars yet?"

"I'm working with one now, but we were talking about you and your Scandinavian lover. What did you say her name was?"

"I didn't say. Let's get back to you. That's far more interesting. What's it like being an actress?"

"What's it like being a photojournalist?"

"Man, for an actress you really don't like to talk about yourself."

"Actor. I hate the word *actress*, and yes, most actors love to talk about themselves, just like most accountants and lawyers and even photojournalists. So talk to me. Tell me about yourself."

"I quit taking pictures for news. Now I just take pictures."

"Pictures of what? Places?"

"No, not places, just people. Pictures of people being themselves. No wars, no blood, no politics —"

"That's a cop-out!"

"Yes, I'm a coward."

"No, you're not. You're brave."

"I am?" He grins from ear to ear.

"Besides, isn't the very act of taking pictures political? Showing people's lives, what they look like, dress like, how they live, their socio-economic backgrounds?"

"They're just portraits, not manifestos. Just pictures of people. They're not doing anything. They're just being."

"That's still active — being, to be."

"Still, they're not fighting or getting shot at or throwing rocks or firebombs."

"You don't miss the action then? Isn't the hunt for the story, the conflict, addictive?"

"The chase maybe, but the conflict itself, nah, it's just —"

"Evil?"

"No, just sad."

Sarah spots a narrow foot-worn path in the grass that veers off the jogging trail and heads directly toward the lake. She takes it, with Andrew close behind her. The path comes to a dead end on a rocky beach. Sarah sits on one of the larger rocks and pats a spot next to her with her palm, signalling Andrew to join her. He obeys, and they gaze wordlessly at the lake.

"You never answered my question," Sarah says to him after a while. "Why didn't you call me? I gave you a small yellow piece of paper with my name and number and you never used it."

"You don't know that. Maybe I did call and maybe you were out and I didn't leave a message. Or maybe —"

"Did you call me?"

"I'm just saying, just because we didn't talk doesn't mean I didn't make use of the number the way you wanted me to."

She sighs. "Now you're just being difficult and abstract."

"Life is difficult and abstract."

Sarah springs to her feet with such sudden force that she becomes light-headed. When she regains her equilibrium, she strides back to the jogging trail. Andrew follows, catches up, and grabs her hand.

Sarah flings his hand away. "Do you remember why I gave you my number? Do you even remember the day I'm talking about?"

"Of course, I remember — it was the day you kissed me."

"You kissed me!"

"No, you kissed me!"

"*Whatever.* What difference does it make who kissed who first? The point is — it happened. It was amazing. I felt something, and I thought you did, too. Clearly, I was wrong. Goodbye." She walks away.

"You weren't wrong. I did, too … feel something."

Sarah stops and stares at him. His large childlike eyes seem so sad and beaten.

"I did call, but I hung up," Andrew confesses. "A man picked up, I got nervous, so I hung up."

Sarah is happy that he did feel something that day, at least enough to call her, but also terribly sad for the missed opportunity. She tries to recall where she might have been when he phoned her and how her life might have been different if she stayed at home that night and picked up the phone instead. Would that phone call have been the beginning of something good, beautiful, and lasting, or would it have only amounted to a lousy date and so-so sex? Sarah would never know. "Must've been my roommate," she whispers, feeling tired.

"I thought maybe it was your boyfriend and that I made a mistake calling you, so I hung up. I'm sorry." Suddenly, he clasps his large hands around her face and kisses her.

After a moment, Sarah pushes him away. "Stop!" she demands, wiping her mouth with the back of her hand.

"Sorry."

"I'm married."

"Sorry."

"And stop saying sorry."

"I'm married, too," Andrew says, her admission giving him permission to do likewise.

Sarah wishes she hadn't stopped him. Their quick kiss, which would have gone on much longer had she not interrupted him, reminds her of their first kiss. How could two kisses a decade apart feel exactly the same?

The basement class was warm. Too warm perhaps, because Sarah's forehead was wet with perspiration as she paced the large room rehearsing Ophelia's "O, what a noble mind is here o'erthrown" soliloquy for what seemed like the millionth time. The wall-to-wall carpeting, the thick concrete walls, and the lack of natural light made her feel cocooned and sheltered from the judging world outside. She had an audition in two days and had come, out of desperation, to her acting teacher, Ella, for an emergency coaching session.

Sarah glanced at her watch, figuring there was enough time to give the soliloquy another go before Ella returned home. She took it from the top and got through it. Sarah remembered every word. She was hitting the emotional beats as she should, but she knew it could be better. Under her teacher's laser-sharp attention to the character's objectives, wants, and needs, telling her to quicken the pace here and extend a beat there, the speech could be made more alive, more immediate. As she finished the last line, "O woe is me t'have seen what I have seen, see what I see," the room erupted into loud applause, followed by a long whistle, the kind people employed at rock concerts.

Startled to discover she wasn't alone, Sarah turned in the direction of the ovation. She found the source at the top of the stairs to the basement. Framed by the open doorway was a man who looked to be in his early twenties. The man was handsome and knew it, too. He stood there shirtless, holding a wrinkled blue dress shirt in his hand.

"Bravo!" he cried. "That was magnificent!"

Sarah was taken aback but pleased. "Thank you. Who are you?"

"I could ask you the same thing." Slowly, he came down the stairs one step at a time, adding a touch of drama to his entrance.

"Ask then."

"Who are you?"

"Sarah Turlington, one of Mrs. Christiansen's students. And you are?"

"Andrew Christiansen, Mrs. Christiansen's son."

They both flashed what-next grins.

"That was amazing," Andrew told her.

"It's not there yet."

"I think it is."

"No, it's not."

"Yes, it is!"

"What do you know? Your mother decides when it's there, and I have a feeling she'll think it's shit."

"You're probably right. My mother can be brutal."

"You're telling me."

"So you're an actress then?"

"Trying to be."

Sarah was still breathing hard from her vigorous delivery of the soliloquy. Her throat was dry, and her forehead shone with sweat. "Sorry. I'm sweating like a pig." She patted the sleeve of her shirt on her face.

"Here, use this." Andrew offered her the wrinkled shirt he was holding in his hand. "I was looking for my mother. I couldn't find the iron. Here, use it."

"No, I can't wipe my face with your —"

"It's clean, if that's what you're worried about."

Sarah stared at his hairy chest and the long trail of hair that ran down his stomach, getting thicker the closer it got to his khaki trousers. Andrew took a couple of steps toward her and stood centimetres away. He folded his shirt and dabbed it on her wet forehead and down the sides of her face. She closed her eyes almost involuntarily and sensed herself falling forward. Sarah wasn't sure if she was leaning in or if Andrew was pulling her toward him. She felt his lips on hers, and they kissed. The thrill of falling, of levitating, lasted longer than any pleasure she had ever known.

When she finally slipped out of this state of — she didn't know what to call it — she found herself in a deep embrace, her arms wrapped around Andrew's naked shoulders and his around her waist. Their tongues were so entwined that for a moment she thought they were one and the same. With a force so abrupt, the bliss she had been in — for how long she didn't know — ended as quickly as it began. Upon hearing his mother's voice calling his name, Andrew suddenly untangled himself from her. When Sarah opened her eyes, she saw him standing in the corner of the room by the staircase, quickly putting on his wrinkled shirt.

Sarah decides she has had enough conflicting feelings for one day and walks briskly in the direction of Andrew's taxi, hoping to make it clear to him that he should take her back to her hotel and never see her again.

"You have no business, you know?" she yells at him when he catches up to her. "You have no business going around kissing people like that!"

"For your information I don't go around kissing everyone."

"The point is, you're completely oblivious to the consequences of your actions."

"Sorry. It won't happen again."

"And for fuck's sake, stop saying sorry."

The weather has been unpredictable all day — the sun beaming one minute and dark clouds threatening to unleash a torrent the next. Now, without warning, it does the latter. Rain comes down heavy and hard and drenches everything it touches. Sarah and Andrew run to the taxi as fast as they can, but by the time they reach the parking lot they are soaked. Andrew opens the door for her, hurries around, and hops in. Although his hair is wet and clinging to his forehead, everything under his red polyester jumper remains dry.

He takes off his coat and throws it onto the back seat. Sarah, on the other hand, is drenched. Her wool sweater is so full of water it feels like a dead body wrapped around her. Seeing her wet and cold, Andrew takes off his golf shirt, leaving his white T-shirt on. He hands it to her without a word, and she takes it silently and uses it to dry herself. They smile at each other as if sharing a joke only they would find funny.

Using the fingers of both hands like a comb, Sarah brushes back her matted hair, revealing her pale, translucent face still glistening with rain. Andrew reaches for his camera and starts taking pictures without asking permission. Sarah turns away from him just as she hears the sound of the first click. The shutter continues whirring with increasing speed. She turns to face him, still holding his shirt to her mouth and nose. Taking deep breaths through his shirt intoxicates her with the scent of his body. She lets the shirt drop from her hands and onto her lap, exposing her face to him, silently acquiescing to his desire to take as many pictures of her as he wishes. When he has his fill, he puts the camera on his lap with a sigh as if exhausted, elated. They regard each other, neither of them willing to chance saying something, fearful of ruining the moment.

"What's your wife's name?" Sarah asks, wishing to take back the words before they fully leave her lips, regretting her clumsy effort to start a conversation when silence would have been ideal.

"Rosemary."

"Any children?" Sarah asks, unable to stop the flood of questions as though overpowered by a strange need to know everything about this man, even things that contradict her fantasy of him as a single man.

"Hanna. She's seven months old." Andrew hoists himself off the seat, takes his wallet out, extracts a small picture, and gives it to her.

Sarah observes the photo for a moment. "She's adorable, Andrew. She has your eyes."

"The best thing that ever happened to me. Every time things get pretty bad with me and her mother, which is pretty often, and I start to regret not having gone back to Helsinki, I think of her and hate myself for even having the thought."

"What was so important in Helsinki?"

"Helli."

Sarah turns away and looks ahead but can't see anything past the pelting rain.

As though sensing that talking about his prior lover in the presence of another woman lacks tact, Andrew says, "We were no Romeo and Juliet. But it was a good, solid —"

"You don't have to explain." *Am I that transparent?* Sarah asks herself. But she isn't surprised by his capacity to pick up on her most subtle body language, especially since he has an uncanny ability to make her feel naked. She wonders how she, a woman so gifted at hiding huge parts of herself while revealing only what is required for any given scene, can also be so incapable of concealing any part of herself in this man's presence.

"What's your husband's name?" he asks.

Sarah regrets having started this line of conversation. She wishes she wasn't married or that at least Andrew didn't know about that aspect of her life. "Michael Haynes."

"That name sounds familiar. Is he an actor, too?"

"Oh, God, no! An actor should never marry another actor. There should be laws against it."

Andrew laughs.

"He's a nose," she says.

"Come again?"

"He's a perfumer for Elizabeth Arden."

Andrew nods. "Ah, I see. He makes a living out of his freaky sense of smell."

"Yep. His sense of smell is pretty frightening."

"Acting and perfume making — they're worlds apart. How did you meet?"

"Through a friend of a friend of a friend — you know, the usual scenario." Sarah is desperate to change the subject. The last thing she wants to talk about with Andrew is her husband. "What about your wife? What does she do?"

"She's a teacher. Special-needs kids."

"That's wonderful. I love teachers."

"She hates it."

"Oh."

"Rosemary's a very unhappy woman."

Sarah remains silent for a moment, as if she knows that affliction intimately. "Aren't we all — on some level?"

"Are you unhappy?"

"Are you?"

"I asked first."

Sarah evaluates her current level of happiness. "Let's just say I'm not as happy as I imagined I'd be."

"You had a vision of your own happiness?"

"Doesn't everyone? Didn't you?"

Andrew shakes his head morosely. "I never really paid much attention to my future. I sort of let my life unfold before my eyes like a movie, like one of those films where you don't know what's going to happen and you sit there clueless, waiting for the next plot twist."

"Maybe that's the way to go."

Andrew shakes his head again, even more glumly. "I wouldn't advise it. More and more, I'm beginning to see the value of participation."

"Participation?"

"Of being a full participant in my life — in its twists and turns, you know? Being the architect of it rather than a viewer.

After all, you did say I should watch out for the consequences of my actions."

"You shouldn't listen to me."

"Easier said than done, though, isn't it — to be a full participant in your life?"

"Is that why you quit photojournalism?"

"Partly. My work was always the result of someone else's actions. I flew from one place to another based on events not of my doing, outside my control. If a friend invited me to his wedding a month away, I couldn't accept because I didn't know where I'd be in week, let alone a month. Surely, that's not the way to go if being a full participant is the goal."

Sarah tries to grasp the notion of participation, of being active in one's life. She thinks about how she, too, is mostly dependent on others for her livelihood. Without someone else to write a play, without some wealthy person to produce it, she wouldn't have a job, and by extension she wouldn't have much of a life. She has devoted so much of her life to her work that without it she wouldn't know who she is. "So what's the other part?" she finally asks him.

Andrew looks perplexed.

"You said that was partly why you quit your work. What's the other part?"

"Oh, right. When Hanna was born, there was no going back."

"She's the reason you didn't go back to —"

"No," Andrew says, cutting her off. "Yes," he corrects himself sadly. "When my mother got sick, I had to come home, and for about a year she was in and out of hospitals. During that time, Rosemary and I … you see, we were childhood friends. We took things farther, much farther than we should have."

"You got married for the baby then?"

Andrew nods.

"You don't love her?'

"Rosemary isn't an easy woman to love."

"No one's easy to love, Andrew. Show me someone who loves easily and I'll show you a liar. But we do it, anyway, don't we? We fall in love and we fall out of love, and sometimes, not often, but sometimes we actually stay in love forever."

They both laugh in a "wouldn't that be nice" sort of way, as if they like the idea, the possibility of love, the kind that lasts forever, but they are too damn grown up to believe in it anymore.

Andrew tries to peer through the windshield. The rain is falling so heavily that it is impossible to see much of anything, and the sound of the drops hitting the roof is hypnotic.

"Looks like it's going to rain for the rest of the day," Sarah says.

"You've done quite a bit falling in and out of love, judging from your theory of love," Andrew says, ignoring Sarah's weather forecast.

"No," she says, shaking her head for emphasis. "I've fallen in love, truly in love, once in my entire life." Sarah takes Andrew's hand from his lap and holds her two small hands around his large one. "And I guess I've never quite fallen out of that one."

Carefully, like a sculptor studying his subject, she examines the thick veins running down his arm. Noticing his long, bony fingers, she lifts his cold palm to her cheek. Andrew stares at Sarah helplessly, neither encouraging her nor stopping her. She looks up at him, and for a moment they lock eyes.

His eyes cloud with tears, and he jerks his hand from her grip with such force that it startles her. Then he turns away from her. Undeterred, Sarah pats his back and slowly runs her palm up and down his spine. Under her hand she can feel him tremble as he gives in. Sarah continues to comfort him, even though she doesn't understand the cause of his tears. The part of her that is most susceptible to fits of fancy, thinks he is crying for her, for all the time they have lost, time they could have spent loving each other.

With a loud sigh Andrew gathers himself and wipes away the tears. "I'm sorry. I don't know what's wrong with me these days. It doesn't take much to get me going."

"Sorry for what?"

There is a long pause, then Andrew says, "I prayed for it to end. Two weeks ago I was in bed awake in the middle of the night and I prayed for it to end."

Sarah is confused but patient.

"The last two months have been so fucking hard, especially for my dad. I watched him as the only woman he ever loved lay in bed, a piece of her dying every day. So I prayed to God or whoever decides these things to end her suffering. I'm happy it's over." Andrew starts to cry again. "It's horrible. It's sick. I know. But you should've seen her, Sarah. You wouldn't have recognized her. It's better this way. I'm sorry, but I really think it is."

"*Shhh,*" she whispers. "You've got nothing to apologize for." Sarah places her hand under his chin and lifts his head, turning his face to hers. They shift closer to each other. Their two previous kisses resulted from an overflow of passion neither was equipped to control. This kiss, on the other hand, is premeditated. Their lips touch again, at first slowly, almost not moving, but with each passing moment their usual frenzy and thirst for each other intensifies.

Sarah has always found penises funny. Male genitals in general perplex her, but the penis in particular causes her to chuckle, mostly because of its ungainliness and strange configurations, the comical bends and peculiar shapes. Each one she has seen thus far in her life has had its own unique characteristic that makes it distinct from others, but the one thing they all seem to share is their comical nature. She has taken this quality as a given. Until today.

It comes as a surprise to her, a very good one, to discover that Andrew's cock is different. She watches him in her hotel room as he puts on the condom with great care. So serious and attentive he is to the task that Sarah thinks if they ever start making TV commercials to show the correct use of condoms, he would be perfect for the role. As she watches him, Sarah sees in Andrew a quality she rarely sees in men his age — a kind of grave solemnity.

This sense of solemnity bleeds into their lovemaking. The silence, the piercing, almost disturbing quiet, alarms her. She has gotten so used to what her husband likes to call "talking dirty" during sex that she has forgotten the power of silence. It accentuates the subtlety of their body language — the arch of the back, the grind of the hips, the hiss of an exhale — all take on the prominence and significance of a shared language.

As he moves in her and she engulfs him with all her limbs, she comes to the realization that what she is experiencing is different than anything she has ever felt with anyone before. *Is it love then?* she wonders. She doesn't know because she has never encountered anything quite like this to compare it with. But she understands for certain that it isn't the great pleasure of mere fucking. She has done a lot of that and quite enjoyed it, but this, she concludes, is something altogether different. The approaching end fills her with dread. She knows all good things come to an end. She also knows that the moment of withdrawal, when he is no longer a part of her, will fill her with pain equal to the pleasure of having him part of her.

What a wonder, Sarah thinks, what a miracle that despite the torrent of feelings and thoughts racing through her head, she still manages to come. What a joke of the body that she can experience such a mind-blowing orgasm with this man she barely knows when achieving the same thing with her husband requires so much effort and manipulation of both body and mind.

Once Andrew finishes, he doesn't move at all. He supports his weight with his knees and elbows as he stays motionless inside her. Neither budges as they slowly descend from the heights of their individual but near-simultaneous climaxes, so close, in fact, that she isn't sure if they came together. Sarah wishes she can relive the experience in slow motion to be certain but instead watches their shared moment already becoming a memory. She is dismayed at how painfully transient the "now" of time is. Just as she becomes conscious of the now of her life, just as she begins to revel in it, it leaps away into the past and embeds itself into one of the many archival compartments of her mind.

Sarah kisses Andrew's neck and strong jaw, which is covered with a three-day growth of hair, and whispers, "I love you," so faintly that she immediately doubts if she actually said the words or merely thought them. When she notices Andrew's lack of reaction, she is convinced he didn't hear her. But what if he did? What if he heard the words "I love you" and chose not to respond?

She wants to repeat those words louder to eliminate all doubt, but her resolve fails. She doesn't have the heart to hear his answer, or worse, absence of one. So she stops kissing him, rests her head on the pillow, and braces herself for the dreaded moment of coming part. When it finally happens, it is as emptying and hollowing as she feared.

Sarah lies on Andrew's back now. They have been in this position for a long time, and when she tries to roll off, saying she must be crushing him, he stops her, telling her that he can barely feel her. She listens to the thunder far away. Kissing his neck absentmindedly, Sarah wonders if he knows what he has done for her today — that he has restored her faith in the existence of the one.

She longs to tell him all this. Sarah wants to tell him what she feels and ask him what he is thinking and feeling. She wants everything to be out in the open, laid out for discussion and analysis, because she is a verbal creature. Sarah makes sense of the world via words, via language. Maybe that is the reason she fell in love with acting when she was ten. It was then that theatre and the drama of language gripped her. She misses the stage so much now that she hasn't been there for a year. Sarah misses being up there, perched on that tightrope night after night with nothing to hold on to but words as her only ally.

As strong as her yearning to ask Andrew if he, too, felt what she did, she doesn't open her mouth, mostly out of fear of destroying the shelter they have found in each other. Sarah is afraid that this man lying under her might believe that to make love is one thing but to speak about it the way one talks about baseball or a novel or a banana bread recipe is base, vulgar even. She wonders if Andrew is one of those people who never talk about *it* because he fears that the minute *it* is taken out of experience and put into language the magic and mystery of the thing evaporates. She couldn't bear to let that happen.

Sarah whispers, "I have to go," into his ear and gives its fleshy pink lobe one last nibble, then kisses him on the back of the neck. "I have to be in makeup soon." Not true. Not for another two hours. But she can't take the not talking, the not addressing this thing that has transpired between them. Slowly, she gets off his back and sits on the edge of the bed. She feels Andrew's warm, flat palm on her back, tracing the long valley that runs down her spine. Sarah delights in his fingers trailing from the bottom of her back to the top of her neck. She glances back at him. They lock eyes. Andrew's gaze has an unhinging effect on her. It makes her feel witnessed — accounted for — for the first time in her life.

"Do you really have to go now?" he asks, sounding oddly vulnerable and needy.

Sarah regards him silently.

"I wish you didn't have to go," he continues. "I wish I didn't have to go. I wish I didn't have to be at a funeral home. I wish I didn't have a —"

Sarah desperately wants him to complete the sentence. But he doesn't, so she finishes for him in her mind. *I wish I didn't have a wife. I wish you didn't have a husband. I wish I had called you again ten years ago instead of giving up. I wish I never stopped kissing you that day in the basement ...*

It occurs to Sarah that she could go on and on in this fashion, making an inventory of all the things she wishes were different, all the things she would change if she had it in her power to alter the past. But what is the use of mourning for what might have been? Things are as they are. With that sobering thought echoing in her head, she gets up from the bed and walks across the room, the cool air hugging her damp skin. She can sense Andrew's eyes on her nakedness as she enters the bathroom, doing her best to conceal the self-consciousness she feels.

In the shower she stands under the stinging force of the hot water as she stares at a little dot on the marble stone of the wall that her eyes have locked onto by accident. Her hands are wrapped around her as if protecting herself from something. She reflects on how badly she ended things as she sat on the bed, her back turned to him, her eyes closed, his hand travelling the length of her.

Sarah regrets not having said something to him when he told her he wished she didn't have to go so soon. She now knows she should have said that she, too, wanted to remain in the warm bed and relish in the afterglow of their accidentally discovered intimacy, the sort of closeness no two relative strangers have any business sharing.

When Sarah comes out of the bathroom cloaked in a thick, luxurious white bathrobe, she finds the bed vacant. The spot on the carpet by the foot of the bed where Andrew's clothes and shoes were is now empty, cleansed of his presence. Waves of regret hit her from every direction. But she feels something else, too. Defeat? Abandonment? No, it is something more, something akin to loss, but heavier still, more intense and all-encompassing — something closer to love.

I 2

the burial

Gregory desperately needs a refuge from the overwhelming and suffocating condolences from people he likes, even loves, people like Ed, his best friend since ninth grade. Or Sheryl, his gossipy but otherwise reliable secretary at the hazardous chemical waste disposal plant in Etobicoke where he was a manager for the past thirteen years until he retired early last year to care for his wife and where he lent a kind and sympathetic ear to the seventy or so workers who came to him regularly with their problems, professional and otherwise. They flocked to his large, cluttered second-floor office for his unique brand of understanding without judgment.

The capacity of these well-intentioned words of sympathy to wound him comes as a terrible shock to Gregory. Sheryl, a short redhead with a penchant for blue eye shadow, grabs his hand as he travels around the living room, thanking the mourners for paying their respects. She hugs him, squeezes his hand, and says, "Ella was a wonderful woman. We'll all miss her terribly."

Gregory wants to remind Sheryl that she met his wife no more than five times during the past ten years and that she couldn't remember the colour of Ella's eyes if her life depended on it. So, given this fact, how dare she stand in front of him and say she will miss Ella. But he doesn't. Instead he simply thanks her and moves on.

He takes two more steps toward the kitchen in order to escape through the back door to the yard. But Joanna Reed, Ella's old friend from high school and one of her bridesmaids, stops him and hugs him with all the affection she can muster. "I'm so, so sorry, Greg." She puts particular emphasis on *so* as if that is all she needs to do to express the magnitude of her sorrow. "At least she's not in pain anymore."

Fuck off! That is what Gregory has on the tip of his tongue. Instead he smiles and moves on. The condolence that takes the cake, however, comes from Father Gleason, who for some inexplicable reason Gregory has always disliked. Maybe it is the thick white spit-bridge that forms between his lips and bounces up and down with each word he speaks that Gregory can't stand. Or maybe Gregory detests him because he had an eerie premonition that one day Father Gleason would stand in his living room, shake his hand, and say, "Rest assured, Gregory, our dear Ella has gone to a better place."

As if watching a slow-motion scene in a movie, Gregory sees his hands go for Father Gleason's neck, grabbing him by the collar, dragging him to the front door, and hurling him out onto the lawn face first. Gregory blinks and is relieved to discover that his hands are still in his pockets. He is already facing an assault charge, and the last thing he needs is a battered priest limping to the witness stand to testify against him.

Do these people really think such vacant words of condolence will make him, or anyone for that matter, feel better? Gregory doesn't want Ella in that supposed better place. He wants her right here where she is loved and cared for. In fact, he hates that she is no longer here more than he hates that she is no longer in pain. Gregory knows it is selfish of him. But going to her hospital room, sitting by her bed, reading to her, creaming the dry, chapped soles of her feet, or simply holding her hand while she slept were for Gregory not just the obligatory duties of a husband but a reason to go on. He wants her here, fighting and eventually beating the last of those poisonous cells even if that means living in a morphine-induced delirium, suspended between this world and the next.

Gregory wishes he could go on performing those acts of devotion because the promise of another day to attend to them sustained him during those long, lonely nights' journey into days when he would get up at six every morning, make his wife's favourite broth, put it in a Thermos, drive to the hospital, and sit with the woman who sat next to him, lay with him, and stood by him for forty years. Without these chores to fill his waking hours he feels hopelessly adrift.

So to hear these ignorant, clichéd phrases of condolence, which to be fair are born of good intentions, makes Gregory shake with anger. He hurries to the back porch in search of fresh air and solitude. Opening the kitchen back door, he stands on the porch, takes a single, deep breath, and exhales loudly, letting go of all the anger bubbling inside him, threatening to implode, or God forbid, explode. With one slow exhalation he feels renewed, somehow restored to his old, happy self, and that is, however fleeting, paradise.

Gregory listens to the wind as it rustles the autumn leaves of the majestic maple tree in the backyard, the tree he and Ella argued about for days. Not about whether or not to put one in the yard but about what kind of tree and where precisely to place it. They both wanted a large, sheltering tree in their yard for their future kids to hang a swing from or build a tree house between its sturdy branches.

He is content to stand here and listen to whatever comforting melody the cool winds from the distant north choose for him, but his peace is interrupted by the voices of a man and woman coming from the alley that separates his house from the Jeffersons' bungalow. Gregory moves closer to the voices and listens intently. It takes him a moment to recognize who is speaking. One of the voices is Andrew's. The other belongs to Natalie.

Gregory inches toward the edge of the porch and spots Andrew leaning against the Jeffersons' house as he faces Natalie, who is standing against the wall of their house. Gregory sniffs the unmistakable odour of marijuana. He watches Natalie take a drag of the joint, then pass it to her brother. Gregory knows his son is a regular marijuana smoker and a fervent advocate for its decriminalization. But his bookish daughter? That is news to him. Not knowing their father is a couple of metres away, they talk openly about matters other than the solemn event they have come to observe: the funeral of the woman who drove them crazy with her nosy, overbearing attention to every detail of their lives but who could also, in the same instant, break their hearts with her unconditional love.

He eavesdrops on the unforced affection between Natalie and Andrew, a tenderness that reveals itself not in what they say to each other but how they say it. Because Gregory grew up as an only child, observing the two of them always makes him happy but also jealous because they have something he always yearned for: a sibling to talk to, fight with and against, someone to share successes and failures with.

"He wanted to come, but I talked him out of it," Gregory hears his daughter tell Andrew as she passes him the joint.

"Why?" Andrew asks.

"I want him to meet Dad, but under better circumstances. That way the odds of him liking Jamal will be on my side."

"When did you get so cunning? I guess you must really like this dude if you care that much about what dad thinks of him."

Natalie nods vigorously like a little schoolgirl.

"Is it *loooove* then?"

She nods again. "It's all so frightening, isn't it?"

"Frightening?"

"I'm always so afraid of something happening to him. You know, of losing him in a flash flood or a freak twister, something like that."

"Don't forget terrorists."

"Shut up! I'm serious here. I know it sounds paranoid, but it's all so new to me."

Gregory listens to his daughter talk about her new boyfriend, and part of him is happy that she has found love. He knows that feeling of being frightened all the time. Gregory experienced that with Natalie's mother. He remembers the delicious sensation of being consumed in equal parts by excitement at finding something so beautiful and the fear of losing it. But Gregory also feels a tinge of sadness that he has to hear about his daughter's new love by eavesdropping. He knows he shouldn't be listening, but he can't help himself.

"So how did you meet this boy?" Andrew asks.

"Boy?" Natalie slaps Andrew lightly on the side of the head.

"Didn't you say he was twenty-two? Is he even old enough to know what love is?"

"He's twenty-eight, and for your information he's the love of my life. Can you say that about Rosemary?"

Gregory senses a slight tension in the air as they smoke in silence.

"I slept with another woman," Andrew blurts.

Natalie smacks him again, this time harder, making her disapproval clear.

"I know, I know. I deserve that —"

"You deserve much worse. How could you? Who is she?"

"Oh, what is it with women and the who-is-she question? Does it matter who?"

"Hell, yes!"

Andrew pauses as if debating the wisdom of revealing the identity of the woman in question. "It was Sarah Turlington."

"You say it like I'm supposed to know who that is."

"Don't you remember? Sarah, Mom's protege."

Natalie tries to recall this particular protege out of her mother's parade of them. *"Oh, my God!"* she cries at last. "You slept with Sarah Turlington?"

"Lower your voice! You still think I should tell Rosemary?"

"Why? What will that accomplish?"

"Wouldn't you want to know?"

"Why on earth would I want to know that my husband, the father of my infant child, just had sex with some hot actress?"

"Don't call her an actress. She hates it."

"Well, *excuse me.* Would she prefer *thespian*?"

"Now you're just being cruel."

"I can't help it. Rosemary is like a sister to me."

"So you think I shouldn't tell her then?"

Natalie ponders the situation. "I can't make that decision for you. But I know you'll do the right thing — whatever that is."

They are silent for a moment.

"God, why are men such pricks?" Natalie says, smacking Andrew on the head again.

Andrew takes another drag. "I know, I know. I should be caned a hundred times or something."

"Too bad we don't live in Saudi Arabia. I'd personally administer the caning myself."

They smoke the rest of the joint, lost in their respective thoughts.

"So what are we going to do with the old man?" Andrew asks, stubbing the spent roach against the wall with his thumb.

"First, we'll have to move him out of this big old house. It was tough enough even for Mom. And let's face it, Dad knows shit about keeping a house."

Gregory continues to listen to their conversation as they talk about, actually more like plan, what practical things ought to be done. True, the house is too big for any widower let alone one who never cleaned a single room of it. Andrew and Natalie also discuss what should be done with all of their mother's belongings, especially her clothes. Their mother's greatest flaw was her inability to walk by a sale sign without purchasing something. Ella was biologically drawn to stores. Shopping was her choice of drug.

Always the generous one, Andrew suggests they donate his mother's clothes. Natalie has other plans. It is true that her mother had a lot of wonderful clothes, garments any woman of taste would be envious of — vintage suits, blouses in every colour, silk scarves, and genuine leather skirts, you name it, she had it, and wore them beautifully. Andrew and Natalie know that clothes of that quality, of that enduring classic style, would fetch good money they could use to offset the astronomical cost of the funeral.

Gregory can't listen to them anymore. It is one thing to hear his son talk about an affair at a time such as this, but to have them chat about what to do with what is left of his wife is too much for him. He wants to stop them, yell at them, hit them even for making plans to remove the evidence of his wife's existence from the house they shared for forty years. *How dare they plan to evict remnants of her?* He leans forward on the wooden railing of the porch where he has been standing for the past five minutes and makes himself visible to them. They turn to see him glaring at them. Gregory scurries toward the kitchen door. Andrew chases after him, with Natalie following.

"Dad, we were just talking," Andrew says as he catches up to his father and grabs him by the hand. "It was just talk."

Gregory shoves Andrew's hand away violently, almost throwing him backward. "How dare you? She's been dead for only a few days and you already want to pretend she was never here. I expected more from you!"

Without waiting to give Andrew and Natalie a chance to defend their good intentions, Gregory hurries into the house. He passes some of the mourners, mostly distant relatives who are standing around the living room, sipping on something or other, reducing their conversations to mere whispers, trying not to offend the memory of the woman they came to mourn. Gregory sprints up the stairs toward the only place in the house where he knows he will be safe.

The bedroom toward which he heads was the most prominent site in the geography of Gregory and Ella's marriage. That union had its fair share of disappointments but was, on the whole, as good as marriages get. However, one year did stand out in sharp contrast. Nineteen eighty-seven was the year they mutually agreed to separate at the behest of Minta Morgan, their therapist. Ella always found it hard to call her Minta with a straight face and treat her professional advice with due seriousness. It didn't help that the therapist had tiny square eyeglasses propped on the middle of her nose, which she constantly had to push back, distracting Ella to the point of annoyance. Minta was a waste of money, they later concluded.

The cause of their marital troubles was distinctly undramatic. There was no affair that shattered the trust, no abuse that broke the bond irrevocably — just plain old coming apart. It happened so slowly, so imperceptibly, until one day they were staring at each other across their mahogany dinner table with the eyes of two strangers who were somehow married, had kids, and shared a history. And it frightened Gregory to realize that the woman who gave him the things he cherished the most in his life, the same woman who used to make him shake with desire, could now, with a single glare, make him feel small and inconsequential.

The marriage had been gradually unravelling since the early 1980s, but at that time both their kids were in their early teens and they had felt they needed to stay together, if for no other reason than to see them through those difficult years with at least the belief of a family still beautifully intact. But by 1987, Natalie had been out of the house for three years and Andrew had left for university the previous year.

With the kids gone, Gregory and Ella only had each other to depend on for happiness. They only had each other to observe, find fault with, and rehabilitate until the finding and correcting of each other's flaws become the only thing that remained. No marriage, however strong its foundation, could endure such microscopic scrutiny and earnest examination.

Even though they spent much of 1987 living in separate places, in their thoughts and hearts they never strayed far from each other. If they weren't thinking about each other, they were sitting in some downtown café, restaurant, or other neutral venue, taking inventory of their wounds, displaying with pride the bleeding scars they had accumulated over several decades of marriage, each giving the other a litany of all the ways he or she was hurt, humiliated, and taken for granted.

It was no surprise then that amid all those arguments and counter-arguments, charges and counter-charges, something got lost, something slipped away without either of them noticing — the reason they were together. It was simple, but neither of them was willing to say they still loved each other, more so then than they ever had, even more than in their first year of marriage when they lived in the perpetual bliss of their hungry, youthful bodies.

But to admit this simple, irrefutable fact would have meant being vulnerable and needy. Neither was willing to do that. But on a cold New Year's Day 1988 they found the courage to talk without yelling, without accusations and tears. They simply spoke on the phone for four uninterrupted hours.

Gregory wore his blue cotton bathrobe with nothing underneath except white boxer shorts, intermittently pacing and sitting on the ugly burgundy sofa he had bought from a flea market. The sofa and a single bed were the only furniture in the Lake Shore Boulevard apartment he was renting by the month. As he and Ella talked, Gregory was astonished at how easily the words came. The big, true, meaningful words that had eluded him for so long, the words that could have spared them a painful separation had he been able to say them, were now coming to him fully formed, ready to be offered, and he could hear his wife on the other side of the line taking them in, contemplating them without interruption, without rebuttal.

All he had to do was close his eyes to see her facial expression as she listened to him. He could imagine the vertical lines that formed between her eyebrows when she listened intently. But Gregory had trouble placing her in their house. He couldn't visualize where she was in relation to everything else in their house and what she was doing.

"What are you doing?" he asked.

"What ... now?"

"Yeah."

"I'm talking to you."

"No, I mean, where are you? What are you wearing?"

"I'm sitting on the cold tiles of the kitchen floor of our house."

Gregory smiled at the words *our house*. He took it as a good omen.

"I'm wearing that red robe you bought me. Remember?"

"Yeah, I remember it," he replied. He closed his eyes and pictured the way black Japanese floral prints played off the red background of the robe. Gregory loved the way the silk material hugged every curve of her body. He felt the flicker of desire for her as he imagined her on the floor, one of her legs popping out of the slit of the robe.

"And I'm eating cheap chocolate that I bought from the convenience store on Bathurst. I've nearly finished the whole box." She giggled the way she did when she was embarrassed.

Now Gregory could see her in his mind's eye, and he found it so easy to say, "I love you." There was a long silence. His heart stopped beating. Or it felt that way as he waited for her to reply, as he tried to interpret the silence. *Does she no longer love me?* he wondered. *Have too many ugly things been said? Have too many cold silences passed between us for love to survive?* Then he heard his wife crying. "I miss you. What the hell are we doing, Ella? I hate being away from you … from our home. I hate this apartment. It's cold and it's ugly."

"I miss you, too," Ella said, sniffling. "I want you to come back, too, but —"

"But what?"

"It can't be the same. We can't go back to the way we were."

"I know."

"I mean it, Greg. No more silences."

"No more silences."

"No more telling me everything's fine when I know it's not."

"I promise." Gregory smiled as he looked out at the snow-covered lake outside his apartment window. It was on that bitterly cold New Year's Day 1988, while he paced the empty apartment

173

and she sat on their cold kitchen tiles, away from each other's harsh gazes, that they both found the courage to put their guns against the wall and lay themselves bare, unprotected, unafraid.

Gregory moved back in with his wife three days later, and the years that followed did have their moments of discord but never without their shared faith that the worst was behind them. And as for the future, well, for them not knowing the precise shape of their future was always half the fun. Gregory knew very well that he was a difficult man, stubborn, not to mention utterly and genuinely lacking talent in all things domestic. He never made a bed, never scrubbed a floor or fried an egg, but he was good and honest, a hard-working man who remained, much to his surprise, resolutely, steadfastly faithful to his wife.

As for Ella, she was the sort of wife whose good intentions gave shape and form to all her actions. She never failed to stand in the vicinity of her husband as he dressed every morning so that she could come over to him and smooth away the creases in his shirt or straighten his tie or simply tell him that a red tie would go better with the white shirt rather than the grey and all this before he even thought to ask. Ella was also the kind of woman who never failed to put him in his place if he had the audacity to step beyond those unspoken boundaries that all good couples observe and confine their words and actions to.

Ella never failed to keep Gregory's toes well within those bounds, and he was grateful for it because he didn't trust himself to be good on his own. She acted for him as a kind of omnipotent, benevolent force, gently guiding him toward his true good nature, reminding him that action was the very definition of character, a simple but profound concept she tried to drill into the parade of young students who wandered into her basement acting studio. And on the rare occasions when Gregory's conscience failed him, Ella was there to inform him that his actions weren't in line with the good man she knew him to be. She was also the sort of wife who tried to be open to whatever last-minute lunacies her husband concocted, like when he came home one day with the craziest idea of all.

Gregory was certain that getting his wife to understand the merits of his new brainstorm was going to be next to impossible, but it was something he had always wanted to do. He walked in from work and went straight to the kitchen where she was making supper. Gregory stood in the kitchen doorway with a childish grin that he knew his wife would register, for he usually returned from work drained. Spending eight to ten hours a day looking out for the safety of everyone who worked in the chemical plant where any number of bad things could happen was no easy task.

"Greg, you've got that look on your face again," she said as she dumped chopped vegetables into a boiling pot. "I know that look. You want something."

"Oh? And what do you think I want?"

Ella smiled. "It's that grin you have when you get amorous."

"This is true. But I've something else in mind this evening."

She sighed. "Oh, God!"

"Promise not to laugh?"

"I'll laugh if it's another one of your loony ideas."

"You make it sound like I come to you with a loony idea a day."

"Just about."

"That's not fair."

"Oh, really? What was it you wanted us to do last month?"

"Millions of people hike the Appalachian Trail. It's adventure."

"And what sort of adventure do you have in mind this evening?"

Gregory breathed deeply. "As you know, our thirty-fifth wedding anniversary is fast approaching."

"You see how I'm not laughing?"

"To celebrate it I think we should go skydiving together."

Ella was quiet for a moment. Much to her credit, she didn't laugh, and Gregory didn't know if that was a good sign or if it was a case of delayed mirth. "Okay. Let me see if I've got this right. You want me to get on a plane, and when it's thousands of feet in the air, I jump headfirst?"

"Well, it doesn't have to be headfirst."

"This is your idea of a good way to celebrate our thirty-fifth wedding anniversary?"

Gregory nodded.

"Why?"

"Because it's fun! Because how often do you get to do something like that? Because it's something I've wanted to do all my life and I can't think of anyone else I'd rather do it with."

Gregory knew that Ella wasn't the kind of woman who needed to jump to possible death to feel alive or happy. A warm bubble bath followed by good, not even particularly great, sex with her husband would have been her idea of a perfect way to usher in a new year of matrimony. But because Gregory didn't stop begging, because Ella likely felt guilty about refusing to take a couple of months out of their lives to hike a good chunk of the Appalachian Mountains when he asked last month, and because there was a small, unexplored part of her that liked the idea of doing something risky for once in her life, a part that longed to be free of fear, she agreed to his scheme. When they came back from skydiving that evening, just as they were about to make love, she admitted she was happy she had done it. And Gregory kissed her and smiled knowingly as though he knew all along she would.

As Gregory trudges toward his bedroom, it dawns on him that he is at the cusp of old age, about to embark on the formidable terrain of seniorhood without his constant companion. His fellow dweller in a two-citizen republic of love, who devotedly and infallibly lobbied for the well-being of their union before her own welfare, has at last abandoned him.

Gregory knows that from now on he has to fend for himself without the woman who loved him as he is — a quiet, unambitious man with no grand passions other than the occasional adventure, and no great desire for success other than to provide for his family. Ella understood and accepted all his shortcomings without ever trying to change his character. She managed to make him feel loved not for who or what he might have been or had the potential to be someday but for the very man he is.

His two children also make him feel he is good enough for them just as he is, even on his off days when he doesn't know which end is up. Which is why it pains him now to be harbouring for Andrew and Natalie the anger, almost hatred, he does as he shuffles down the long hallway that leads to his bedroom, a hallway whose baby-blue walls bear photographic witness to all their Christmases, birthdays, and anniversaries.

Once inside the bedroom he shared with Ella, Gregory locks the door, leans against it, sinks down, squatting at first, then crashes onto the hardwood floor. He renounces that innermost part that speaks to him like a sermon, that appeals to his pride and sense of manhood, that preaches the virtues of stoicism. He lets go of all that and simply surrenders. He weeps, at first quietly, almost inaudibly. Then slowly, incrementally, the waves of grief gather strength until they overflow and manifest into glorious sobs of eulogy.

After a long, messy cry, Gregory composes himself, rises from the floor, and drags himself to the walk-in closet in which he and Ella often dressed side by side as they got ready for a dinner party or a new play, asking themselves which item of clothing went better with which, their elbows occasionally touching.

Inside the closet Gregory looks at his wife's clothes, those expensive garments Natalie wanted to sell. They are the physical evidence he needs to be certain Ella was once here, that she wasn't an apparition or the heroine of some lovely dream he had. He touches the hem of her navy blue ball gown, fingering the texture of its fabric. Each item he gazes at floods him with memories of how it came into their lives. He gathers the cream silk blouse she bought at Bloomingdale's during a weekend trip they took to New York four years ago and drapes it over his shoulders.

From a hanger he slips off a pashmina shawl he bought for Ella at Boston's Logan Airport as an apology gift for some unkind remark he made on the phone during their nightly conversation, a tradition they tried hard to keep anytime one of them was out of town. Gregory tries to remember what he said to her that he felt the need to apologize for, but he can't. He holds the pashmina to his nose, filling himself with the scent of his wife. Gregory can feel the tiny particles of Ella's scent running up his nose and into his head where they swim and dance like happy children.

He scoops up the heavy, beaded cerulean dress Ella wore to Gregory's best friend's wedding and wraps it around his neck. Then he snatches a black jacket and the red-and-gold scarf with the frayed edges she used to love wearing with the dress. He continues to take his wife's clothes off the hangers in this manner until most of them adorn him. These pieces of clothing are all he has left of Ella, and he isn't about to relinquish them.

Gregory goes over to the bed and dives into the middle of it. He feels empty, drained, as though he has endured a hundred years of mourning. His limbs are weak, immovable, and his head aches as if every atom in his brain has come undone and is spinning around in his skull, crashing into one another. He wants more than anything to sleep ...

When Gregory wakes up, it takes him a while to realize where he is and why he has all of his wife's clothes on and around him. He glances at the radio clock on the night table on his wife's side of the bed. It reads 6:03 p.m. Gregory listens for the voices of the mourners downstairs, but all he hears are the chirps of the birds that nest in the huge tree in the backyard. Getting up with some of his wife's clothes still on his shoulders, he shambles over to the bay window that overlooks the backyard.

The late-afternoon sun bathes his wife's beloved garden in a soft pink glow. The rain of the past couple of days has given the iris garden a new life despite the recent night frosts. One of the things he admired most about his wife was her devotion to her irises. They never had pets, but to Ella these flowers were as alive and worthy of her love as any dog or cat. Throughout the year she spent endless hours tending to their needs, and every spring they repaid her in kind with a stunning tapestry of lavender, blue, and yellow.

It was in this garden that she spent most of the summer afternoons and early evenings where they took their coffee and talked or sat side by side and listened to the rustling leaves of their tree, a sound Ella used to say reminded her of the gentle waves of the sea at Larnaca in Cyprus where she grew up until her parents immigrated to Canada. The garden was Ella's favourite spot in their house, possibly in the world.

For the past two days Gregory has been wracking his brain, trying to think of a fitting way to dispose of Ella's ashes. He thought about taking a trip to Cyprus, but she always considered Canada her home, so he discarded that idea right away. Then there was the honeymoon trip to the Grand Canyon where Ella, tears in her eyes, was so touched by the haunting vistas that stretched for many kilometres before them that she asked him to bury her there. Remembering this again, Gregory decided to take Ella's ashes and spray them from some beautiful cliff in the Grand Canyon so that her resting spot would be the only place that ever moved her to tears. When he told Andrew and Natalie his idea, they both endorsed it enthusiastically and suggested they make it a family pilgrimage. Gregory secretly looked forward to having one of those cinematic moments where each family member dips into the urn, takes a fistful of ashes, and surrenders them to the air right at the crescendo of a lugubriously heart-breaking symphonic score worthy of an Oscar.

Gregory stares at the garden below from the window of his bedroom as the tall, bearded irises blow in the wind. *This is where she belongs,* he thinks. What remains of his wife shouldn't be shipped to some faraway place whose beauty, while undeniable, she had nothing to do with. The beauty of her garden, on the other hand, she was wholly responsible for.

With this thought still forming in his head, Gregory rushes out of the bedroom and down the stairs to the living room. Thankfully, all the relatives and friends who were gathered here are now gone. Gregory looks around for the green urn with the gold engraving, then recalls putting it somewhere in the living room so the mourners could look at it and pay their respects if they wished. He scans the room, spies the urn atop the fireplace mantel, and goes for it.

Urn in hand, Gregory crosses the living room carefully, making a great effort not to be heard by Andrew and Natalie who he can see in the kitchen washing the mountains of dishes left behind. He is certain that if they spot him his plan will be ruined. The closest way to the garden is through the kitchen back door. But they are in the kitchen. So he does the next best thing. He opens the front door quietly and walks around the house to the backyard. Once in the garden, he can see his son and daughter standing under the golden glow of the kitchen light, framed by the window that looks out onto the yard.

Gregory knows they could easily discover him if they take their eyes off the dishes even for a second. So he takes the lid off the urn, grabs fistfuls of the finely grained ashes, and sprinkles them over the garden.

He would love to take his time to distribute the ashes evenly over the entire garden so that every plant and flower has a piece of her, but he knows that at any moment Natalie or Andrew could glance away from the dishes and catch him. Just as he is thinking this, Andrew looks up from the sink and they lock eyes. The expression on Andrew's face, which he can only interpret as betrayal, hits Gregory like a punch in the gut. Then Andrew runs out of the frame of the kitchen window, followed by Natalie.

Gregory knows it is only a matter of seconds before they reach him. As Andrew and Natalie approach, he turns the urn upside down on the garden and shakes it with all his might. A cool breeze comes to his aid and blows the dusty contents of the urn over the area. His children stop and stare at him helplessly, their anger and dismay giving way to resignation.

"What the fuck, Dad!" Andrew yells. "We had a deal. We were going to take her to —"

"This is where she belongs!" Gregory shouts back.

"And only you get to decide?"

"I'm her husband. And I say this is where she belongs. In this house!"

Andrew turns away, as if the sight of his father is enough to make him sick. He walks away, but after several steps comes back and stands face to face with Gregory. "So that's what this is about? This is some sort of a territorial marking?"

"What the hell are you talking about?"

Natalie glances back and forth between her father and brother as if watching a tennis match.

"You overheard us saying you'll have to sell the house, so this is some sick way of making sure you never sell it by turning it into Mom's graveyard." Andrew stalks back into the kitchen without waiting for his father to defend himself.

His son's words make Gregory dizzy, so he sits on one of the four white Adirondack chairs in the garden, cradling the empty urn like an infant. Natalie perches on the chair next to him. She doesn't say a word. He wants to know if she, too, shares her brother's view, but doesn't ask. They hear the sound of Andrew's taxi leaving the driveway. For the first time since getting the idea to bury his wife here, Gregory doubts the purity of his motives.

13

when things fall apart

Having at last put Hanna to bed, Andrew wants nothing more than a bottle of beer, if he has any in the fridge, or failing that, a glass of whiskey, which he thankfully does keep at home but hardly drinks for fear of getting another one of Rosemary's looks. The expression that says: *Oh, sweetie, being a drunk at your age isn't pretty.*

As Andrew strolls into the kitchen, he sees his wife washing the pile of dishes she has uncharacteristically left in the sink on account of being busy with the funeral. He is so amazed and proud of the way she chipped in at the service earlier in the day.

Rosemary woke up at six in the morning, baked two different cakes, dropped Hanna off at a friend's house, and went over to his father's home where she and Natalie set up the tables with flowers and the food that relatives and neighbours brought. Andrew was particularly impressed with the way his wife walked around the room, asking the mourners if she could get them anything to eat or drink or simply thanking them for coming. Every time he surveyed the room, there she was, with her long, elegant black dress, her normally curly blond hair solemnly straightened for the occasion, shaking hands with everyone, making them feel comfortable, their attendance appreciated.

Andrew once turned away from his friend Zakhariye whom he was talking to and caught a glimpse of his wife bringing a cup of coffee to his father's snobby Aunt Julie, who never liked Rosemary and made no attempt to conceal it. But Rosemary managed to put her feelings aside, at least for this one day, and extended herself to his aunt. At that moment he wanted to walk over to Rosemary and hug her for the kind, decent woman she is, but he let the opportunity slide. Instead he stood there and admired his wife from afar and drowned in the tide of guilt that washed over him.

Ever since his accidental meeting with Sarah and their subsequent lovemaking in her hotel room, Andrew has been getting attacks of guilt when he least expects them. Early this morning he suffered a bout when he was standing in front of a mirror and putting on his only suit, a navy blue one that Rosemary had bought for him.

She stood behind him, straightened his crooked tie, and smoothed out the crease at the back of the suit, giving him three consoling little pats. At that instant Andrew wanted to confess, get down on his knees, beg for her forgiveness, and promise he would never see Sarah again.

But something stopped him. He desperately wanted to confess, but he couldn't. How could he when he spent much of the previous night tossing and turning in bed, replaying the short, intoxicating time he spent with Sarah and how beautifully alive he felt making love to her? Promising his wife that he would never see Sarah again would have been a crime, considering he would have abandoned the funeral and everything else planned for the day if Sarah had called him and asked to meet him somewhere. Of that he is now certain.

Andrew is sure of another thing as he opens the fridge in search of a cold bottle of beer. He is positive he is in love. Of course, he has loved other women before. There was Zadie, the Trinidadian he met in his second year at McGill University, and Helli in Finland. And in some ways he does love Rosemary. But for the first time in his life he is beginning to comprehend the distinction between loving and being in love. This is no longer semantics to him. Andrew always felt people were playing with words whenever he heard that silly distinction. Now he knows the difference. He feels the difference.

Just his luck. No beer in the fridge. For an instant he thinks about driving over to the nearest liquor store and bringing home a case or two. Instead he walks through the other doorway of the kitchen that leads to the living room and over to a shelf they pretend is a bar where they keep a tray of various alcohols.

Andrew pours a generous glass of whiskey — his wife's disappointment be damned — and takes a couple of big gulps. He tries to shut out the voices in his head, like the one that commands him to call Sarah and tell her he is in love with her. The other voice, the grown-up one, orders him to stop being foolish. *How could you be in love, you buffoon?* it whispers to him. *How could you love a woman you know almost nothing about?* For now he listens to the latter voice.

Sure, Andrew met Sarah many years ago when they were young. Sure, they shared a kiss, the kind he compared to all other kisses that followed. And certainly seeing her again, kissing her, and making love to her reawakened a part of him he was convinced had perished. But is that really love?

Andrew pours another shot and saunters back to the kitchen where his wife is impossibly absorbed in the simple task of washing dishes. Rosemary, it seems to him, has a singular talent for losing herself in menial chores. Andrew often looks at her as she disappears into these daily tasks and wonders what is going on in her mind. He yearns to know about her inner life, if she has one, and what she thinks and dreams about. What, for instance, does she fantasize about on the rare occasions when they have sex?

"We have a dishwasher for that you know," he says instead.

"I know," Rosemary says without turning. "But I like washing dishes, unlike you."

"I don't dislike doing dishes. I just don't get off on it like you do."

Rosemary smiles at him wearily, as though unsure how to read his comment. She snatches a folded dishtowel from the top of the fridge and throws it at him, hitting him in the face. Andrew smiles back at her, uncertain how to interpret the force with which she threw the towel.

"Make yourself useful," she tells him.

Obeying his wife, Andrew sets his drink on the counter and starts drying. As he puts away the dried dishes, it occurs to him that he and his wife haven't fought since she found out about his mother's death a week ago — a record, actually. Through the stressful ordeal of the viewing, the funeral services, and everything else, she has somehow managed to conceal her anger at all the little things that usually make her furious. *Is this what death does to people?* Andrew asks himself. *Does it make all else inconsequential?*

This brief period of peace feels good to him, but it also fills him with dread. It is temporary, and he knows it. And it only reminds him of its opposite, the way they have lived their lives ever since they got married — a constant interplay of anger and disappointment at him and his often childish defiance, which he is certain is the result of her attacks on everything he does, from his method of changing Hanna's diapers to the way he drives, down to the little bagel crumbs he leaves on the kitchen counter in the morning.

These nights of peace have shown Andrew there is another way to live besides the alternating bickering and out-and-out war he has gotten so used to. The calm reminds him of how his parents lived, how he and Helli were in their cozy apartment in Helsinki, how he and Sarah could live if they ever got the opportunity. Without any premeditation or thought about the consequences, Andrew hears the words coming out of his mouth quite independent of his control. "I had an affair."

Rosemary stops rinsing the plate in her hand.

"Did you hear me?" he asks.

She shuts off the water and places the plate back in the sink. "Who was it?"

"No one you know."

"*Who is she?*" Rosemary screams, causing Andrew to recoil.

"What difference does it make who she is?" Andrew was under the naive impression he could direct the course of his confession. *I should've prepared myself better,* he thinks. His wife is now in charge of the conversation, and there is no telling where it might go.

"When?" she asks, more composed, but steelier, more ominous.

"On Thursday."

"This past Thursday?"

Andrew nods. Rosemary backs away from him with an expression of horror and sadness he has never seen in his wife or in any other woman before.

"You're unbelievable!" She paces the small kitchen, her breathing shallower as if struggling for oxygen. "A hooker?"

"What?"

"Was she a hooker?"

"No! Of course not."

"Oh, of course not? Why of course? You think you're too good for a hooker?"

"No ... I don't know. Why are we talking about hookers?"

"News flash for you. No self-respecting hooker would fuck the kind of man who'd go cruising for sex while his mother lies in a funeral home."

"I wasn't cruising for sex. It just happened."

"Really? I get out of the house every day and that never happens to me."

"It was the last thing on my mind," Andrew says, desperate to deflect the conversation back to more predictable terrain such as what all this means for their marriage, or any other line of questioning that doesn't involve what kind of hooker would sleep with him. For instance, a discussion about the quality of their marriage and the fact that it started off shaky and only got worse with time would be a much more fruitful field of discourse. But he can't figure out how to steer things in that direction. It seems to Andrew that not only is he a failure at fidelity but he is also a failure at confessing to infidelity.

"Explain that to me," Rosemary says without a trace of the sadness that was in her voice a moment ago. Now there is cold, menacing rage. "Explain to me how something like that just happens, because I'm just not getting it."

"I can't explain it. I don't know how to."

"*Try, asshole!*" she screeches, giving Andrew another violent jolt.

"Could you not scream like that, please? You're going to wake Hanna up."

"*Aww*, how sweet! Suddenly, you're concerned about Hanna."

"What do you want me to say, Rosemary?"

"I want you to explain to me as clearly and as rationally as possible how fucking another woman just happens to you."

"That's just it — it's not clear or rational to me. I was devastated and confused."

"Confused?" Rosemary repeats, seemingly exasperated and confused herself. "Just what were you so confused about, exactly? That you're a married man? That you're married to me? Oh, I see. You mistook her for me. Is that it? It was really me you wanted to fuck, but you just got too goddamn confused?"

"You're twisting everything," Andrew says, edging out of the kitchen.

"Where the fuck do you think you're going?" Rosemary yells, grabbing his arm.

Andrew is impressed and a little frightened by her strength.

"You don't tell your wife you just cheated on her and get to walk away."

"What do you want from me, Rosemary?"

"I want you to tell me what you were confused about."

"Okay, maybe *confused* isn't the right word. I was devastated. My mother just died —"

"Oh, honey, you don't really want to go there with me. Your mother dies so you go and find yourself a consolation fuck?"

"That's not what I mean."

"Tell me, Andrew, did this poor chick know she was just pick-me-up pussy?"

"Would you please stop talking like that?"

"Why? Is that too vulgar for your refined sensibilities? Am I being too crude?"

Andrew, feeling dizzy and shell-shocked, stumbles over to the breakfast nook and sits. This isn't the way he envisioned the evening would unfold when he came home after his fight with his father about his mother's ashes. He looked forward to a quiet evening after a long, crappy day. Now he wonders what on earth possessed him to confess. True, he was drowning in guilt, but now living with his guilt seems like a far better alternative to this interrogation. Too much guilt — that is his weakness. How do some people chop up other human beings and go on with their lives, shopping for socks and raking leaves? He wished he could be one of those people, unsullied by remorse.

Rosemary comes over to where he is sitting and glares at him. "How many times did you sleep with her?"

"Once. Just once. That's what I mean when I say it just happened. I didn't plan it. You have to believe me." Part of Andrew is convinced of the truth of his words. But another part knows it was a deliberate act. He did, after all, stop by a drugstore to buy condoms.

"Did you know her?" Rosemary asks.

"She was one of my mother's students — a long time ago. I bumped into her by accident. I swear it was —"

"Does she live here?"

Finally, Rosemary is asking questions whose purpose he can understand. How he answers this one could give his wife some peace of mind. "No, she lives in New York. She's here briefly, probably till the shoot is over."

"The shoot?"

"She's making a movie here. She's an actress."

"Oh, she's an actress," she says, mimicking him. Then her voice switches back to fury. "How very nice for you."

Oh, shit! Andrew thinks. Just as she was calming down and perhaps even beginning to see the whole thing as an unplanned, honest-to-God mistake, he had to tell her the female in question has a glamorous occupation. He really should know better, considering how much Rosemary despises glamorous women.

"Is she hot?"

"What?" Andrew asks in a desperate attempt to buy a few seconds to come up with an answer that won't trigger another verbal attack.

"Is she hot? Is she sexy, beautiful, fuckable, or whatever other sick adjective you men use to categorize women."

Andrew isn't used to hearing feminist polemics from a woman who doesn't think twice about spouting misogynistic insults at other women. It was only three weeks ago that they were driving home from his mother's hospital and a beautiful redhead in a silver Mini Cooper made the mistake of cutting Rosemary off. In a fit of righteous fury she rolled down the window and yelled "Cocksucker cunt!" at the poor girl.

Andrew realizes that how he answers the "Is she hot?" question might well determine the outcome of this evening. "No," he lies.

"Bullshit!"

"Then why did you ask me if you're not going to believe me?"

"Because you're a liar."

Having tried all his life to be honest and conduct himself with integrity, Andrew is deeply hurt by her remark, but even he knows this isn't the time to defend his character.

"What's her name?" Rosemary asks.

"Her name isn't important."

"Don't tell me what's important, asshole. I'll ask again — what the fuck is this chick's name?"

"Her name is Sarah Turlington."

"Thank you!" Rosemary bolts out of the kitchen and into the living room where the black computer they share sits on a tiny work desk. The machine is turned off, and as she waits for it to boot up, Andrew approaches the desk to see what she is up to.

Rosemary types Sarah Turlington into the Google search engine, and Andrew puts his hand on her shoulder. "Honey, please stop this. It's not important who she is or what she looks like."

She flings his hand off her shoulder. In no time Rosemary finds a fan website devoted to Sarah, probably run by an unemployed theatre freak. At the top of the site are various links for awards, interviews, and photos. Rosemary clicks on the photo link. Instantly, a large picture from a magazine spread fills the screen. In the photograph Sarah wears a white T-shirt and blue jeans. Her shoulder-length brown hair is pulled back, giving her face and liquid blue eyes the camera's full attention, her stunning beauty unencumbered by big hair and makeup. Rosemary studies the photograph intently, then reaches for the mouse and closes the screen. Turning to Andrew, she regards him gravely. "Tell me it was just sex. Swear to me that's all it was."

Andrew is unable to speak. Rosemary patiently waits for an answer. When it becomes clear that the words she wants to hear won't be said, she gets up and stands before him, eyes filling with tears. Andrew stares at his feet, while his wife shuffles off as if each step causes physical pain.

He watches her disappear into the hallway to their bedroom. Then, suddenly, she returns and strikes him with her open hands on his face, chest, head, and any other part of his body she can reach. Andrew doesn't flinch or defend himself. He takes every blow as though it will bring him one step closer to absolution. When the sting becomes too much to bear, he covers his face with both hands, but she continues until she is heaving, exhausted. At last she stalks away, leaving him in the middle of the living room. Feeling a stinging pain in his bottom lip, Andrew runs his tongue over it. The rusty, metallic taste of blood fills his mouth.

Moments later he hears a suitcase hitting the floor with a loud thud. Andrew enters their bedroom and finds Rosemary packing his clothes in the large black suitcase he bought when he moved back to Canada from Finland. He watches his wife dart back and forth between the closet and the suitcase until it is stuffed with every piece of clothing he owns. She struggles to close it, but it is too full. Even stepping on it doesn't help.

"Close it," she orders.

"Honey, please —"

"Close it!"

He obeys silently as she watches. Once the task is complete, she flees to the bathroom and locks herself in. Andrew knocks on the door softly. "Honey, please open the door. Please let me in ..." He leans against the door and lets the weight of his exhausted body, still burning from her blows, completely rest on it. It isn't until he hears the sound of his wife's muffled sobs that the extent of the damage he has caused dawns on him.

Andrew has spent his adult life proud of the fact that although he might have hurt some people, he never did it out of malice. He never knowingly inflicted pain on another human being with his actions or words. But now, listening to his wife weep, he will never think that about himself again.

For close to an hour Andrew has been sitting in his taxi. He turned off the ignition long ago, and now his hands and feet are unbearably cold. When he pulled into the driveway of his parents' house, he decided to sit in the car and wait until his father was asleep. The only thing worse than being kicked out of his apartment is to face his father. Gregory's disappointment has always had an inexplicable power over him, and on a night like this it could unravel him. So he waits in the cab until he is certain he can sneak up to his old room and deal with his father and sister in the morning.

Glancing out the windshield, Andrew sees no sign of life in the house. All the windows are dark. He gets out of the car, closes the door quietly, takes his suitcase out of the trunk, and heads for the front of the house. Getting his suitcase over the steps that lead to the front door and entering the house without making a sound prove more of a challenge than he imagined. He still has the key he used when he visited his sick mother at all hours of the day and employs it now.

Andrew hauls the suitcase in at last, leaves it in the middle of the foyer, and stays there for a moment as he tries to figure out how to carry it up the stairs without waking his father or sister. It seems impossible. Standing in the dark foyer makes him feel like a thief. He decides to leave the suitcase where it is and deal with it in the morning. In the dark, with the only light coming from the large living-room window, the only thing he can think of is Hanna.

She will wake up tomorrow, and for the first time in her short life she won't be lifted out of the crib by him. *Will she wonder what happened to him? Do babies have thoughts?* He wishes he knew the answers to those questions. Or not, for the answer might break his heart even more. *So this is what it feels like when things fall apart.* Tears come accompanied by waves of nausea. He sits at the foot of the staircase. In the dark foyer, with no fear of ridicule or pity, Andrew sheds the tears he didn't for his mother's final defeat, for his father's loss, for his sister's sadness, and for his betrayed wife.

The house explodes with light. Andrew jumps up, turns around, and sees his father at the top of the staircase in striped pajamas. Quickly, he wipes away his tears with the sleeve of his sweater. They stare at each other without a word for what feels to Andrew like eternity. He notices the dreaded look in his father's eyes, and it pierces him like a blade. "I'll explain it all in the morning, Dad. I just want to go to bed now."

Before his father responds, Natalie comes out of her bedroom, wearing a long white T-shirt down to her knees with large red letters that read: I LOVE ME. She stands next to her father, and they both stare at Andrew from the top of the staircase. Gregory returns to his bedroom without saying a word. As soon as her father's door is closed, Natalie joins Andrew in the foyer. She hugs him. "Are you hungry? Want me to fix you something?"

Andrew nods. They walk into the kitchen and turn the light on. He sits on one of the three high stools by the island counter in the middle of the kitchen as Natalie rummages in the fridge, which is full of Tupperware containers of leftover food from the funeral service. She takes out one with lasagna in it, puts some on a plate, and warms it in the microwave. Pouring a glass of juice, she places it and the lasagna in front of Andrew, sits on the stool next to him, and watches him eat.

"You just couldn't keep your mouth shut," Natalie says. "Had to blab it all away."

Andrew looks up from the plate. "I've fucked up big time, haven't I?"

Natalie nods sadly.

"Do you really have to go tomorrow? Can't you stay for a few more days?"

"I'm so behind as it is, sweetie."

"Don't leave me with him, please. He can't even bring himself to utter a word to me. I disappoint him."

"Well, he disappoints us, too, sometimes. That's what families do — we disappoint each other."

"What time's your flight?"

"Eleven. Drive me to the airport?"

Andrew nods. Natalie sees him eyeing her T-shirt.

"I love me?" he says, wincing.

"I have self-esteem issues — deal with it."

Andrew tries to laugh, but it comes out a tired chuckle. Natalie gets up, kisses him on the forehead, and heads upstairs. Before she leaves she grins at him. "So does this mean I'll have a famous sister-in-law?"

Andrew grabs the paper napkin next to his plate, crumbles it into a ball, and throws it at Natalie, who runs out of the kitchen before it hits her.

———

After Natalie checks in her luggage and gets her boarding pass, she and Andrew stroll around the new Pearson International terminal until she has to go through security. He wears his regular work clothes, which today consist of dark blue jeans, a white T-shirt, and his beloved brown leather jacket that Helli bought him as a going-away present when he took a freelance job for *Stern* magazine to do the photographs for a cover story on Romanian girls forced into prostitution in Italy.

In his opinion the pictures from that assignment are by far the best work he has done in his career: hundreds of portraits, in colour and black and white, taken on the streets of Rome and Palermo, showing girls as young as fourteen, their baby faces caked with makeup to appear older and sometimes to hide the bruises received from their johns and pimps. He keeps all these photographs in a portfolio that he would one day like to publish as a book.

The cold front that has swept in early this year gave Andrew an excuse to take his leather jacket out of the closet where he had put it last April. He is surprised at how good it looks after so many years and how many memories it conjures up of his past life as a photojournalist and especially his time with Helli.

As Andrew and Natalie wander in the terminal, the huge glass-and-steel structure is ablaze with the sunlight that seeps in from every corner.

"Want to sit down?" he asks his sister, pointing at the sitting area where two men in black business suits are drinking coffee. He overhears their conversation, something about the need for restructuring and layoffs. *Bastards,* he thinks as he passes them.

"Let's keep walking," Natalie says. "I want to see more of this new terminal." She was in no state to see anything when she flew in. But now that their mother is dead it seems as if the ordeal of the past two years is finally over. Although she is still in the grip of sadness that her mother is no longer in her life, Andrew is amazed at the dignity with which she is handling her grief and the compassion she has shown to both him and their father.

He admires his sister's determination to find pleasure in small things like making popcorn for her and her father last night, taking it to him in his room, and having as she put it, "a good heart-to-heart." And now, rather than feeling sorry for herself, she wants to see what small consolation a good ramble in a shiny new airport terminal can bring. Andrew indulges his sister's request, and they walk from one end of the terminal to the other.

"Coming for Christmas?" he asks, finally breaking the comfortable silence of the past few minutes.

"Yeah, unless —"

"Unless what?"

"Unless something big comes up and I can't make it."

"Something big like what?"

"Like if I decide to elope with Jamal."

"Before Dad even meets him? Wouldn't that be something? I'd pay to see his reaction."

"Come on now. Go easy on him. Please promise me you'll be nice to him."

"I just think sometimes you worry too much about what he thinks."

Natalie releases a sardonic laugh. "This coming from the man who fled his entire life because of a single phone call?"

"Somebody had to."

"What the hell is that supposed to mean?"

"Oh, come on, Mom was seriously sick, Dad was alone and couldn't take care of her by himself, and you —"

"And me what? Finish it."

"You could've taken one semester off, but you didn't, did you?"

"Screw you, Andrew. I finally got the grant I've worked so hard for. I was in the middle of research. Some of us don't have the luxury of taking well-paying assignments whenever it suits us."

"What are you saying? That I didn't have to move, that I had a choice?"

"I'm just saying you didn't have to be so drastic about it and drop everything."

"Oh, and just what was I supposed to do — hop on a plane back and forth from Helsinki to Toronto every weekend?"

"All I'm saying is —"

"What?"

"It was classic Andrew."

"Classic Andrew? What the fuck does that even mean?"

"It means it was so *you*, always being the good son who drops everything for his mother."

"It wasn't even Mom who called me and asked me to come back. Just goes to show you how little you know about it."

"Oh, don't be dense now. Do you really think Dad asked you on his own accord? You don't think Mom had something to do with it?"

"What are you saying — that she asked him to talk me into moving back?"

"You know how Mom felt about you being so far away … about your job. She always worried sick you might get hurt. Her biggest fear in life was that she would one day pick up the phone and the person on the other end would tell her you were killed by a stray bullet or some shit like that. It was the perfect way to make you come home, and you fell for it."

This version of the story, or at least the possibility that his return was his mother's doing rather than his own honourable decision, is a most unwelcome revelation, and he is furious at his sister for planting doubt in his mind, for muddying what was once to him a clear case of benevolence and sacrifice on his part. "You know what, Natalie? I don't need this shit. Goodbye." He begins to walk away.

"Oh, that's really mature, Andrew. Go ahead, run."

He quickens his pace.

Natalie goes after him. "C'mon, stop! Don't say goodbye like this. Please."

Andrew slows down until he comes to a gradual stop. He turns and kisses his sister on the cheek. "There, happy? Have a safe trip. Goodbye." He sets off again.

"No, *stooooop!*" Natalie whines, reaching for his hand and holding him. "I'm sorry. It's all in the past now." She glances at her watch. "I have ten minutes left — just stay for ten more minutes. Walk me to security." As they proceed side by side in silence, Natalie wraps her arm around her brother's waist. "You should be flattered, really, not angry."

Andrew glares at her. "Really, and how do you figure that?"

"She didn't orchestrate anything to get me back home. It was you."

"Yeah, because she knew I would, the good obedient son that I am."

"No, because you're the one Mom loved more than anything else in the world."

"What are you talking about? Mom loved you, too."

"Of course, she did, idiot. All mothers love their daughters. That's not the point. But you know how it was with us. We could only take each other in very small doses. Every time I came home for the holidays, the first couple of days were amazing, and then one of us would say something and everything would go to shit from there."

Andrew snorts. "Right, you disliked each other so much, that's why you talked on the phone at least once a day."

"I know she meant well, but she never understood me ... or tried. I guess I never really tried to understand her, either. I guess we're even. She didn't get a single aspect of my life. My work, my relationships ... even my damn hairstyle was a puzzle to her. And look, I don't even have a hairstyle. Everything about me disappointed her, so I just stopped trying."

"Maybe that's the trick," Andrew says. "Maybe I should do the same with Dad."

"What are you talking about? You don't disappoint him. You said it last night and you're saying it now. I don't know where you get this stuff from."

"Easy for you to say. You turned out to be everything he ever wanted — an Ivy League doctor who's probably going to end up curing mad cow disease or something. All I end up with is the look."

"What look?"

"Oh, that look he gives me. The one that says I'm the only non-immigrant cab driver in town. The one that says he had a fully paid mortgage and ten grants in mutual funds by the time he was my age."

"He just wants you to be happy."

"He wants me to be him."

When they arrive at the security gate, they face each other. "Be kind to him," Natalie says. "He really needs that now more than ever."

"I'll try, but I'm not making any promises."

"And give my beautiful niece a big kiss."

Andrew nods.

"And call me every day. I want all the dirt on you and Rosemary."

Andrew nods again, this time with a feigned sigh. "Anything else?"

"I love you."

"Yeah, yeah, yeah. Go. You're going to miss your plane." Andrew hugs his sister with a sudden urgency he doesn't fully understand. They hold each other tightly as travellers buzz around them. Finally, he breaks off. "Go. Go."

Natalie proceeds through the security gate, walks behind a frosted glass wall, and disappears from view. He misses her already. First his mother dies and now his sister leaves. Andrew's knees buckle a little under the sudden sensation of being orphaned.

He ambles toward the parking garage where he parked his cab. On his way out, just in front of the revolving door, he spots a large information screen listing all departing flights. Andrew studies the long list of flights going to every corner of the globe. For many years these departure screens were his Bible as he travelled the world, hopping from one airport to another, departing here, arriving there, connecting at Heathrow, resting at Jomo Kenyatta, off to God knows where else after that. As much as he hated the complex choreography of travelling, he did love the getting away part that allowed him to escape whenever things got too heavy in one place. A part of him, the old one, yearns for that now. Things have never gotten as overwhelming as they are at the moment, but the option of escape is no longer on the table.

Andrew glances at the flight numbers to destinations he knows like the back of his hand, places like London, Rome, and Amsterdam, as well as flights to cities he has never been to but would love to visit one of these days — Lima, Reykjavik, Kuala Lumpur. As his eyes dance to the bottom of the screen, he finds the flight uppermost in his mind: AC876 — Toronto to Helsinki.

What if? Andrew thinks. What if he went to the Air Canada counter, took out his Visa, and purchased a one-way ticket to Helsinki to resume his interrupted life? Hundreds of men, thousands, disappear every year. He is always reading news reports about sane, normal men who wake up one morning, put on their clothes, get into their cars, and flee. People do such things.

Andrew wonders what Helli is doing now. He calculates the time difference. It is late in the afternoon there. She has just had dinner and is probably taking Henry, the dog he got for her birthday, for a walk in the nearby park where they used to spend most of their summer weekends lying on a blanket, she reading a John le Carré novel in Finnish, while he read whatever English newspaper he could get his hands on. *Would Henry still recognize me?*

He sees the time, 11:13 a.m., flashing at the top of the screen, and remembers he has to take Hanna to the pediatrician this afternoon for another shot. What is it this month? Tetanus? Mumps? Rubella? Haemophilus influenza? There are so many shots she is supposed to get before she is five that he can't remember which is which.

Andrew also has a betrayed wife to deal with and a grieving father to be kind to, and then there is Sarah. He must find her. He hasn't been able to stop thinking about her. No matter what time of the day it is, no matter what urgent matters need dealing with, thoughts of her and their brief time together bubble up against his will. *I must see her. I must talk to her! I must kiss her!* These are his thoughts as he slips through the giant revolving glass door and heads toward the parking garage.

14

come in from the cold

Dufferin Gate Sound Stage, 11:30 p.m., scene 185, take 19.
Christopher Hastings, the director, and Allen Lawrence, the cinematographer, have their eyes glued to the monitor. They watch as
the cameraman follows Sarah pacing a large drawing room, lav-
ishly decorated in late nineteenth-century American splendour.
They are shooting night for day. The klieg lights placed outside
the fake windows on both sides of the room give the impression
of a beautiful sunny day outside.

"And when did you begin with him?" asks Liam Rouch, who
is sitting in a wheelchair and playing the part of Clifford Chatterley.

"In the spring," Sarah answers softly, her voice brilliantly con-
veying a combination of Constance's remorse but also her dignified refusal to feel cheap and dirty.

"And it was you then in the bedroom at the cottage?"

"Yes."

"My God!" Liam cries. He collects himself and regards Sarah
with repulsion. "You ought to be wiped from the face of the Earth."

With that line Sarah loses it again. The tears she has been resist-
ing throughout the scene stream once more without warning.

"Cut!" Christopher shouts. Without leaving his seat behind the monitor, he says, "No! No, no, Sarah, you're crying again. Let's take it from 'in the spring,' but this time, do it as we've discussed."

Sandy, the makeup artist, runs over and freshens up Sarah's eye makeup, hiding all evidence of tears. While Sarah has her makeup retouched, a technician measures the colour temperature by holding an instrument in front of her face.

They have been shooting this climactic confrontation scene for the past five hours. Liam's coverage took less than two hours to complete, but Christopher remains unsatisfied with Sarah's close-ups. They have covered the scene in every conceivable way: contrite, angry, pleading. Nothing seems to please Christopher. His direction to Sarah was to let her eyes well with tears but not let them actually fall.

Unfortunately, Sarah has managed either not to cry at all or to weep uncontrollably. She feels the pointlessness, the lunacy of what he is after, but she has indulged his whims for hours now and is at her wits' end. The lights are giving her a headache. Her tight corset is crushing her lungs, and every time she breathes deeply her ribs feel as if they are going to snap. And under all the hair extensions her head itches, but she doesn't dare scratch lest she pluck out one of the countless pins holding everything together.

With each take Sarah's exasperation with Christopher and his fixation on her tears increases. She has always hated the way most filmmakers fetishize women's tears on film, making the falling of them equivalent to the money shot in porn flicks. But trying to please Christopher, she gives it another try with the purest intention of serving her director, of helping him realize his vision, even though she no longer has any idea what that might be.

They start another take and get to the line, "You ought to be wiped from the face of the Earth," but this time Sarah's eyes don't fill with tears. She is too distracted by the pressure to produce the right amount of tears — just enough to mist the eyes but not too much that they roll down. It is impossible to inhabit a moment fully when she feels reduced to a tear-producing machine. Instead of listening to her scene partner and being in the moment with him, she is thinking about the amount of tears she needs to manufacture.

It's a lost cause, Sarah thinks. She has no faith in what she is doing anymore, and as a result all she feels is numb. Her aim tonight, on any night, in any scene, is to simply *be.* That is all she wants — *to be,* not to put on a show. She wants to be Constance, not Sarah performing Constance. She longs to evoke what she experienced with Andrew as they made love in her hotel room. They weren't performing. They weren't trying to turn each other on the way she and her husband do. They were merely two people sharing a few moments of *being.* That is the feeling she wants to summon — the simple act of *being* — as she tries to play this difficult scene. If only Christopher would get the hell out of the way.

Instead her director wants a song and dance whose convoluted choreography she hasn't learned or cares to discover at this point. So when he yells "Cut!" for what feels like the millionth time, Sarah loses it. She won't be reduced to a crying machine, so she storms off the set, shouting at Christopher as she steps over the electric cables taped to the floor, "Enough is enough. You have a million good takes. Use one of them. I'm not a goddamn tap you can shut on and off. I'm a human being. Treat me like one, for fuck's sake." Then she walks off the set, leaving a stunned director and his helpless crew.

Sarah requested a change of room at her hotel. When the manger asked why she was displeased, Sarah didn't go into the details and simply pleaded with him to move her. Her husband called yesterday to tell her he would be able to visit her in Toronto for the weekend, and Sarah's first thought was to switch rooms. The idea of being in the same bed with her husband that she shared with Andrew unsettled her in a way that felt beyond reason. But because the hotel room was fully booked for the weekend, Sarah had to accept the inevitability of sleeping with her husband on the same bed she and Andrew had made love on.

It is in that very bed that Sarah and Michael lie now. Michael has already fallen asleep and breathes heavily but without the faintest hint of a snore. The lamp on the night table on her side of the bed spreads a ring of light. Sarah has always been jealous of her husband's ability to fall asleep with the lights on. She once did a full rendition of "My Favourite Things" from *The Sound of Music* that would have made Julie Andrews proud just to test her theory that her husband could sleep through a military invasion. She was right.

Sarah gazes at Michael's naked, hairless chest rising and falling with each breath. Softly, she pulls the white duvet over his shoulders, exposing only his boyish face, which looks much younger than thirty-four.

Only twenty minutes have passed since they made love, and now he appears comatose. *What is it about sex that makes men fall asleep so fast?* she wonders. *Is the act of making love to a woman so gruelling, so unimaginably draining, that an involuntary stupor can be the only outcome?* She resolves to ask Michael in the morning. Sex has the opposite effect on her. She feels more energetic, more alive, as if every cell in her body receives its own wake-up call, urging it to come to life and rejoice.

Just then it occurs to her how different sex was with Andrew than with her husband. What she had with Michael twenty minutes ago was, as always, fun and filled with naughty banter as they tried new tricks they had learned from the Kama Sutra book they had ordered online. To their lovemaking Michael brings the spirit of inventiveness his job as a perfumer demands. His dogged determination to be the best lover he has the capacity to be often leads them to experiments that result more in laughter than sexual ecstasy. Like the time a particularly convoluted position resulted in Michael falling off the bed and getting a nasty bump on the forehead. They laughed so hard, for so long, that Michael lost his erection and couldn't regain it.

Sex with Andrew, on the other hand, took on a sober, more reverent tone. She remembers that not a single word was uttered. With her astounding sense-memory, a technique honed for years in her acting classes, Sarah recalls her body's reaction to his touch and how with every kiss on the palm of her hand or the small of her back or the tip of her tongue resonated with a kind of solemnity that made her think of God and of death and of all the weightier matters of *being*. With these thoughts racing through her mind, Sarah reaches for the lamp on the night table and switches it off.

The room now pitch-black, Sarah turns her back to her husband and abandons herself in thoughts of Andrew. This isn't the first time she has immersed herself in this activity. Off and on over the years she has contemplated that day in the basement of his mother's house when she experienced her first real adult kiss. She has wondered what her life would have been like if she and Andrew had become lovers.

A realization that she has made a terrible mistake marrying Michael suddenly comes to her with stunning, church-bell clarity. *I should've said no,* Sarah thinks. Four years ago, when Michael nonchalantly asked if she would marry him, she should have said no.

Sarah recalls the day so clearly. She was sitting in the bathtub of their new brownstone in Harlem, washing Michael's back with a sponge the colour of clay. They were so tired from moving in, arranging the furniture, and hanging paintings and the

black-and-white photographs Sarah has collected over the years.
After eating the pizza they ordered, they decided to take a bath and
took turns sipping red wine straight from the bottle as they soaked
their tired limbs in the 1920s clawfoot bathtub. Michael placed
his head on her breasts, looked up at her, and unceremoniously, as
though asking her to pass the butter, said, "Marry me, Sarah."

At the time they had been living together for two years and
had just moved into their beautifully renovated townhouse. The
frantic activities of putting together a new home had made her
feel adventurous, on the cusp of some great pinnacle in their lives
that would usher in better, brighter versions of themselves. She
and Michael had, and continue to have, a kind of easy, carefree
relationship that exists in the absence of real love, the kind of love
that demands serious reflection and brutal honesty.

For instance, if they are both honest, they would admit they
like each other. They might even love each other in the way that
people who like each other a great deal love, which isn't really
that much and therefore shouldn't lead to marriage. She once
almost asked Michael why he proposed to her, but she didn't
because part of her already knew the answer. He wanted to marry
her not so much because of who she was or what he felt for her
but where he was in his life. He had just turned thirty. He was
professionally successful. What else was there for a man to do?

Equally, if Sarah is honest enough with him and with herself,
she would tell him this: she agreed to marry him because it was
easier to go with him in the direction he was headed than to
forge a new and unknown one for herself. Her work gave her
enough uncertainties and required her to make so many difficult
choices that in her private life she was thankful to have someone
else carry that burden.

It was the summer of 1998 when she and Michael started living together. The days were long and warm and the economy solid.

The market bubble was still intact, and their stocks were strong. It was happy days all around. Bill Clinton was in charge, and Harlem was experiencing its second renaissance. All that brightness and happiness made her feel that she, too, was happy or at least could be if she gave it a chance, if she closed her eyes and let the feeling carry her. It was too much hard work and uncertain results to alter direction, so she acquiesced to Michael's vision of a happy future.

Sarah tries her best to lie still and quiet the voices in her head that replay memories of being in this bed with Andrew. The voices compare and contrast the two men, and her desire to numb her thoughts is no match for her need to relive everything. So she tosses and turns while Michael lies beside her, oblivious.

She begins to panic, fearing Michael might have sensed something in her manner, in the way she related to him, to his touch when they made love. It hits her that she was different with him than her usual cheery self. She wasn't the version of herself that found enthusiasm for whatever new thing he wanted to try, that went along with his need for role play and dirty talk. Sarah could only imagine how foreign she must have seemed to him when she pressed her palm against his mouth, telling him to stop talking as he started his usual litany of raunchy phrases whose utterances brought him to the brink and he believed did the same for her. Tonight she yearned for silence.

Sarah wanted to re-create the silence of her earlier encounter with Andrew, and Michael did give her the quiet she longed for, probably thinking it was some new way of doing it that she had read about somewhere. But silence with Michael was just that minus everything that had made the experience so powerful with Andrew.

Missing was that intoxicating, unnerving stillness she had felt, and Sarah knew instinctively that her husband sensed something was amiss. She saw it in his eyes, the way they became vacant and ice-cold. As she was pressing her hand against his mouth, she felt him sense on some deeper level she didn't even know he possessed that he was making love to a different woman tonight, a woman whose exterior was the same but whose interior was wholly foreign.

Michael might not be a man of great depth, Sarah knows, but he isn't so dimwitted as not to feel that the woman he was inside wasn't the same woman. He must have sensed it, she is now convinced. He must have detected something transformed in his wife — a shifting on a molecular level that had taken place in his absence. That must be why he rushed to finish the act, not pacing himself the way he normally did, savouring every thrust, but instead pushed himself harder and faster, then quietly withdrew from her and went to sleep.

When Sarah wakes up from a long, exhausting dream in which she wandered aimlessly in the Arctic, adrift in an endless, flat expanse of whiteness, she sits up on the bed and notices Michael isn't lying next to her. She turns on the lamp. Nothing. She glances at the washroom. It is dark. A cold breeze hits her. The door to the balcony is open. She gets out of the bed, peeling the white duvet and wrapping it around her naked body.

Sarah stands on the metal track of the sliding door that divides the room from the balcony that faces Lake Ontario. Michael is near the black metal balcony railing, his nude body shivering as he gazes at a thin ray of light breaking through the otherwise solid grey clouds over the indigo water. In the east the morning sun raptures a thin red line in the clouds like a wound.

Slowly, as if bored by the violence of the burgeoning sunlight, Michael turns and looks at Sarah. Tears linger in his eyes
on the verge of falling, just as Christopher demanded of her. She
can't tell if the tears are the result of the cold wind blowing in
Michael's eyes or if they are the real thing.

"Honey, come back in," she says. "You're freezing."

Michael returns his gaze to the fissure in the clouds. Sarah
doesn't repeat her request. She knows how stubborn her husband
can be.

"You're going to leave me, aren't you?" he asks without glancing at her.

"What are you talking about, Michael?" She realizes her voice
is strained under the weight of her determination not to reveal
anything that might cause her husband any more anguish, or
God forbid, do something stupid like take a step forward.

"I wouldn't hate you, you know?" he continues. "Even if you
left me, I wouldn't. I could never hate you." At last Michael turns
to her, as if to see the effect of his words.

"I know, sweetie." Sarah moves closer to stand behind him,
holding her arms wide open, the white duvet spreading like two
giant angel wings. She wraps her arms around him from behind,
the front of her body pressing against his naked back, sending
shivers through her.

At some point Michael will have to know about Andrew,
Sarah concludes. But at this moment she doesn't know how
much she should divulge. Should she simply reveal the basic fact:
that as much as she cares for Michael, she doesn't love him? Or
should she go into the more painful details: that she has fallen in
love with another man, that she has, in fact, been in love with
that man ever since the day she kissed him or he kissed her?
Should she try to make him understand how her love for Andrew
has stayed dormant much like the way some tropical viruses do,

staying harmless for years, but then, with the slightest provocation, attack with ruthless force? Her love for Andrew has taken the form of an insidious virus, and now all her body can do is surrender to it and be consumed.

As she hugs her husband tighter from behind, kissing his cold neck, letting her lips run over the goosebumps, she vacillates between these two desires: confess and destroy or drown in secrets and lies.

Sarah knows she has the ability or talent or whatever it is that would enable her to take from her husband what she needs from him, whatever that might be, while getting from Andrew what she can't obtain from Michael — love. It is this ability that makes her the great actor she is — her capacity to alter and augment parts of herself as the occasion calls for so that she can be different things to different people while at the same time keep intact that part of her that makes her who she is, whoever that might someday reveal itself to be.

"Let's go in, honey," Sarah says after a lengthy silence, lost in the contemplation of the unfathomable days ahead. "Come in from the cold."

After a moment, as if weighing the wisdom of her suggestion, Michael accepts. They go inside, close the sliding door, and slip into the warm bed that waits.

15

scar tissue

Zakhariye has no regrets yet. When he sat in front of his boss, Alan Norrad, and told him he was quitting his job as managing editor of *Scio*, a magazine to which he has devoted almost a decade of his life, the ordeal wasn't as horrible as he imagined. Had he known it would be so amicable, he wouldn't have bothered rehearsing his speech.

The speech he prepared for his boss might come in handy in a few minutes. Zakhariye sits at a window table in Trattoria Vaticano, an opulent Yorkville restaurant, the sort of establishment the likes of Sophia Loren and Catherine Deneuve dine at when they come to town for the film festival, if the pictures on the walls are to be believed. A place like this would normally make him feel at best strange and at worst downright ostentatious. But tonight is a special night, so he finds it easy to forgive himself for this overindulgence. And as he waits for Thandie to walk through the door, he is fidgety with anticipation.

Zakhariye hopes breaking the news to his wife will go as well as it did with his boss, but he realizes the odds are against him. This is personal now. Emotions and financial worries might get in the way. At least he will walk away with a decent severance pay to cushion the blow. Thandie is ten minutes late, but that is understandable, considering he told her to dress in "something sexy and elegant." "Something sexy and elegant," she warned him, would require going home after her shift at the hospital to see what her modest closet had to offer. *Modest* is too generous a word to describe Thandie's wardrobe. Shopping has always been a mysterious, unpleasant chore for her. No telling how long "sexy and elegant" could take.

The tall, sinewy waiter has already come twice to ask Zakhariye if he wants to see the drink menu. The man wasn't thrilled when he told him he doesn't drink but that his wife might have a glass of wine. Checking his watch again, Zakhariye sees Thandie speaking to the hostess, who points her in his direction. They lock eyes and wave to each other quickly. She has decided to wear her long ivory trench coat, and for a moment he holds his breath, dying to know what she is wearing underneath. He doesn't have to wait long. Thandie unbuttons her coat, takes it off, and hands it to the coat-check woman.

As she moves toward him, she takes confident, graceful steps. Her long navy slip-on dress, her single chain of large white pearls, and her hair tied in a tight, low ponytail work to create the picture of a cosmopolitan *fashionista* who has never had a rainy day in her life let alone four broken bones, a fractured pelvis, and a buried child.

Zakhariye stands, gives her a kiss on the lips, and pulls out the chair for her. "You look stunning."

"Thank you. Since you did say it was a swanky place, I decided to go all-out."

"I'm glad you did. You look very beautiful."

As she sits, Thandie surveys her surroundings. She looks so pleased, and he is happy about that. He has forgotten the sweet thrill of making her happy, something he once did quite often, more than most husbands ever manage.

"I'm on pins and needles," Thandie says with a radiant smile. "You were terribly cryptic on the phone."

"I was trying to surprise you."

"Mission accomplished. So what's the occasion? Have we won the lottery?"

Zakhariye intended to delay the news to the latter half of the evening, perhaps during dessert, but it looks as if he has no choice but to adjust his strategy. *Why don't things ever go as planned?* he wonders. "I have something I need to tell you."

"Sounds ominous. Should I be worried?"

He wants to say she has no reason to be concerned, but he knows better. He is aware of his wife's dislike of change and her inability to cope with it. Zakhariye prides himself on, if not his love for change, then at least his capacity to live with it, even thrive because of it. The death of his father when he was a year old and the subsequent financial troubles of his family ultimately made him a man when he was a boy. Immigrating to Canada and learning to master a foreign language were other changes that he not only coped with but thrived as a result of. He wishes his wife possessed some of his ability to roll with the punches, as the saying goes.

"No, it's not ominous," he tells her. "Depending on how you see it, I suppose."

"That doesn't sound very comforting."

Just as Zakhariye is about to tell her his news, their waiter, Mr. Tall, Dark, and Handsome, makes another appearance. "Have you decided on drinks?" he asks of no one in particular.

"Yes, I'll have a glass of Cabernet Sauvignon," Thandie says without looking at the wine menu.

"And I'll have a cup of coffee," Zakhariye says, ready for his wife to tease him about never drinking alcohol. The first time he told her about his abstinence from all alcohol she didn't believe him. It was on their first date. They were both students at the University of Toronto — she a poor medical student, he an even poorer English graduate student. They went to a cheap steak house on College Street where she spent the entire night trying to get him to take a sip of her drink, determined to break his will. Such a temptress she was.

Tonight, though, she forgets to tease him. All her thoughts, he expects, are focused on the reason he called her this afternoon at work and asked her to put on her best dress and meet him after work at this restaurant in Yorkville, especially since he hasn't taken her out to dinner since their son's death.

"So will I have to beat it out of you, or are you going to tell me what this is about?" Thandie asks. This time the smile has vanished. In its place is an expression of cold curiosity tinged with worry.

"I quit my job."

She leans back in her chair and wraps her arms around her chest as if suddenly chilled to the bone. "When?"

"This morning."

"Why didn't you tell me you were going to quit?"

"I didn't know I was until —"

"Fired?"

"No, of course not."

"So you planned it then?"

"No. Yes. Well, as you know, I've been unhappy at work for a long time, but it wasn't until this morning that I made the decision." Zakhariye hates lying to his wife, but it is either that or get into another fight, and he is tired of the bickering and the days, sometimes weeks, of silence that follow. One of the reasons for quitting his job was the hope that one major change in his life could be the instigator of another transformation, that a fresh

start in his professional life could somehow trigger a new beginning in their marriage. But judging from his wife's reaction now,
he might have hoped for too much.

"I know it's sudden, but we've got some savings, and with
some luck it won't —"

"Honey, I don't care about that. We'll be okay, for a while at
least. I just wish I'd known about it, that's all. I had no idea it was
so bad at work."

"It was. I dreaded going into that building every day."

Thandie reaches over the table and holds her husband's
hand. Softly, she rubs her thumb in his palm. Her earlier radiant
smile reappears.

"You're not angry with me then?" Zakhariye asks, trying but
failing to hide the incredulity in his voice.

Thandie shakes her head. "I wish I could help. What can I do?"

"This is helping — your understanding, your support."
Zakhariye smiles at her and shakes his head with disbelief. Just
when he thinks he knows all there is to know about his wife, just
when he is convinced she could never surprise him, she does
something like this. She acts in a way that is the opposite of what
he has come to expect from her. And it makes him want to get to
know her all over again.

After they finish the main course of Dorset leg of lamb with
chopped creamed goat cheese and roasted veal bone marrow
and maitake and cinnamon mushrooms, Thandie and Zakhariye
move on to dessert. Not familiar with most of the fancier items
on the menu, they decide to share an old favourite — baked
vanilla cheesecake.

As they take slow, luxurious spoonfuls of their cake, Zakhariye
feels a tinge of guilt for dreading this evening. All day long he
was in the grip of anxiety about his wife's reaction. Would she
blow up at him and storm out? Would she break into tears and

call him selfish for keeping her in the dark about a decision that would affect both of them, or fall into another one of her impenetrable silences?

But now as he sees her enjoy the cake with girlish abandon, head tilted to one side the way she did back in the days when they flirted in public and went home to make groping, hungry love, Zakhariye wonders why he imagined the worst about her. Has his feeling for his wife changed so much that he can no longer see the good in her? Has he prematurely given up on her and their marriage? These questions fill his head as he watches her across the table and is reminded of the day they met.

Zakhariye was frustrated with the pop machine on the main floor of the Wordsworth College building. He put in the money, but nothing came out. The shop where he normally got the strong cup of coffee that helped him through the mind-numbingly boring bibliography seminar was closed, and he was certain that if he didn't get some caffeine into his system, he would start snoring in class. Coca-Cola was the next best thing. Out of desperation he gave the bulky machine one final good kick, hoping it would cough up the can of Coke it was refusing to surrender. The last jolt did the trick.

He listened with joy to the sound of something heavy falling through the intricate system of tubes and passageways. A can of Orange Crush fell with a thud. Zakhariye extracted it and studied it as if it were a foreign abject. Did he press the wrong button by mistake, or was the machine playing a cruel joke? It was as if the contraption knew how much Zakhariye hated Crush and its fake citric taste. At that moment he saw her staring at him the same way he was gawking at the can, as if he, too, was a foreign object.

"You look like you've never seen a can of pop before," she said with a bemused smile.

Zakhariye was taken aback. He wasn't used to beautiful women speaking to him without a long, arduous effort on his part. "I put in all the change I had for a can of Coke. I got this instead." He immediately regretted the inanity of his words.

"A fitting allegory for life, I think."

"I'm afraid I fail to see the allegory."

"One never gets exactly what one wants."

Beautiful and philosophical — what a combination, he thought. She was still smiling, Zakhariye noticed. "Let me guess, a philosophy major?"

She laughed and shook her head. "Not even close." She fished for change in the side pocket of her bag. "Tell you what, since I like Crush, I'll buy a Coke and then we trade. What do you say?"

Zakhariye grinned like an idiot. "I'd say you're an angel." She turned away from him toward the machine. *Fuck, went too far with the angel bit,* he thought. Then she turned around with a can of Coke and exchanged it with him. "Thank you … um?"

"Thandie."

In that instant Zakhariye knew he didn't want to return to his stupid bibliography class. He would miss bibliography or any other kind of class to continue talking to her. And he did. In the weeks that followed he did something so uncharacteristic, so shocking to him — he cut numerous classes to spend many afternoons with her in the single bed in her tiny dorm room.

Something about the ease with which they talked on the day they met reminds Zakhariye how effortless it used to be between them. Could it ever be that uncomplicated again?

Things will never be the way they were. No couple endures the death of a child and emerges unscarred, but tonight for the first time since the accident he feels hope.

"Want to get out of here?" she asks as she ceremoniously wipes her mouth with a napkin.

He nods with an involuntary smile.

It is ten o'clock, and the streets of Yorkville are practically deserted. To get a cab they would have to walk south to Bloor or go west to Avenue Road or east to Bay or Yonge. They decide to head to Yonge and walk home. The cold, rainy first half of October has given way to warm, breezy weather.

"Must be Indian summer," Thandie says as they stroll side by side, hands clasped.

"Yeah, it must be. Wish it would stay like this all year."

Thandie chuckles. "You think Canada would let us in if the weather was like this all year long?"

"You think Canada welcomes immigrants because of its weather?"

"On those twenty minus Celsius days I think — no wonder they're so damn welcoming."

Zakhariye laughs half-heartedly. Part of him agrees with her, but another part doesn't like anybody taking cheap shots at Canada, not even his wife. "Hey, just remember, Canada took us in when no one else would — two broke immigrants from Somalia and Tanzania. This country gave us access to a first-rate education and a decent crack at our professions, not to mention the freedom to live in peace and dignity without having to melt into that hideous proverbial pot." He knows he probably sounds like a politician, which makes him cringe.

"That's true. But what's so wrong with assimilating, becoming one with your new country and its people? You make it sound like a concentration camp."

They continue their friendly, albeit slightly pointed banter about immigration and identity and the loss of it. More and more, Zakhariye has been thinking about the question of identity and what it really means, not just theoretically but his own identity. Does he have one? Is identity like a kidney or a gallbladder, innate, given to all, or is it like wealth, attained through genealogy, hard work, or luck? What is it based on — religion? If so, he is seriously screwed. There is nothing muddier than a Sunni Muslim with a serious fetish for Sufism — something he became fascinated by after seeing the whirling dervishes in Istanbul — and New England Transcendentalism thrown in for good measure.

Is identity based on race? He is a black man, more precisely an African-Canadian man, something he has never had a moment of doubt about and nothing but pride in. But he has never had a whole lot in common with most of the black men he has met either in school or the few he encounters in his line of work. Nor has he ever been completely at ease with his white colleagues. He doesn't drink beer or watch hockey or bitch about paying too much taxes, all of which seem like prerequisites to be like one of them.

As for his Somali community, he feels equally estranged from them. He has always been too much of an independent thinker in all matters religious, political, and sexual, and that has gotten in the way of maintaining a truly intimate relationship with Somalis in Toronto. His two cousins have tried on many occasions to involve him more in the community, inviting him to weddings of various relatives. In the rare instances when he did go, he felt lonely and out of place. They tried to take him to coffee shops on Weston Road and Lawrence Avenue West where current Middle Eastern politics and tribal conflicts back home are discussed until two in the morning. The heated debates and circuitous arguments seemed too aimless and uninformed to his Western-educated ears. So he stopped going altogether. To Zakhariye it appears that this is his lot in life: being an outsider among his own people in the living rooms of Etobicoke high-rise buildings just as he is sitting in posh downtown bistros with his white co-workers, watching them get sloshed.

So identity, as far as it means finding a place to belong, has been his struggle, his particular test, in life. For some people the crucible is the fat cells in their bodies. For others it is gambling or drugs. But figuring out who he is deep beneath the brown pigment of his skin and just where the hell home is has always been his one true foe.

His wife asking him what is so wrong with a little assimilation strikes at the heart of the matter. It sounds to him as if she is saying: if a person's identity is strong enough, it should withstand a certain amount of watering down for the good of society. Is the implication of her question that his identity is so shaky that a little assimilation would render him unrecognizable to others, or worse, to himself?

They reach the intersection of Yonge and Bloor. The area is alive with crowds going in every direction. As they wait for the red light to turn green, they face each other and lock eyes. Zakhariye leans down a little and kisses her, oblivious to the swarming mass of people around him. He feels so light and weightless he might just fly.

When they finally come apart, the light turns red again. It doesn't feel like it, but apparently they were kissing on the sidewalk long enough for the light to turn from red to green and then back to red. Now they have no choice but to wait for the next green light. As he stands there, still holding her hand, the unexpected rush of desire for Thandie envelopes him, and it feels so good and so foreign at the same time. It reminds him of the maddening way he wanted her on their wedding day when they stood in front of a judge at City Hall, impatiently waiting for the official to pronounce them husband and wife so they could run back to their barely furnished apartment.

Zakhariye had just abandoned his Ph.D. career and was looking for real work, and she had begun her first job at Mount Sinai Hospital. The idea of a big, expensive wedding was out of the question, but they both wanted more than anything to start a married life. So one morning, as they sat across from each other and ate breakfast, she took the newspaper he was reading, put it on the table, and told him they should go to City Hall and do it. It wasn't the most romantic moment of their life, but it was unplanned and unsentimental. It was real life. He didn't get down on one knee, and there were no flowers or diamond rings — simply a good-fashioned agreement to share lives.

So tonight, as they approach their townhouse, Zakhariye still holding her hand and the mint taste of Thandie's lip gloss lingering in his mouth, he wants more than anything else in the world to return to that time in their lives when they had more hope than prospects, more love than money, more laughter than silence. As he turns the key to the door of their home, Zakhariye senses his wife's weight on his back. She leans on him even more as her mouth finds the nape of his neck. He turns, and their lips touch again. Much to his surprise, he feels Thandie's hand dig into his trouser pocket and grip his erection. She giggles in his ear when she discovers how hard he is and gives him another loving squeeze. Zakhariye hasn't seen this side of her for such a long time that he was certain it was gone for good. He has never been so happy to be proven wrong. Their lips rarely come apart as they make their way up to their bedroom.

When they finally fall onto the cool duvet of their bed, Zakhariye switches on the night table lamp. In their past life they made love with the lights on. Something about seeing each other's bodies made the experience all the more intoxicating. Now Thandie reaches for the lamp and turns it off. When he manages at last to slip her dress off, he is so desperate to get a glimpse of her body that he instinctively gropes for the lamp. Her hand intercepts his and guides it back to her breasts.

"I want to see you," he whispers, making another attempt for the lamp.

She holds his hand to her breast, this time hard. He tries to wiggle out of her grasp. "Don't," she mutters irritably.

"I just —"

"Please don't," Thandie interrupts, her voice cracking.

Zakhariye knows that tears can't be too far behind when her voice breaks like that. "Hey, hey, it's okay, baby. We don't have to turn the lights on."

They continue kissing, but the hunger has slipped away. Their touches become softer, more tentative, sexless. A certain eggshell fragility smothers everything. As he reaches down to take her panties off, Thandie's insistence on darkness becomes apparent to him. His fingers brush the scar tissue running from her upper inner thigh all the way to the back of her knee. Since he hasn't seen her naked thighs in such a long time, he has completely forgotten about the gash she received when the paramedics tried frantically to remove her from their mangled Honda for fear it might catch fire.

Despite the invasion of many unwanted memories, Zakhariye continues, determined not to let this beautiful night be contaminated by the past. Once inside her, the hunger slowly returns. Their bodies remember how to get back lost passion even if their minds don't. Amid their moans and kisses, Zakhariye hears his wife say something, but he can't make it out. "What is it, sweetheart?" he asks, the tenderness in his voice surprising him.

"Let's do it," she says, this time clearly.

"Do what, sweetie?"

"Have a baby. I want to have a baby with you."

Zakhariye freezes.

"Please, Zhaki," she whispers in his ear as she grabs his buttocks and tries to move his hips.

It is no use. Zakhariye feel himself softening. He rolls off her and lies lifelessly next to her.

16

the lavender dress

Gregory hasn't gotten out of the house in five days. Eight, cold, lonely weeks have passed since his wife's funeral, and every day he wakes up with the intention of getting dressed, going out to get a haircut, and buying some mangoes from the grocery shop on his way. For some inexplicable reason he has been craving mangoes. Somewhere between showering and getting dressed, however, Gregory always loses focus, his will evaporates, and he abandons the plan completely.

It seems that lately a task as simple as making his bed requires an extraordinary effort. The other day Gregory tried changing the sheets on his bed. He stripped off the old sheets, took out fresh ones from the linen closet, then lost interest in the task halfway and simply covered the bed with the comforter. For two nights he has been sleeping on a bare mattress.

Gregory can sense the same thing happening to him now as he stands in the walk-in closet of his bedroom and stares at his side of the closet. Earlier, while eating dinner with Andrew, he told his son that he intended to go out for a haircut, and when

Andrew left for his evening shift, Gregory came upstairs with the sole purpose of making himself look presentable.

He put on his favourite Frank Sinatra record, shaved, and took a long, luxurious shower. When he left the bathroom, he was filled with the sense of possibility that comes from the thrill of a mission. But now, in his closet, having just put on his underwear, the sense of possibility that was so enthralling a few minutes ago has vanished. Instead he gapes at his clothes, unable to remember what he planned to do. For many long minutes he looks at his clothes until he turns to the other side of the closet where his wife's garments still hang. *Must do something about them,* he thinks as he touches one of his wife's dresses, a formless egg-white cotton summer dress. He can't remember Ella ever wearing such a frumpy frock.

Gregory tries to picture her in this dress, but his mind is blank. He moves on to one of her blouses, but it, too, conjures no memory of her. Panic grips him. The more he tries to think of his wife in any of these clothes, the blanker his mind becomes, as though someone has taken a giant eraser to his brain.

Desperate, Gregory indiscriminately pulls whatever item of clothing he can get his hands on off the hangers. Fingering them, holding them, he attempts to place them in the proper context. Perhaps she wore them at a dinner party or on a weekend trip. Maybe if he had one memory of Ella in one of these dresses, his terrifying fear of erasure would stop. At last he comes to the lavender dress Ella wore to Andrew's wedding last year, and instantly, as if a switch has been turned on, there she is in his mind's eye, as real and fully embodied as she was on that late summer day.

It was a beautiful August Sunday in the garden. Ella wore the lavender dress that matched many of the irises in her garden, its asymmetrical tail flowing behind her as she stood beside Gregory, watching Andrew and a four-month-pregnant Rosemary exchange vows. By then Ella was at the front end of a rigorous chemotherapy regime that her oncologist had recommended as a last resort. As a result, she had lost every strand of hair on her body. She made herself two long, arching eyebrows where there was nothing but bare flesh above her eyes, put on her prized gigantic, round white straw hat, the kind only Audrey Hepburn could get away with, and topped everything off with a pair of black oversize sunglasses.

Gregory remembers observing her instead of his son. He can still see the single teardrop that rolled down Ella's cheek as Andrew kissed his new wife. No one else cried that day except Ella. It was as if she were witnessing the realization of a dream only she held: Andrew and Rosemary, at last husband and wife.

He holds up the dress and imagines the way it hung over his wife's thin frame. Back in her healthy days, it would have emphasized her every beautiful curve. *Ah, what a vision,* he thinks. The next thing he knows he has his hands up and is squeezing the dress down his wide shoulders. It hung beautifully on his wife's body, but on him it clings to his broad back, round waist, and chunky, hairy thighs. The material cuts into his armpits, and his arms tingle from loss of circulation.

But Gregory doesn't care. He carries on. Nothing must interfere with the recovery of the vision he has of Ella in this dress. As long as he holds on to that beautiful picture on that sunny August day, she isn't gone.

Curious to see what he looks like, Gregory walks out of the privacy of the closet and into the bright light of the bedroom. He struts over to the mirror on the dresser and glances at himself. The tight lavender dress that clings to his belly and shoulders and the white chest hair that peeks out of the low V cut of the dress would have made him scream in horror had he been in his normal state of mind, but tonight all he sees is the image of his wife from that day, so alive and happy even as her organs were surrendering one by one.

More than how she looked, it was her determination to celebrate the wedding of her only son to a girl she loved and her desire to enjoy herself despite her physical deterioration and the approaching end it signified that made Gregory fall in love with her all over again. And now, as he sits on his wife's makeup chair in front of the dresser where all of Ella's lotions and perfumes remain untouched, Gregory only has a crazed hunger to re-create that picture.

As he sings along with Sinatra's "My Way," he reaches for a container of foundation powder, takes out the soft pink powder puff, and dabs some on his face. Not knowing the right amount to use, he goes overboard and makes himself look like a geisha on crack. Next he turns his attention to the lipsticks. There are four different kinds on the dresser. He opens each one and examines it carefully.

Finally, he settles on the last lipstick he opens, scarlet red, the kind women wore when he was a horny teenager. Using more force than is required for this delicate task, he puts on so much of the substance that his lips become heavy with what feels like a layer of cold grease. *This can't be right,* he thinks.

Gregory recalls kissing his wife after she did her lipstick and liking the thin layer of that substance whose taste changed depending on which type she was wearing. He wipes his lips and reapplies, this time delicately, precisely, until it is just right. Encouraged, he picks up the eyeliner pencil and gently traces it around the bottom of his eyes.

There are several other kinds of makeup paraphernalia whose purpose and how to use them is a mystery to him. So he stops while he is ahead and looks at himself in the mirror. The makeup seems okay, but something is amiss.

Then it dawns on him — hair is missing from the equation. His short white hair is ruining his hard work. He gets up and searches for his wife's brown shoulder-length one-hundred-percent human hair wig that she started wearing after she began chemotherapy. Ella had many wonderful virtues, but lack of vanity wasn't one of them. He remembers her telling him once: "Just because I have cancer doesn't mean I have to walk around like the kids in those damn save-this-child commercials." No one could have ever accused Ella of soliciting sympathy because of her illness.

Gregory finally finds the wig in the bottom drawer of the dresser. He feels the rush of locating the last missing piece. *It's all coming together,* he thinks as he carefully places the elastic ring of the wig around his head and adjusts it a couple of times. It is still lopsided, so he gives it several nudges this way and that, then leaves it alone. *Focus on the big picture,* he tells himself.

He gets up and takes several steps back to see the "big picture" in the mirror. The thick bush of chest hair sticking out of the V neck line of the dress is ruining the effect, he concludes. As he tries to come up with a way to remedy this problem, he hears two gentle knocks on the door, followed by Andrew saying, "Dad?"

Gregory turns toward the door as a wave of panic hits him. "Wait! Don't Come in!" He runs toward the closet, but it is too late. Two steps toward the safety of the closet, and the door is wide open. Their eyes lock, and for Gregory the moment lasts a lifetime. All he can see is his son gawking at him. It is an expression completely devoid of recognition. His son, his own flesh and blood, stands before him, eyeing him as if he were a deranged stranger.

"Don't look at me like that!" Gregory demands.

"What the fuck are you doing, Dad?"

"Go away!" Gregory screams as he scurries into the closet and slams the door. Once inside the closet, he tosses the wig and tries to peel the dress off. He lifts it over his head, but it gets stuck around his thick shoulders. In his eagerness to remove the garment he rips the fabric. He attempts to slip it off with all his strength, but it doesn't budge. Gregory gets hot and sweaty under the dress, and his breathing becomes rapid and shallow. He wants desperately to call out for Andrew's help, but the mere thought of standing in front of his son with his wife's dress pulled over his head makes him wish for a speedy, violent death. So he struggles in the closet by himself. Finally, he manages to get the dress off. Exhausted and on the verge of tears, Gregory slumps onto the cold hardwood floor of the closet.

Later that night Gregory finally emerges from his room. After removing the last trace of his wife's makeup from his face and back in his own clothes, he tiptoes out of his room, desperate for something to eat. On his way downstairs to the kitchen he passes his son's room. There is light under the door, and he hears Andrew's voice. He stands close and listens.

"I really think he's losing it, Natalie," Andrew says. There is a long pause. "I haven't got a clue what he's feeling. He rarely comes out of his room, and when he does, he barely talks, so how the hell should I know?"

There is another pause, this one longer. Gregory would love to hear what Natalie is saying. He wonders if his daughter is defending him.

Andrew chuckles. "Right, I could just see Dad sitting on a couch spilling his guts to some therapist." Another pause. "Hold on. I'll see if he's still up."

As soon as Gregory hears Andrew say this, he tiptoes back to his room, but Andrew swings the door open before he can reach safety. Gregory turns around. His son is holding the cordless phone.

"It's Natalie. She wants to talk to you."

"Tell her I've gone to bed."

"Nat, here he is. Now you can tell him he needs a shrink." Andrew passes the phone to his father, who snatches it, goes into his room, and slams the door like a petulant teenager.

At eight in the morning after a restless night Gregory comes downstairs and goes into the kitchen to find Rosemary handing Hanna to Andrew. He is getting used to her morning visits when she drops off his granddaughter for Andrew to look after while she is at work. At five o'clock most afternoons she picks up Hanna so that Andrew can work the evening shift in his cab. It is a shaky arrangement, but it seems to be working so far. Oddly enough, Andrew and Rosemary appear to get along better now that they are separated.

"Bye, sweetie," Rosemary says, kissing Hanna on the forehead. "Mommy will see you later."

Hanna smiles contentedly in her father's arms. Gregory is amazed at how undisturbed she is watching her mother leave. He remembers how, as infants, Andrew and Natalie wailed hysterically whenever their mother left them in his care. Every morning he marvels at the way Hanna is just as happy to be with Andrew as she is to be with her mother, and for that he envies his son.

Not seeing Gregory outside the kitchen door, Rosemary almost bumps into him as she exits and he enters. "Oh, hi, Dad. Sleeping any better?" She pecks him on the cheek quickly.

Gregory takes silent delight in the fact that Rosemary still calls him "Dad" even though she and his son are separated. "I'm all right. It could always be worse, right?"

"Yes, it could. Take care of yourself." She heads for her car, while Andrew stands at the front door, holding Hanna's hand and waving it at her mother.

In the kitchen Gregory fixes himself breakfast. Fried eggs are what he craves today. For weeks now he has been eating the whole-wheat crap his wife used to force on him, and he is sick of it. *Fuck fibre!* he thinks. Since Ella's passing, Gregory has continued to eat the so-called healthy cereal partly out of respect but mostly out of fear, as though she can see what he is doing from the grave. Now he takes out a skillet, pours oil into it, and turns on the stove. By the time he cracks the eggs, the oil in the skillet is burning and the kitchen fills with smoke.

"Dad, what are you doing?" Andrew demands as he enters the kitchen.

"Making fried eggs and toast. Want some?"

"The only thing you'll be making is a house fire. Here, hold Hanna. I'll do it."

"I can fry eggs, for crying out loud. I'm not an imbecile."

"No one's saying you are, Dad. Just sit down and hold her for me."

Andrew hands Hanna to his father. Gregory takes his granddaughter, sits at the table next to the big window, and watches Andrew fry eggs and make toast and coffee simultaneously. He zigzags between these tasks with a grace that amazes Gregory, making him jealous.

Hanna wiggles on Gregory's lap, desperate for freedom. He realizes he has been holding her too tightly for fear of dropping her. "Oh, don't cry. Don't cry, little girl," he says to her in a high-pitched singsong that makes him sound more frantic and nervous than soothing and fun. The more he talks to her that way the more she tries to escape. Gregory bounces her up and down, but the jerky movement makes her even more agitated. He glances at Andrew for help. "I don't think she likes me."

"Make funny faces at her. She likes that."

Gregory pouts and opens his eyes as wide as he can while making little kissing sounds. Hanna cries.

"You're scaring her, Dad."

"You said to make faces."

"Funny, not scary faces. Here, I'll show you." Scooping his daughter out of Gregory's lap, Andrew sticks out the bottom half of his jaw à la Marlon Brando in *The Godfather* and says "What's the matter for you, huh?" in a bad Italian Mob accent. Hanna quits crying instantly.

Gregory feels the sharp pang of failure as he watches Hanna's crying face give way to her usual happy, wide-eyed expression. He hates being one of those people children recoil from. He would love to soothe his granddaughter the way his son does and vows to learn how.

Andrew puts a plate of fried eggs and three slices of toast on the table in front of his father, then goes over to the coffee maker, pours a cup, and brings it to him while still making faces at Hanna, who is now completely riveted.

"Thank you," Gregory says sheepishly.

"You're welcome."

Andrew sits on the opposite side of the table with his own cup of coffee. After several hungry mouthfuls, Gregory turns away from his food. "About last night —"

"Dad, you don't have to explain. I understand."

"You do?"

"Well, no, not really, but I'm sure you had a good reason. This is your house. You're entitled to do whatever you want in it."

"You don't need to say it like that."

"Like what?"

"'This is your house,'" Gregory mimics his son. "'You can do whatever you want.' You make me sound depraved, like I was torturing little kittens up there."

"No, Dad, I just don't want you to feel like you have to justify yourself."

Gregory feels his son's eyes on him as he devours his breakfast.

"Taste good?" Andrew asks.

"Very good," Gregory mumbles through a mouthful.

"Did you start looking for a lawyer?"

Gregory shakes his head. Hanna gapes at him across the table. He wonders what the little girl thinks when she tilts her head and stares at him like that. *Do they have thoughts at that age? Do they have a consciousness?*

"Dad, the trial's in two months. You better find a lawyer. You need a damn good case for why you beat up that poor man."

"The man was twice my size, for crying out loud. I merely pushed him."

"You don't seem to be taking this seriously. Battery's a serious offence."

In his mind Gregory scoffs at the word *battery.* "I've decided to do it," he says suddenly, changing the subject.

"You've decided to do what?"

"I'm going to donate them to Goodwill, your mother's clothes, I mean."

Andrew lights up with a smile. "I think that's a great idea, Dad. Want some help?"

"You've got your hands full with Hanna. Besides, it'll give me something to do."

Andrew hoists his daughter and smells her diaper. "Good girl," he says as though filling her diaper is akin to winning a Nobel Prize for chemistry. "C'mon, let's get you cleaned up."

Getting up, Andrew leaves the kitchen with Hanna. Gregory gazes out the kitchen window at the garden as he eats the last mouthful of eggs. It is the time of year when his wife would work in the garden to prepare it for winter. *The clothes first, then a lawyer,* he thinks. Once he takes care of that, he will cover the plants in the garden, rake all the leaves in the yard, then learn how to make funny faces to entertain his granddaughter.

Gregory composes a mental list of the chores he will have to perform without Ella by his side. This isn't how he envisioned he would spend his retirement days, but there is no point in wasting time yearning for what was. Sighing, he sips his coffee and watches the autumn leaves blow in the wind.

17

the magic of thought

Perfect, Andrew thinks as he studies the eight-and-half-by-eleven photograph of Sarah. This is the fifth exposure. He threw away the first four because he either overdeveloped them or under-developed them. Andrew is surprised he used nearly an entire roll of film on Sarah that day. He recalls reaching for his camera as she dried herself with his shirt. Something about the way her face shimmered with rain or the gentle light that shone on the wet windowpane of the passenger seat that backlit her or her slight, nervous, but genuine smile inspired him to immortalize the moment. *Even if I never see her again,* he now thinks, *at least I'll have something of her.*

Andrew hasn't seen Sarah since that day, and hardly an hour has passed that he hasn't thought about her. Mundane recollections of the way her wet, matted hair clung to her neck or her tendency to emphasize her words with sharp, elegant gestures randomly drift in and out of his mind as he goes about his day. These remembered details of Sarah give him a lift, a degree of levity to his current situation, which has been particularly cheerless since he made the mistake of confessing adultery to his wife. His depression has only been compounded by moving back to his boyhood room in his father's house and sleeping in his creaky single bed surrounded by swimming trophies and other souvenirs from his past.

When he thinks about Sarah, however, not so much the possibility they might one day end up together, for that seems more unlikely than ever, but the fact that she exists, that she is out there somewhere and he has known her, however briefly, gives him the one thing he doesn't have much of these days — hope.

Using a small clothespin, Andrew attaches the photograph of Sarah to the long, thin rope he has hung across the basement from one wall to the other. The rope is lined with numerous portraits. He asked his father last week for permission to turn the basement into a temporary dark room to develop the photographs he has been shooting for months.

When Andrew finishes hanging the new batch of photos, he turns off the red light and switches on the regular bulb, wincing from the brightness as he takes down several photographs he developed two days ago. These are the pictures he has selected from the contact proof sheet using his beloved antique loupe that his old boss at Reuters gave him as a going-away present. Carefully, he checks for light, shadows, subject expression, tone and mood, and thematic consistence.

Andrew doesn't quite know what he wants out of these pictures, but he discovers what he is aiming for by process of elimination. Sometimes a photo is cut because of something as simple as a streak of street light in the background that ruins the mood of the picture. At other times it is precisely because of the way street light from the rear or side windows of his taxi casts a glow on the subject's face that brings out some unique quality that makes an otherwise okay picture beautiful, even haunting. Andrew takes from the rope one such photograph — a picture of Pauletta Jean-Baptiste. She is his favourite and most memorable subject to date.

_____

Andrew met Pauletta at one o'clock in the morning on a dry, breezy July night. He had dropped his last customer of the night and planned to head home and collapse into bed when at the corner of Adelaide and Jarvis she hailed him. Andrew wanted to pretend he hadn't seen her, but she seemed lonely and distressed. So he made a quick U-turn, and in a flash she was in the back seat as if desperate to get away from something or someone. She told him she lived pretty far away — all the way to Rexdale in the northwest — and gave him the address.

As he drove, he stole glances through the rearview mirror: early thirties with luminous brown skin; a strong, almost masculine jaw; and large black eyes that displayed fierce, world-weary intelligence that didn't have to be spoken or declared. Andrew watched as she rummaged through her fake Louis Vuitton purse.

"Fuck me," she muttered with annoyance, then looked up at him. Their eyes met. "Sorry."

"Bad night?"

"The worst. And now I can't find my fucking cigarettes. Got any?"

"Nah, sorry." He drove for a couple of blocks, occasionally peeking at her as she dragged her long, colourfully decorated nails through her hair, looking pissed. "I have a joint if you're really desperate for something." Andrew was surprised by his casual willingness to offer narcotics to a complete stranger.

"I sure could use it after the night I've had."

Andrew extracted a joint and a lighter from the pocket of his leather jacket and handed them to her.

She lit the roach and rolled down the window halfway. "Thanks, honey."

"No worries."

Suppressed giggles escaped from her that turned to full laughter. "You're a man ..."

"Guilty as charged," he said with a smile.

"Then explain this to me — what the fuck's wrong with y'all?"

"What?"

"You heard me. Your whole sex is fucked!"

"You're beginning to sound like my wife."

"Sounds like my kind of girl."

"So why the man-hating? Did something bad happen tonight?"

"I ain't man-hating. Just saying it like I see it, and believe me, I seen it all. Every fucking night I see how twisted y'all are. Lord, y'all are twisted."

Andrew laughed, partly because he found her funny but also to show her he took no offence on behalf of his sex.

"Like tonight, this dude with his fancy apartment and pictures of his little blond wife and cute kids all over the place, prob-. ably a banker or a politician or something big like that, and what does he ask for? A massage? A blow job? A little light spanking? 'Cause I be down with that. But, no, he just had to bring out this nasty, motherfucker dildo the size of my arm and had the nerve to ask me to use it on him."

Andrew tried to contain his laughter, but it was no use. He got a mental image of an old white man on all fours asking this fierce, sexy, no-nonsense black woman to fuck him with a giant dildo. "So ... so did you do it?"

"For $300? You better fucking believe I did! These rich white folk, man, they unreal. No offence or nothing."

"Hey, none taken. I may be white, but I'm not rich, as you can see."

"I hear you, hon."

"So the other guys don't ask for, you know ...?"

"No! It's always the rich white dudes. Hispanics or brothers or even the working-class white dudes just ask for regular stuff. But the rich white men —" she shook her head "— better watch out for those. They wanna be stepped on, slapped, strapped, penetrated, and anything else their fucked-up minds can think of."

"Sounds like an interesting job," Andrew said. "Doing it long?"

"Two years now. About a year and eleven months longer than I thought I would."

"Yeah, some jobs have a way of sucking you in."

"Tell me about it. It ain't too bad, though. Not as bad as they make it out to be. I get to choose who, when, where, what, how much, and ain't no motherfucker pimp taking a cent from me."

"But the burnout rate's pretty high, no? It's not really the kind of job you can do for a long time."

"True, true. But every job got its downside. What they say, dentists have the highest suicide rate?"

"No shit!" Andrew was genuinely surprised.

"Read it some where. Couldn't believe my eyes."

"Why dentists?"

"Why not dentists? Spending their whole lives looking at nasty teeth and infections and shit. Honey, I'd shoot myself, too."

Andrew laughed again. There was something about the way this woman's mind worked that intrigued and delighted him. "Is it true that most girls have plans? Something they're saving up for?"

"Yeah, but some are just lying to themselves." She switched to a perfect Valley Girl accent. "'I'm just doing this, like, until I finish medical school, so I can, like, open my own practice and work with kids because, like, I really, really, really love kids.'"

Pauletta's ruthless realism and indifference to other people's perceptions fascinated Andrew. He wished he could get to know her better, find out her backstory, how she ended up becoming the fierce woman with artificial nails and a fake Louis Vuitton bag. "What about you? Do you have plans?"

"Sure do. But I don't kid myself. I save my money, invest."

"Invest?"

She snorted. "Hell, yeah. Stocks. Bonds. Even got me an adviser. Darnel, my fiancé, he's saving, too. Got our eyes on this five-room bed and breakfast outside Kingston."

"Fiancé?"

"Yeah, fiancé. Why, you surprised?"

"What does he do?"

"A bouncer. Ever heard of For Your Eyes Only?"

"Yeah."

She laughed. "I bet you have. Probably go there every night. I know your kind."

"Nah, I don't go. I take a lot of businessmen there, though."

"Yeah, that place is crawling with them business types. That's another thing about men I don't get — strip joints. It's just tits-and-ass people. Ain't nothing special there you aint never seen before."

"I know, I know. It's another one of those baffling things we men do. So does your fiancé mind?"

"Mind what?'

"Oh, come on, you know what I mean."

"Yeah, I know. Nah, he's cool with it. He knows where my heart's at."

"Sounds like a smart man."

"Sure is."

Andrew turned onto Martin Grove Road at Finch Avenue. "Are your evenings always so adventurous?"

"Yeah, always. Always something new, man. I tell you, in this line of work, nothing surprises me about people no more. Everything they ever told you about people turns out to be a lie.

Ain't nobody what they seem like. Just when you think you know them, *bam*, they turn around and show you a different side."

"I take it you like it then, your work, I mean."

She was quiet for a moment as if trying to construct the perfect response. "What you say your name was?"

"Andrew. And you?"

"Pauletta Jean-Baptiste. Now, Andrew, you look to me like a smart man ..."

"I like to think I am."

"So why you go and ask me a dumb-ass question like that?"

Andrew was taken aback by her sharp change in tone, but he understood it. "You're right. That was a dumb-ass question. I apologize."

"No apologies necessary. I just know you know better, is all."

Their eyes met again through the rearview mirror, and they smiled at each other, a kindred spirits, comrades-in-the-night sort of smile. As Andrew pulled into the driveway of her home, one of many public housing two-storey red-brick townhouses in the development, he looked around while she fished for money in her purse. He pondered what the urban planners and city officials were thinking when they built this sorry excuse for low-income housing. It was clear to him they, whoever they were, thought the poor had no need for beauty, no room for aesthetics in their lives. Pauletta handed him two crisp twenties and a ten. Andrew double-checked the meter, which read $35.40.

"For the conversation," she said.

"Thank you. It was great talking to you, too."

Before she stepped out, Andrew summoned the courage to ask if he could take some photographs of her. She stared at him as if he had solicited a lock of her hair, but then she smiled. "Sure thing, honey."

It took five minutes or so to get some shots of her gazing straight into the camera, her large black eyes sad and fierce with a hint of mischief. Andrew also requested a few profile pictures, which he obtained by getting out of the car and shooting from the open windows of both sides. As he was taking the pictures, he explained to her about the project he was working on and the kind of photos he was attempting to get. She didn't appear to understand the purpose or value of what he was doing but seemed to trust him and wished him well when he slipped her a cheap business card he had printed at Office Depot. When he was done, she got out of the taxi, opened the front door of her townhouse, waved, and disappeared from his life.

Andrew stares at the photo of Pauletta and wonders where she is and what has become of her dreams. As he walks the length of rope across the basement, he thinks about all the people he has photographed and the stories they shared with him. Like the wacky Nigerian philosophy professor with the bushy Einstein hair he picked up from the airport last spring on the way to a Nietzsche conference to give a lecture on the immorality of suffering. He and Andrew got into a debate that almost turned into a shouting match about the professor's theory that home-less people were hostile toward those better off simply to inflict suffering on them. The man seemed to believe that the homeless were on the street for the sole purpose of pissing him off.

The next photograph on the rope is of Liam and Anthony, a young, clearly in love couple who fought relentlessly from Woodbridge all the way to their loft on King Street East and Portland. Liam was hurt by a comment Anthony's mother had made, and Anthony either couldn't or didn't want to understand

Liam's point of view. Desperate for an ally, Liam asked Andrew's opinion. As much as Andrew didn't want to get involved in the private affairs of his customers, that day he found himself playing peacemaker.

Andrew managed to show Anthony how hurtful his mother's words might have been for Liam and was also able to get Liam to see things from Anthony's perspective. Liam told Andrew, "That was the best therapy session we ever had, and we've had plenty."

As Andrew studies the picture of Liam and Anthony he selected from the fifteen he took of them that day, he understands why he chose it, even though there were five others that were better. He shot this one through the closed window of his taxi from the outside. It was a beautiful spring day, and there was enough light to let him play with the composition a little. He focused on the couple through the window and captured both of their profiles: Liam leaning back in the seat, Anthony a little forward.

The result is a portrait of a loving couple as seen through the glass of a car window. *This could very well be the best of the collection,* Andrew thinks as he moves on to the other photographs. There is one of Zakhariye and his wife, Thandie, that he took on a rainy afternoon back in March. Large raindrops dot the glass behind his friends, giving the photo a romantic Parisian atmosphere.

There is a picture of a nun Andrew gave a free ride to on a bitterly cold day back in January when he saw her shivering at a bus stop at the corner of Bathurst Street and Dupont Avenue at the edge of the Annex, with no bus in sight. When he dropped her at her convent, she blessed him, and Andrew remembers feeling happy even though he no longer believes in God.

The downsides are, of course, numerous. There is the lack of respect, the bouts of boredom, and the random risk of danger. Last month in Toronto a cab driver was stabbed to death. There are also the drunk twenty-somethings he often picks up on Saturday nights who puke in the back seat; the corporate snobs who look down their noses at him; and most disturbing of all, the racists who spout hatred like the Aryan Nation guy who said to him as they drove through Little Jamaica, "This town's turning into fucking Niggerville."

Normally, Andrew restrained himself, but he had spent much of that morning listening to Nina Simone's anthem "Mississippi Goddamn," which must have inspired the righteous militant in him. Andrew stepped on the brakes, turned to the bigot, and snarled, "Get the fuck out of my car!" The man got out, called him a nigger lover, and slammed the door so hard he almost broke the window.

Despite all the shortcomings of his job, it is the only one he can think of that keeps him constantly in touch with people from every walk of life: a Catholic nun one day, a prostitute the following night, an immigrant from New Delhi one afternoon, followed by a managing director of a Fortune 500 company. In this fashion Andrew presides over a moving portal through which humanity walks for seven hours a day. He roams the city and encounters innumerable scenes that entice him: an old hunchback Chinese woman crossing the street in Chinatown; a scrawny, tattooed teenager with a Mohawk washing windshields for a buck; a little boy in a Superman outfit trailing behind his father on their way to trick or treat; a black teenage girl with an iPod dangling from her ears in a bus shelter, dancing to a beat all her own. Andrew captures these scenes with a quick roll of the window and several snaps.

He loves taking pictures of people on the street who are unaware they are being photographed. It is photography at its least conscious and at its most honest and visceral. Taking these candid shots always reminds him of *Faith and Confidence*, William C. Beall's Pulitzer Prize–winning 1957 photo depicting a quiet moment between a cop and a two-year-old boy amid the chaos of a Washington, D.C., parade. That picture inspired Andrew to become a photographer. He encountered it when he was six-teen during a school trip to the Toronto Reference Library on Yonge Street.

Andrew studied the photograph, which he found in a book, for what seemed like hours, so touched was he by the big cop bending to look into the eyes of the little boy who leans forward playfully, keenly. He wondered what the boy and the cop had said to each other and wished he had a time machine to whisk him to the scene that had taken place before he was born. That a com-plete stranger would treat a child with such respect and sympathy, and that a little boy would regard that stranger without a trace of fear or distrust, moved him profoundly.

He photocopied the picture, took it home, pinned it on the wall of his bedroom, and contemplated it every day. Later he bought a print of it and still has it. To him Beall's photo is the gold standard to aspire to. However, it wasn't until he came across the staggering work of war photographer James Nachtwey, whose book *Deeds of War* is Andrew's Bible and one of his most prized possessions, that he focused his general aspiration to take pictures into a career as a photojournalist.

Andrew has hundreds of candid moments of strangers in the middle of their lives from cities around the world. He keeps them in several banker boxes. One of these days he plans to sift through the shots to see what can do with them — perhaps a book of photographs that does for others what *Deeds of War* did for him. *One day.* But tonight he has other, more urgent matters on his mind.

He leaves the basement, carrying the photo of Sarah. She told him principal photography for her film would wrap up in a week and that she would return to New York right after. Initially, she refused to see him again, but after a whole lot of cajoling she agreed to meet him before leaving town.

Now Andrew has less than two hours to shower, get dressed, and go to a photo shop to have her picture framed. He wants to give it to her as a memento of that rainy day they last met, hoping that having it in her possession will keep those moments they spent together fresh in her mind.

Andrew goes through two changes of wardrobe: first, a navy suit that makes him look too desperate, followed by blue jeans and a sports jacket that scream, "Trying too hard to be casual." Finally, he settles on ivory dress pants, a light blue shirt, and his ubiquitous brown leather jacket. The overall effect projects a confident, carefree man about town, which is far from the way he feels. Still, looking the part is half the battle. As he grabs his car keys from the mahogany table in the foyer, Andrew checks himself one more time in the mirror that hangs over the table. He smoothes his combed-back hair with his palm more out of habit than to improve anything.

"Off to see the girls?" his father asks from the doorway to the kitchen where he stands holding a cup of coffee. He is still in his pajamas.

Andrew forces a smile. His father knows that since Andrew has Hanna all morning and Rosemary takes her home in the evenings, it is unlikely he would be going over there. But it seems Gregory is attempting to express disapproval in his own not-so-sly manner. "No, Dad, I'm not off to see the girls."

"I was just wondering. You're looking pretty swanky."

"I'm just going out. Nothing special." Judging by the way Gregory is staring, he is obviously curious about what Andrew is holding in his hand. Andrew has covered Sarah's photo with flimsy gift wrap to protect it until he gets it framed. "See you later, Dad."

Andrew makes for the door. Just as he opens it, he glances at his father, who is fixed to the same spot, still wearing an expression of fatherly disapproval.

———

Twenty minutes have elapsed, and Andrew is getting agitated. He has played this scene in his head over and over since Sarah agreed to meet him. Now he just wants to get on with it and see if the reality lives up to his fantasies. He stands across King Street, directly facing the front entrance of the King Edward Hotel where Sarah told him the *Lady Chatterly's Lover* company is staging a wrap party for the cast and some of the other talents such as the cinematographer and the costume designer. Since Sarah is returning to New York City in two days, seeing her has an added urgency.

At last Sarah crosses the street and comes toward him. She is wearing a long cream dress studded with numerous shiny beads that look like tiny diamonds and has a navy shawl draped over her for protection against the harsh wind. Andrew notices he is holding his breath and has to remind himself to inhale. He feels light-headed from lack of oxygen as she stands before him, face flushed from the evening chill.

"Hi," she says almost shyly.

"Hello," he replies, finally taking the deep breath he has been denying himself.

They consider each other silently for a few moments until Sarah kisses him on the cheek. *I hope she likes it,* Andrew thinks about the Polo cologne he bought yesterday for this encounter. He has never worn cologne before. But as she breaks the hug, she seems not to have noticed the scent.

"It's good to see you." Andrew produces the photograph he developed for her, which he wrapped in a red-and-gold paper. "For you."

"A gift? I have nothing for you. Now I feel bad."

"No, please don't. It's nothing really, just ..." Andrew gives her the present.

Sarah opens the package carefully as if afraid to break what-ever is in it. "You've wrapped it so beautifully that it's a shame to tear the paper." She raises a hand to her mouth, holding the tips of her fingers to her lips when she sees the photograph. "It's gorgeous. Thank you. This is … I don't know what to say." She hugs him unexpectedly, wrapping her arms around his neck and kissing his cheek again. "You've made me look so beautiful."

"I can't take credit for that."

Sarah finally lets Andrew go as pedestrians manoeuvre around them.

"Can we go some place less —" Andrew begins to ask.

"I really must get back to the party."

"Let me drive you to your hotel after you're finished here."

"I don't think that's a good idea."

"No funny business. I promise. I just want to talk."

"We can talk here."

"Are you afraid of me?"

"No, of course not."

"You sound afraid."

"Don't be silly."

"Then what is it?"

"I just don't think it's a good idea — you and me alone."

"Then you *are* afraid of what might happen."

She frowns at him. "And just what do you think might happen?"

"The same thing that happened the last time we were alone."

"That was a mistake."

"That's bullshit and you know it."

Sarah shakes her head and begins to walk away.

He goes after her and stands in front of her. "You don't really believe it was a mistake."

She pushes him out of the way. "Don't do that, okay? I hate it when you do that."

"When I do what?"

"Tell me how I feel."

"Then *you* tell me how you feel."

"How I feel is none of your business," Sarah snaps, frustration getting the better of her. She leans against a wall, and he slouches beside her, making sure their shoulders touch. "Why are you doing this?" she asks, not looking at him.

"Doing what?"

"You're not stupid, so don't act like it."

"I love you," he says, gazing at her intently. "That's why."

"Fuck you, Andrew!" She crosses the street as fast as she can. A speeding minivan narrowly misses her as its driver honks his horn.

Andrew watches helplessly, his heart jumping into his throat. He dashes after her and seizes her by the arm before she enters the hotel. "I'm sorry. I shouldn't have said that. Please don't go in. Not yet. Please."

"What is it you want, Andrew?" Sarah cries, prompting the stares of several pedestrians. "Just what do you want from me?"

"I want to talk to you. Come with me. Ten minutes — that's all I'm asking."

She doesn't budge. They move away from the door to allow a well-dressed elderly couple to exit.

"Where?" she asks.

"Your hotel room."

Sarah heads for the King Edward door again.

"Okay, okay, no hotel. Just some place less awkward. There's a park nearby."

She thinks for a minute, then nods. Andrew suppresses the grin he wants to flash, knowing that will spook her. Everything he does or says seems to irritate her. As they head eastward past Church Street toward St. James Park, Andrew's spirits rise at the thought of spending a little more time with her. It will give him another chance to appeal to her, to speak to that part of her he knows he touched the day they made love. When they enter the park, Andrew is surprised at how pleasant it is even at nine o'clock at night in mid-November.

"It's pretty here," Sarah says. "I've passed this park many times, but I've never stopped to see it, certainly never at night."

"In the summer if I happen to be around the park at noon I bring my lunch here. It's very nice."

There is a long, uncomfortable silence.

"What are we doing here, Andrew?"

"You just said you liked it here."

"I don't mean the stupid park. God, why do you insist on being so obtuse tonight? What I mean is, what's the point of this? I'm married. You're married. It's hopeless."

"It doesn't have to be."

"Really? How do you figure that?"

"I've left my wife."

Sarah covers her face with her hands as if horrified, embarrassed, ashamed, or a combination of all three. "Oh, my God, I've broken up your marriage!"

"Give me a break. You haven't broken anything that wasn't already broken."

"So I had nothing to do with it then?"

"Of course, you did. You had everything to do with it."

"Are you deliberately trying to piss me off? One minute you tell me I had nothing to do with it and in the next breath you say I had everything to do with it." She turns around and heads in the direction they came from.

Andrew stops her. "I'm sorry. All I'm trying to say is that you have nothing to be guilty about. My marriage was a mess way before I met you. But to stay with Rosemary would be cruel and unfair when all I think about day and night is you." The instant the words leave his lips he feels his face burn as her open palm hits him. Blood rushes to his face. His first instinct is to return the blow, but he doesn't and is surprised to hear himself laugh instead. "You can slap me all you want, Sarah, but it doesn't change the fact!"

She wraps her shawl around her shoulders and paces before him. "What do you want me to say to that? That I love you, Andrew, and that I'll leave my husband for you? Is that what you expected to hear tonight? Is that why you dragged me to this park?"

"Yes, that's exactly what I want you to say."

"Then you're wasting your time."

"I don't believe that."

"You're so sure of yourself, aren't you?"

"Tell me I don't have a good reason to be. Tell me I'm a fool and imagine things that aren't there. Go ahead and tell me that and I promise I'll never bother you again."

Sarah is silent, as if she has given up on words, as if they have ceased to be of use to her. Andrew knows he has her where he wants, that he might never corner her like this again. Clasping his hands around her pale face, he kisses her, feels her pull back, but holds on as though his life depended on it.

As he kisses her, she gives up the fight and kisses him back with equal ferocity. *This is all the proof I need,* Andrew thinks as he takes her by the arm and leads her to a dark, secluded area behind a tree. They resume their frantic kissing against the tree. The hard, jagged trunk pricks the flesh of his back, but Sarah's soft, warm body pressing against him negates any discomfort. Cold air enters his trousers as Sarah opens his zipper. Her cool hand feels good on his erection. Just as he surrenders to the sensation, the sound of laughter disturbs them.

"Yo, man, check that out!"

Andrew spots four teenage boys in baggy jeans and large hooded parkas. Quickly, he turns away from the kids and shoves his erection back into his pants. Before he can say anything to Sarah, she is on her way out of the park.

"Wait, goddamn it!" Andrew cries. "Will you just wait a minute?"

"Let's have some shame here, Andrew."

"Fuck shame! You can't leave like this."

"Don't you think we're a little too old to grope each other in public?"

"I won't feel ashamed for loving you. I won't!"

"You won't feel ashamed for loving me? Do you even hear yourself when you say these things?"

"So that's it. You won't even give us a chance?"

"A chance to what? To hurt innocent people who don't deserve to be hurt? I'm sorry, but I'm not prepared to do that."

"At what cost then, Sarah? At what cost are you willing to spare your husband's feelings?"

"Whatever it takes."

"That's fucked-up morality."

"So be it."

"You'd rather be good and moral than have something real?"

"Love and morality are one and the same, Andrew. One can't exist without the other."

"Where do you come up with this stuff? This can't be you talking."

"And what do you know about me?"

"I know more about you than your husband will ever know."

"Go to hell, Andrew!"

"Yeah, that's right, run. Run back to sniffer boy!"

Sarah hurls the framed picture he gave her at him. Andrew jumps out of the way in time, and the photo crashes into a nearby iron bench. As he watches, Sarah runs out of the park and disappears from view. Andrew scoops up the picture from under shards of glass. He is overcome with dizziness, and his breathing is shallow as he slumps onto the bench. The cold metal stings his thighs. Andrew has heard about the thin line between love and hate, but now as he struggles for air he knows he has reached that edge. One more step and he might hate Sarah for the rest of his life.

Three hours have passed since Sarah walked away from him, and as he lies in the long, narrow bed of his teen years, all he can do is miss her. He wishes he could submerge himself in the pool of hatred that beckons in order to be cleansed of this malignant, consuming desire for her. Even now Andrew can feel her cold fingers on him as they kissed in the park, her body pressing him hard against the tree trunk.

He got into bed an hour ago and has since twisted every way the narrow bed allows, vividly imagining the excruciating pain of his thumb being smashed with a hammer or a soccer player kicking his testicles, all in a vain attempt to banish his erection. Finally, he gets up, turns on the night table lamp, and opens the drawer where he deposited the smashed picture of Sarah. He stares at the photo for a long time. As if out of his control, his hand moves to his cock, his fingers feeling more like those of someone else. *Her fingers, her touch.* Part of him wants to fight the urge to turn Sarah into a pin-up girl for his self-gratification, but the stronger, more male part wins and before he knows it he is in that peculiar bliss that comes with years of dedicated practice.

Perhaps he might have heard the knock on his door had he not been mesmerized by the image of Sarah, but it takes the noise of the door opening and his father standing there to jolt Andrew out of his trance.

"Fuck, Dad!" he yells, reaching for the comforter to shield himself.

Gregory closes the door and says through it, "I'm so sorry. I saw the light on and thought you were reading."

"Never mind, Dad. Just forget it."

"I knocked. I did. I guess you didn't —"

"I said it's fine. We don't have to have a town hall meeting about it."

"Good night then. I'm sorry again."

"Good night!"

Andrew tosses the photo back into the night table drawer and slams it shut, furious with his father. He knows it was an honest mistake, but Gregory is the closest target he can direct his anger at. Andrew tried to be mad at Sarah and to hate her for turning him into a desperate, pathetic loser who jerks off to artsy black-and-white photographs, but he can't despise her. Every time he thinks about Sarah his rage morphs into an aching desire to be with her and to devote his life to making her happy. Sighing, he switches off the lamp, covers his face with the comforter, and silently prays that he will wake up tomorrow in another life.

Andrew cooks breakfast for himself and his father as Hanna sits obediently in her high chair across the kitchen next to her grandfather, who has developed a habit of reading the morning newspaper out loud to her. It started two weeks ago when Gregory enthusiastically read the politics section to entertain her while Andrew made breakfast. Much to his father's shock, she not only stopped crying but actually focused her eyes on him and smiled as if she understood as he read the column on the Canada/U.S softwood lumber dispute.

Since then, reading the paper to her has become a morning tradition. Rosemary drops Hanna off, gives her a kiss on the cheek, and runs off. Andrew whips up breakfast while Gregory reads Hanna the latest in world news. But this morning their tradition has a harder, less congenial edge to it. Andrew and his father avoid eye contact. Ever since last night when Gregory caught his son masturbating, something between them has changed that makes Andrew feel like a pervert guest who was caught sniffing his host's panties.

The air is cold and still. Andrew lies on the dry ground, gazing at the late-night sky. He can't remember the last time the stars shone so brightly. *How could something that died so long ago be so brilliant and beautiful?* he asks himself.

Andrew has always been haunted by the stars, the Milky Way, the cosmic stuff of life. If he still believes in anything resembling God, it would be based not on angels, purgatory, or paradise, but more on the big bang and the gases and substances that make up the little pearls that shimmer above him.

Maybe the joint he is smoking is causing him to see things, but the stars seem so close that he is tempted to reach out, scoop them up, and become one with the force that willed them into being. *How marvellous a thought is,* he thinks. It amazes him that he can look at something, anything, and grant validity to its existence and imbue it with meaning by the simple act of ruminating upon it. Andrew is convinced that the magic of thought makes the whole enterprise of living worth the trouble.

"Nice night," his father says from the back porch, breaking into his reverie. "Can I join you?"

"Sure, Dad, grab a seat." Andrew taps the bristly grass next to him with his hand.

Gregory, who is wearing a winter coat over his pajamas, sits cross-legged next to his son. "So are we going to keep ignoring each other?"

"Works for me," Andrew shoots back.

Gregory laughs and reaches for the joint in his son's fingers without asking. Andrew is shocked.

"Don't look at me like that," Gregory says. "I wasn't born yesterday, you know." He takes a long drag, holds his breath expertly, then releases a blue plume of smoke that lingers in the chilly air. After handing the joint back to his son, he stretches out on the ground and contemplates the starlit sky. "I take it the girl in the picture is the one you went to see last night?" Gregory asks.

"Yup."

"You love her then?"

"She's married, Dad."

"That's not what I asked."

"Shouldn't you be scolding me and telling me that my actions are disgraceful?"

"Your actions are disgraceful."

"C'mon, you can do better than that."

"Your actions are disgraceful!" Gregory repeats harsher, louder, but no more convincingly.

Andrew is quiet for a moment, trying to think of the best way to make his father say what he really feels about the situation. "I know I disappoint you."

"You don't disappoint me, son. At least no more than I disappoint myself."

"You, the model husband, worker, and citizen?"

Gregory chuckles. "You mean aside from being the guy who beats innocent people in bowling alleys, who wears his dead wife's clothes, and who reads the newspaper to his granddaughter because he doesn't know any children's stories?"

"But I bet you never cheated on Mom."

Gregory doesn't answer right away, and for Andrew those brief seconds of silence are excruciating.

"I was at a convention in Philadelphia once. You were seventeen. There was this young woman, this beautiful girl. She had the most stunning smile. For some reason she took a fancy to me. We were both there for the convention, and we had dinner together at the hotel restaurant."

Andrew closes his eyes as his father tells the story. It is too bad he can't stop hearing, as well. He asked the question, but now he wishes he wasn't here in the backyard where his mother's ashes were scattered, listening to how his father screwed a girl in a hotel room in Philadelphia.

"We talked about everything," Gregory continues. "She told me about her dream of quitting her job and doing a Ph.D. in organic chemistry. I told her about your mom and Natalie and you. I told her about what a big mistake your mother and I made buying you that camera for your birthday and how you drove us all nuts, sneaking up on us and taking our pictures."

Andrew remembers those days when he walked around with his camera all day, snapping pictures of everything he came across: grass, caterpillars, daisies. Nothing was too small or unworthy of his observation. He was convinced he was documenting the world for the first time in human history.

"Your mother and I, we weren't doing so well then," Gregory says. "It was a pretty bad time. The only one we ever really had."

"Dad, you don't have to explain."

"We ended up going to her room. I won't lie to you. The passion or chemistry or whatever draws two people together was there. But I had one of those moments. We all have those when you could do something you really want to do and you know it's wrong, but if you did, it was okay because no one would ever know. No one would ever judge you for it." Gregory pauses. "But I couldn't do it."

Andrew opens his eyes and looks at his father, whose gaze is focused on something among the stars that only he can see.

"The strangest thing happened," Gregory says. "At some point, as if I left my body, I could see myself on this large bed making love to this beautiful young woman. It was like an out-of-body experience. That's all I needed. That little change of perspective. So I got up, put my shirt back on, heard myself say, 'I'm sorry,' and left. I knew your mother would never know or even suspect, but I would know. That was enough to stop me."

So it wasn't an illusion, after all, Andrew thinks. His father and mother did have the real thing. It is possible, he realizes, for a marriage to survive the passage of time. And the fact that he couldn't have the same with Rosemary says more about him than it does about the institution. This new revelation about his father is a gift. If he is ever lucky enough to have Sarah in his life, he has something achievable to aspire to.

the end of all things good

Susan: Well, we have tried over eighteen months, that's right? And we have failed.

Mick: Right.

Susan: Which leaves us both feeling pretty stupid, pretty wretched, I would guess, speaking for myself. And there's a point of decency at which the experiment should stop.

Mick: Susan ...

Susan: We have nothing in common, never did, that was part of the idea ...

Mick: It just feels bad ...

Susan: The idea was fun, it was simple, it depended on two adults behaving like adults ...

Mick: It feels very bad to be used.

Susan Traherne is proving to be more of an enigma than Sarah bargained for. After a month of exacting rehearsals of David Hare's *Plenty*, Sarah still doesn't understand Susan. The very thing that drew her to this character is what is frustrating her now. As if watching on a screen, Sarah can see herself going through the motions. The lines are simply lines. She doesn't want to stop the scene but also doesn't see the point in continuing.

Thankfully, her director comes to the rescue. "Okay, let's stop for a second," she says from the darkened theatre seats.

Radhiya Davies, the outrageously youthful director, is only twenty-eight. The South African helmed her first Broadway play at the ridiculous age of twenty-four. She is a short, compact woman with a long, thinly woven mass of brown dreadlocks that match the colour of her skin. Radhiya sprints up to the stage where Sarah and her scene partner, the seasoned Broadway actor Clifton McGowan, stand.

"What's bothering you, Sarah?" she asks, traces of her South African accent still lingering in her speech. "You have that look on your face again."

"I can't seem to get behind the words. Do I have to be this close to Clifton when I say my lines? Can't I do something instead of talking to him?" Sarah isn't certain what she means. She despises this helplessness but knows she must trust her director fully.

Radhiya faces the stage and gazes at the empty seats as though conjuring up an audience. "Let's try this. Speak the lines while you work. Don't get up from the desk. Ignore him as you say the line and let's see what happens."

Sarah nods, grateful for any suggestion. She and Clifton do the scene again, this time as the director suggested. And suddenly the subtext changes. The lines stay the same, but the meaning is completely different. By not looking at Clifton when she speaks the lines but instead writing in her notebook and smoking with the other hand, the tension in the words is apparent in the action of ignoring him, of belittling him. *Another perfect case of action releasing emotion,* Sarah thinks.

She can hang almost everything she knows about acting on that one principle. Her director has confirmed for her the wisdom of what her mentor Ella Christiansen taught her all those years ago. To Sarah's delight Radhiya, like Ella, is very much interested in the "physicalization" of a character's internal life. The South African directs by creating a language for the characters based on gesture, movement, and action. But despite this small victory, Sarah is still plagued by doubt and anxiety.

After principal photography wrapped up on *Lady Chatterley's Lover*, Sarah relished the thought of time off from work where she could stay at home, read a little, try out some of the recipes she has been collecting, and spend time with Michael. However, two weeks into what once used to be a blissful decompression following the run of a play or in this case shooting a movie, a necessary period to shed remnants of whatever character she was immersed in, lost its charm this time and left her feeling adrift. What used to be a slow and delicious easing back into herself took the form of despondent moping around the house, and all her items of comfort, like her bathtub or her favourite armchair by the window, where she spent hours curled up with a good novel, became suffocating anaesthetics.

All the activities Sarah looked forward to such as sleeping until eleven, catching up on her reading, and finally learning to bake perfect banana bread proved futile. Insomnia, a problem she never had before, became her enemy in the night. To make matters worse, Michael developed a strange and maddening need to pamper her, to treat her like the sort of high-strung, artsy type they both used to mock. No longer was he the "get-over-it" man she relied on to keep her neuroses in check; instead he became an enabler of all that she hated about herself and her profession.

In the middle of a particularly bad day, Bobby Greenberg, her agent, called and told her about the Broadway revival of Hare's

Plenty and that the actress attached to it had jumped ship three weeks into rehearsals due to creative differences with the director. Bobby asked Sarah if she would consider taking the role. So she read the script and was immediately attracted to the role of Susan Traherne. Perhaps it was Susan's anger, contempt, or disillusionment with the way things turned out not only in her own life but also for Great Britain after the Second World War, that spoke to Sarah. Susan's idealism, intelligence, and capacity for bravery and cruelty in equal measures fascinated Sarah.

The fact that she also didn't understand Susan or rather her psychology was also a major draw. Susan is not the kind of woman Sarah encounters a lot in the scripts and plays she reads for consideration. Traherne doesn't beg for the audience's sympathy. She doesn't grovel for their love or understanding. She just is. There is no backstory, no long, tedious monologues in which she justifies why she is the way she is. If Susan has a philosophy, it is: I do, therefore I am.

The scene that clinched it for Sarah is the one in which Susan says: "So I tell you nothing. I just say look at me — don't creep round the furniture — look at me and make a judgment." As soon as Sarah read those lines, she knew she wanted to be this woman for a while. Susan, Sarah thought, was the kind of woman who could teach her something.

Now, however, as she stands on the stage of the Booth Theater in New York, she has serious doubts about her agreement to take on this play. She still likes the script and its many technical demands such as the need to master a British accent, and she continues to be gripped by Susan Traherne, but the pressure to understand her character in order to perform it with conviction has become more and more overwhelming with each rehearsal day that passes. There are only six weeks left until previews, and Sarah can already hear the critics sharpening their knives. The fact that the original U.S. run of the play in 1982 with the brilliant Kate Nelligan, a fellow Canadian actress playing Susan, was such a resounding success only adds to her fear of ridicule.

"Good work," Radhiya now says, bringing Sarah back to the present. "See you tomorrow."

As Sarah heads for her dressing room, she reflects on what makes good theatre. She once heard a famous actor, she can't remember who now, say in an interview that good theatre causes molecular disturbance in its audience. Glenn Close, that is who it was, she remembers at last as she puts her coat on and leaves the Booth. *Molecular disturbance.*

No point in putting on a play that doesn't pose hard questions or provoke fierce debate, Sarah thinks as she gazes out the subway train window at the dark, subterranean world on her way home to Harlem. *Provoke.* What an interesting word. It occurs to her that provoking is something she has shied away from in her life. In fact, despite her line of work, being confrontational and asking tough questions is something she has avoided for the sake of peace, for the sake of not disturbing the status quo. But at what cost?

Does she really think that if she doesn't pay attention to the facts of her life that somehow they will cease to mean anything? She has spent weeks now trying to erase all thoughts of Andrew and his words in the park that night in Toronto. Her plan, though too unconscious to be called that, is that if she ignores these thoughts, then eventually they will wear off, their mark gradually vanishing much the same way the henna she put on her hands during a trip to India with Michael three years ago faded without her noticing. Brilliant red one day, a week later a mere shadow, until she woke up and her hands were as clean as a newborn's.

Could her feelings for Andrew suffer the same fate? More than a month has passed since he kissed her under that tree in the park, and the taste of his kiss is still in its brilliant red stage. Time nor distance nor all her efforts to throw herself back into love with her husband have yet to take their intended antiseptic effect.

This isn't the time or the place for these thoughts, Sarah instructs herself like a misbehaving schoolgirl as the train hurtles her homeward. Out of her bag she takes out this week's *Time* that she bought from the newsstand in front of the subway entrance. A picture of a bloody scene after a roadside bomb in Baghdad is the cover story. She plunges herself into a report about the deadly insurgent attacks in Iraq and the ongoing attempts to put Saddam Hussein on trial after his capture by the Americans at the end of 2003. But even the potential trial of a murderous dictator doesn't have the power to expel Andrew from her mind.

Sarah and Michael sit at the dinner table in the large kitchen they spent thousands of dollars renovating. It was half its current size when they bought the place. Sarah always dreamed of a cozy, colourful Mediterranean kitchen in which to entertain their many friends, but Michael, whose taste in interior design leans more toward austere Japanese minimalism, convinced her they should opt for big silver metal commercial appliances and a metal island counter to match the appliances. All their dishes are placed on long shelves that run along the walls of the kitchen, and no matter how much she tidies up, the room always looks messy. It has a chaotic restaurant look that she thought she would grow to love eventually, but she still hasn't.

She watches Michael open a bottle of wine. Much to her annoyance, he has brought out from their modest cellar in the basement the 1995 Lafite Rothschild Pauillac they decided to keep for several more years until it fully matured. He made the steak to perfection, just the way she likes it, medium rare with minimal herbs and spices, accompanied by basmati rice and baked vegetables.

Lately, Michael has gotten into the habit of making these elaborate, unexpected dinners, often with candles and music. She longs to ask him what the hell is going on, but always stops short of saying the words. Sarah abhors confrontations, but every day these seemingly spontaneous romantic gestures get more intricate. Two days ago Michael put a single rosebud in the pocket of her winter coat. It wasn't until she got to the subway on her way to rehearsal that she discovered it. She spent the duration of her commute fingering the soft, velvety petals, vacillating between guilt and anger. Each of Michael's gestures makes her guiltier about what happened between her and Andrew, and the guiltier she feels the angrier she gets at Andrew, but even more so at herself.

"How are the rehearsals going?" Michael asks, disturbing the silence she was enjoying.

"Fine. Good, I suppose. I don't know."

"Okay …" he whispers with a raised eyebrow.

"It's frustratingly slow." She pushes back her chair and tries to stand.

"What's wrong?"

"Nothing. I'm just getting the salt-and-pepper shaker for the salad."

Michael leaps to his feet and snatches the shaker from the island counter. Sarah extends her hand to take it from him.

"I'll do it for you, hon," he says, sprinkling salt and pepper on her salad. "Just say when." He grins.

"That's enough."

He stops and returns to his chair. "You were supposed to say when."

Sarah ignores him and starts pecking at the salad with her fork, her agitation increasing with each jab at a slice of tomato or a cucumber as if they were her enemies.

"Are you okay?" Michael asks.

"I'm fine."

They resume their silent eating, punctuated by animated chewing on Sarah's part. Finally, she puts down her fork and glances at Michael.

"What?" he asks.

"We weren't supposed to open this bottle of wine for two more years."

"We could be dead in two years. There could be a nuclear holocaust in two years."

"Or not."

"Why take the chance? Why not enjoy the things we have now?"

"Yes, but we had an agreement, an understanding."

"We also agreed to live every day like it's our last, remember?"

"I don't remember making any such agreement."

"It wasn't an explicit agreement, more like a new way of life, a philosophy of sorts. We talked about this, hon, remember?"

"That's a dumb philosophy."

Michael sighs like a father frustrated with a stubborn child. "Honey, you're stressed, you're under a lot of pressure —"

Sarah slams her fork against the salad bowl so violently that it jolts Michael. "Don't do that! For God's sake, don't do that!"

"Do what?"

"Enough of that —"

"Enough of what, honey?"

"Screw you, Michael! You know exactly what I mean. 'Oh, honey, you're under a lot of pressure. Oh, sweetie, let me get the salt for you. Oh, baby just say when.' What does that even mean — *just say when*? Who says such a thing?"

"I'm just trying to be considerate ..."

"*Considerate?* How about weird, freaky? I feel like I'm married to a complete stranger."

"How am I a stranger, sweetie?"

"Ever since I came back from Toronto, you've been a different man. Breakfasts in bed and little flowers in my coat pocket. Who puts a goddamn flower in people's coats?"

"I thought it would be romantic."

Maybe he's had an affair, Sarah thinks, ignoring her own infidelity for the moment. *Oh, God, that makes perfect sense.* It would certainly explain the doting-husband syndrome he seems to have contracted. "Are you having an affair?" she blurts out loud.

Michael breaks into hearty laughter that borders on hysteria. "You crack me up, honey. Really, you do." He wipes tears from his eyes, still chuckling.

Sarah feels absurd for even broaching the subject. But then why is the notion of her husband sleeping with another woman so absurd when she did so with another man? Is he a better person, more virtuous, more honourable, than she is?

"Why is that so funny?" Sarah asks. "Oh, I see, you're better than all those pathetic losers who cheat on their spouses. You're above that."

"Maybe I am. Maybe I'm not. Why are we even talking about this?"

"And I bet you look down on those who make mistakes."

"Since when is cheating a mistake?"

"It can be."

"Not looking where you're going and falling on your face, that's a mistake. Taking your panties off and having sex with someone, that's a decision."

Sarah starts to clear the table, dumping the contents of her plate in the trash can and putting her dirty dishes in the dishwasher.

"Is there something you want to tell me?" Michael asks.

Sarah freezes. Slowly, she closes the dishwasher. She is in the middle of one of those moments she has heard people talk about. Sarah can seize it and change her life, make a fresh start, and in the process inflict undeserved suffering on her husband, or continue to betray him, and worse, herself.

By the time her eyes meet his, it is pretty evident he knows. She doesn't understand how he does, but the pure hatred she now detects in his expression renders words superfluous. For a fleeting moment she thinks Andrew must have called while she was out and talked to Michael, or perhaps her husband opened the mailbox and found a love note or some other incriminating item.

"Who is he?" Michael asks, still sitting at the table.

"Would you believe me if I told you how sorry I am?"

"I would."

"Thank you."

"So what?"

This question puzzles her. "What?"

"I believe that you're sorry. So what? What good does that do me?"

"You at least know I'm not indifferent to your feelings, that I'm not heartless."

"I'll ask again. What good does that do me?"

Tears form in her eyes. "I know you're angry, but —"

"Actually, I'm thankful, if you must know."

"Thankful?"

"For weeks I waited and waited. Every day, I thought to myself, today will be the day. This is the day she'll stop taking me for a fool."

There is a cold malevolence in his eyes she has never seen before, and even as he speaks calmly, thanking her for her honesty, he looks as if he might pounce at any moment and strangle her with his bare hands. She can't bear the loathing in his eyes, so she turns away.

"At least have the decency to look at me when I talk to you. That much I deserve."

Sarah glances at him. "How did you know?"

"Oh, honey, you're a good *actress*, but you're no Meryl Streep." His face crackles with sardonic rage. "You know what the problem has always been between you and me? You always assumed I wasn't as smart as you."

"That's not true, Michael."

"And maybe you're correct. Maybe I'm not as clever as you'd like me to be, but I assure you, I was never so dim-witted that I wouldn't notice my wife becoming a different woman in front of my eyes."

Sarah knows he is right. Everything between them has changed since that day with Andrew in her hotel room in Toronto. She came back to New York determined to make her life with Michael work, but she returned a different woman. Their normal chatty existence has taken on an inexplicable gravity as if contaminated by a fatal virus.

"Why didn't you say something?" Sarah asks, leaning against their large two-door fridge, the appliance's cold metallic surface almost burning her skin. Now his behaviour over the past few weeks suddenly makes sense. Were those gestures, like slipping a rosebud into her coat pocket, the desperate actions of a man trying to hold on to the woman he loved, or was there something more sinister behind them? Did he realize that each romantic gesture made her guilt all the more unbearable? Was that, in fact, what he was attempting to achieve?

"I wanted to see you crack," Michael says as if reading the questions she has been posing in her mind. "I wanted to see how long you'd keep up the deception."

"Deception? Is that what you think I've been doing all this time?"

"*Yes!*"

"It wasn't deception. It was absolution, not deception."

Michael laughs. "*Absolution?* God, you're so fucking bourgeois! This is New York, babe. You don't need absolution. If you wanted to fuck another guy, you could've just asked for it. We would've made the necessary arrangements, sweetheart. After all, we're cosmopolitan folks, right?"

"You're angry. I —"

"You bet I'm angry!"

Michael moves toward her, and for a moment she thinks he is going to hit her, something he has never done before. But he stops just in front of her face.

"You know what hurts more than the fact that you're a lying, bourgeois cunt? I would've done anything to make you happy. I would've agreed to anything."

Sarah winces at his words, but remains silent.

"Anything!" he yells again as he storms out of the kitchen.

Feeling dizzy, Sarah hobbles over to the kitchen counter and holds on to it for support. *Is this the end,* she wonders, *the end of all things good between them?*

I9

the boy who loved ants

"Goddamn It! Fuck! Shit!" Zakhariye growls at the TV as he watches the live coverage of John Kerry's concession speech.

Two minutes ago he was stretched out on the couch that has officially become his bed, high with the anticipatory thrill of turning on the television to hear that George W. Bush has been defeated, that the most powerful nation in the world would no longer be headed by a man he has come to loathe to an extent that if it were possible for him to be objective about his own feelings he would surely find irrational, even demented. For Zakhariye, Bush has become the living, breathing personification of all that is evil in the world.

He stayed up until three in the morning to find out whether or not Kerry carried Ohio, thus giving him the needed electoral votes to oust Bush. But after no definitive news by 3:00 a.m., Zakhariye turned off the television and hoped he would wake up to a better world, as though the condition of the planet depended on one man's defeat in an election.

The shock and injustice Zakhariye feels as he listens to Kerry's words of surrender are soon replaced by venomous rage as he watches Bush deliver his victory speech. The fake conciliatory words Bush utters to the half of the electorate that didn't vote for him, the promise to bring the country together that will no doubt be broken the minute the cameras are turned off, and the barely concealed arrogance and sense of entitlement that ooze out of every pore of Bush's face, produces in Zakhariye a fury he didn't know his body was capable of.

His natural response to unwanted occurrences has always been melancholy, but the kind of wrath boiling in him now is completely foreign. It feels like barbed wire being dragged through his intestines. Yet, strangely, it also generates the sensation of being alive — something he has lately learned to do without.

Zakhariye gets off the couch and starts pacing. Then he sits back down. His limbs seem on fire, so he rises and paces some more, never taking his eyes off the television screen, convinced Bush is smirking at him personally, actually taunting him.

As though watching someone else, Zakhariye sees his leg extend and hit the coffee table with full force. The table tips over, sending the blue antique bowl with the gold engraving, the first serious purchase he and Thandie made as a couple, fly off to the corner of the room where it hits the wall and breaks into three large pieces. The bowl is one of his wife's favourite possessions. They bought it in Damascus on their first trip as a double-income couple.

Zakhariye knows this accident could spark an all-out-fight with Thandie. He squats over the bowl's fragments and places them together in a way that resembles their former shape. Zakhariye is convinced that with some Krazy Glue and careful attention he can repair the bowl. He gathers the pieces, takes them to the kitchen counter, retrieves the Krazy Glue container from a drawer, and starts working. Then he remembers that Andrew invited him to his father's sixty-sixth birthday party. Zakhariye initially turned his friend down, but Andrew persisted, almost begging him, saying that at the rate everyone was bailing out only four people would probably show up. He got an image of four bored individuals standing around a cake mumbling, "Happy birthday to you ..." Zakhariye couldn't do that to Andrew.

Now he wishes he hadn't said yes. He has a bowl to repair and doesn't have a present for Gregory. What to buy a man he has met only once? A book? Is Gregory a reader, and if so, what does he like? A tie? God forbid! Zakhariye tells himself to think of something interesting in the shower as he leaves the broken bowl on the counter and runs upstairs. He has to be at Andrew's father's place in an hour.

The guests, no more than ten, mostly relatives and friends of Gregory, all of whom Zakhariye remembers seeing at Ella's funeral a few months ago, are scattered around the living room, sipping wine and taking careful bites of appetizers. Perhaps the guests are confusing this gathering with that other more sombre previous one, because for some reason their small talk is peculiarly soft, almost hushed. The only people speaking normally are Andrew, his father's best friend, Ed, and another person Zakhariye doesn't know. They are all assembled around Hanna, the centre of attention. It seems she has been given the task of bringing some levity and joy to this otherwise dreary party. The poor girl is passed from one group to another as if she were the original miracle child. Even the music in the background can't lift this sorry scene. The Miles Davis CD playing at the moment, which in a different place and time would sound buoyant, now only adds to the sense of wrongness ... of defeat.

To Zakhariye the sight of Andrew holding Hanna in his arms, her back on his belly as he shows her off to the people around him, is a sad attempt to make people forget his mother is the essential missing piece from what should be a celebration. At the very least Ella would have brought light and colour to this occasion.

Zakhariye knows all about essential missing pieces — his household is flooded with the eerie silence of absence. He is intimately familiar with that absence's texture, its smell, not to mention the futile efforts to fill it, like playing video games by himself as he did one overcast Sunday several months after the accident when he could no longer bear the quiet hum of the house. His wife refused to play with him, so he went into the living room, sat on the carpet in front of the television, and played by himself. The little robotic sounds, the cheesy background music mixed with explosions and gunfire, were what he missed so badly. Their Sundays had once been infused with the frivolity and banter of harmless competition between a seven-year-old Nintendo expert and his father who brought more enthusiasm than skill to the matches.

He can't help the overflow of sympathy he feels for the people here today, especially Gregory. Zakhariye notices Andrew glancing at his watch as if expecting someone to arrive. Their eyes lock, and Andrew comes over to him, smiling. "Hey, man, do me a favour? Hold Hanna for me? I have to make a quick call."

Before Zakhariye can process what is happening, little Hanna is in his arms. "Wait, don't. I'm not good with babies …"

Andrew chuckles. "That's ridiculous. You love babies." He heads for the telephone on the end table between the sofa and loveseat and checks his watch as he punches in the numbers.

Hanna stares at Zakhariye with large, watery eyes, so clear and open they are startling, almost disturbing. There isn't a trace of fear in them. She is neither happy nor troubled to be in the arms of this stranger — just an acceptance of him, a blind trust that Zakhariye doesn't know how to receive, which is what hurts him the most. This is the first time he has held an infant since

Alcott was a baby. It is all so familiar — the weight, the smell, the texture — but holding her feels wholly and utterly wrong.

His instinct tells him to put Hanna on the floor or hand her to the nearest person and bolt out of the room. But before he can do so the light in the room dims, causing everyone to gasp softly as if something magical has happened. Rosemary enters from the kitchen carrying a large round cake with tiny candles all around it. The flickering circle of flame casts a warm, liquid glow, and the room comes to life with the deep, reverberating voices of people crooning "Happy Birthday."

Zakhariye is surprised that he can distinguish Natalie's thin, distant voice singing "Happy birthday, dear Gregory." He looks around to locate where her voice is coming from, then realizes Andrew has called her and put her on the telephone speaker. It must have been pre-arranged. *How sweet and clever,* he thinks as he sings the last notes of the song.

As the flurry of clapping fades, Natalie's voice fills the room with "Happy birthday, Dad." Everyone gazes at the telephone as if she really were in the room. "I'm so sorry I couldn't be there in person," she adds.

Gregory picks up the telephone to say thank you. Everyone turns away to give the man and his daughter some privacy, while Andrew cuts the cake and serves generous slices to the guests.

Zakhariye feels cold, wet lips on his knuckles as Hanna tries to bite him. And she would, too, if she had any teeth. She is at that pre-teething age, Zakhariye figures, when babies nibble on anything they can get their mouths on. He remembers Alcott at that age, the comical way his mouth was always half-opened, always on the prowl for something to soothe his aching gums with. A tie, a hand, a shirt sleeve, the TV remote control — it didn't matter.

He has never had an asthma attack, but this must be what it feels like, Zakhariye is convinced, as he tries to breathe deeply.

Instead of that pleasurable feeling of his lungs expanding with oxygen, all he experiences is heavy airlessness, as if someone is sitting on his chest and squeezing. The harder he tries to suck air in the shorter his breathing gets until it is reduced to the quick panting of a Chihuahua. Then dizziness overtakes him.

So this is death, Zakhariye thinks when he is jolted out of his swoon by Hanna's crying. She must have sensed something ominous and unwell with the man whose arms she was perfectly content in a moment ago. In his last fully conscious moment Zakhariye sees an alarmed Andrew snatch Hanna out of his grip.

The next thing he knows everyone is gathered around him, staring at the floor where he has fallen. All he wants to do is get to his feet and run away from their pity and fear.

"Hey, Zakhi, are you all right?" Andrew asks. "Are you feeling okay?"

Zakhariye can hear his friend, but the words seem slow, muffled, and stretchy as though each syllable is travelling through muddy waters.

"Nod your head if you can hear me," Andrew says.

"Fresh air, give him some fresh air," Zakhariye hears a voice from behind.

"Panic attack?" Zakhariye repeats, confused and slightly angry after the doctor has told him the nature of his freak-out at Gregory's birthday party. "Panic from what?" he asks the old doctor, who has also informed him there is nothing wrong with him physically and that too much stress might be the problem. "Are you saying I have a mental problem? And stress from what? I'm unemployed and I've spent the past month on my couch surfing twenty-four-hour news channels."

The doctor suggests therapy and anti-anxiety medications. As soon as the *T* word is mentioned, Zakhariye reaches for his coat, ready to bolt for the door. He has come to fear and loathe *therapy* like the plague. He and Thandie went to a grief counsellor for two months after the accident until Thandie refused to go. Silently, he thanked God for her rejection of the sessions because he hated every minute he was there and only went because he thought she wanted them. There was something about the sort of verbal revelling in the morbid details of their grief that he found masochistic. As for medication, he has seen what the alternating regimes of antidepressants and sleeping pills have done to his wife and wants no part of that. So he gives the doctor's hand several hard shakes, assuring him he will be fine, and escapes.

Cringing embarrassment is all Zakhariye remembers of the party. He finds it hard to believe he actually fainted in front of people. As far he is concerned, fainting is something skinny Victorian women in tight corsets did, not a big black man in his late thirties. He also feels terrible taking Andrew from his father's birthday party, even though he did his best to convince Andrew that he was perfectly fine and didn't need to see a doctor. Andrew wouldn't hear of it and drove him to the emergency room.

Now he lies on the couch in his living room in front of the dark television, having turned it off, unable to stomach the news coverage of George W. Bush's re-election. The electoral defeats and the general misfortunes of other men in faraway places that used to be abstract and unaffecting have lately become inseparable from his own troubles.

His wife, who just returned from a double shift at the hospital, comes out of the kitchen wearing a bathrobe, a towel around her wet hair, and walks into the kitchen. When she came home, she said hello to him and went straight to their bedroom. She didn't ask him how his day went, probably assuming he never left the house, and he in turn felt no need to tell her about his meltdown at a birthday party. Lately, even their attempts at recapping their days have become one-sided, with Thandie being the only side to have anything worth reviewing.

Thandie returns to the living room carrying the pieces of the bowl and stands over him. She doesn't speak, but her obvious distraught desire for an explanation makes words redundant.

"I'm very sorry, honey," he says. "It fell from the table."

"How does a bowl just fall from the table?"

"Okay, I hit the table. The bowl fell as a result."

"You hit the table?"

"I'll fix it. A little Krazy Glue and it will be as good as new."

"That doesn't explain why you hit the table."

"I had a ..." he says, looking for the right word, "an episode."

"An episode?" Thandie glares at him. "I'm going to bed now." She heads back to the kitchen.

Don't you want to know about my episode? Zakhariye wants to scream. Instead he watches as she disappears into the kitchen. A moment later he hears the sound of the fragments of the ceramic bowl hitting the bottom of the garbage can and breaking into even smaller pieces.

It is three o'clock in the morning. For the past two hours Zakhariye has been sitting at the kitchen table, bent over the pieces of the bowl, gluing them together with careful, almost obsessive attention. At last the mission is completed. He feels the rush of satisfaction and pride that doctors must feel when they coax a patient back from the brink of death.

Zakhariye senses the presence of something or someone and glances up. Thandie is at the kitchen door. She is still wearing her robe. It doesn't look as if she has slept. Her eyes are red and puffy. It is clear to him that his wife has been crying.

"Look," he says, holding the bowl up.

Thandie replies with a weary smile as though it would hurt to speak. She goes over to the fridge, takes out a carton of milk, grabs two glasses, and sits at the kitchen table next to Zakhariye. Without a word she pours them both a glass of milk. They take slow, childlike gulps as they lock eyes. He finds gazing at her inexplicably painful, but he doesn't look away.

"It looks good," she says. "I hardly see the cracks."

He nods, and they remain quiet for a long time.

"I can't do this anymore," he says at last. His face burns with shock at the ease with which the words have slipped out. "I went to the emergency room this afternoon."

"What happened?"

"An anxiety attack. That's what the doctor said."

"First time?"

"It happened before … at work mostly. But this one was the worst by far."

"Did the doctor suggest medication?"

Zakhariye chuckles and shakes his head. *Amazing,* he thinks, *the way she goes into doctor mode.* Her faith in medication and its ability to cure all human maladies is astonishing even when all she has to do is observe herself in a mirror to see its shortcomings.

"What?" Thandie asks. "Why are you laughing at me?"

"Nothing. He suggested meds, but I declined."

"Medication isn't the enemy, you know. It doesn't mean you're weak, either."

"I know."

"Do you really? I don't think you do."

Zakhariye shrugs, either unable to defend himself against her accusation or just no longer caring to.

"So what do you want to do then?" she asks.

"I want to go away."

"We decided to go to Mexico in the summer, didn't we?"

"On my own, I mean."

"I see." She takes a sharp intake of breath. "Where?"

"Home. I mean, Somalia."

"As far as that?"

"I haven't seen my mom and sister in three years."

"You've been thinking about this for a while then?"

Zakhariye shakes his head. It is a lie, and he knows it, but he wants to spare her unnecessary pain. The truth is for some time he has been considering returning home, partly to see his mother and sister and the few remaining relatives, partly to see what has become of his homeland, but mostly to get away.

The closest he has been to Somalia since he left in 1986 was three years ago when he and Thandie went to Nairobi so that Alcott could finally meet his grandmother who was brought there for minor surgery. From what he has read and heard his homeland is unrecognizable now.

"When would you be coming back?" Thandie asks.

"I don't know." Another lie. A long trip, one of those perspective-shifting, life-altering journeys, is what he has in mind — the kind measured not in weeks and months but years.

Thandie turns away and gazes at a spot over the fridge. "You blame me, don't you?" she says, returning her attention to him, fighting back tears.

"What?"

"You blame me. You think I'm to blame for Alcott."

"Stop it! Please, just stop it, Thandie. I won't listen to you saying such things."

"Why not? It's what you feel."

"*I don't!*" he cries, surprised by the vehemence of his reaction.

Thandie shakes her head in disbelief. "Sometimes I see the way you look at me." The tears she has been denying stream down now. "You wish it was me."

"What are you talking about?"

"The one who died that night … instead of your son, you wish it was me."

Zakhariye leaps to his feet and stands at the far corner of the kitchen to put as much distance between himself and her words as their small kitchen allows. "You don't know what you're talking about."

"I know you. I know how your mind works."

"You know nothing about what I feel, what I go through."

"Then tell me. Talk to me. I'm here for you."

Zakhariye laughs and shakes his head. "Here for me? How could you be here for anyone when you're not even here for you? You medicate yourself and sleep through it all and you have the nerve to tell me you know how I feel?"

"You're abandoning your family — that much I know!"

"*What family?*" Zakhariye shouts back.

Thandie scurries out of the kitchen, leaving Zakhariye standing against the wall. The dizzy spells come again, making him feel as though he is walking on a waterbed. He stumbles back to the kitchen table where the half-drunk glasses of milk sit next to the repaired bowl. Zakhariye rests the side of his head on the table, hoping the action will make the dizziness go away. The cool surface of the table is comforting to his flushed face. His cruel, uncalled-for words rush back, nauseating him with shame and regret. *"What family?"* Those two simple, otherwise benign words are so nullifying when posed to a woman mourning the death of her only son. He keeps his head flat against the wooden table, amazed at the wounding power of words. When he feels steady enough to check on Thandie, he stands, picks up the bowl, and leaves the kitchen.

In the living room Zakhariye carefully places the bowl in its original spot in the middle of the coffee table. Standing over it, he studies its interior. Not a single crack is visible.

When he goes upstairs, Zakhariye hesitates at the door to the master bedroom. Taking a deep breath, he knocks to let Thandie know he is coming in. *This is what nine years of intimacy is reduced to — knocks on the door before entering.* He twists the doorknob, but it refuses to turn. "Thandie, please open the door. Honey, please let me in." There is no answer.

He bends to see if the light is on in the room. It is pitch-black under the door. He knows she wouldn't be sleeping tonight. Nor would he. He heads back to the living-room couch but changes direction and goes toward Alcott's room.

Zakhariye hasn't set foot in this room since they buried Alcott. He knows what he will find: a cold, dusty room that was once an oasis for a little boy who loved animals. Opening the door, he switches on the light. The first thing that strikes Zakhariye about his son's room is the absence of the Vicks vapour scent that used to hit him as soon as he opened the door. For so many years in the winter Thandie put liquid Vicks in a humidifier that she turned on every night. That scent must have seeped into the very substance of the room because it was present year in, year out, summer or winter. But now, as he looks around the room, there isn't a trace of it. The narrow single bed with a blue-and-white-striped comforter is against one wall, and opposite it is a small table with a lamp where Alcott used to draw pictures of animals.

Sitting on the edge of the bed, Zakhariye is surprised at how strangely empty of meaning this room is now. He once bestowed an almost mystical, otherworldly profundity to it.

He sees that the room is merely four walls containing a bed, a desk, a bookshelf, and some toys. Zakhariye is also amazed at how clean the room is. He runs his index finger over the night table. Not a speck of dust. Thandie, he realizes, must have been cleaning it all along. Another wave of nausea hits him, this time out of compassion for his wife. He wishes he could know what she feels when she cleans this room. Does she cry when she dusts? He peels the comforter off the bed, gets in, and lies down, facing the ceiling. The walls of the room and the ceiling are covered with cut-out pictures of animals.

Zakhariye and his wife thought hard about what they wanted to get Alcott for his sixth birthday. They both admired their son's passion for animals and wished to encourage it, so they decided to repaint his room. Their initial idea was a mural or a fresco like the ones he had seen in churches all over Italy, but of animals instead of saints or holy figures. To their delight they discovered a shop that sold wallpaper that featured all sorts of animals, trees, and grass that could be pasted on the walls and ceiling in a way that simulated wildlife in natural habitats.

The weekend before Alcott's sixth birthday Zakhariye and his wife dropped off Alcott at Thandie's sister's place and then put up the pictures in their son's room. On one blue wall, fish and other animals of the sea swim around coral reefs of all colours. On another wall, lions frolic in the Serengeti while large colourful ants march on rolling sand dunes. On the ceiling, beautiful ladybugs crawl on flat green leaves next to tiny hummingbirds in treetops. A gaggle of butterflies float about the room. One of them is a rare transparent butterfly. When he and Thandie saw the pictures of these butterflies in the store, they instantly knew that the butterfly with the transparent wings was the one must-have item that would add the last magical touch to the whole fantastic arrangement.

Alcott gasped when he saw the transparent butterfly. He didn't know they existed. As much as Alcott liked butterflies, though, ants were by far his favourite animals. Zakhariye could never figure out what it was about ants that Alcott found so fascinating. But it all started when he was four years old and they were walking to the nearby daycare.

Alcott hated having his hands held when they walked. It was one of the first signs of his fierce independence, and Zakhariye, though he enjoyed holding his son's hand, indulged Alcott's need for freedom. Every morning, on their way to the daycare, they strolled side by side like two adults. As Zakhariye walked a step or two in front of his son, thinking about all the things he had to do at work, he sensed that Alcott wasn't immediately behind him. When he glanced back, he saw his son squatting and gazing at a long, frantic procession of brown ants. Zakhariye stood over his son and said, "C'mon, buddy, we're going to be late."

"Look, Daddy," Alcott said, looking up, "they're carrying a bug."

Zakhariye squatted next to Alcott and watched the ants rally around a bug five times their size as they carried it toward a hole in the sidewalk a couple of metres away. Like Alcott, he found himself riveted by the scene before him.

"Where are they taking the bug, Daddy?" Alcott asked.

Zakhariye thought for a moment. He didn't want to tell his son that they would eat it. Alcott would find that out for himself soon enough. "Bury him," he said. "I think they're going to bury him."

Alcott seemed satisfied with the answer and didn't pose any more questions. He just watched the ants struggle to get the bug into the hole. That was the beginning of Alcott's love affair with ants. Later that night when they got home they went on the Internet and discovered that the insects they encountered that morning were most likely carpenter ants. They read about the ants' life cycles, nesting habits, and physical characteristics. That was one of the many things he missed most about being a dad: the constant process of education about things he would otherwise never learn about on his own. Without his son's interest in ants, it would have never occurred to Zakhariye to read about their lives.

Being in this room gives Zakhariye the impression of entering a floating animal kingdom. No matter how many times he has entered his son's room, it always takes him a moment to get used to the world he has stepped into. Now, lying on his son's bed and gazing at the ceiling, Zakhariye is reminded of something he and Alcott used to do, especially on those nights when his son was being difficult and refused to sleep. With his left hand Zakhariye reaches for the light switch near the door. The room turns dark. With his other hand he feels his way around the top drawer of the night table where Alcott kept a small flashlight. On the nights when the boy didn't want to sleep, they would lie in bed and point the flashlight at the pictures on the ceiling and the walls. Doing this always gave them the impression of watching a procession of moving animals.

As Zakhariye does the same thing now, the circle of illumination the flashlight supplies is so sharp and small that it only reveals one thing at a time while keeping everything else shrouded in mystery. He pulls the covers all the way up to his neck like a little boy and traces the light around the room. Then it hits him. Grief envelops him, not so much for the actual loss of Alcott but a different sort, a quieter kind, less cutting, something closer to a requiem for what might have been. What he feels now is more liquid and permeates him on a molecular level. It hugs the spiral contours of his entire DNA. The initial mourning of the days and weeks that followed the accident was more concentrated. It had an excruciating sharpness like a burning blade piercing flesh. He remembers it as if it were yesterday.

It was a rainy Saturday. He was at the office that whole weekend readying a new issue of the magazine for the printer. Maria, Thandie's younger sister, called him, and just the couple of seconds of silence that followed her shaky "Hello" gave him enough of a hint that something was horribly wrong.

It took him thirty hellish minutes to get to North York General Hospital to discover just how horribly wrong. He never saw it coming. As the taxi sped toward the hospital, all of his fear and prayers were for Thandie. The other possibility didn't even enter his mind. It was too unthinkable, too unnatural. When an official took him to the morgue to identify his son's body, he couldn't bring himself to do it. He stood by the large steel drawer-like bed the official dragged from the wall. A thin blue sheet lay over the familiar shape. Zakhariye was by himself then, the man who brought him there having left to give him some privacy.

He reached to lift the sheet so he could know for sure that it really was his son, but he couldn't summon the strength. Zakhariye imagined Alcott's open eyes staring at him with their combination of innocence and perspicacity. Instead of lifting the sheet, he placed his palms on his son's face and felt the spiky crew cut. Three days earlier Zakhariye had taken Alcott to the barber. For some reason his son always hated getting a haircut. He used to weep inconsolably every time Zakhariye took him to the barber. To cheer Alcott up Zakhariye always took him to the ice-cream shop afterward. This became their tradition: the barber, then ice cream.

Zakhariye ran his fingers over Alcott's ears, large and fleshy, too big for the slender features of his face. He always worried that kids would tease his son about his ears once he started school. But they never did, or if they did, Alcott never told him. The boy had a strange way of being above the silliness and stupidity that plagued others, as if somehow he knew he had a short stay on Earth and wanted to focus on things of substance like the lives of animals. Alcott had a hunger to know about their lives in a way that went beyond childhood curiosity. He had for animals a love that didn't need reciprocity. Alcott expressed this love the best way he knew — a devotion to learning about their lives.

Having felt Alcott's head, face, and ears, Zakhariye had all the assurance he needed — this was his son lying in the cold morgue. He turned, left the room, and thanked the official waiting for him on the other side of the door, then took about twenty steps toward the elevator and collapsed.

As Zakhariye passes the flashlight over the marching ants, he wonders about their lives, too, the way Alcott must have done. *Where are these ants going to? They always seem to be in such a hurry. Do they have a sense of time?*

Magically, the landscape painted on the wall changes. Zakhariye's eyes glide over an ocean as big and blue as the real thing. The map of Africa, large and muddy, dances before his eyes. He hears Alfie, his neighbour's golden retriever, barking in the distance, followed by the roar of a motorcycle speeding away on Jarvis Street, its noise gradually dying. A warm tear streams down the side of his face and disappears between his ear and the pillow. He turns the flashlight off and goes to sleep in his son's room for the last time.

20

the woman with tangerine hair

One morning Gregory awakens with a thought: *What if I redeco-rate Natalie's old bedroom for Hanna?* So he gets up, dizzy with excitement, and drives to the nearby Home Depot. The salesman in the home renovation section is an odd-looking fellow in his forties wearing two black dime-size rubber rings in each earlobe and shoulder-length white hair tied in a ponytail. Gregory tries hard not to stare through the holes, but it is hard not to. The man suggests a shade of pink for Hanna's room. Gregory does his best to suppress laughter when the man says, "Misty rose, that's what I see for your granddaughter. What's her name?"

"Hanna," Gregory says.

"*Aww*, how precious." He then launches into a mystifying dis-sertation on the subtle variations of pink. "All men may be cre-ated equal," the man says, "but there's nothing equal about pink. It's a truth universally acknowledged that certain shades of pink are better than others. Don't ask me why. They just are."

Gregory has no intention of asking why and just nods and lis-tens to the man as he goes on and on about the subject. He tries to keep up with the clerk as they walk around the paint aisle. There is pink raspberry and Easter pink and pink peony and pale iris and dog's ear. But it is a shade called razzle dazzle that finally breaks Gregory's attempt not to laugh. After the man finishes, Gregory finally says, "The misty rose will do, thank you." Razzle dazzle is out of the question.

For almost a week Gregory spends each evening working on the room without Andrew knowing. Every night when Rosemary picks up Hanna after work and Andrew leaves for his evening shift, Gregory puts on an old pair of jeans and a T-shirt and goes to work on the room. This secret project becomes his salvation, a little private endeavour of his own that makes the silence of the evenings bearable, almost enjoyable.

The silence throws him for a loop. Crushing and endless, the house hums with it every evening between supper and bedtime. It reminds him of his failures and thwarted dreams and sickens him with disappointment in himself but mostly with life in general. During those long, silent evenings, life itself seems like too much trouble for too little in return.

Where was all this silence before? Gregory often wonders. Why didn't he hear it when Ella was alive? Gregory tries to drown the silence in many ways. He plays his wife's jazz records as loud as he can, neighbours be damned. But no John Coltrane or Sarah Vaughan is an equal match for the silence in his home.

Gregory also attempts to become one of those people who organize evenings around prime-time television shows. News reports from blood-soaked cities in the Middle East, sleek dramas about how to extract forensic evidence from decomposing bodies, and reality programs in which people eat worms for $50,000 only add to his growing sense that everything is topsy-turvy.

To his surprise, though, the slow, painstaking work of clearing out his daughter's childhood room, stripping the walls and repainting them, carpeting the floor and assembling a crib and changing table, all the while hiding everything from Andrew, turns out to be more of a gift to himself than the present to his son and grand-daughter the project started out as.

Gregory has been thinking of a meaningful way to thank Andrew for the effort to put on a birthday party for his sixty-sixth birthday. That was ultimately a failure. No one, it seemed, could ignore the fact that they were all recently in that very room for a funeral a few months ago. With each attempt they made at celebration the room sank deeper into mourning. Zakhariye's fainting spell didn't help matters. In short, the party was another failure to add to the many fiascos of his son this year, but the intention was genuine, and for that Gregory is grateful to have his son back in his life after so many years of living abroad.

When Andrew told him about Zakhariye's story that night as they were putting leftover food in the fringe, he asked, "Why didn't you tell me? I could've —"

Andrew frowned. "Could've what?"

"I don't know, been nicer or kinder to him. Given him a hug or something."

His son laughed. "You would've given him a hug?"

"Well, I don't know. Anything to let him know how sorry I am about his son." Then Gregory asked him a question that sur-prised him as much as it seemed to astound his son. "Have you ever hugged him, your friend?"

"Yeah, Dad, I did. I do. We hug each other practically every time we get together."

Why don't we hug? Gregory wanted to ask his son that night, but he didn't. Many things puzzle Gregory about himself, none more so than his inability to show his feelings physically with his son. He was always physically affectionate with his wife and daughter, and God knows he actually has to remind himself not to smother Hanna with kisses. But hugging his son seems next to impossible.

Gregory has always been proud of his son and even a little jealous of him. Andrew possessed, even as child, a kind of fearlessness of human emotions whereas Gregory has always been afraid of them. At age twenty-three Andrew got on a plane and landed in Johannesburg for his first assignment with nothing more than a passport, his beloved camera, and a hunger to know the world, how it worked, and the people who made it work. When Gregory was that age, a combination of fear and desire for security drove him into a job at a chemical plant he wasn't crazy about, as well as into a mortgage and a marriage.

Back then Gregory wanted to tell Andrew how much he admired him for his dangerous missions to tell people all the horrible things that were happening in the world. And likewise, now that Andrew is no longer out there putting his life at risk, Gregory marvels at how he puts his heart on the line for his daughter. He sees Andrew get up early every morning to be at the front door when Rosemary pulls into the driveway with Hanna in the back seat. He watches his son change, bathe, and feed Hanna with nothing but enthusiasm for the task of caring. This fills Gregory with shame because even on the rare occasions when he did those things for his children, he did them because they needed to be done not because he found purpose and pleasure in the boring minutia of daily childcare.

Every day they live together produces for Gregory new evidence of his son's many admirable qualities that he, as his father, can't help but be proud of, but as a man, can't help be envious of. *So why can't he say how he feels?* Gregory thinks. *Must be generational.* Certainly, Andrew doesn't suffer the same malady.

When Gregory finally finishes his secret project for his granddaughter, he asks Andrew to come upstairs. His son arrives with Hanna and meets him in the hallway outside what used to be Natalie's room.

"What's up, Dad? Something wrong?"

"I want to show you something, a little present for Hanna," Gregory says as he reaches for the doorknob.

"Did you hear that Hanna?" Andrew says to Hanna. "Grandpa got you a present."

Hanna gazes at her father with an expression of indifference as if she has already received too many gifts in her short life and is thoroughly bored by all the fuss over her.

Gregory swings the door slowly to reveal a light-filled room of pink, or rather misty rose, as the clerk at Home Depot called it. The sheer pink curtains transform the mid-morning sun coming through the large window into a pink liquid glow that blesses every part of the room. Except for a pale lavender crib, a changing table, and a rocking chair by the window, the room has been emptied of all the clutter of its past. It is light and airy, a perfect new space for a new life to flourish in.

Gregory glances at his son, who has a bemused look that he doesn't know how to read. Is he surprised? Moved? Confused?

Without warning Andrew moves in and gives Gregory one of his trademark unselfconscious, open, unreserved bear hugs. "Thank you, Dad!" he whispers.

Gregory makes a third trip to his car. He has already taken two large plastic bags to the small office on the second floor of the Goodwill Store on St. Clair Avenue near Bathurst Street. A thin, haggard woman with wispy blond hair and a missing front tooth who strikes Gregory as a woman recovering from something terrible instructed him to put the bags in the office so that Gale Franklin, the store manager, can have a look at the clothes.

When he enters Ms. Franklin's office, he puts the third bag next to the first two, takes a seat, and waits for the manager to arrive. It took several hours and three large bags to get all of his wife's clothes out of the closet. He sorted old from new, dresses from pants, sweaters from scarves, securely tightened the bags, and put them into the trunk of his Volvo. Andrew offered to help him, but Gregory felt this was his job, and his son agreed.

The idea percolated in his head ever since he overheard his children talking about what to do with their mother's clothes and Andrew suggested donating them. At the time since Ella's funeral, and this morning he woke up and knew what he had to do.

Just then Gale Franklin enters the office and brings him back to the present with a jolt. Her tangerine hair is the first thing he notices about her, then the long dreadlocks. He has seen young women with interesting hair colours before — blue, green, even purple — but those were girls, teenagers who have the right to look as deranged as they wish. *But a grown woman is surely too old for tangerine hair,* he thinks as he gets to his feet and shakes hands with the manager.

"Gale Franklin, pleasure to meet you," she says.

"Pleasure to meet you, too," he says, trying not to stare at her dreadlocks. He has seen individuals with hair like that before, but they were mostly black people, like Sandra, one of Ella's close friends from her drama school years. But he isn't used to seeing a white middle-aged woman with dreadlocks to the middle of her back. *Interesting,* he thinks, *very interesting.*

"You have quite a donation for us, I'm told," she says as she moves around the large, cluttered desk and sits down. "Please, have a seat."

"Thank you. Yes. The clothes belonged to my wife. She … passed … she died about three months ago."

"I'm so very sorry for your loss."

"Thank you."

"May I?" she asks, walking over to the three bags near the wall by the door. She opens one of the bags and puts some of the clothes on a table. Sweaters and several winter coats fill the first bag. She opens the next bag packed with dress pants and blouses. With each new beautiful piece of clothing she sees, the manager seems more surprised.

"Are you sure you want to donate these clothes? I mean, don't get me wrong, we'd love to take them. It's just … this is awfully generous of you."

"It was actually my son's idea. We could either give them away to relatives who can afford to buy clothes, or give them to people who really need them. That's what he said."

"You've got a very kind son. You have no idea how many women will benefit from all this." She comes over to him and shakes his hand again. "Really, thank you so very much."

"I'm glad we could help," he says, getting up.

Gale realizes she is still holding his hand. "Oh, God, I'm sorry." She releases him.

"Well, I should let you get back to work," Gregory says. He is fascinated by this woman. What sort of white lady in her fifties has tangerine dreadlocks, large brown African beads for a necklace, and works at a Goodwill store for a living?

Outside, on St. Clair Avenue, Gregory walks toward his car, which he parked on a side street about a block away. It is two weeks into December, and many of the stores on both sides of St. Clair are festively decorated. He has been so busy these past couple of weeks putting together Hanna's room and meeting with his lawyer about the upcoming trial in January that he has completely forgotten about Christmas.

He has met a rather young but seemingly clever lawyer that a friend recommended, and at the end of their meeting he told him he wanted to plead guilty. Gregory has decided to take full responsibility for his actions. No contesting, as the lawyer suggested, no excuses. Plain old guilty of wrongdoing and pray that the judge will see the incident at the bowling alley for what it really was — ugly and out of character.

Gregory glances at the sky. It is bright silver and low and hints that snow is coming. His thoughts turn to all the things he has to do to prepare for Christmas. Natalie is coming next week and is bringing her boyfriend, Jamal, possibly his future son-in-law. He wonders what he should get Natalie for Christmas. Then there is Hanna and her father, Rosemary, his best friend, Ed, and Doris, his wife's sister. He has to get a Christmas tree, too, not to mention put up lights all around the house. And he still needs to prepare the garden for winter. The irises have to be covered, and the garden furniture has to be moved into the shed.

"Thank God for chores," he whispers as he opens his car door and gets in.

Later that afternoon, after a short nap, Gregory decides to start on the garden. He has seen his wife shelter her flowers by covering them with evergreen boughs, so he does likewise. The overcast sky at last releases the snow it has been threatening all morning. Gregory stops covering the plants and watches the falling snow. Large, feathery flakes, whiter than he has ever seen before, seem to hang in the air, suspended as if the snow has forgotten how to fall.

Gregory focuses on one particular flake as it hovers in the air. He thinks about the journey of the snowflake as it makes its way down from supercooled clouds. Gregory can still remember learning about the formation of snow in the natural science courses he took in university. Such a perilous journey a flake of snow makes. *And so beautiful, too,* he thinks. *How so beautifully the snow falls.*

He and Ella once took out his magnifying glass after a major snowfall and walked around their backyard, observing the flakes that clung to the tree branches, the windowsill, and the porch railing. They were astounded by the intricacy of their shapes — needles, plates, and the most beautiful of them all, the six-sided crystal flake. Watching the snow fall would have made her so happy. Then it hits him. Ella will never see snow like this again.

21

they come running

At eight o'clock every morning the children come running into the classroom. Zakhariye checks his watch. It is 7:43. That gives him just enough time to hang a huge map of the world on the front wall of the classroom next to the blackboard. He unfolds the map carefully as if it, too, is as fragile as the real world. It came yesterday, along with enough pencils, rulers, sharpeners, crayons, and notebooks for his entire class. Two weeks ago he sent an urgent email to Andrew in Toronto, pleading with him to send supplies for his pupils as soon as possible and that he would reimburse him later. Two days later he received an email from Andrew:

> Howdy, teacher man ...
> The school supplies should be with you in eight days. Oh, and if you say another word about reimbursement, I'll fly all the way there just to kick your ass. Cheers! Keep up the good work.
> Your ever-admiring friend,
> Andrew

Once Zakhariye finishes putting the map on the wall, he turns his attention to sorting the supplies. Each student gets a notebook, a pencil, a sharpener, an eraser, a ruler, and a box of crayons. He looks at the twenty-five empty desks lined up in five rows that will shortly be filled with third-grade students. Painted white with cheap, dusty paint that is already fading, the square classroom has two large windows with no panes or even shutters. The windows are sufficient, since they let enough sunlight in while allowing cool breezes to act as an air conditioner, a blessing during afternoon classes when the temperature can reach the mid-thirties Celsius. The local NGO that built this two-classroom school for boys and girls in Jowhar, Somalia, a small town ninety-five kilometres northeast of Mogadishu, only had enough money for the bare necessities: a simple box structure to keep the rain and dust out. Everything else Zakhariye improvises as he goes along. Education guerrilla-style, he likes to call it.

In a few minutes the more eager of his pupils will start to trickle in, decked out in their khaki shorts and white, cotton shirts. They are mostly boys age eight to ten. He tries to convince more parents to enroll their daughters, sometimes going to nearby houses to tell the parents about the school and to bring their daughters in free of charge, but most girls that age start taking care of their younger siblings and help their mothers around the house. Kids looking after kids is quite normal in Somalia.

He tries not to compare these parents to North American ones, but Zakhariye is still frustrated that these girls are being denied education not because their parents are terrible or careless but because more is expected of girls rather than less. Without their daughters' help, many of the mothers here wouldn't be able to take care of their families and work outside the home.

Zakhariye is excited about the lessons for the day. He will start with geography for the first period. They have already covered the names of all the countries in Asia and their capitals. Today he will turn their attention to their own beautiful and troubled continent. Zakhariye will teach them about the Sahara to the north and the rainforest in the centre and Mount Kilimanjaro in Kenya. He is also excited, almost giddy really, about next week's geography lesson focusing on Antarctica. Zakhariye knows it will be mind-blowing for the kids. When he showed them pictures of Canadian winters, their eyes lit up. Farah, a nine-year-old boy with a permanent mischievous smile, asked if people in Canada ate snow. The other kids laughed at him, but Zakhariye thought it was a clever deduction, since ice is such a highly sought commodity in Somalia.

Geography will be followed by a fifteen-minute recess after which he will give English lessons. Next comes lunch and then rudimentary mathematics. This is the subject that gives him nightmares. Having dropped math in grade ten, he could barely multiply when he started teaching here. The science he teaches is equally elementary, a fact that fills him with regret.

Zakhariye would love to add another subject to the schedule — world religions. There is no reason why they shouldn't learn not only about Islam but the other faiths that came before it — Christianity, Judaism Hinduism, Buddhism. But he has to tread carefully here. Maybe talk to the parents beforehand and explain his intentions, for if word got out that he was teaching the kids about Christianity or any other faith, there would be hell to pay.

Teaching. Now there is something he never thought he would end up doing. It started out quite by accident. His brother-in-law asked him if he would teach at the new school they had built. The teacher they had hired was shot in the pelvis by a khat-chewing, gun-wielding teen. What started out as a favour to his sister's husband has now developed into a most earnest and benevolent obsession and a source of daily pleasure and adventure.

It amazes Zakhariye how far these kids have come. Most of them have never sat in a classroom before this school was opened. But in five short months they have become intimately acquainted with the wondrous gift of waking up each day with the possibility of learning something new. Until now school was a fairy tale for these children. They congregate in this little square classroom with almost non-existent supplies and sit all day on uncomfortable chairs. But every day, as though going to the beach, they come running, hungry for more.

Ever since he returned to Somalia, Zakhariye has been very busy, first spending time with his aging mother, who lives with his sister and her husband, then travelling around the country, trying to see how much it has changed. And it has. Years of civil war is bound to transform a nation. But he is astounded at how amid all the violence and lawlessness the people have changed so little. They are as disputatious and generous and violent and proud as they have always been. If anything, they have only become more of themselves.

He would like to think that he, too, has become more of himself, though he doesn't quite know what that is. Until recently, Zakhariye believed he carried around with him an authentic, fully formed identity and that it was his duty to excavate it. He also believed that coming back to his birthplace would unlock the secret. But to his great sadness and relief, actually, he has discovered that there really is no such thing, that identity is as slippery as happiness. The harder one tries to grasp it the harder it is to hold on to.

Change. That is something Zakhariye finds himself thinking about these days quite often. Sometimes dreaded, sometimes welcomed, but it is the one constant thing he can always count on. This is what he has come to understand about the subject — change comes and hits us like a tsunami. We can either adapt to the obvious hardships and hidden pleasures it can bring, or we can fight it and wither away.

He once read somewhere that the human body, on a cellular level, changes every seven years so that essentially everyone is a different person every seven years. And if that is the case, he reasons, why cling to a lifestyle, a career, a house, a city, and all the other stuff we desperately embrace to define who we are and what our place in the world is? Why not evolve and mutate along with our cells?

Whenever he ponders his current life in Jowhar, he reflects on his past in Toronto, which inevitably makes him think about Thandie. He received the divorce papers from her weeks ago. His hand shook a little as he signed them. Another thing he has discovered about change is that it is like death, universal and inescapable. For to live is to change. No one or thing gets immunity, even old Mr. O'Brien. On his way back to Somalia, Zakhariye made a stopover in Dublin to see what became of the old man he met many years ago on a train to Dublin.

He had seven hours to kill until his connecting flight to Nairobi, so he took a taxi from the airport and asked the driver to drop him at the intersection where the old man had told him his cigar shop was located. An upscale apartment complex was being built on the very spot the store was supposed to be. Zakhariye asked around and discovered that the old man had retired to a small town in the south of Portugal where his nephew lives. He walked around downtown Dublin for a couple of hours and went back to the airport as he replayed in his mind images of Mr. O'Brien outside the train station on Amiens Street, striding away and disappearing into the crowd.

Sometimes it hits Zakhariye: it isn't just the geography of his life that has changed. His inner life has also been rearranged by the outer changes. Gone is his obsession with the self, with interior life. Metaphysics don't interest him as much as the physical, tactile, dirty, and muddy world around him. He hasn't read a novel or a poem in a long time, and to his amazement he doesn't miss them. At last he has become the philistine he always dreaded, and now that he knows what it feels like to be a philistine, it isn't as bad as he thought it was.

Instead he spends his days wandering the dusty roads, past the few small rice fields that dot the outskirts of town, past dilapidated villas covered with bullet holes the size of his fist, houses that once belonged to middle-class families who must have fled the battles waged here not too long ago. On these long walks he tries to recover, to no avail, any memories from his early childhood of playing in gardens in this once lush, tranquil town.

One of the excuses he told himself for coming back to Somalia was that he might take a crack at translating some of his favourite Somali poems. His people, though marred by illiteracy, have a rich legacy of oral literature, and one of his dreams has always been to introduce Somali poetry to English readers. But old dreams have a way of morphing into new dreams when we aren't looking.

Zakhariye hears the voices of two kids coming from outside. *Must be Nuruddin and Ibrahim,* he thinks. He could pick out their high-pitched giggles anywhere. They are always the first to come to class. Their curiosity about the world and hunger to know the way it works are matched only by their talent for mischief. They remind him so much of Alcott. There are more Alcotts in the world than he ever imagined, and that knowledge brings a smile to his face as the boys run into the classroom.

"*Subax wanagsan, macalin,*" Nuruddin and Ibrahim greet their teacher in unison.

"*Subax wanagsan,*" Zakhariye says with a smile.

2 2

something remains

Gregory's feet ache. He has been standing since nine this morning.
On Mondays, Wednesdays, and Fridays, 9:00 a.m. to 3:00 p.m., he
works at the Goodwill store. He sorts clothes, helps customers
find what they are looking for, and assists Gale, his supervisor,
who sucks at Excel, with spreadsheets for her monthly reports.

He came here back in February after his trial for assault. The
judge found him guilty and sentenced him to three hundred
hours of community service and counselling. His lawyer milked
the "the grieving widower" angle for all it was worth. The judge,
a widow herself, was very understanding. It helped that he had a
cleaner criminal record than Mother Teresa.

Gregory welcomed the community service part of his sentence. He always wanted to do volunteer work but just never got
around to it. However, he hated the forced counselling bit and
thought it was overkill. Being forced to sit on a couch talking
about his feelings with a complete stranger is his idea of purgatory.
Gregory still finds the weekly visit with Dr. Benoit strange and
slightly unbecoming, but he has loosened up a bit. He doesn't feel
as naked as he did the first couple of visits and is even beginning

to see the value of therapy, at least for the people who really need it. Which, of course, doesn't include him, he thinks.

He hangs new skirts and matching jackets that came in yesterday on a long metal rack. His eyes catch a beautiful navy women's business suit. The price tag reads $36. He wonders who this suit used to belong to. Perhaps a generous woman in Rosedale, someone who wished to help other women better their lives? Or more likely a dead woman whose children decided to dump all of their mother's belongings at the nearest place they could find so they could get on with their lives. He imagines a young woman, dirty blond hair, a former heroin addict, going to her first job interview wearing this very suit. They love her sense of style. She gets the job and can now get full custody of Tiffany, her nine-year-old daughter. He smiles as he conjures up these happy scenarios.

"What are you grinning about?" Gale asks suddenly.

Gregory turns to find her smiling at him. She has taken a liking to him, that much is clear to Gregory. She teases his conservatism, his quiet attention to the mundane details of his job. "Jesus, fucking Christ, relax, will you?" she said to him the other day when she caught him sitting on a stool and he stood up and apologized, saying that his back was giving him trouble. "Man, you need to get laid," she told him. He felt his face flush. "Dude, you're as red as a baboon's ass."

This sort of teasing has become a daily ritual, which he has learned to tolerate, even find secret pleasure in. Gregory has officially considered her a friend ever since she cried in front of him in her office. He walked in and noticed that she looked distraught. Gregory asked her what was wrong, and she told him she had just found out that her ex-husband of twenty-seven years, the father of her two daughters, had actually married his twenty-five-year-old hairdresser mistress.

"You're supposed to fuck the little bimbos, not marry them," she said to Gregory as she wept. He handed her a tissue. "Thanks. You know the part that really infuriates me?" she asked as she blew into the tissue. "The ink hasn't even dried on our divorce."

Ever since that day she has kept him informed about the grisly details of the fight over their five-bedroom house in the Annex and all the other who-gets-what melodrama. Gregory tries to be supportive and listen, but he finds it hard to follow her train of thought, which moves more like a tornado than a train.

"So what's got you smiling like that?" Gale asks him again, breaking his reverie. Her hands are on her hips as she watches him fix the clothes on the rack.

"Oh, nothing, just thinking about these clothes. Where they came from, who's going to wear them. Silly stuff."

"No, it's not silly. It's called an imagination. Most men don't have a fucking iota of it. So who do you see wearing this little number?" She touches the navy blue suit.

"A former heroin addict struggling to get a good job so she can stand before a judge and ask for custody of her child."

"God, you're corny."

Gregory concurs with a nod and a smile.

"Corny but sweet," she adds. "What do you say we go to Timmy's across the street and get ourselves some coffee? That glazed motherfucker doughnut is calling my name."

"Sure," he says, wondering why she feels the need to curse so much.

After they get their coffee and Gale gets her doughnut, they sit on a bench in front of the Goodwill store. It is an unseasonably warm mid-May afternoon, with the sun blessing everything under it. Gregory figures his pasty white skin can use some rays. Squinting at the sun, he looks over at Gale's profile. She brings the honey-glazed doughnut up to her mouth, takes a huge bite, and releases a long, orgasmic moan. Gregory laughs and wishes he, too, had something that made him feel that good.

"Here, have a piece," Gale says.

Gregory shakes his head.

"Oh, c'mon."

He shakes his head again.

"You know you *waaaaant* it," she sings, then laughs.

Since it is such a beautiful day, Gregory decides to do some work in the garden. The late-afternoon sun is now behind the large tree, forming long, ever-changing shadows on the lawn. Andrew is already dressed for his evening shift. While he waits for Rosemary to pick up Hanna, he plays with his daughter on the lawn. Andrew stands at one end of the garden and encourages her as she wobbles over to him, each step emphasized with a squeal of delight.

Gregory smiles as he watches his granddaughter fall all over the place. He has been thinking about telling Andrew what he did three days ago, but decided this morning that he won't. Gregory did what his wife failed to do: he prepared for the end and drew up a will for himself. In it he stipulates that upon his death the house will go to Hanna to do with as she pleases when she turns twenty. If he tells his son, Andrew will probably have a fit and see it as another effort to cement them for life to this house, to this small piece of land. But Gregory doesn't care. It is the only thing of value he has to pass on to his granddaughter.

He turns his attention from Hanna and her father and back to the work at hand, inspecting the garden for signs of rhizome rot such as sick, yellowing leaves. Gregory finds one and cuts it away, then dusts the severed surfaces with dry Bordeaux mixture.

He is amazed at the work that goes into keeping a garden beautifully alive. Lately, he has gotten into the habit of going to the neighbourhood library and signing out books on growing irises. He also listens to gardening shows on the radio and has become fascinated by such things as timed-released fertilizers, cross-pollination, propagation, and many other things new to his untutored ears. Gregory wonders why he never developed these absorbing hobbies that everyone else seems to have.

Why did it take losing his wife to discover the world of gardening and volunteering? Since last winter, Gregory has begun educating himself on everything to do with growing irises, the only flowers his wife ever grew in her garden. It has always struck him as odd that Ella never wanted to try other flowers. But now he sees why. Just a few weeks into spring, and already the combination of irises in full bloom is a magical sight. He is also beginning to understand the passion he saw in the iris growers he met at the Canadian Iris Society annual meeting that his wife took him to once. At the time he thought they were a bunch of crackpots, but now, as he looks at the magnificent flowers that his hard work has brought into being, he can see why they would want to get together and share stories, ideas, and techniques.

As his eyes follow a dead flower he has clipped fall to the ground, Gregory sees two entwined, slimy, brown worms digging themselves into the mud. He scoops a fistful of the mud around them and brings them closer to his eyes. The scientist in him loves to observe things up close. As he watches these creatures doing what they have been designed to do, taking their part in the glory of nature, it occurs to him that his wife's ashes are all over this garden.

He remembers that day when out of sheer desperation for a proper place to bury Ella's ashes he scattered them in her beloved garden. A small part of him wishes he had conducted the act with more deliberation, perhaps taken her remains to the Grand Canyon, but he immediately dismisses the thought, knowing she is where she belongs. As he cups the cool soil in his palm, he catches his breath, moved by the knowledge that this is what remains of his wife. But deep down he knows this isn't all that remains of his wife. A lifetime of memories remains. Gratitude for those memories remains. Always, always something remains.

Gregory scatters the soil back and wipes his hands with a cloth. He needs to burn all the material infected with rhizome rot and sterilize the equipment but decides that can wait. Now is the time to play with his granddaughter. He gets up and joins Hanna and her father.

23

a pledge

Sarah sits cross-legged on the hand-scraped Brazilian walnut hardwood floor of her now-empty townhouse. As she waits for the movers to carry out the remaining items, she gazes at the large window that reveals a beautiful early spring afternoon in New York City. Last week Michael moved his furniture, and this week it is Sarah turn to empty her belongings from this once beautifully decorated house before it goes on the market. She decided to let Michael have all the furniture as long as she keeps all of the large collection of black-and-white photographs that took her over a decade to collect.

She looks at the suitcases and picture frames that line the walls of the living room, waiting to be moved into a storage place somewhere in Queens. Recently, she moved into a tiny sublet on Sullivan and West Houston Street, a couple of blocks from Washington Square Park, where she plans to stay through the run of the play, which finally begins in two days after several delays for technical reasons.

Sarah has no time or mind to figure out where she wants to make her home. What she knows for sure is that she will miss this home and this part of Harlem. Every corner is full of the history of this place and the people who made that history. One of her favourite things to do in this neighbourhood is to visit the famous Harlem Renaissance landmarks. Just last month she went to see the home of Langston Hughes, probably her favourite of all the poets she admires most. And though it saddens her to be leaving this neighbourhood, it distresses her almost as much to think of all the native families who were displaced in order for well-to-do home buyers like her and Michael to purchase historic homes like this one.

Sarah isn't even sure if she wants to remain in New York. Once the play closes, she will be unemployed with no other commitments to keep her in any one place. As she checks her watch, it hits her that she is in that precarious place she has always tried to avoid. One phase of her life has come to an abrupt end, but the next phase still hasn't revealed itself. How she feels about that depends on her mood: she is either at the cusp of a great, thrilling possibility, or she has destroyed the only life she knew and has nothing to anchor her. Before she can figure out which version is the truth, she hears the moving men coming back to the house. She springs to her feet and heads for the front door where she sees the two men, a short, stocky guy with a goatee and a New York Mets cap, and an even shorter fellow with a goatee and a Yankees hat.

She shows them what still needs to be moved and watches them carry the suitcases first and then make several trips for the photographs. Finally, they come for the last two large frames, and before they pick them up, the guy with the Mets cap turns to her. "Is that all, ma'am?"

She stares at the man blankly.

"Ma'am? Is that all?"

Still no answer from Sarah.

The man in the Mets cap comes closer and lightly touches her shoulder as if to make sure she is awake. Without warning a short, almost inaudible cry escapes her. She puts her hand to her mouth to prevent a full-blown breakdown.

"Are you okay?" the mover with the Mets cap asks.

"Yes, I'm fine." Sarah quickly wipes away the sudden tears that fill her eyes.

"Want us to call somebody?" the guy in the Yankees cap asks.

"That won't be necessary. Really, I'm fine. Thank you." Sarah walks toward the front door and opens it wide to usher them out. She watches them load the photographs into the back of their van and then waves at them as they drive away. Once the door is closed again, she weeps in private.

Eight hundred people are on their feet clapping. Some cheer, a few whistle, and others appear shell-shocked. *So this is what it feels like,* Sarah thinks amid the deafening applause in the Booth Theater. She has done five plays in her career so far: her first at the Stratford Festival in Ontario, one in Toronto, an off-off-Broadway piece that earned her a Tony nomination, one in Chicago, and a play in London's West End. The last was Harold Pinter's *A Kind of Alaska* in which she played a woman old enough to be her mother and for which she won the Laurence Olivier Award. But never has she gotten a standing ovation of this length and enthusiasm. The ovation she got for playing Nina in *The Seagull* in Chicago was more for the famous actress who played Arkadina. But this one is all hers.

Sarah can feel the presence of Anne Bancroft, Henry Fonda, Blythe Danner, and all the other greats who have performed on this very stage. It feels as if she has at last joined that select company of real Broadway actors. Many have come from all over the world to play here and many more will come after her, but tonight it is her turn.

Her director, who is standing in the wings, practically pushed her onstage to receive the audience's gratitude. She had them in her palm all night and could do no wrong. Whatever reprehensible thing Susan Traherne did or said, they hung on her every word and gesture, and Sarah in turn gave them everything she had. At last the curtain goes down and the rest of the cast stands by her side. They join hands as they wait for the curtain to rise again to take another bow, this time as an ensemble. The applause is even more deafening as they stand in one long line and face the audience.

Sarah wishes every night for the entire run could be like this, but she knows better. There will be performances when she will wish she were anywhere else but standing here and saying the same lines for the umpteenth time. There will also be those evenings when the other actors on whom her performance depends will give her nothing. They will lounge around and wait for her to say her lines so they can say their bit and go home, and she will wish she had something very sharp to stab them with. And, of course, there will also be those nights when she will be doing the lounging, while the other actors fantasize about strangling her. It is a business of hits and misses in more ways than one — that is the nature of the beast. But she can't think of anything else she would rather do with her life.

They take their bows in unison. The curtain comes down again, and it is over. Months of gruelling work, arguments, and frustrations come down to fewer than two hours followed by applause, wild and heartfelt, but still just the mere clapping of hands. Sarah can't help but feel the disappointing anticlimax of the whole enterprise. *Two hours of what?* she wonders. *Two hours of entertainment, diversion?*

In those two hours the world wasn't changed, somehow made better. Nobody's bad liver was transplanted, no cancerous tumour removed or defective heart healed, no child was taught the alphabet, and no tree was planted. Just two hours of a sort of communal experience in which, she hopes, questions were posed and thoughts were provoked, and ideas were brought forth inspiring debates or at least discussions in the theatre foyer, in a nearby bar, and most important, in the minds of those who have paid their hard-earned cash.

In her small white dressing room Sarah fixes her hair in front of the large vanity, her face illuminated by little light bulbs around the mirror. A respectable bouquet of roses sits in a vase on the counter.

When she first saw the flowers, her heart skipped a beat. For a moment she thought, or rather hoped, they were from Andrew. She snatched the card and discovered that Stan Silverblatt, the executive producer of the play, had sent them. Sarah flung the card onto the counter and resumed brushing her hair. She could swear she saw Andrew. In the middle of the second act the light from the scene illuminated the stage for no more than three seconds, and she thought she saw Andrew in the second row, several seats left of the middle. Blood rushed to her head. For an instant she forgot her next line, causing one of the other actors to repeat his line a little louder than usual, thus snapping her out of the trance and saving her from a fate worse than death.

As she changes into her black dress for the opening night party, she thinks about the reviews. Somewhere deep inside her she knows she will never match the legendary reviews showered on the brilliant Kate Nelligan, the fellow Canadian who originated the role on Broadway, but at least Sarah is confident they won't accuse her of ruining the part or the play.

Sarah vowed at the beginning of her career never to read her own reviews out of self-protection more than anything else. So as much as she wants to know the verdict, she decides to stick to her rule. She wants nothing more than to go back to her apartment, take a long bath, fall into a deep sleep, and have a lush dream in which she and Andrew do a two-hander of their own creation. This has become her nightly ritual. After a long day at the theatre, she prepares herself for bed as she thinks about him, what he is doing, who he is with, if he is thinking about her. By the time her body gives into sleep, her consciousness is so saturated with Andrew that communing with him in her deepest sleep is inevitable.

She stands back from the mirror, looks at herself, and decides she is good enough for the party. Sarah leaves her dressing room and heads for the exit. Once outside in the warm, airless summer night on West Forty-fifth Street, she tries to find a taxi to take her to the party somewhere on the Upper East Side. There is no cab in sight, so she walks in the direction of Seventh Avenue. At the intersection she hails a taxi, and as she gets in, she makes a pledge: *When this play is over, I'll take my suitcase and drop by Andrew's house unannounced. And if he's not there, I'll sit on the steps and wait patiently.*

24

everything put back together

"It's a hit! It's a hit!" Or at least that is how Hilary Dean, the owner of the gallery on Queen Street West that specializes in portraits, sums up the evening for Andrew.

It isn't what Andrew imagined it would be like. He doesn't know exactly what he expected for his first showing, but in his imagination the night was different. More? Bigger? Somehow grander? Who knows? Over a year of photographing some of the hundreds of people who found their way into the back seat of his taxi, months of meticulously developing the black-and-white pictures in the basement of his father's house, and weeks of discussions with the owner of the gallery have all come down to a couple of hours in a small space full of people, some he knows well and many others he has never met before, mingling about, looking at his portraits, eating cheese, and drinking wine.

"They're all here," Hilary whispered to Andrew earlier in the night, referring to some of the art critics and writers from local publications who bothered to show up to see the work of a complete unknown former photojournalist turned cab driver. "Oh, God, there he is," Hilary hissed, discreetly pointing at the influential Samuel something or other whom he was told writes for the arts section of the *National Post*, or was it the *Globe and Mail*? He can't remember which.

As Andrew glances around the large square gallery whose walls are lined with his photographs, he can't help but feel out of place. He makes several rounds as Hilary instructs him to do and attempts one-sided conversations with the oh-so-chic crowd that packs the room. They do the talking. He does the nodding.

"Love the sense of claustrophobia," a woman raves. "It's like they can't escape your microscope," she adds as she sips white wine rather dramatically like a bad 1920s actress.

A man says, "It's so intimate yet formal, distant yet close enough to touch."

Another man in his fifties who appears to be channelling Tom Wolfe in a white suit says, "Dark and grainy, almost sinister."

Andrew can't help but chuckle at this summation. *Yeah, dark and grainy, that's what happens when you take pictures in the back seat of a cab with no lighting,* he wants to say, but instead he smiles and moves on.

Then he comes upon an old, frail lady with a brown wig that reminds him of his mother's wig. She seems particularly taken with the photo of Pauletta, the call girl who told him about the strange sexual proclivities of wealthy white males. "The loneliness is heartbreaking. It's in her eyes. It's just there. You don't have to put a spotlight on it, really. Lovely, just lovely." She gives Andrew's hand a gentle pat as if to say, "Well done, you."

Andrew wants to hug her. "Thank you," he says, leaning in. "Just between you and me, it's my favourite, too." He exchanges a conspiratorial smile with her before moving on. But it is true. He isn't just charming the old lady. Of the twenty-five portraits the gallery chose to show, the one of Pauletta staring out the window, the street light illuminating the left side of her face, leaving the other side obscured, is one of the best of his career and by far his favourite.

As much as he likes the photo of Sarah he took on that rainy day when she stormed back into his life like a warm tropical front, the one he tried to give her as a present, he decided to keep it out of the collection. He knows Sarah would have probably allowed him to use it if he asked, but he wanted to keep everything that happened between them that day for himself. He is selfish that way.

Andrew glances at one corner of the room and sees Gregory with a wineglass in one hand and gesturing with his other hand as he talks with Gale whom he asked to accompany him to the show.

This morning as they were having breakfast Andrew caught his father staring at him nervously. "What?" Andrew asked.

"Nothing." A long pause. "Well, I invited a friend tonight. Hope it's okay."

"A lady friend?"

"Don't say it like that."

"Like what?"

"A lady friend? Like it means something. It doesn't."

"But it could, yes?"

"No, it couldn't."

"Why not?"

Gregory didn't answer. He stuffed toast into his mouth as if that would prevent him from having to give an answer. "She has tangerine hair," he said at last.

And Andrew and his father laughed like old friends.

Now Andrew watches his dad and the tangerine-haired lady friend talking as they study the photo of Liam and Anthony, the couple who fought relentlessly in his cab. Less than a metre away from his father and Gale stands Rosemary, who is looking at

Zakhariye's portrait. He watches her move on to the next picture, that of Nuura, the Lebanese girl.

Rosemary seems even more out of place than he does. This is certainly not her scene, but she seems to be making an effort to be here, if not for her cheating, soon-to-be-ex-husband, then at least for the father of her daughter. Their eyes meet, and she gives him a shy wave. Rosemary was the first person he told about the exhibition, and when he asked if she would come, she smiled sadly and said, "Wouldn't miss it for the world."

Andrew is a little disappointed that his sister, Natalie, couldn't make it tonight. Her research is at a critical stage, and he didn't want to tear her away from it, so he downplayed the importance of the evening and made it sound as if he had gallery showings every weekend. Glancing out the huge glass facade of the gallery, he realizes he needs to feel fresh air on his skin.

Quietly, he puts his wineglass on a nearby table and discreetly makes his way out of the gallery. It is a beautiful Saturday night in early June, and the cool evening breeze brushes his face. *Heaven,* he thinks, *this is what it must be like if heaven exists.* He scans both directions on Queen Street. Westward it seems dark and deserted. Eastward the street is abuzz with humanity. It teems with life. He heads eastward.

By the time he realizes he should get back to the gallery, he has already reached Queen and Bathurst. The bars on either side of the street are crammed with people out on a warm summer night searching for all the pleasures life has to offer. For some reason Andrew experiences everything anew tonight. The lights, the traffic, the smell of a spring breeze mixed with hot dogs being cooked on the sidewalks, mingled with the unmistakable scent of pot, is intoxicating. He listens to the conversations of people on the street, hip hop coming from the boom box of a street vender,

Hindi music drifting from a car with its windows rolled down carrying Indian teens on the prowl.

A middle-aged couple kisses on the street as Andrew passes them. They seem oblivious to the world around them. He thinks about Sarah. The last time he saw her was a month ago at the opening night of her play on Broadway. Late one night when he couldn't sleep, he got up, turned on his laptop, and Googled her name, searching for any information about her. When he came across a website advertising *Plenty*, he read about the play, its origins, run dates, theatre location, ticket prices, et cetera.

Andrew bought a ticket for opening night online, rented a car, and made a weekend road trip to New York. He dressed up in his navy blue suit, white shirt, and red tie. Andrew didn't really understand the play, but he sat there mesmerized by Sarah's performance. There was a brief moment when he forgot to breathe, so astonished was he that Sarah, his Sarah, could be this other woman onstage in front of hundreds of people.

He hadn't seen a play since his twelfth-grade English teacher took his class on a field trip to see Arthur Miller's *Death of a Salesman*. After seeing Sarah that night, Andrew vowed to see more theatre and make it a regular part of his life.

I should've fought harder for her, he thinks as he approaches the intersection of Queen and Spadina. It is even more crowded here. His feet ache, but he presses on. Andrew looks around at the people on the street. Three young black males stroll together. Behind them an old Chinese couple holds hands. To their right a young WASP couple pushes a stroller. Across from Andrew is a Muslim woman in full hijab waiting for the light to change.

He wonders if actors can see their audience, and if so, did Sarah see him that night? Sometimes he also fantasizes about going home after a long day of driving his cab, pulling into the driveway, and discovering the figure of a woman sitting on the front steps. As he gets out of his car and comes closer, he realizes that it is Sarah.

Andrew passes Queen and Yonge and stops near St. Michael's Hospital. He can't walk anymore. He is tired and sweaty. His dress shirt that he bought for tonight sticks to his back. He spots several empty park benches in front of Metropolitan United Church. Andrew ambles over and sits down. He loosens his tie and slips off the dress shoes that he almost never wears. The air through his thin black socks is soothing. Behind him is St. Michael's Hospital. Before him, in the direction of Church Street, are wooden chairs and tables where a group of older men has gathered to play chess. They seem jubilant, grateful for a warm summer night and a few friends to share it with.

Loud laughter erupts from the front steps of the church. He glances in that direction and sees four teenage boys. From the look of them it is clear they are homeless, maybe even drug addicts. They jostle and banter. Two of them chase each other and fall to the ground wrestling. "Get off me, you faggoty-ass motherfucker!" the boy on the bottom yells. The words are harsh, but the tone is warm, brotherly even. Andrew smiles. Why, he doesn't know. He wishes he had his camera so that he can photograph them.

This morning when he woke up he didn't know where he was for a brief moment. He looked around and realized he was sleeping in his boyhood bed. His mother bought the bed when she redecorated his room for his fifteenth birthday. And everything in his room, the five swimming trophies, the bookshelf on which his university textbooks still stand, the poster of Pele on the wall that his father got him for Christmas when he was fourteen, all reminded him of how things have fallen apart in his life.

Never did he see himself in his mid-thirties sleeping in the same bed he slept in every night until he left for McGill University, the same creaky bed on which he lost his virginity with Mandy Stephenson from his eleventh-grade history class.

Yes, things really do fall apart, he thought to himself as he rubbed his eyes and stretched in bed, his feet pressing against the footboard. He never envisioned for himself a future in which he moved back with his widowed father, spending his mornings with his daughter, driving around town in a cab at night, and thinking about the woman he loves and can't have. But as he got out of bed and stumbled over to the bathroom across the hallway, he had for the first time in years a moment of pure faith that one of these days he *will* wake up and find everything put back together and he *will* marvel at how the pieces of his life have reconfigured themselves in a way he never saw coming.

The toll of the church bells pierces the layered din of the street. He checks his watch — it reads nine o'clock. Ah, how he loves the sound of bells. It is one of the things he loved most about living in Europe. As happy as he is to hear the chiming, it carries with it a soft sting of sadness, for it reminds him of the dwindling away of the hours.

But he doesn't dwell on this for long. He has that melancholy thought, revels in its truth, and files it away in one of the many compartments in his head for later use. For now he is here, his feet ache, his forehead is cool and clammy with sweat, and his mind is full of great, revelatory thoughts, mundane, pedestrian thoughts, and his heart overflows with desire. Desire for more time with his dad, desire to see his daughter through to womanhood, desire to make love to Sarah again, but mostly, a desire for more of everything he finds around him now — life.

More Great Fiction from Dundurn Press

Valley of Fire
by Steven Manners
978-1-55488-406-3
$21.99

John Munin is a rational man, a gifted psychiatrist who believes that the soul and psyche are interesting only in dissection. More susceptible to Munin's searching analysis, though, is Penelope, who suffers from obsessive-compulsive disorder and is Munin's star patient. Munin plans to present Penelope's case at a major medical conference in Las Vegas. But tragedy strikes on the eve of the event, and the probing psychiatrist's orderly world crumbles in the crucible of the desert.

The Postman's Round
by Denis Thériault
translated by Liedewy Hawke
978-1-55002-785-3
$19.99

Nominated for the 2009 Governor General's Award for Translation

Using dazzling descriptions of lush, tropical landscapes and subtle evocations of the sober, precise art of the haiku, Denis Thériault conjures up the solitary daily life of Bilodo. He's a postman who, as a result of his indiscretion (the steaming open of personal correspondence), becomes involved in an exchange of haiku between the woman of his dreams and Gaston Grandpré, an eccentric intellectual whose mail Bilodo delivers.

Woodstock Rising
by Tom Wayman
978-1-55002-860-7
$21.99

In this extraordinary black comedy shot full of the social and political issues of 1969–70, a group of college students sets out to put a satellite into orbit in homage to the recent Woodstock Festival. Accompanied by a young Canadian graduate student, the activists break into a mothballed missile silo and have big plans for their loot, including a nuclear warhead, which might culminate in the Light Show to End All Light Shows over the Nevada desert.

Available at your favourite bookseller.

DUNDURN PRESS
w w w . d u n d u r n . c o m

Tell us your story! What did you think of this book? Join the conversation at
www.definingcanada.ca/tell-your-story by telling us what you think.